BAY OF
ALL SAINTS
AND
EVERY
CONCEIVABLE
SIN

*ANA MIRANDA*

# BAY OF ALL SAINTS AND EVERY CONCEIVABLE SIN

Translated from the Portuguese by
Giovanni Pontiero

**VIKING**

*For Rubem Fonseca*

VIKING
Published by the Penguin Group
Viking Penguin, a division of Penguin Books USA Inc.,
375 Hudson Street, New York, New York 10014, U.S.A.
Penguin Books Ltd, 27 Wrights Lane,
London W8 5TZ, England
Penguin Books Australia Ltd, Ringwood,
Victoria, Australia
Penguin Books Canada Ltd, 10 Alcorn Avenue, Suite 300,
Toronto, Ontario, Canada M4V 3B2
Penguin Books (N.Z.) Ltd, 182–190 Wairau Road,
Auckland 10, New Zealand

Penguin Books Ltd, Registered Offices:
Harmondsworth, Middlesex, England

First American Edition
Published in 1991 by Viking Penguin,
a division of Penguin Books USA Inc.

1  3  5  7  9  10  8  6  4  2

Translation copyright © HarperCollins Publishers, 1991
All rights reserved

Originally published in Brazil as *Boca do Inferno* by
Companhia das Letras, Sao Paulo. © Ana Miranda, 1989.

Grateful acknowledgment is made for the support given to
the English translation by Vitae — Apoio a Cultura,
Educacao e Promocao Social and by INL —
Instituto Nacional do Livro/Fundacao Pro-Leitura —
Ministerio da Cultura, Brazil.

LIBRARY OF CONGRESS CATALOGING IN PUBLICATION DATA
Miranda, Ana Maria.
[Boca do inferno. English]
Bay of All Saints and every conceivable sin / Ana Miranda.
p.  cm.
Translation of: Boca do inferno.
ISBN 0–670–83455–6
1. Salvador (Brazil)—History—Fiction.   I. Title.
PQ9698.23.I618B613   1991
869.3—dc20          90–50759

Printed in the United States of America
Set in Bembo

# CONTENTS

# TRANSLATOR'S FOREWORD

Ana Miranda's absorbing tale of murder and revenge is set in seventeenth-century Bahia, the capital of Brazil from its foundation in 1549 until 1763, when the seat of colonial government was moved to Rio de Janeiro. Renowned for its tropical exuberance and volatile inhabitants, the *Bay of All Saints and every conceivable sin* became a bustling metropolis where fortunes were quickly made and lost, where white settlers consorted freely with blacks and mulattos on the plantations and in the brothels. Recognized as the second city of the Portuguese Empire, Bahia was the seat of Governors-General and Viceroys, of the all-powerful *Relação* or High Court of Appeals. The city boasted an Archbishop and its own curia, sumptuous baroque churches and convents, fine public buildings and stately homes worthy of their aristocratic occupants. A strict hierarchy of soldiers, lawyers and priests which was based on caste and privilege dominated every aspect of secular and ecclesiastical activity. Pomp and ceremony, feasts and processions, helped to distract the impoverished, unruly populace and make them forget their woes under a corrupt administration obsessed by wealth and power. In the words of one contemporary historian, Bahia was *a hell for blacks, a purgatory for whites and a paradise for mulattos*. It was also a haven for dreamers and men of ambition.

Its agricultural wealth made Bahia and Northeastern Brazil one of Portugal's most valuable assets. Heavily dependent on African slaves for its labour force, the region played a prominent role in the triangular pattern of trade that flourished between Portugal, Angola and Brazil.

Sugar became the mainstay of the economy and the distilling of rum and sugar cane brandy were important by-products. The so-called sugar barons formed a rural aristocracy whose economic power was to remain unchallenged until the end of the century when tobacco-growing proved to be more profitable.

The events in Ana Miranda's novel take place against a background of political turmoil and social unrest. The impact of the Dutch invasion of Pernambuco in 1630, and the bitter warfare that followed until the last of the invaders' strongholds capitulated in January 1654, had left its mark. Portugal's "Holy War" against the heretical Dutch had proved to be costly. The plantation owners resented being exploited by Lisbon and fiscal authorities who levied crippling taxes. And the constant smuggling and piracy caused them further problems.

Senior administrators (captains-general, governors-general and viceroys) were generally members of the high nobility. Some were professional military men with little experience of the law or administration. The excessive bureaucracy and a Byzantine legal system resulted in widespread negligence and inefficiency and as the colony's fortunes declined, tension and resentment grew between the *filhos da terra* or "sons of the soil" and the Portuguese settlers. Law and order collapsed. Crime and immorality became all too common and the activities of the government's secret police and officers of the much feared Inquisition created a stifling atmosphere of fear and mistrust.

This turbulent chapter in Brazil's history has provided Ana Miranda with a plot reminiscent of "cloak and dagger" drama in Renaissance literature. She skilfully builds on historical incidents and introduces important figures of the period into the narrative.

When the city's Captain-General, Francisco de Teles de Menezes, is ambushed, stabbed to death and mutilated, fierce reprisals ensue. Old feuds are rekindled and a reign of terror begins which sweeps both the innocent and guilty into a maelstrom of treachery and violence. The dominant presence of two strong personalities connected with the colony's future – namely, the Jesuit orator and preacher Padre Antonio Vieira (1608–1697) and the Brazilian satirical poet Gregório de Matos (1636–1696) – allows the author to penetrate the mind and spirit of an age much given to subtle reasoning and lively debate.

Antonio Vieira had been taken to Brazil as a child. He studied at the Jesuit College in Bahia and subsequently entered the Order. As Professor of Rhetoric at Olinda in Pernambuco, he soon attracted public attention as a preacher of unrivalled eloquence and his famous sermons were to prove a powerful political weapon at home and abroad. In 1641 he returned to Portugal, where he won the admiration and esteem of Dom João IV. The King made him his confidant, involved him in affairs of state and sent him as his personal envoy on diplomatic missions. A staunch believer in Portugal's glorious destiny, Vieira preached the gospel according to Vieira, and used the pulpit to utter prophecies and voice his opinions on a wide range of topics: religion, patriotism, war, justice, race, and morality. Audacious and militant, he relished controversy. His support for the Jews and his plea that they should be allowed to return to Portugal aroused fierce opposition and made him many enemies. Undaunted, he argued that the persecution being waged by Church and State against the Jews was unjust and contrary to divine and human law.

By 1652 he was back in Brazil where he worked indefatigably for the Jesuit missions in Maranhão and Grão-Pará. He defended the Indians against the abuses of the colonists and argued persuasively for protective legislation. By learning to speak and write native languages, he was able to win their confidence and trust. But his insistence on a more humane regime for the Indians in the colony made him few friends among landowners and even brought criticism from his fellow missionaries.

When the Jesuits were expelled from Maranhão in 1661, he returned to Portugal under a cloud, accused of heresy and publicly rebuked for his stubborn campaign on behalf of converted Jews. Frail and weary of conflict, he moved to Rome where he was to spend six happy years. His powers of oratory had not diminished with age, and in the Italian capital he found new friends and admirers. When he left Rome in 1675, Vieira was granted a Papal brief protecting him from any further investigations by the Inquisition. His enemies, however, continued to persecute him and the reluctance of Dom Pedro II to come to his defence caused him much bitterness. In 1681 he returned to Bahia for good, and this is when we meet him in the novel. His last years were dogged by serious illness, but he went on revising his sermons and essays until he died. Venerated by monarchs and slaves, he was seen by his enemies as a devious meddler and opportunist. He was certainly no saint and political expediency occasionally influenced his opinions, but no one could deny that he was a man of remarkable courage and vision, who truly believed in tolerance. He once confided: "My life has been one great farce." In fact, it was often closer to tragedy with its struggles and reversals.

Gregório de Matos, the poet, was no less colourful a personality. Another restless spirit, his life was also one of glaring contradictions. The son of wealthy parents, he was born in Bahia. Like Vieira, he studied at the Jesuit College before graduating in law at the University of Coimbra in Portugal.

Once back in Brazil, he embraced a bohemian existence. His rebellious spirit brought him into conflict with the Authorities and he soon became better known for his daring satires than his competence as a lawyer. And if the poet's friends and allies saw him as an amusing rogue, his enemies found him a disreputable charlatan. Foolhardy and incorrigible, he became the symbol of bourgeois revolt against the colony's feudal aristocracy. His political sympathies belied his privileged background. And while he himself was guilty of many of the vices he denounced, he genuinely deplored the hypocrisy and arrogance of the gentry in the realm. He consistently preferred nobility of character to that of blood.

Like Vieira, he made as many enemies as friends. His reckless behaviour and lack of commitment in carrying out his professional duties meant that he was frequently penniless. Having squandered his inheritance, he was reduced to hardship and poverty. And a period of enforced exile in Angola made him resentful and despondent.

His verses fall under several headings: lyric poems which sing of love, nature, and human destiny, and outrageous satires, often blasphemous and obscene, which attack the rich, the powerful and the clergy, and sacred poems which are often deeply moving. Gregório de Matos has never been considered a great poet, but his verses even when improvised pulsate with life and vivacity. These were rare qualities in a literary tradition that favoured artifice and discouraged spontaneity. His satires not only mirror the follies and pretensions of his age, but also expose the deep contradictions in his own soul. The transience of life's pleasures is never far from his thoughts:

*The sun appears and lasts but a day,*
*Its light soon followed by darkest night.*

Like Vieira, he suffered deep disappointments in later years. Hostilities increased and several attempts were made on his life. The tone of his poetry became more bitter and rancorous. The archetypal rake, he repented on his deathbed and made his peace with God. His poems, which only survived in manuscript, many of them apocryphal or of dubious origin, were not published until 1882.

Antonio Vieira had castigated the evils of the day from the pulpit; Gregório de Matos derided them in the verses he jotted down in taverns and brothels. The priest was austere and prophetic; the poet licentious and irreverent. Yet for all their differences of background and outlook, both men give voice to similar frustrations. Their idiosyncratic interpretations of things sacred and divine reveal the same thirst for experience, the same uncompromising allegiance to everything they believed in. Both men were to learn the vagaries of success and good fortune. Both priest and poet ended their days in sadness, convinced that their dreams and aspirations had come to nothing, haunted by a sense of failure and rejection as they faced the horrors of old age. Their decline marked that of the colony itself. A wondrous age of discovery and conquest had passed never more to return and the poignancy of its demise is somehow heightened by the cool, dispassionate tone of Ana Miranda's prose.

The other characters in her novel are loosely based on historical figures or are entirely fictitious. Parallels can be found for Samuel da Fonseca, Luiz Bonicho and Donato Serotino, whereas the women in the novel are drawn from the various muses of Gregório de Matos.

*Bay of All Saints and Every Conceivable Sin* is not merely an imaginative evocation of a unique city with a proud history. The factual and fictional are ingeniously woven together. The novel's characters, whether real or fictitious, find their own truth amidst the shadows of fate. Winners or losers, their separate destinies attest to Gregório de Matos' conviction that "Nothing escapes mockery" and that human destiny is the greatest mocker of all. These men and women embody the best and worst of human nature. But in the final analysis, the important thing is to have lived and dreamt and loved. For all of these characters Bahia remains that city where heaven and hell are often indistinguishable.

*Manchester March 1991*                    GIOVANNI PONTIERO

# TRANSLATOR'S NOTE

The term *Captain-General* may be judged an arbitrary rendering of *Alcaide-mor* (the title and rank held by the ill-fated Francisco de Teles de Menezes who is assassinated at the beginning of the novel). But after due consideration, it seemed entirely appropriate within the context of the plot.

To avoid any confusion and to appease historians, the following distinction should be made between the functions of the *Alcaide-mor* and those of the *Capitão-mor* in colonial Brazil. The *Alcaide-mor* was in charge of all garrisons and fortifications in a province; the *Capitão-mor*, on the other hand, exercised much more power and influence as the military administrator of a captaincy or municipality.

G.P.

# The City

THE CITY HAD BEEN BUILT at the southernmost tip of the peninsula, thirteen degrees south and forty-two degrees west, on the Brazilian coast. It stood facing a wide, sheltered bay from which it received its name: Bahia.

The bay, little more than two leagues across, extended from St Anthony's Point, where a fortress named after the same saint had been built, to the land beneath the Hermitage of Our Lady of Montserrat. At the mid-point of the bay stood the city, perched on a flat-topped mountainous rock, cut sheer on the slope that faced the sea; the rock itself was surrounded by three lofty hills scattered with villages. To the south, the houses came to an end in the vicinity of the Monastery of St Benedict; to the north, near the Monastery of Our Lady of Mount Carmel. To the east, the city was sparsely populated.

Three fortresses, two landward and one by the sea, defended the narrow shore of Bahia. The long strip of coast with its row of warehouses, stores and workshops was connected to the upper part of the city by three steep roads. A noisy windlass owned by the Jesuits hoisted heavy cargo from one part of the city to the other.

There were still signs of the destruction caused by the wars against the Dutch nearly sixty years before. The ruins of burnt-out houses, abandoned cannons, the wreckage of a ship on the beach. In more deserted places, one could still come across spiked iron caltrops concealed among the undergrowth. Near the entrance to the Carmelite church there were high ramparts and deep caves which had once been used as trenches.

Set in a pleasant region divided by clean rivers and blessed with blue skies, fertile lands and forests of leafy trees, the city was the image of paradise. Yet demons prowled there, luring souls to hell.

# I

GREGÓRIO DE MATOS looked out of the window of a two-storey house in the square in front of the Jesuit Church. "This city is finished," he thought. "Bahia is not the same. People used to be respectful. Nowadays, you could be assaulted in the street, under the noses of the military and the clergy, even in front of the gallows."

He remembered his favourite Spanish poet, Góngora y Argote; in his portrait the poet was dressed as royal chaplain in his religious habit: the long, austere face, the cleft chin, the temples shaved to behind the ears. Góngora had been ordained to the priesthood at the age of fifty-six. On the third finger of his left hand he wore a magnificent ruby ring kissed by all. Gregório, like the Spanish poet, wished to write verses which would be grand and ornate rather than banal. But could he? He felt an emptiness. Should he succumb to it, where would he end up? Had Góngora not been trying to establish a link between man's exalted soul and the earth's carnal sorrows? Here was Gregório on the dark side of the world, feeding off the rotten leftovers from the banquet of life. What would be his theme? *Rejoice, rejoice in the glittering light of gold.* Would things have been easier if Gregório had been born in Spain? Would it have made any difference?

At six o'clock in the morning, the Governor, Antonio de Souza de Menezes, left the palace. He crossed the main square in which the administrative buildings were located: the seat of government, the prison, the Council Chambers, the Tribunal and the Royal Armoury. He made his way to the Jesuit church for the sacrament of penance. He liked to confess in the morning. He had his own

4

confessor who belonged to the Franciscan Order, but he found the Jesuits better trained to dispense spiritual guidance.

As he knelt at the priest's feet, he liked to imagine that it was the much revered Father Antonio Vieira himself who was hearing him confess. For these were his most intimate secrets. He would confess the crimes he had committed, his sins and omissions. But there was one thing he never mentioned: the twenty-four years he had spent in seclusion on an estate at Olivais. No confession could bring greater relief than this mystery. No one, not even a priest, was to learn what had happened during that period of his life. Even he himself did not wish to be reminded of it.

Most of the people walking through the square at that hour were black slaves or mestizo workers. Summoned by the pealing of bells, many were on their way to church.

From the window, Gregório watched the Governor pass among people from different worlds and kingdoms. They were referred to as rogues, fugitives or exiles from their own countries because of crimes committed there, paupers who had been starving in their own land, men seeking their fortune, adventurers, descendants of slaves, petty criminals, penniless desperadoes who landed daily in the colony. Some arrived in a state of extreme poverty, barefoot, dressed in rags, even naked, and within a short time they returned to their own country as rich men with landed property, money and ships. Even those who were penniless, without plantation or mistress, wore silk and powdered wigs. As Pietro Caroldo had prophesied in 1533, men sentenced to death would come to this land in order "to tame the country so that upright men might face no danger". The majority of those who came were Christians and they doffed their hats and bowed as the Governor passed. There were also Persians, Mongols, Armenians, Greeks, infidels and other races. Myrmidons, Jews and Assyrians, Turks and Moabites. The city received them all.

At night, the same people who attended Holy Mass practised *calundu* and other forms of witchcraft. Men and women gave themselves over to these magic rituals in the hope of securing good fortune. They squandered their money on the priests of *candomblé*. They fell into a trance and such was their dancing that onlookers believed they were seeing Satan himself. They concealed these practices from the priest who heard their confession, although it was not uncommon to see members of the clergy attending voodoo ceremonies, too.

The faithful brought rosaries and prayer-books to church. Many made the sign of the cross before entering, although Gregório noticed that some crossed themselves contrary to the teaching of the catechism. Once inside, they genuflected briskly, one knee touching the ground, like archers prepared to take aim.

Waiting for Mass to begin, some admired the saints in their niches, others preferred to watch the comings and goings of the congregation. One man was dozing against the wall, while a group of youths eyed two beautiful black girls as they passed by carrying bundles on their heads.

Women bedecked in earrings, brooches and dresses with gauze sleeves and embroidered petticoats bustled along to the chimes of the bells from the Carmelite monastery, the church of St Benedict, the Jesuit college and the church of St Francis. Many commented that the women were going to Holy Mass to curse their husbands or lovers, or perhaps to yield to unworthy temptations.

The church entrance was crammed with beggars and madmen. But even with so much wealth, there was a great deal of poverty and many people were starving to death.

The Mass began. In the pulpit, the priest pulled out a long sheet of paper on which were written the names of those Catholics who frequented the church. The Archbishop João da Madre de Deus had ordered that they should be read out loud. Those who were present responded: the priest wrote down the names of the absentees and, after rebuking them in public, promised that they would subsequently be punished and ordered to do penance.

The slaves remained outside the church. Many of them showed piety and contrition while others raised havoc. Few settlers attempted to educate their slaves. Some even refused to feed them. Many of the gentlemen posing as aristocrats sported moustaches and sideburns like those of King Fernando, led degenerate lives and treated their female slaves like prostitutes.

The latter, also, remained outside, some kneeling in the patio.

The most desirable creatures on earth, thought Gregório, lovelier
. . . even lovelier than the stars. But what did the stars have to do
with it? Lovelier than white women, (little madams from Portugal
and grand ladies from Spain).

Indoors, at a distance, someone was strumming a guitar. A mother
and daughter emerged from a side street and passed in haste.
Young women were accompanied everywhere by their mother or
a woman slave. Caution had to be observed. Girls were at risk,
smitten by love, they could easily be led astray by secret missives.
Gregório had often resorted to these stratagems. During Holy
Mass, a young fellow took the opportunity to slip poems or a
*billet-doux* to a young lady, or, as in Portugal, to pinch the bottoms
of the girls.

Even in church the men were armed with swords and daggers.
In this city a man's valour was paramount. It was no longer common practice to hang thieves and murderers; still less, perjurers
and scandalmongers. People boasted that Bahia was free of
notorious bandits; but nearly everybody did a little pilfering. Few
pick-pockets and bag-snatchers roamed the streets, and thieves
who resorted to violence were rare, yet dishonesty was rife and
taken for granted. Runaway slaves prowled the roads and certain
streets were known to be dangerous. Getting rich and securing
positions of power and influence were common ambitions. Many
wished to see the aristocracy discredited and impoverished, or
killed off in relentless conflict. Nothing sacred was respected, be
it king or bishop, priest or cloistered nun. They all came under
attack, all became the victims of cruel and wicked intrigues.
Gregório sighed. Life was difficult in the colony. Why had he
returned?

Pedlars were selling trinkets and wares in the square and all
around the church. The commotion was getting louder. People
were out in pursuit of pleasure. Some were heading for the
countryside, others simply enjoying themselves or criticizing the
government while inventing their own laws and decrees. And
although it was still early morning, some were already unsteady
on their feet.

Single or married, all men liked to get drunk, however good or bad the wine. They would drink themselves senseless, reducing their wives to poverty and their children to starvation. Drunkards could be seen lying in the streets each morning. Boots with untied laces, fragments of broken tankards, empty kegs lay scattered everywhere, left behind from the night before.

Two prostitutes walked by, worn out by their excesses. They made their way uphill and into the square before vanishing from sight. One of them was barely twelve years old. To which brothel did she belong? A pretty girl with tiny breasts. The other prostitute was dressed with more ostentation and style than most courtesans. In the morning, after a night of frenzied activity, these women crawled back to their hovels. During the night droves of them paraded brazenly through the streets. With their gentlemen friends they would sing lewd songs and perform suggestive capers.

The women experienced in the pleasures of the boudoir were unlike those prattling virgins who filled their hours with idle chatter and were frivolous and stupid. Virgins could only be seen behind shuttered grilles and peepholes. They held up bunches of onions to the men, staring them out of countenance. *Ah, sweet, wicked copulation, full of phlegm and wine.* Gregório de Matos could be enslaved by those depraved black beauties.

A tipstaff, carrying his staff under his arm, ran toward the church, late for Mass. He was responsible for maintaining order within the sanctuary and usually walked ahead of the priest during the ceremony. But Mass was already over. The crowd was coming out of church.

Some of the more prosperous settlers got into their litters or palanquins. There were very few chaises or carriages because the steep inclines made wheeled traffic difficult. The Governor was one of the last to leave.

Antonio de Souza de Menezes, known as Braço de Prata, entered the palace. He walked stiffly, no doubt because of the heavy artificial limb in solid silver. He had lost his right arm in Pernambuco while serving with the armada of the Count of Torre, after a battle which lasted for four days. The artificial limb which had earned him the name Silver Arm had been made in Oporto by a famous silversmith Adelino Moreira. The fingers were perfect, even the nails and veins had been faithfully copied by the skilful and meticulous artisan. Besides the rigidity of that arm, which seemed to pervade his entire body, the pristine dignity of the Noble Houses of Sarzeda and Alvito had to be taken into account.

He walked through the corridors to the private study where he carried out his duties, barely acknowledging the footmen and major-domos who were lined up to await his arrival. All knelt as he passed, a ritual he insisted upon, although he was neither bishop nor archbishop.

On his desk, De Souza found some papers put there by his trusted manservant, Mata. They contained details of the day's business. The Governor glanced through them.

# The Crime

THE CONSPIRATORS were all too familiar with the habits of Francisco de Teles de Menezes. They knew that at sunrise, on certain days of the week, the Captain-General of Bahia would leave to visit his favourite whore. Gossips commented that he was impotent and had to take advantage of his early morning erection. Or perhaps in order to get sexually aroused he needed the silence of the streets at an hour when even bohemians and vagabonds were fast asleep. Perhaps he liked the hot breath and flaccid flesh of whores as night drew to a close.

In fact, Teles was an early riser and he had plenty of time during those empty hours to satisfy his lust. The Captain-General frequently absented himself from his work, to go off and get drunk or play backgammon with faithful comrades. He visited his mistress's house accompanied only by a few unarmed slaves. Then he would confer briefly with the Governor and briskly settle any other matters, leaving himself free to pursue his pleasures. But that morning he would meet his sad fate.

Fornicating with prostitutes, or former prostitutes, as in the case of the Captain-General's mistress, and the snares laid by his enemies, were activities associated with the shadows of night, when God and His sentinels withdrew and the Devil went on the rampage; weapons and phalluses were raised in the name of pleasure or destruction, because the two were often enlisted for the same purpose. Thieving, the city's favourite pastime, also went on at night. By day, the faithful flocked to church to ask forgiveness for their sins before committing more: illicit unions, incest, gambling, blatant immodesty, drunken orgies, prostitution, abductions, rape, polygamy, robbery, blasphemy, adultery, sloth, idolatry, sodomy, lesbianism and gluttony.

# I

BEFORE GETTING INTO the prostitute Cipriana's bed, the
Captain-General took off his white wig and blue military
cloak, to which was pinned a cross of rubies.

A little bag of coins jingled at his belt. To be powerful was not
enough. Gold could also arouse desire.

He embraced Cipriana, kissed her softly on the lips, clasping
her by the waist.

"Can you feel my pike?" he demanded. "Come."

"Not just yet."

"Don't you want it?"

On a sudden impulse, the Captain-General got up, went to the
window and opened it. The street was almost deserted. A skinny
little urchin was standing on a corner. Teles sensed something odd
but dismissed it. He saw his footmen relaxed, propped up against
the wall, near the palanquin.

He closed the window carefully and stretched out beside Cipriana. She had never seen him without any clothes on.

"We haven't got much time," he said, covering her with his
body.

The conspirators pulled back their hoods; they carried daggers in
their belts. A pact had been sealed between them.

"It's almost time. A scoundrel like him is bound to fornicate as
fast as a rabbit."

The men laughed.

"I'm sure he's been castrated."

"Let's take this seriously, my friends. Knowing what we do
about rabbits, we'd better be prepared."

"I'm not convinced. I know the little runt. He takes his time, then falls asleep. Sometimes he even drops off before doing anything."

They roared with laughter. They were nervous.

Teles was lying beside Cipriana. They gazed at the ceiling. The Captain-General remembered he must call at the palace and have a word with the Governor. De Souza was expecting him; he was bound to have some matter to discuss, and as usual, something disagreeable. Teles found anything connected with work extremely tiresome. That morning they would discuss a matter about which he had already been warned. A letter.

Teles had known De Souza many years ago in Lisbon where he had been sent as a prisoner. No guilt had been proven, and Teles was free to return to his native land, and now had the rank of Captain-General, bought at an absurdly low price. He came back intent on taking his revenge against those who had denounced him to the Count of Óbidos, against his detractors, his former enemies.

When he learned that his friend Antonio de Souza would be arriving to govern the colony, he began plotting the downfall of his enemies. André de Brito, Gonçalo Ravasco, Antonio Rolim, Manuel de França, João de Couros, and many others, were already paying for their opposition to the Captain-General. All of them had sought refuge in the Jesuit College.

An anonymous letter had fallen into Teles's hands warning him about the assassination plot which was being hatched at the College. He would show the letter to the Governor.

"What are you thinking about?" Cipriana asked him.

"Nothing of interest to a woman."

One always had to be prepared to kill, or to die. Even to go around without guards might be imprudent, his fencing-master, Donato Serotino, always reminded him. He looked at his weapons on the table and felt more reassured. He had always been able to put up a good fight ever since enlisting at the age of eighteen. And he had perfected his fighting skills in the battalion led by Captain Sebastião de Araújo e Lima, then as captain of the regiment, and assuming the post of commandant of the infantry battalion soon after. He got out of bed and grabbed his double-edged sword. He raised it shoulder high and brandished it in the air with a swishing noise.

"Tarasque!" he exclaimed. "The famous sword Renaud de Montauban used to slice cheeses and chop off heads."

Cipriana remained in bed. She could still feel the warmth of her lover's body between the sheets.

Perhaps because he had laid aside his sword, Teles went back to thinking about the risks he might be taking. In fact, various people had warned him about Antonio de Brito's intentions, but he couldn't believe that any member of that family would go through with such a daring plan. André de Brito was in prison along with the black slaves and sentenced to exile. He had been taken in secret to the fortress on the hill named after St Paul. The De Brito brothers, he decided, were harmless. Otherwise, why should the oldest of them have taken refuge in the Jesuit College? It was Antonio de Brito who was facing danger, hidden away like a common thief.

The Captain-General sighed. The Vieira Ravasco clan – Bernardo, his son Gonçalo and Antonio the priest – might join forces with the De Brito clan; after all, they were related. But they wouldn't get involved in such intrigues. For while they might have political motives for opposing the Menezes faction, they had never been known to resort to violence. As for Padre Vieira, he was in favour of conciliation. He had called on the Governor to try and restore peace. When all was said and done, the Ravasco clan were a bunch of cowards. They wouldn't have the courage to carry out a murder.

The Captain-General mentally listed his enemies, but they all seemed fairly harmless. Teles considered himself omnipotent; he could count on his troops, officers, swordsmen, arquebusiers, all the cannons, ships and fortresses. Anyone who tried to oppose him would come up against all this military force.

"I feel thirsty," he said.

Cipriana got up.

"What do you want to drink?"

"Brandy."

"That won't take away your thirst."

"But it'll take away this anxiety. I detest water."

Cipriana brought a mug of brandy.

"You shouldn't have too much to drink today, Francisco."

"Why ever not?"

"There are days when one shouldn't drink."

Teles downed the brandy in one gulp, then smacked his lips and gave a grunt of satisfaction. He drew on his cloak and secured his weapons to his belt. He took a coin from his purse and threw it on to the bed.

"Until tomorrow. Wait for me, washed and ready."

"Are you really coming tomorrow?"

"If I can."


The party of armed conspirators emerged from the Jesuit College and crossed the slippery road covered in putrid filth.

"At least let him have his morning fuck."

"That's more than he deserves."

"It's the one thing a man should be allowed before he dies."

Tense and on their guard, with hoods over their heads and weapons at the ready, the eight men found hidden corners along the Rua Trás da Sé and there they waited in pairs to make a surprise attack.

The Captain-General's palanquin appeared in the square. It came to a halt before the palace entrance. Teles entered.

Some twenty minutes later, he reappeared. He stretched, arms extended, and got into the palanquin. It travelled for several blocks along the Rua Trás da Sé.

When the urchin raised his hand to warn them that the Captain-General's palanquin was approaching, the conspirators pulled their hoods down, concealing their faces. The urchin, a lad in his teens, took a few steps forward and stood alone in the middle of the street. He made the sign of the cross, joined his hands briefly in prayer and waited. He was paralysed with fear.

He took a few more steps, approached the palanquin and signalled to the footmen to stop.

"Your Lordship, Your Lordship," the little slave called out.

The Captain-General popped his head through the curtains.

"What do you want, boy? Money?"

Then, on seeing behind the terrified face of the young slave the hooded men emerge from their hiding-places, he realized this was an ambush.

"Death to the Captain-General Francisco de Teles de Menezes, that bootlicking toady who panders to Braço de Prata," called out one of the conspirators, as they advanced on the palanquin. There was a glint in the Captain-General's eye as he watched the hooded men surround the litter. He shut the curtains. The slaves barely had time to defend themselves; struck by gunfire, they fell to the ground.

Blood flowed over cobblestones and men's clothing. Everything had happened so quickly.

Concealed by his hood, Antonio de Brito drew back the curtains of the palanquin.

"Is it gold you're after?" Teles asked. He took out the little bag hidden beneath his cloak: "Gold," he repeated, holding out the small, burnished coins. He threw them on to the ground. The coins scattered at the feet of the hooded men, but no one stirred.

Antonio de Brito removed his hood. The Captain-General recognized the enemy he had but recently tried to eliminate and turned pale. For a moment everything seemed to come to a halt. The men stood petrified like stone statues.

"Get on with it," someone shouted from behind, shattering the bewilderment.

"You bastard," shouted Antonio de Brito.

"Coward," replied the Captain-General.

He reached for his belt, pulled out a pistol and fired, hitting De Brito in the shoulder. Now one of the conspirators drew his sword and with one stroke chopped off the Captain-General's right hand.

Teles shrieked in pain. He drew the dagger from his belt with his left hand, and desperately tried to attack his enemy, but De Brito was too quick and stabbed him, opening a deep gash in his throat. The Captain-General uttered a moan and fell from the palanquin to the ground. Antonio de Brito bent over him and dealt another blow, this time to the chest. Close to death, Teles lay sprawled on the ground, covered in mire and blood, but found enough strength to mutter: "Braço de Prata will avenge me." His face assumed a terrible look of hatred and fear.

"Let's go," someone shouted.

One of the hooded men approached and pulled the ruby cross from the corpse's cloak. De Brito wrapped the Captain-General's severed hand in a rag and took it with him.

The conspirators fled in the direction of the Jesuit College.

Once inside the building, they were taken to a cell crammed with books, many of them worm-eaten; delicate spiders' webs glistened in the corners of the roof-tiles; cassocks eaten by a locust plague which had recently attacked the kitchen garden, were folded over chests. Along one wall stood several beds covered with clean sheets.

A thin ray of light came through the windows, casting reflections on the writing table.

Here the fugitives, some sitting on the beds, others standing about nervously in silence, listened for any sounds from outside. They were remote from the shouting and uproar. In the College all was peaceful and quiet.

The Governor was in the habit of clutching his silver arm and in this manner (with flesh gripping precious metal) he received Mata and the Archbishop João da Madre de Deus. They came into the room looking drawn and solemn.

"Did I hear shots?" De Souza asked.

"Your Excellency," Mata began nervously, "we have some terrible news."

"Out with it."

"Francisco de Teles de Menezes."

There was a moment's silence.

"Misfortunes are the fatal outcome of human passions," remarked the Archbishop, summoning his courage. "The Captain-General is close to death."

Mata narrated the details of the attack.

For a few seconds, De Souza remained silent. He stared at his artificial arm. Then banged softly on the table. He looked at the men standing before him in silence.

"Does your Excellency feel unwell?" asked the Archbishop.

"I have suffered pain so great that I couldn't feel it. But moral pain is bearable. It wounds the soul and causes suffering which ultimately makes one even stronger. Physical pain, on the other hand, can destroy the bravest soldier. Only women can withstand it."

He paused.

"To lose my arm came as a terrible blow."

"*Having known misfortune, I can succour the afflicted.* Don't forget those words spoken by Dido," said João da Madre de Deus.

"I shall never forget the pain of that wound inflicted by a cannonball. I was lying on a filthy pallet on a caravel overcrowded with wounded soldiers. I opened my eyes, tried to speak, to call for help. I raised my arm, realized there was scarcely any weight. I could still feel the pain of the shrapnel in my flesh. I raised it a second time and looked for it but could see nothing. I thought I was hallucinating. I lifted my other arm with great difficulty. It seemed as heavy as an iron beam, the hand of a gorilla, my wrist all swollen up like a balloon. It was my left arm. I was alive, although part of me was missing. Such a strange feeling to have an arm that doesn't exist. Francisco must be feeling exactly the same at this very minute, his soul circling his body in search of his hand."

"There were eight assassins," Mata told him. "One of them was Antonio de Brito. We have witnesses."

"I warned Francisco. It was a great mistake to allow De Brito to go free. Did the witnesses recognize any of the other assassins?"

"Only De Brito, Your Excellency," said Mata. "The others kept their faces covered. They took refuge in the College."

"It was that damned Vieira Ravasco lot." He banged on the table once more, this time with force. "They will pay dearly for this."

# II

THE NIGHT HAD BEEN COLD with a gale blowing and Maria Berco had stayed up, filled with foreboding and unable to sleep. She listened to her own footsteps echoing through the house, the sound of distant voices, horses' hooves trampling the turf, their teeth tearing the grass from its roots.

She was exhausted, with dark rings under her eyes. Moving to the dressing table, she looked at herself in the mirror. There was a curious lack of symmetry between the two sides of her face. Her hair was in plaits drawn on to the crown of her head and gathered into a bun. She dressed quickly, in order to be on time for work that Friday morning. She was the companion of Bernardina Ravasco. The Secretary's only daughter, Bernardina had been widowed without children and, although still young, her delicate state of health required the utmost care.

The palanquin moved rapidly up the slopes. The main streets were broad and covered with gravel. There were public parks near the main landmarks and within the city and on the outskirts, lots of gardens were located, with fruit trees, medicinal herbs, green vegetables and a wide variety of flowers. Many churches appeared along the route, some under construction, nearly all of them built in cream-coloured and rose-veined imitation marble imported from Portugal. The convents were spacious and imposing.

Now and then, Maria would pop her head through the curtains and order the slaves to go faster. But on reaching the Rua Trás da Sé, they found the road blocked by the Governor's guards. Maria inquired what was happening. Her palanquin took another route and made a detour before arriving at the

Ravasco residence. She paid the slaves and got out of the palanquin.

Bernardo Ravasco had sent word that he would be spending the night at Tanque, his country estate, but would call at the mansion early next morning. Why was he so late?

Bernardina opened the door of her brother's room. No one was there, the bed had not been slept in and there was a faint smell of mildew in the air. For some nights now, young Gonçalo had not slept at home, having sought refuge in the Jesuit College to escape the sentence of exile passed by Judge João de Gois, who might be called the Governor's right arm, had he not already had one made of silver.

Anxiously Maria entered the Ravasco mansion. Like most of the buildings in the upper part of the city, it was spacious and consisted of three storeys, each with four balconies, a roof covered in curved tiles, and the stonework around the entrance with ornamental carving in the style of the old palaces of Alfama. There was scarcely any furniture in the rooms, but the walls were covered with paintings.

"What's wrong, Maria?" asked Bernardina.

"The city's in an uproar. They've killed the Captain-General."

"God help us, where is my father?"

Maria went to the kitchen. Bernardina followed her. "Why are you out of breath?" she asked.

"It's nothing, Dona Bernardina, nothing." Maria whispered as if afraid of being overheard. She threw open the door to the backyard. A gust of cold air swept into the kitchen. She sat down on the stone bench, pensive, waiting. Bernardina sat down beside her.

"You can't hide anything from me. Tell me what you know, Maria."

Maria remained silent, eyes lowered.

"I must know what happened. Maria, tell me at once."

"It's just that with your weak heart . . ."

"My heart is certain to fail me one of these days, I know. But I'll die this very minute unless you tell me what's going on."

"Very well, Dona Bernardina. People are saying Gonçalo killed the Captain-General."

"My brother? But how if he's been shut away in the College for weeks now . . . How dare they? Tell me about the murder."

Maria recounted all she had learned about the Captain-General's death. Looking silently toward the sea, they waited for Bernardo Ravasco to arrive.

*Ah, that unfortunate city, the terrible fate of an ignorant and irresponsible race.* Gregório was told of the Captain-General's death. It distressed him to see how badly the colony was being managed, but he realized that the devil had taken possession not only of those in government but of the entire city. Wherever one looked there was vice and depravity. He picked up his pen and started making notes.

The nobleman who lived next door found it too embarrassing to borrow money and preferred to steal to keep up appearances. His unmarried daughter, who clearly preferred finery to honour, had become a concubine. The nobleman's wife paraded in extravagant clothes. A house filled with knick-knacks while the husband goes around in rags can only imply he's a cuckold.

A lawyer occupied the house on the other side. What can one say of such a man? The idle rich in the colony turned villains into victims and obtained favours from both. This lawyer prevaricated and when called upon to answer for his actions he insisted he was defending the family honour. The previous week, he had revoked a sentence with bribes and embraces.

The lawyer's brother, a greedy merchant, had made a two hundred per cent profit on everything he bought or sold. He had been killed in an ambush and left his widow penniless and the house mortgaged, having squandered all his ill-gotten wealth on prostitutes. In an effort to keep up apppearances, the widow received one friar after another into her home. And how she moaned and shrieked and worked herself into a frenzy of excitement.

One of the priests who visited the widow was the abbot of a nearby monastery. It was rumoured that he stole the order's revenues to support his whores; to safeguard his reputation, he silenced his critics with generous payments from church funds.

Gregório stopped taking notes. As Góngora y Argote once wrote, it was necessary to *"speak the truth about nations in every age"*. He left the house and made his way to the College.

Bernardo entered the house. His daughter was waiting for him at the door with Maria. The Secretary was formally dressed in court attire, a tight-fitting jacket, fine cloth breeches, shoes with pointed toes.

He embraced his daughter. "You look down-hearted, child," he said, kissing her on the forehead. "Maria, bring me the small trunk."

"Did you know the Captain-General has been ambushed?" Bernardina asked. "Apparently Gonçalo is involved."

"Who told you that?"

Bernardina hesitated before replying.

"Maria."

Maria lowered her eyes and withdrew, sorry that she had spoken.

"You, too, father, must be under suspicion. All eyes are watching what's going on here."

"But there's nothing going on."

"Of course there is. Gonçalo has taken sanctuary in the College, you spend your nights away from home, you've stopped going to the Secretariat, you've vacated your seat on the Board of the Misericórdia Alms-house which has now been filled by your enemy Gois, you keep the strangest hours and turn up when least expected. And now you're going off carrying a trunk. One would think you were taking flight. Why are you running away? From whom?"

"But how can people be so well informed when we are living behind locked doors?"

"There are spies posted on every corner, listening, watching." She broke off, perplexed. She looked at Maria as she dragged the trunk into the room. She whispered: "Father, you must leave at once. You must go far away from here and avoid our country house."

Bernardo lowered his head.

"I cannot abandon my son at a time like this."

"Gonçalo was right to kill the Captain-General. Teles deserved to die," said Bernardina. "The man was hateful."

"My child, this has nothing to do with hatred. It's simply a matter of politics. Besides, Gonçalo didn't succeed in killing him. He's still alive."

"But he isn't expected to survive. He might be dead by now."

Bernardo put his hands round his daughter's shoulders. "Try not to think about it, will you?"

"How can I stop thinking about it? You hide everything from me, but I've always suspected you were mixed up in a plot against the government."

Maria Berco served her master a bowl of hot milk with sticks of cinnamon. Seated at the table, Bernardo drank with noisy gulps.

His brother, Padre Antonio Vieira, enjoyed ecclesiastical immunity, but the post of Secretary of State did not carry similar privileges.

"I'm frightened. They're determined to kill you."

"Keep calm, nothing will happen to me. The country house owned by the Jesuits offers safe sanctuary. I'll send someone trustworthy to escort you to Samuel da Fonseca's plantation at Recôncavo. Someone you know."

"You mean the Jew?"

"Yes, the Rabbi. He's a kind man."

"Do you think I'm in danger, father?"

"No, it's simply a precaution. We have to think of your health."

"Why don't you come with me to the plantation?"

"I have some essays I must finish writing at our country house," Bernardo answered, rising to his feet. "They're almost ready. Perhaps no one will ever read them. And before setting off for the estate I must call at the Secretariat and collect my papers."

"Isn't that risky?"

"Probably. But I can't leave them there."

"I sometimes regret I wasn't born a man."

Bernardo kissed his daughter's hand. "The fact that Semiramis was a woman didn't prevent her from ruling Assyria," he said. Then he whispered into her ear:

"I'll teach you to read yet."

She remained thoughtful. Then she studied his face closely, and was moved by the grief she saw there.

"God, how weary I feel."

"Weary?"

"Yes, weary of everything."

"This city is heartbreaking."
Stroking his face she asked:
"Are you suffering like me?"
He smiled and pondered.
Then he said to her: "Take a good look at my face, my child. Take a really good look. Look at these dull eyes which were once bright and eager. Look at this wrinkled skin, this broken nose and this sparse white hair of mine. There's neither respite nor remedy. There's no turning back."

# III

I N THE COLLEGE OF THE JESUIT FATHERS Gregório de Matos wrote: *"When you disembarked from the frigate, My Lord Braço de Prata, I thought as I looked at this nobody masquerading as Governor, that the Inquisition had sent a statue to this foolish and fatuous city."*

He grinned and handed what he had written to Gonçalo Ravasco. Gonçalo read it, enjoyed the joke and handed it to the alderman.

The paper passed from hand to hand.

"The god you worship is slander," they told him, smiling.

"I must be off now," said Bernardo glancing at the clock on the small table.

"When shall we see each other again, Father?"

"I don't know. Wait until I send for you. Stay indoors, be careful no one sees you at the window. I'll ask Doctor Gregório de Matos to escort you to the plantation. He'll oblige me, he's a good friend. You can rely on him for everything. Well, for almost everything."

The nobleman left a pouch filled with gold and silver coins beside the clock.

"Should anything happen, Bernardina, you will surely need this."

Bernardo's carriage drove off. His daughter watched as he disappeared round the corner of the street.

Bernardo arrived at the Jesuit College. He went straight up to the attic where his son was waiting, pacing up and down, staring at the floor, his boots echoing on the wooden boards. On seeing his father arrive, young Gonçalo went together with his fellow conspirators to meet him. He helped his father to remove his jacket.

"Where are the hoods, Gonçalo?" asked Bernardo.

The youth fetched the hoods out of hiding.

"Burn them."

Gonçalo gathered up the hoods and made his way to the kitchen.

Bernardo pulled up a chair and sat down. The men gathered round expecting news.

"Well?" asked Antonio de Brito.

"We must wait. The square has been cordoned off, there are soldiers posted in all the streets."

This news appeared to make the men even more tense.

"What happened?" asked Bernardo.

"Everything went as planned," replied De Brito. "Two of us were slightly wounded, nothing serious. That swine Teles didn't die at once, he still had time to ask forgiveness for his sins."

"I have my doubts about the outcome of this venture," said the Secretary.

"Ah, no, Dom Bernardo," said a man standing beside De Brito. He had a tonsure but was dressed as a layman, elegant and well-groomed with an amber-coloured waistcoat made of fine leather. The man was Gregório de Matos.

"Braço de Prata," he continued, "set up a powerful snare, strongly backed by three forces: himself and his fawning allies in the Treasury and Administration; the judges Palma and Gois who support him in the Courts, herding together all the venal judges; and finally the deceased Captain-General, who dominated him and assured him of supremacy in the municipal sector. Without Teles, one of the three legs of this brute creation, the whole thing will start to collapse."

"I hope it won't collapse on top of us," remarked João de Couros.

"Of course it will collapse and on top of us. That's obvious," said De Brito. He ran his fingers over the scar on his face. (It had been inflicted during an ambush set up by the Captain-General. His arm was also covered with scars from the same attack. On his shoulder he still had an open wound.)

"I hope Francisco Teles recovers. We knew each other in the dungeons many years ago when we were thrown into prison. But I'm convinced your actions were justified," said Bernardo. "Someone had to put a stop to this situation. Things couldn't go on as they were. I hope it'll teach Teles a lesson."

"Dom Bernardo, aren't you afraid of what might happen?" João de Couros asked.

"At my age you no longer fear. If we're capable of the direst evil, we're also capable of the greatest good. I've thought long and hard about what is just and worthy, and what is not; my conclusion is that sometimes you have to commit an injustice to see justice done."

"I don't believe any injustice has been done," interrupted Gregório.

"Can't you see these scars of mine?" De Brito asked him.

"And what about the scars on our souls?" said Gonçalo. He looked from one to the other with his small dark eyes. "The ancients say one shouldn't repay evil with evil. But we're being exterminated."

"If only the Prince had listened to us . . . ," Bernardo said sadly. The Secretary affirmed that the Regent was not as unworthy a ruler as some imagined. He could even be described as considerate and good-hearted. But if all men had their weaknesses, His Royal Highness's was his love of power. He didn't abuse it in order to enrich himself or to attract women, or even to destroy his enemies. He rejoiced in his title and status, that was all. It gave him great pleasure to parade through the streets of Lisbon escorted by his guards, in a carriage bearing the royal coat of arms. He enjoyed receiving his subjects, not to lord over them, but to grant them favours. A generosity that was disinterested after a fashion, a question of personal vanity. Playing with power amused him. For although Pedro, the Peace-Maker, had entered the Palace of Ribeira by violent means and forced the abdication of his brother, mad King Afonso, he had listened to his people and signed the peace treaty with Spain, thereby ending the War of Restoration. And although he had seduced his sister-in-law, Maria Francisca, the daughter of the Comte de Nemours – or, as many believed, had been seduced by her – and imprisoned his mad, inept brother,

29

despite the intrigues of the French cabal with the Marquis de Saint-Romain, Louis XIV's secret envoy, the Regent was loved by his people, for he had not betrayed them.

"You know, my friends," confided Bernardo, "when I was very young, I dreamed of being a Jesuit like my brothers, but finally decided to become a soldier, swept along by sentiments and ambitions I scarcely understood. I had fanciful dreams like all students."

Perhaps Bernardo saw the assassination of the Captain-General as a noble and, therefore, poetic gesture. He did not consider himself a poet, although he wrote some verses in Spanish, "pale imitations of Camoens" as he described them. Lyrics on the theme of love, epic poems in a classical vein, poems about loving God, about religious zeal and Christian resignation. He had not become a Jesuit but considered himself more religious than his brother Antonio, who possessed all the traits of the true politician. Padre Vieira, how-ever, was now an old man and wished nothing more to do with politics, preferring to devote his life to philosophy and writing.

"But he's still a sly fox," said the Secretary. "We should change places. I'm convinced that, like me, he would really love to have been a poet."

"Poets have been the curse of our language," exclaimed Gregório.

"And as we know, the Jesuit Order has never produced any poets. It has formed soldiers. And here am I mixed up in politics, the victim of circumstances."

"You've always been a fighter," De Brito reminded him.

"True. I only regret that things have turned out like this. But we might as well accept the situation."

"We might as well," repeated Gregório, placing his hand on the old Secretary's shoulder.

"What excuses shall we offer to God to convince Him that we don't deserve to be thrown into hell?" asked João de Couros.

"Ah, now you're touching on a subject I really know something about," interrupted a man who was sitting in a corner. "It's some time since we last saw each other, is it not, Dom Bernardo?"

"Oh, it's you, Councillor. Forgive me, I hadn't noticed you."

"No need to apologize. I'm used to being ignored."

Councillor Luiz Bonicho rose to his feet. He was small and pale. He had an enormous nose and a hunchback. "But as I was saying, you are now touching on a subject I know better than anyone: The Land of the Dog. We're at the gates of the Eternal Fire. I'm not saying this to torment you, to sting you like the wasp I so closely resemble; I'm simply stating a fact: We're entering the House of Damnation. We know there's no harm whatsoever in stabbing a scoundrel to death, all the more so when it's an act of revenge. So long as the scoundrel isn't one of the Governor's friends. But this one was, so be careful, gentlemen, make sure your breeches are securely laced, for Braço de Prata will try to pull them down and kick you in the backside. And don't worry about the Captain-General's fate. In fact, we'll have done him a great favour if he's been dispatched to Satan's palace. Anywhere would be better than this hole."

"Come now, Dom Luiz, I can see you're as bitter as ever," said De Brito.

"Bitter?" replied Bonicho. "I'm simply facing up to reality. Bitter is the spittle of that criminal, the Governor. Bitter will be the sentence passed against us by the Judges Gois and Palma. They'll be the next to attack. Doctor de Matos couldn't have given a better description of Braço de Prata than in these lines: *'The slave curses you, the white man damns you, but nothing wounds you. Colourless churl that you are, you'll be slandered and mocked until the cannonball that knocked your arm off comes back and gets you in the face.'"*

These words were received with mixed cries of approval and derision.

"The third to die," continued Bonicho, "will have to be Braço de Prata himself. Either we eliminate him or he'll eliminate us. The judges need watching. As councillors, we think the Tribunal is on our side, but we're soon proved wrong. They're rogues. We must keep up our efforts to have the Court of Appeals abolished. After all, we were responsible for having it set up in the first place in 1652. The judges and magistrates were barred, and the councillors wiped their feet on that scum. But back they came and now those same swine who should be on their knees and licking our boots have no respect for us. They accuse us of being ignorant and corrupt. Some councillors are. If they appoint the sons of disreputable merchants and unscrupulous plantation owners who are only interested in money, what else do they expect? But to refer to me, Luiz Bonicho da Gama, as ignorant? To hell with the lot of them!"

Some of the men chuckled. They were taken aback by the councillor's outburst.

"Don't those fools know that I studied Theology in Portugal?" ranted Bonicho. "I spent years in France, I'm a qualified theologian! Don't they understand? They're so stupid that they can scarcely compile their own reports. They draft them with such awkward phrasing and illegible signatures, that you can only surmise what's been written there. Corrupt? Very well, we're corrupt. But who in this city isn't? Do they really believe it's possible to mete out justice equally? Only some bastard of a priest could believe such hypocrisy. No, no, it simply isn't possible. So what are we aldermen supposed to do? The next best thing: if we can't benefit everyone, then let's benefit some. Who? Well, the sugar barons, for one, the landed aristocracy who own plantations and slaves. And who else? The Captain-General. The judges. The Governor. And then? Ourselves, of course. Where's the corruption? Did Christ not say: Love thy neighbour as thyself? That's precisely what we're doing. If we can't love our neighbour, at least let's love ourselves. Palma, Gois, Teles, Braço de Prata, they've all given us nothing but trouble. We're sinking in shit up to our eyebrows. But then so are they. Things have clearly got out of control on both sides. Those cuckolds have not settled their debts in all these years I've been protecting them. At the first opportunity, they tried to stab me in the back. No, no, I don't feel any remorse. I've never had any inclination to play the saint."

Bernardo listened. Having heard what Bonicho had to say, he decided they should proceed. "Well, gentlemen, I think the alderman's right. We must be more cautious than ever. The fact that we're all gathered here together could make things easier for them. Let's get back to leading our lives as if nothing had happened. João de Couros, Piçarro, Francisco Amaral, Barros de França, Rolim and Antonio de Brito will remain here in the College to avoid arrest. Doctor Gregório de Matos is also out of favour with the Governor and should take every precaution, though I see no reason to remain here. You can go to Samuel da Fonseca's plantation in Recôncavo. You can take my daughter with you. Dona Bernardina is alone and in poor health. What do you say?"

Gregório thought for a moment and said he had no desire to leave the city, but he was willing to accompany Dona Bernardina to the plantation.

Turning to the Councillor, Bernardo asked: "Dear friend, surely there's no further need for you or your fencing master to remain in hiding?"

"I'd no intention of rotting away in this dark hole. Besides, I can look after myself."

"My son Gonçalo will remain here since he's been sentenced to exile. I'll go to the Jesuit Fathers' country estate until things calm down. As for your families, they should be taken to places of safety."

They agreed that the men should go into hiding. But no one believed that the Governor would do anything to the women, the elderly or the children.

"We can't afford to take any risks," warned Bernardo.

"Couldn't our families stay here in the College? It's the safest place of all."

"I'm not so sure it is. I saw soldiers prowling around when I came in."

"But surely the Governor, villain that he is, wouldn't dare force his way into the College. He would have the entire Church against him, the entire population, all of Portugal, His Majesty and even the Pope," argued De Brito.

"Then we must act," said Bernardo. "There's one more thing. The Captain-General's hand."

"We'll make a gift of it to the people. They will carry it in procession through the streets and up the slopes. Let them hang it on the door of Braço de Prata's mansion as a reminder of our revenge," suggested De Brito.

"I don't think that's such a good idea," said Bernardo. "We don't know if the people are on our side. And Teles' death shouldn't be seen as revenge. Please, I beg you, entrust me with the Captain-General's hand. It can only be used to incriminate us. The Fathers have also requested that no weapons should be brought inside the College. This is the house of God. They want no daggers or swords. No guns."

33

The men surrendered their arms to Bernardo who locked them in a chest. Those who were about to leave would take arms with them. Antonio de Brito went to the writing desk. He opened one of the compartments and took out a small bundle swathed in blood-stained rags. He placed it on the table and unwrapped it. The men gathered round to watch. Inside the rags lay the rigid, black and blue hand of the Captain-General with an emerald on the ring finger. They stood in silence examining the sinister, mutilated hand. The flesh gave off a slightly bitter smell.

Bernardo wrapped it back up in the rags.

"I'll look after this."

With words of reassurance he took his leave.

Gonçalo was waiting for him at the door.

"You didn't surrender your weapons, my boy."

"I don't want to be unarmed, father."

"All the others agreed. You know that the Jesuits won't allow it. Hand them over. You have nothing to prove to anyone."

"Really father, this is hypocritical. Lots of priests go around the streets carrying a dagger in their belt."

Gonçalo clutched his dagger. He handed it to his father. Carefully he removed his firearm from his belt. The pistol was heavy for its size, perhaps because of the silver butt. He raised it to eye-level. Then closing one eye, took aim at an insect on the wall. At that distance he might hit it.

"Your ammunition," ordered his father.

The youth handed him the weapon and a leather pouch.

"Such acts are not for us, my boy. We have to think of our reputation. I know we're being persecuted and I understand how you feel, but our family tradition is one of precept and learning. Let those who know no better dishonour themselves with violence. You must devote your life to books and study rather than waste your time with artefacts of destruction. We must cherish values and aspirations that sustain life. How often I've begged you to give up this pursuit of violence. Why didn't you heed me? Now you're in serious trouble."

"Yes, father, I know. Forgive me, but I can't resist this thirst for adventure."

"Then you must try harder. After all, you are a Ravasco."

Maria was waiting for the Secretary at the gates of the College.

As he came out, she stopped him:

"Dona Bernardina sent you this, sir." She handed the Secretary a fine gold chain with a medal. "She beseeches you to wear it at all times, for protection."

"Thank you, my child," he told her. "Now go home and stay beside your mistress. As you know, Dona Bernardina should not be left alone."

"Yes, sir."

Maria was turning to leave when Bernardo called her back.

"Would you do something for me?"

"Yes, sir."

"Something which could be very dangerous."

"I'm not easily frightened, sir. I'll do anything you ask."

Bernardo handed her the bundle containing the Captain-General's hand.

"Get rid of this. No prying. Just throw it away tonight, in some place where no one will find it. Then meet me in the College chapel and tell me how it went."

"Very well, sir. I'll do as you say."

Bernardo took a gold coin from his purse and held it out to Maria.

"There's no need, sir. I earn as much as any of the Queen's ladies-in-waiting."

"Never mind, girl, take it."

Carved inside the entrance to the College chapel was the emblem of the Company of Jesus, IHS, *Iesus Hominis Salvator*. And on top of the tall building with its numerous rectilinear divisions were marble statues of Francis Xavier, Ignatius Loyola and Francis Borgia. Bernardo entered the sanctuary built with stone brought from Alcântara. The nave was flanked by four side-chapels separated by a broad transept. At the far end, the high altar with its impressive proportions looked solemn and austere.

Some priests were kneeling at prayer, others were walking about. Young pupils played quietly in the vestibule. The smell of burning incense pervaded the building.

Bernardo knelt before the altar. A child scampered out of the church.

A few moments later Antonio Vieira entered by a side door. He was wearing a simple faded black habit tied at the waist with a thin cord. In his right hand he was carrying a quill, as if he had just stopped writing that very second.

The brothers embraced each other and went into the sacristy, a spacious room with dark, polished furniture.

"I suppose you know what happened yesterday? Apparently because of me," said Bernardo.

"I'm kept informed. Sin is part of man's nature. The idea no longer exists that *'He who does not hate his father and mother, and wife, and children, and brothers and sisters, and his own soul, cannot be my disciple'*, – it's a medieval precept of virtue for those who relinquished everything to follow God. Virtue must be subordinated to the interests of the Kingdom. Religion for me no longer means distancing oneself from the world. The greatest sin is that of omission. So don't grieve. It's for God to judge human actions and for men to act in accordance with their own conscience."

"But I am grieving, Antonio. I'm different from this world, we're both different from the men who inhabit this earth."

"I don't believe we're different. We're simply on the other side."

"No, Antonio, we're different. That's why we're on the other side. Otherwise there would be no conflict."

"We are all equal in the eyes of God. Stop moaning and don't lose heart. As a devout man, lament your misfortunes, but if they hadn't done what they did, our adversary wouldn't have been satisfied with just the city and its wealth. He would have tried to possess our souls, and no one could have stopped him. You're defending the Holy Roman Catholic Faith and putting your life at risk out of loyalty to the Crown. As for me, they're trying to goad me into behaving like Dom Marcos Teixeira, who exchanged his rosary for a lance, his religious habit for a coat of mail, and gave up being a prelate of the church to become an army captain. But they won't succeed, I shall never leave this place of retreat."

He paused.

"Was Gonçalo one of the hooded men who carried out the crime?"

"Well . . . he didn't tell me anything, but you know what my son is like, always trying to wash over the stains of past injuries with blood. What about our leaving tonight? I still have a matter to settle. Is it wise to go out in the night air? It can get so cold in these parts."

"Tonight is fine, I'll be well wrapped up. By then everything should be sorted out."

"Do you know what I've been thinking? I'd like to enter the Jesuit Order."

"It's been on your mind for some time, Bernardo. That's why you never married and left all your children illegitimate."

"I could never forgive Filipa. But don't let's talk about that right now, I've more serious problems on my mind."

A little crop-haired Indian boy crouched beside Padre Antonio without stirring, fascinated by a tiny insect that was running between the feet of the wooden benches.

"This is our best choirboy," said Antonio Vieira, pointing to the child. "Sing my boy. *Ere-î-kuab xe nde r-ausuba.*"

"What were you saying, Antonio?"

"I'm very fond of this child."

The boy got to his feet, looking up at the priest with his big round eyes, and intoned the low notes of plainsong. His pure voice seemed to come from heaven rather than from his tiny human throat.

"Ah, if only one could undo the past, turn the clock back and achieve the impossible, if only what has happened had never taken place." Looking at the little Indian boy, Padre Vieira remembered his misfortunes in Maranhão. Despite everything, those had been the best days of his life. He had gone around dressed in a coarse, black habit woven locally, its colour faded; he existed on corn meal, slept little; he had covered miles on foot for there were no animals to ride in that region. The Jesuit used to work from morning to night. He spent much of his time commending himself to God (my friend, it isn't fear of hell that will carry me to heaven); he never left his cell except to save a soul; he wept for his sins, made others weep for theirs; and he devoted any time left over to reading the works of Teresa of Avila and other such holy writings.

It was important to convert the natives of Maranhão, to ensure that the faith of the Portuguese settlers should be sustained and that the native Indians be persuaded to believe in God.

The vast number of Indian savages living in the hinterland spoke a wide variety of dialects. Some of those who lived amidst the Portuguese, foreign immigrants and Brazilians, were slaves while others were already free.

Widespread greed, especially among the powerful landowners, resulted in one military expedition after another into the hinterland where Indians were taken captive and brought back in ropes. They were tortured, and one village chief had his fingers burned until he delivered more slaves. The married women were dragged from the villages and set to work in private homes without any hope of ever seeing their loved ones again. Captives lived in abysmal conditions and were forced into hard labour, growing tobacco; they were not granted any free time to cultivate their own smallholdings nor given food, so they and their families suffered and died of starvation. Nor were they allowed to practise their own religion or to be catechized by the missionaries. These atrocities led the Indians in the hinterland to loathe the very name of the Portuguese. They retreated further and further into the forests until they finally fought back in desperation, causing as much damage as they could. Vieira tried to forget, but these memories continued to haunt and torment him.

He had struggled to close off the hinterland and to prohibit any more ransoms, and tried to ensure that all the ransomed slaves should be declared free. But it seemed to be an impossible task and experience proved him right: mutinies were justified on the pretext that the Indians were the only means of support the settlers possessed.

Within forty years, on the coast and inland, they had massacred more than two million Indians and destroyed more than five hundred large settlements, as Vieira had reported to King Afonso VI. That year had witnessed the outbreak of the savage War of the Barbarians, a most cruel and vicious assault on the Indians who resisted the expropriation of their lands. No one was ever brought to justice for causing all this death and destruction.

# IV

A CHOIR OF PRIESTS walked in procession through the city streets reciting the *proficiscere anima Christiani*. Their voices, solemn and in harmony, filled the air with a well-rehearsed symphony.

A novice with a sad expression appeared to be self-absorbed, his lips uttering no prayer, his eyes raised to heaven, his mouth open, clearly distressed, as he stumbled over the cobblestones in badly tied sandals. He came to a halt as if walking in his sleep. The priests behind him also came to a halt, puzzled by the youth's odd behaviour.

The coadjutor approached and questioned the novice.

"I've had a vision," said the youth.

"More visions?"

"One yesterday, Reverend Father, and another one today."

"And what have you seen this time?"

"God. God in armour with a fiery sword raised against the city of Bahia."

Midday. The dairyman passed, leading his cow; he paused to watch the priests. Then as he made his rounds, he told others of the novice's vision. Some saw it as an omen of impending evil; according to others, the apparition betokened a punishment about to be inflicted unless vice was eradicated. The blind man with the concertina sang a little ballad about a deluge of molten iron that would destroy everyone. Merchants believed that prices would rise because of the shortage of money. Manufacturers predicted that workshops would burn to the ground. Speculators decided that the sword was pointing to seams of gold in the mountains.

Many, absorbed in their own affairs, simply ignored the warning.

Padre Vieira declared: "Nonsense. Better to guard both sea and land than to lose one's mind in heaven."

The first guards appeared at two o'clock in the afternoon. People started coming out on to the streets to watch the parading cavalry and hear the foot-soldiers sound their trumpets and bugles. Flags waved from their staffs, long pennants and unfurled banners touched the ground.

The soldiers took up their positions overlooking the city; from the watch-towers of the fortresses they aimed their arquebuses. From the jutting ledges of the ravelin on the Fortress of São Pedro, towering above the surrounding houses, the bronze cannons were angled to aim at the streets.

Antonio de Souza had spent the last hours in session with his advisers, poring over maps of the city, charting the places for attack, discovering the vulnerable points where his enemies were located. In the higher part of the city, to the west, the Archbishop was watching from the bridge which connected his palace to the Cathedral. The Cathedral was neither massive nor imposing. It had a stone façade and convoluted pillars, two tiers of windows, square towers. Beneath the panelled and painted ceiling, rows of simple benches, all of them empty. The outer door was locked.

The square and the palace forecourt swarmed with soldiers and onlookers.

There was the most extraordinary bustle in the city. From the Hospice to the College, from the Cathedral to the windlass, from the door of the Carmelite church to that of St Benedict, people gathered, watching.

The crowd jostled their way through the streets, entered the taverns to chat and drink, admired the troops on horseback in pursuit of suspects.

When the Governor passed on his stallion, lots of people fled in terror.

"It's Braço de Prata."

Others stifled their fear and stayed rooted to the spot as they confronted the terrifying apparition of this man with his inert arm resting on his lap, the black-gloved hand visible beneath his cuff.

The Governor was supervising the search in person. His face impassive, he headed the posse of soldiers.

He drove his horse into the crowd which scattered in panic, muttering curses under their breath, or giving loud cheers. There were lots of soldiers on horseback, though most of them, dressed in brown linen uniforms, with sharpened swords and good pistols, were on foot.

The group divided and carried out house-to-house searches. They blockaded the roads, cordoned off squares, interrogated passers-by, looked for witnesses, gathered information.

When they were refused entry to homes occupied by Ravasco family relatives, they broke down the doors. They ransacked houses, smashing up anything which was of no interest to them, throwing furniture out onto the street and setting it alight. Numerous supporters of the Ravasco faction escaped into the countryside and hid in shacks concealed among the trees, or sought refuge on farms or plantations, some still in their night attire, barefoot, and carrying nothing except a sack with their valuables. They escaped at great risk by river, sea, or into the ravine. The older fugitives recalled having similar experiences during the Dutch invasion.

The city gates were under guard and no one could enter or leave the port without being searched and identified.

By the end of the day, thousands of suspects from every corner of the city had been taken to the dungeons, including soldiers from the Governor's private army.

"No one saw anything, no one knows anything, no one has uttered a word," the captain of the garrison informed the Governor.

The Captain-General Francisco de Teles de Menezes died at six o'clock in the evening. The tolling of bells echoed throughout the city, spreading along the headland and over the black rocks at St Anthony's Point, the white sands of the bay. The sun low, almost resting on the water, sending golden rays across the sky. The entire province, from the southern shore of the São Francisco River to the northern shore of All Saints Bay and Padrão Point, was in mourning by order of the Governor.

Religious ceremonies to mark the Captain-General's death would be held throughout the night. The burial in the crypt of the Church of St Francis would take place the following morning. Vigil over the corpse was held in the chapel inside the church. Accompanying the cortège, a choir of Franciscan friars intoned a funeral dirge. There was an atmosphere of melancholy and unease.

In the College church, while the search went on for their friends, Padre Vieira and Bernardo were informed of Teles' death and of the blockade around the city.

"Was it for this that we sailed unknown seas?" asked Padre Vieira, staring with beady eyes into his brother's face. "Was it for this that we discovered new lands and climates? Was it for this that we braved winds and storms with so much daring? There is scarcely a sandbank in the ocean that has not witnessed the most awful shipwrecks and the drowning of Portuguese sailors. Was it so that after so many perils, so many disasters; devoured by monsters, wild beasts and sea-creatures, so many painful deaths without burial on deserted beaches, we should witness the lands we conquered come to this?"

That same night, after attending the funeral service, the Governor rode up to the stable gates. He had an escort of soldiers.

The guard opened the dark wooden gates and the squadron entered, making its way down a tree-lined path illuminated by torches, to the coach-house.

Riders, grooms, peons and stable-boys gathered round. The soldiers dismounted and their horses were led away to a nearby stream.

The moon appeared, casting a reddish glow on the dark mountain slopes with their motley vegetation. The sky gradually became clearer, the stars disappeared.

The horses were watered and scrubbed down by coachmen. Stable-hands cleaned the saddles, the crimson covers, the hide straps, bridles, reins, stirrups; they beat the leather leggings against the wall, sending up clouds of dust. Then with sand they polished the metal fittings.

Under a wattle roof, a tall man waited, holding an oil-lamp

which gave off poor light; he was dressed in linen robes, the sleeves puffed at the shoulders and his collar trimmed with ermine that extended to the hem. The curvature of his long neck made him look like a bird of prey.

The Governor went to him, and the robed man, Judge Manuel da Costa Palma, asked him: "Now then, Dom Antonio, has the cordon round the city achieved anything?"

The Governor looked despondent.

"Nothing."

"I feel very sorry for Teles," said Palma. "He was a decent fellow. He didn't deserve this."

Antonio de Souza observed in the distance the shadowy forms of the horses splashing the silvery water.

"He was a brave soldier," he said. With measured strokes, he lashed his whip against the edge of the verandah. His thoughts seemed to be elsewhere.

"He had his own ideas about most things," Palma continued. "Had circumstances been different, he could have become a real hero. He was born, and died, at the wrong moment. Had he been a few years older, he could have proved his worth in the battle against Sigismund."

A carriage drawn by four magnificent chestnut horses had been stationed in front of the small shed. A soldier, still in his teens, held the horses by the reins.

"What does your Lordship intend to do?"

"To arrest the Ravasco clan."

"The priest has immunity. The Secretary is in hiding and there's no proof against him."

"I'll find a way. Gonçalo Ravasco has been given asylum in the College. The other assassins, too. They've been gloating at the windows, showing their contempt for authority and justice."

"Are there guards at the College gates?"

"Yes, but what's the use? The criminals can remain there in safety, and escape whenever they like without being seen. Students and priests come and go all the time."

"We could use the Courts. I've enlisted the support of half the judges."

"I'll invade the College."

The Judge looked at De Souza.

"What's the matter? Why do you look so shocked?" asked the Governor.

"Invade the College?"

"Precisely. We'll trap the wolf in his lair."

"But, Dom Antonio, that's somewhat rash."

"What's rash about it? One would think you were hand in glove with the Ravasco mob. I am the Governor, after all."

"And what about the Archbishop?"

"He won't open his mouth. He's only been here a month but he's already shown himself to be a scoundrel. I need your help."

"But . . ."

"I need a warrant to arrest the Ravascos."

"Even Antonio Vieira?"

"Him, too."

"That's impossible."

"Nothing is impossible."

"On what charge?"

"Murder."

"But that would mean starting a lawsuit."

"Then get on with it."

"But Antonio Vieira didn't kill Teles."

"He's the brains behind it all."

"He has friends at Court. He'll defend himself tooth and nail."

"I also have allies in Lisbon."

"I'm unhappy about the idea of invading the College."

"If you don't want to cooperate, that's up to you. But I'll consider it disloyal. Where's your spirit? Are you afraid? Even if you don't cooperate, you'll still be held responsible. Everybody knows we're in league. You're also an interested party in this affair, and besides, you're in no position to deny me anything."

Palma looked into his eyes, trying to detect any hint of a threat. The Governor's opinion carried weight. Not because of the position he held, nor because of his intimidating presence. But because he usually had his way.

"Let's suppose a day has already gone by," De Souza told him. "Let's suppose this is no longer the fourth but the fifth of June, 1683. You look at yourself in the mirror and which would you prefer to think? Palma, you're a coward, you didn't do what was expected of you. Or: Palma, you're a heretic, you invaded the Jesuit College although it was only to take revenge on your god-son's assassins? There's nothing to fear. An ocean divides us from the Prince and two oceans from the Pope. A murder has been committed which gives us every right and we'll have no difficulty in convincing them. Besides, something tells me that the Ravascos are also plotting against us. I've no doubt that we're their real target. Padre Vieira would be perfectly capable of plotting my death. Let's get rid of him. We'll be doing a great favour to many men in power. He's cursed and hated as much in Lisbon as in Rome."

"In Rome? He's held in great esteem there."

"He was. Now he's old and decrepit. He's finished. Why else would he have come back to this god-forsaken place? If he had any strength left, he would be conniving elsewhere, filling the ears of the mighty with his malicious 'half-baked schemes', as the Count of Ericeira remarked. There's no reason to fear him. He himself admits that he's vulnerable."

*"To him who consents no harm is done*, as the saying goes."

"Another foolish maxim invented by the law. Go now, and do what has to be done."

# V

BEARING TORCHES the police made their rounds. Maria walked silently through the dark streets, carrying inside a leather bag the bundle which Bernardo had asked her to dispose of. She was curious to know what it contained. She touched it and felt something rigid, yet smooth. It gave off a most unpleasant smell. Unable to contain her curiosity, she opened the bag, and unwrapped the rags. She was overcome with revulsion and fear. She knew where that hand had come from; after all, the circumstances of the Captain-General's death were common knowledge in the city. A precious green stone sparkled on the ring finger of the left hand. Peering closely, she saw that the initials FTM were engraved on the gold band. Francisco de Teles de Menezes. Maria's heart was pounding. She put the bundle back inside the bag.

It was drizzling. She had to tramp through mud. Whenever she passed a beggar or pauper on the street, she pressed the bag to her bosom. She had never thought that a human hand could be so heavy.

She wandered through the city, shivering, clutching the fetid bundle, feeling quite sick, and steering clear of the guards who were patrolling the streets and searching passers-by. She skirted the walls of São Tomé de Souza, made her way through the maze of houses, then up to the top of the hill until she reached the huge double doors of St Benedict's. The dark precipice gaped below. If she threw the hand down there, it might be discovered by daylight. She descended the slope of São Francisco, went along the Rua do Thesouro, skirted the friary, passed by the Carmelite church, then the College; once in the square, she gazed down on the lower part of the city with its buildings, three and four storeys

high, at the uncultivated plots, the marshes, the puddles of stagnant water and the scrubland.

Shadowy forms passed amidst the darkness as in a dream. A
black maid emptied rubbish on to the street. Maria waited until
she had finished this disgusting ritual and was back indoors. She
then went up to the heap of litter. There were gnawed bones,
scraps of food, fruit peel, leftovers turned to mush, all mixed
together and beyond recognition. With one foot, she cleared a
tiny space among the refuse and threw the Captain-General's hand
into it.

She ran quick as lightning along the street. Remembering that
there were patrols guarding the roads, she slowed down. If she
were to be seen running, she would be detained. In the shelter of
a dark alleyway, she sat down, leaning back against a wall.

She took a deep breath.

It was a mistake to have thrown the hand on the rubbish heap.
After all, although only a hand, it was still part of the dead man's
body. The Captain-General's ghost might come to haunt her.
There were many ways for a dead man to take revenge on the
living. In dreams. By placing curses on them. She had made a
terrible mistake leaving the hand behind. Besides, it might be
discovered next morning.

She remained there motionless for some time, imagining she
could hear horses clattering on the cobblestones. A cold sweat
broke out on her forehead.

A faint light filtered in from a window. Words, visions of the
orphanage, meaningless phrases came into her head.

She rose to her feet, almost slipping on the muddy ground. Her
hands, feet and the back of her skirt were caked with soft, reddish
mud. She wiped her hands on her blouse. She must look dreadful
and might easily attract attention. She tidied her hair and inadver-
tently smeared mud on her forehead.

Trying not to walk too quickly, she retraced her steps.

In the distance she could see that pile of rubbish. A dog was
sniffing the blood-stained bundle and struggling to dig it out with
one paw. She shooed the dog away and retrieved the hand which
now smelled really foul. Shoving it hastily into her bag, she felt
her stomach heave.

Unsure of which direction to take, she continued to wander through the streets. The best solution would be to throw the bundle into the water. Should she make for the dyke? For the sea? She drew her veil closer, raised the collar of her cape and headed towards the shore, feeling more reassured now that she had a route to follow.

Descending the slope of the Pau da Bandeira, where she saw signs saying *boats for hire*, she arrived at the lower part of the city. The streets were even more narrow, polluted and badly lit. She caught a faint smell of alcohol.

A man was urinating against a wall. A whore standing in a doorway whistled at him and he turned to look at her. The woman then opened her cloak and exposed a stocky body, tightly clad in a brown dress. She was young with firm breasts.

Maria pressed on cautiously. Shaking with fear, she passed a group of soldiers. Conscious that they were staring at her, she opened her cape as she had seen the prostitute do, exposing her body. The soldiers lost interest. They were not on the look-out for whores. Maria quickened her pace, heading for the harbour.

At the shore, she made certain that she had not been followed and that no one was watching her. A cat was sniffing dead fish swept in by the tide, caught between hunger and the foul smell. Through the gaps in the clouds, a white light descended.

Maria spotted a small boat on the sand and approached. A man lay outstretched inside the boat, covered with a tattered blanket that reeked of spirits. He was restless and holding a metal flask.

"Are you asleep?" Maria asked.

The sailor jumped.

When he saw who had spoken, he relaxed.

"You must be joking. Would you like some rum, my pretty one?" He stroked the flask as if he were embracing an old friend. "Rum." His voice was hoarse and grating.

"What are you doing here, my flower? Wearing out your sandals?"

"I'd like to go for a sail."

"For a sail?" chuckled the man, sitting up. "For a sail?"

"The sea's calm."

"If you think you're going to rob me . . . What have you got in that bag? Eh? Cherries!" The man took a swig of rum, spilling it over his clothes. He raised his cloak and revealed a red leather holster on his belt, with the butt of a pistol sticking out.

"I've got this," Maria told him, showing him the gold coin she had received from Bernardo Ravasco.

The man thought for a moment. Looked around. No one. "That'll pay for a short trip." He grabbed the coin, examined it, bit it, and popped it in his pocket. Then he got up, stored the flask and blanket at the bottom of the boat.

Maria noticed there was a skull tattooed on the man's hand. Pressing the bag to her bosom, she waited until he had dragged the boat over two rounded tree-trunks down to the water's edge. Once afloat, he helped her to clamber aboard and pushed the boat out before swiftly jumping in, drenched to the waist. He sat down and began rowing. He never took his eyes off Maria who, still clutching the bag, watched the oars hitting the water.

They were some thirty to forty metres from shore, passing between the tall hulls of sailing vessels and cables grinding on the timbers.

They remained silent. The sailor looked at the leather bag, sizing it up. It was not uncommon to see girls with swollen bellies on that bleak shore, trying to get rid of an unwanted baby with the assistance of an old woman practised in abortions. He was accustomed to taking some of them out in his boat to dump the foetus, sometimes even a stillborn child, in the sea. But this girl didn't look as if she had had an abortion, nor did she utter a word, and the way she was holding the bag suggested she was carrying something valuable. Stolen goods perhaps? How had she come by that rare and precious gold coin she had paid him for the trip? Could she be a thief in trouble?

"I know what you're carrying there," he said.

Maria turned pale. "No. No, you mustn't."

"Either it's something you've stolen or an abortion."

"No, it's nothing of the kind."

"Well, what is it then?"

Maria stood up, steadying herself.

"Stop, stop rowing. This is far enough."

49

"Let me see what you've got there," demanded the sailor, suddenly reaching out and snatching the bag.

"No, for the love of God, give it back to me!"

"Let me have a look, my pretty one. Where's the harm? I'll be as silent as a man with no tongue." The sailor opened the bag and pulled out the bloodstained bundle with a look of disappointment. So it was an abortion after all. He unwrapped the rags. His feet tapped nervously on the planking and he shook from head to toe. Suddenly he paused. A glint flashed in his eye. He had spotted the ring with its emerald stone. He immediately forgot the stench coming from the hand.

"You're going to throw it into the water? That's not such a bad idea. But I'll keep the ring. It'll be more useful on my finger than stuck in the guts of some fish."

"No, please. I must throw everything into the sea. The ring, the rags, everything."

The sailor took the pistol from his belt and pointed it at Maria.

"This ring is mine."

He eased the ring off with some difficulty and threw the hand into the water. He slipped it on to his finger and stared at the precious stone in admiration.

"An emerald! Gold!" he howled.

Then he paused.

"Who could have worn this ring?"

"For heaven's sake, don't breathe a word to a living soul. Throw the ring into the sea," Maria implored.

The man remained silent, looking at Maria, mulling it over. He drank more rum. He seemed to be pickled in rum. The clothes he wore, made of leather, also reeked of alcohol. Yet he didn't appear to be drunk.

The sailor turned the boat and began rowing towards land. He had his back to the shore, and would periodically look round to see where he was heading. As he rowed, he sang along to the rhythm.

Suddenly Maria turned pale, her eyes fixed on something in the distance.

The man stopped.

"What? Have you seen a ghost?"

They had reached the surf line.

"It's nothing," replied Maria, looking ahead to the shore where men bearing torches awaited their arrival.

The sailor turned round. "Bah. They're only soldiers. You're scared of them, eh?" Then he became serious. He removed the ring from his finger and handed it to Maria. "Hide it. Not a word, do you hear? If you so much as open your mouth, I'll cut the tongue from your head. You'll give me back the ring later. Don't get any ideas about making off with it. For I'll pursue you to the gates of hell. Is that clear?"

"Yes," she murmured.

Maria thought of jumping from the boat and escaping to some other shore. But she could not swim, and would drown at once. The soldiers had their guns aimed at them. There was nothing for it but to disembark. They pushed the boat on to the sand, and over the tree-trunks.

"What's this? What's this?" cried one of the soldiers. "What are you two up to? Smuggling? Whoring?"

The soldiers searched the sailor and confiscated his pistol. They found the gold coin and kept it. They opened Maria's leather bag, now empty.

"Speak up or I'll arrest you," the officer warned.

"We haven't done anything," replied the sailor. "I was resting in my boat when this wench appeared and we went for a sail. Where's the harm in that? She's no virgin, as you can see."

The soldier held his torch up to Maria's face. She was pale and numb. She looked pleadingly at the sailor.

"You've been hiding tobacco," accused the soldiers.

He put his gun to the sailor's head.

"Speak up, or you're as good as dead."

"I was satisfying this bitch, Captain," the sailor whimpered, "that was all, nothing else."

"Is that the truth, girl, eh?"

Maria said nothing.

"Speak up, damn you," the officer bellowed.

To rid herself of the sailor would mean falling into the hands of the guards and, worse still, with the ring hidden in her belt.

"That's the truth, sir," she said.

The sailor sighed.

"This man's a smuggler, sir," interrupted one of the soldiers. "He's from the Van de Saande brigade that's been looting the sugar-mills at Recôncavo. I know him."

"Off to jail with this rogue," said the officer.

"But Captain, I haven't done anything. I'm not a smuggler, I'm a privateer!"

"And as for you, my girl! You'll spend the night in the cells."

The guards howled with laughter. They prodded Maria and the sailor and marched them off, keeping their guns trained on the prisoners.

"I'm innocent, Captain!" the sailor pleaded.

"Shut your mouth, vermin," said the soldier, poking him in the ribs.

Maria was alone in the cell. Should they search her, all was lost. Bernardo must be getting anxious, waiting for her in the College chapel. If they did not search her, she would hand over the jewel to the Secretary on her release. But the ring did not belong to him. She put her hand to her waist and ran her fingers over the ring. How much could the gem and gold be worth? How often she had dreamed of having money. If only the ring were hers, she could sell it and give some of the money to João Berco in recompense for everything he had spent on her since rescuing her from the Misericórdia Alms-house. Her husband could be a brute at times but Maria was deeply grateful to João for having chosen her from among the orphans to be his wife. She could never abandon him, now that he was almost blind, without so much as a farthing to hire a street urchin to look after him. If she sold the ring, the money would help her support her husband until he died, and there would still be enough money to pay her passage aboard a ship sailing to Lisbon, a dream she cherished. Fashionably dressed in widow's weeds, she would cross the ocean on the flagship of the armada, and from the square in front of the Palace of Ribeira, she would wave to the Regent and watch real nobles parade by in gilded coaches.

So dreaming, her hand resting against the cold wall of her prison cell, she fell asleep.

It was midnight when the brothers left the church, crammed into their chaise. Bernardo had waited for Maria to come with news of her risky mission but his daughter's companion never appeared.

The scribe, Padre Soares, perched on the edge of his seat, drove the carriage, keeping a watchful eye on the road.

The streets were deserted.

They had gone to the Ravasco mansion to look for Maria but the building was in darkness. All they found was Bernardina asleep with her maids beside her bed.

The wheels turned with difficulty, the chaise shuddered along, when suddenly they were stopped by soldiers patrolling the roads.

"We're on our way to administer the last rites," said Padre Vieira.

"Let them pass," the captain ordered. "They're priests on their way to save souls."

The soldiers removed their hats and bowed.

The chaise continued uphill.

"Hypocrites," muttered Antonio Vieira. "Today they're bowing as I pass and tomorrow they'll be after my blood. They'll rant and rave, bite and claw until they've completely destroyed me. *The more one is admired, the more one is envied.* But I'd sooner be envied than pitied. Wretched is the man who has no enemies. To have enemies may seem unfortunate, but to have none is a sure sign of even greater misfortune. Bernardo, let me tell you a little story: Themistocles went around looking very sad and people asked him why, since he was so dearly loved. He assured them this was precisely what was wrong. No worse fate than to be loved by all Greece! To win enemies is to win fame."

"Come, brother," said Bernardo, "you don't have many enemies. You're far more loved than hated."

"You're so naive. They hate me because I'm not some hermit from the desert, I'm here working myself to death because I'm not certain of saving anyone's soul, least of all my own."

"Your reward in heaven is assured."

"I detest tiresome litanies. I'm not one of your friars with hairy legs celebrating Mass with a chalice made from a bull's horn."

"I know, brother. But tell me, how are your sermons coming along?" Bernardo asked, anxious to change the subject.

"You're right," rejoined Padre Vieira, "there's nothing left for me except to shut myself away and get on with my writing. That's all I'm left with. But I intend to go on living for some time yet in order to haunt these loathsome Christians. These barefoot cynics, forever carping, they disgust me. I am wading in mire, as St Bernard once said, or was it the Abbé Guillaume de Saint Thierry? I'm incarcerated in my cell like a lizard. But I mean to stay there, for me it's still the best place on earth. Anything better is down below."

"Come, Antonio, you mustn't say such things. That's precisely what your enemies want."

"Kempis is milk-and-water, the holier-than-thou-brigade is the plague of salvation and one's conscience, the churches should be turned into prisons and hospitals. Our public figures are either contemplatives or thieves. To steal a coin makes a pirate, to plunder a city and its palaces makes an Alexander. The world is full of thieves. Especially here in the colony. Not that people here are any different or worse than elsewhere. Men are the same everywhere. But here there is no shame in committing a crime, no remorse, no conscience. Today's degenerates are a bunch of shameless extortionists."

As he spoke, Antonio Vieira raised his voice, grew hoarse, then recovered; his eyebrows went up and down, his eyes began to gleam.

"Men teach us how we should not behave."

He spoke about his opponent's bravado. Braço de Prata had shown himself to be a villain, but he had his qualities. He was tough. The Governor's greatest folly was to have involved himself with a barbarous and ignorant man like the Captain-General. The death of such an individual, like so many other deaths, would bring more good than evil. Only his mistresses will weep for him. Perhaps not even them.

"But any man, however bad, has someone to mourn at his graveside," said Padre Vieira. "Even the greatest villain, even a hermit. Teles could have written a treatise on the verbs *to steal* and *to hate*. He knew everything there was to know about theft, hatred, blackmail and extortion. It used to be said of those aides or *laterones* in the service of kings, that soon they became thieves or *ladrones*. They will all go to hell, hand in hand. The magnet attracts both iron and gold. Brazil is being torn apart by the claws of those who govern her. Here people suffer because they're ignorant riffraff, each and every one of them. God's poor little goats are the creatures who go to heaven."

The chaise came to a halt in front of the palace.

The building was in darkness, everything seemed peaceful. Bernardo was about to disembark when Padre Vieira gripped his arm.

"Don't you think it's much too quiet? Shouldn't there be a guard on duty?"

Bernardo waited.

"Can you hear horses neighing?" Padre Vieira asked him.

"Yes, Antonio, I can."

"I think we'd better go. We can send someone to fetch your papers later."

"Ah, no, how will anybody know where to find us? We're here. I'm going inside."

Bernardo got down from the chaise and entered the palace. Antonio Vieira and Padre Soares waited for him outside the main entrance.

The Secretary walked through the darkened corridors. He groped his way along, skirting the walls, until he reached the staircase, and then cautiously crept up to his room. He opened the secret compartment in his writing desk. The papers were there.

When he heard the sudden noise of horses' hooves, the clanging of metal and frantic cries outside, he immediately realized what was happening. He locked the papers back within the secret compartment. He went to the window and looked out. A patrol was approaching.

He sighed, straightened up, adjusted his attire and waited.

Padre Soares rushed in, gasping for breath.

"Braço de Prata's down there, Dom Bernardo. He's coming up the stairs like someone possessed."

Bernardo returned to the window. The soldiers were surrounding the palace.

The Governor entered accompanied by two soldiers carrying

torches, and remained quite still, a hand resting on the table. The glare from the torches accentuated his livid expression.

"The honourable Secretary of State for War is under arrest," announced the Governor. He was followed by a posse of soldiers with guns aimed at Ravasco.

Confusion broke out. Soldiers began searching the rooms, opening doors, drawers, cupboards, tossing documents into the air, overturning furniture. Ravasco knew they were looking for the papers. He stepped aside and confronted De Souza.

"May I know why you are arresting me, Governor?"

De Souza stared at him coldly.

"Your Lordship murdered the Captain-General of the city of Bahia." His silver arm, dangling at his side, began to sway gently, reflecting red tinges of light.

"You can't prove anything. And never will. I'm innocent. I was with my brother on the estate at Tanque at the time the murder was committed. Everyone knows that."

"That's not all people know."

Antonio Vieira entered in a towering rage.

"This cannot be right. It's illegal and arbitrary. Arrested?" fumed the Jesuit after his brother told him of De Souza's intentions.

The Governor turned to the priest.

"Well, would you believe it, the deaf defending the deaf! I'll pack you both off to jail at one go."

"Your Excellency knows perfectly well that you can do me no harm."

Padre Vieira, dwarfed by the man whom Gregório de Matos had once described as "a sack of melons", folded his arms.

"You're right, Padre," the Governor replied. "For the moment I'll have to be satisfied with the Secretary here. But your turn will come. Mark my words. And I won't be the one to throw you into jail. It will be the Prince Regent himself. What's more, he's been waiting for such an opportunity for a long time."

Antonio de Souza turned to his men.

"Take the Secretary away."

"No!" protested Antonio Vieira. "You will do no such thing."

"Let them, brother," intervened Bernardo. "Better not resist.

We'll settle things later once this matter has been cleared up."

"The Prince will hear of this outrage," Antonio de Vieira insisted.

"I shall write to His Royal Highness myself, Padre Vieira," said the Governor, "reporting your crimes and informing him of the secret meetings at the College in the cell of Diogo Torto, where you gentlemen have been conspiring against the government. One of these days you will find yourself sent into even greater exile. But please try to understand, Padre Vieira, I represent the Prince here in Bahia."

Bernardo Ravasco was led through the square on foot, flanked on either side by mounted soldiers. Antonio de Souza led the way, triumphant, as if parading a hunting trophy.

De Souza had directed operations in battles at sea. He had held administrative posts in Estremoz, in Olivença and Campo Maior. He had sailed to India with the armada of the Count of Sarzeda and had been First Admiral of the Fleet. For someone who had spent so much time at sea, he rode supremely well.

Padre Vieira departed in haste for the estate. José Soares stared at the road.

"Brazil is being torn apart by the sharp claws of those who govern her," said Padre Vieira. "Brazil's problem is that any unjust or arbitrary act carried out here never reaches the right ears in Portugal. Even the thieving doesn't seem to be noticed back in the metropolis. So the people struggle on in the greatest misery. And Brazil is no more than the image and reflection of Portugal, a hotbed of vice and corruption, of infinite extravagance without any financial resources and riddled with all the other contradictions of human nature. As for the Governor, I'll get even with him when I'm ready."

"Be careful, Padre," said José Soares. "The man is extremely dangerous. Let's go, Padre, let's withdraw to the estate and join the rest of the community. You mustn't get excited or you'll make yourself ill. Try to detach yourself from the indignities of the outside world."

"Detach myself and remain among our fellow priests? Are they not also men? I shall only be rid of human indignities when I meet my death, Padre Soares. The clergy of today are worthless and behave like laymen."

"Don't be unfair, Padre Vieira."

"Today this is the situation: Take a youth without a father, ill served by nature, lacking the courage to join the army or the brains to study, and with no initiative to earn his living in any other profession. Is he dishonest because he goes into government? Is he honest because he becomes a priest? These youths enter the monastery where they're fed and clothed, enjoy themselves and while away the hours in idle conversation. They can scarcely make the sign of the cross or tell you whether they believe in Christ's Resurrection."

All that day and the next, Padre Vieira continued to rant and rave; he barely slept three hours during the night, thinking about the wickedness of men, and broke into one frenzied tirade after another, quoting St Thomas of Aquinas, St Paul, the entire Bible, to justify his outrage.

## VI

WITH THE FIRST RAYS OF SUNLIGHT, Maria awoke. An officer opened her cell door and, after rebuking her and giving words of advice, he sent the girl on her way. She felt a weariness in her bones as she rose to her feet. She adjusted her skirt and tidied her hair. Suddenly she remembered the meeting with Bernardo in the church, and ran there but did not find him. A servant boy told her he had left for the estate the previous night with Padre Vieira. Maria sighed. The ring! What was she to do with it?

She knelt before the statue of Our Lady set in a niche on a side-altar and prayed. She begged the Mother of God for guidance.

Maria left the church and wandered the streets. She thought about João Berco. She thought about Lisbon. She thought about the widow's weeds of black lace, about the sea, the flagship, the noblemen, about her feet covered in mud, about poverty.

She found herself outside the premises of Dom Balthasar Drago, the jeweller. After some hesitation, she went in.

People of rough appearance, probably paupers, stared at her. Maria sat on the edge of the bench and waited her turn. One by one, clients were being served. They were either selling or pawning jewels, watches, chains, lengths of damask.

Maria's turn came. She went up to the counter and placed the ring on a small velvet cushion. The man on the other side of the counter, a stocking filled with hot salt round his throat, raised his eyes and studied her.

"Are you selling or pawning?" he asked.

"Pawning," she blurted out.

He took the ring between his pale, tapering fingers and held it up to his eyes. He stared at Maria again. With a tiny magnifying glass he examined the gem against the light.

"Ten thousand réis in silver hundreds."

"Fine."

The old man smiled. He had fully expected that the girl would not question the valuation. A reaction which nearly always meant that the object had been stolen.

Ten thousand réis was not worth much more than the coin Bernardo had given her in payment for this mission; she had handed the coin over to the sailor and it was then confiscated by the soldiers. A gold coin was worth four thousand and four hundred réis. Melting down the gold ring would get her at least two such coins. The gem must be worth about a hundred thousand réis, the equivalent of two months' salary for a colonial governor, or a judge's offering on the Feast of São João, or the wages earned by a smelter in six months.

"Name?" he asked her.

"My name?"

"Yes. Your name. Or don't you want a receipt?"

"Yes, yes, I do. The name's Maria."

"Maria what?" he snapped impatiently.

"Berco."

The jeweller wrote the name on a slip of paper and popped it and other details into a little velvet sachet. He got up and disappeared with the sachet through a door at the far end of the room, guarded by an armed man. After a seemingly endless few minutes, he returned with another sachet and emptied it on to the counter. The silver coins fell onto the wooden surface in packets of ten. The jeweller counted them out, signed the receipt and handed the lot to the girl.

Maria departed, without so much as checking the amount.

"Next," the jeweller called out.

On the way home, Maria entered a tavern. She examined the wares set out on the counters. She was starving.

"How much for a meat pie?"

"A farthing," said the landlord.

"Can I have a small one? Don't bother to wrap it."

The man handed her the meat pie. She devoured it and paid.

"Nothing else?" the landlord asked. "We have some nice sweets, candied lemon peel, boxes of quince. Silk stockings."

Maria looked down at her grimy feet. She wasn't wearing any stockings and her shoes were in tatters.

"Do you sell shoes?"

"We have these in fine leather."

She slipped them on. They felt so comfortable.

"And how much for the stockings?"

"In silk, two hundred réis."

Maria left the tavern carrying a large package. In addition to the shoes and stockings, she had bought a silk dress, a linen shirt, a hat in the finest beaver for her husband, a silk hood, a roll of tobacco, a thick pork sausage, a carved box and other knick-knacks.

João Berco sat in the room wrapped in a coarse woollen shirt that had seen better days. His skin had the same rough appearance. His shirt was the same colour as his skin and made him look like a pile of clothes tossed on to a chair. On hearing his wife enter, he twitched his nose ever so slightly as if trying to detect her smell. He was clutching his walking-stick with both hands. As Maria approached, her husband lashed out with his walking-stick, hitting her.

"Bloody bitch," he yelled. "You've been off whoring again. I woke up in such agony but what do you care? Leaving a man who's practically blind all alone in the dark in this hovel. You'll end up in jail. Why am I always being deceived? Ah, what a miserable life, I can just imagine what the gossips must be saying."

"Listen," said Maria, "I've brought you something."

The man didn't reply. He simply turned his face expectantly in her direction, seeing nothing except a shadowy form. He lived in a dark poky house, crammed full of old things, broken furniture everywhere, things scattered all over the place, grotesque angels carved in wood, as if everything had been picked up from a rubbish dump.

Maria looked at her husband slumped in the chair. His head of white hair was thrown back as if his neck could scarcely bear the weight. She put the beaver hat on his head.

"How soft," he said, stroking the pelt.

She unwrapped the tobacco, chopped a small amount, put it inside the carved box and handed it to him. João raised the tobacco to his nose and inhaled.

"Smells good! What else have you brought? Money?"

"Yes, I've also brought you some money," Maria said.

"What would I do without you? Don't ever leave me. You'll be rid of me when I die. And that won't be long. I'm worn-out and decrepit."

"You won't die for a while yet."

"I'm afraid of dying, for your sake. Where would you have as easy a life as you have with me? You would have to pay for your food and clothes. In any other house you'd wither like a dying flower, you'd finish up with dirty nails from washing dishes and scrubbing floors, and smell of garlic instead of lavender. That's what happens to whores and common women like you."

"I'm neither a whore nor common. My father was a gentleman."

"You're common all right. And your father abandoned you. I bought you from an orphanage in exchange for corn and junk. That was all you were worth. You were as skinny as a starving rat. Here at least you've got me to give you shelter." His tone softened: "You're still no more than a child."

"The life I lead is no child's life."

"But it's a good life. At least nobody treats you cruelly. Your back was black-and-blue and covered in welts when I rescued you from that orphanage. And your feet? And legs? I've seen your scars. Irons. Burning tongs. Boiling fat. Whiplashes. Your father almost killed you. Some gentleman!" João Berco paused and cleared his throat. "You're doing no more than your duty when you provide me with a little comfort. I've spent a lot of money on you. Food, clothes, the services of a barber-surgeon. You've ruined me. You smell of bogs, of rotten fish." His nostrils twitched.

"One day I'll pay you back everything I owe you." Maria removed the bag from inside her skirt and shook it close to João's ear. The coins jingled.

The man reached out to touch them. His dull eyes seemed to shine. He grabbed the coins and counted them one by one. "Where did you get these? You've been stealing! Even if you'd slept with every sailor in port you couldn't have earned all this money. Have you a lover? If you run off with any other man I'll have you done away with. You know it'll be no great loss. For me you're no better than a slave."

"Next time, I'll bring even more money."

"Why are you giving me money? You don't give a tinker's cuss about me," João muttered.

"I'm going to hire a negress to take care of you while I'm out working."

"Out with it. You have a lover. I ought to smash your face in. There's someone behind all this, someone who's trying to exploit you. I've taught you what life's all about, but you're not very bright, Maria. If you leave this house, you'll spend the rest of your life whoring with sailors, students, tramps. Those fellows will soon finish you off. Did a man give you this money? Young or old? Young men don't waste much time, do they? Then they want to fool around, start haggling about the price." João fell silent for a moment. He could not see that Maria had put on the linen chemise and silk hood, fascinated by the soft feel of both garments.

"I'll never be a prostitute," she said. She thought of telling her husband the story about the ring but felt ashamed. Just as soon as people began to forget the Captain-General's death, she would redeem the ring and return it to Bernardo. Yes, that's what she would do.

"Filthy, tainted money," scowled João, pocketing the coins as Maria retired to the bedroom.

Light filtered through the shutters and cast a soft glow over the tapestries, the jacaranda sideboards, the metal chest. Luiz Bonicho was seated at his desk in the Council Chambers, reading the document in his hand for the umpteenth time.

"I can't believe it," he said.

Donato Serotino, resplendent in his brown uniform and dark boots, paced back and forth, agitated and close to tears.

"What shall we do, Luiz, what shall we do? He's sure to discover everything and he'll be able to incriminate us."

"That isn't a problem."

"Not a problem? Are you mad?"

"No. Teles was the only person who could have testified against us."

"And isn't that enough? He must have left papers behind. Proof. Why didn't you give in to his demands? It wouldn't have cost us all that dearly and we could have silenced him once and for all."

"Silence Teles? No, he would have gone on threatening to denounce us and made more and more demands. He was the biggest rogue I ever knew," said Bonicho. "The only way to silence him was to do away with him."

"In fact you deceived him, Luiz," continued Donato. "When he instructed the auctioneer handling the sale of arable land, tools and slaves, that all offers were to be made in ready cash, he hoped such a ploy would eliminate all competitors, except you. You got a real bargain this way, but you know full well whose money it was. Those acquisitions were intended for members of the Menezes family. You held on to them! It was to be expected that they would react as they did!"

"Perhaps this was a cunning snare to catch me out. What I know about that one-armed . . ."

"It's not a question of what you know. If you so much as open your mouth, he'll swear that you're questioning his honour in order to lower the value of shares. Even if he can't prove the accusation, he *is* the Governor. That's all that matters. Besides, not every corrupt deal in a bureaucracy is necessarily illegal."

"You're forgetting one important detail: a governor only holds office for three years. Whereas as a councillor . . . I can remain in office for the rest of my life."

"He'll be in power for quite a while yet. He could give us a bad time. How often have I warned you not to trust him?"

"I've never put any trust in that walking silver mine. Nor he in me. That's why we've remained friends. He did the plotting and planning, then I made the deals and we shared the profits. Everything was in my name. The villain knew that at any moment we might be caught red-handed, and that I alone would pay the penalty. Mine was always the greater risk. And frankly, I needed the money. But now . . ."

"Now . . . Is there really no other solution?" asked Serotino.

"No there isn't." Bonicho whispered in Serotino's ear: "It won't take him long to discover that we're up to our necks in this conspiracy and he'll have us removed. But you'll finish him off first during today's fencing lesson. It shouldn't be difficult to overcome a fat old man with one arm. Then we can get away from here."

"There are guards everywhere. The port is being watched. And suppose things don't work out?" Serotino ran his fingers through his hair. His face was flushed.

"If things don't work out . . . that will be that. At least we'll have tried. If men hadn't put their powers to the test, we'd never have had any of our great navigators. Braço de Prata won't succeed in throwing us into jail. We're not alone and we are powerful. It's not a case of one man exterminating another: we're a group of men determined to see justice done."

"Antonio de Souza may already be suspicious. He won't let us escape so easily."

"He's an arrogant fool. He believes no man is brave enough to murder him. He gives himself airs. Surrounds himself with flatterers which is why he hates me. I refuse to grovel. The blood that runs through my veins is not that of some lily-livered parasite. I'm sick of these politicians, I'm one of them and I know what they're like. False to the core. I cannot breathe in this foul atmosphere any longer. Take a good look at me. I'm on my own. But we'll see who has the last laugh."

Serotino looked at the clock.

"Time to go," he said.

Antonio de Souza was in the habit of practising with his fencing master every morning. The manuals of Marosso, Agrippa and Giganti had helped to make the Italians the best fencing instructors in Europe. But a French invention, a light rapier with the tip buttoned like a flower, *fleur*, which they called *fleuret*, was fast surpassing the popularity of the sword.

Bearing in mind the Governor's disability, he could be considered an above average pupil.

"Let's get on with our lesson, Serotino. I'm in fine fettle today."

"Allow me to point out, Your Excellency," he replied, "that one has to be quite composed in the art of fencing, a theory that can be traced back to the warriors of ancient China or to the Romans who duelled with swords."

"I don't believe it, Serotino, I don't believe it. Aggression sharpens the wits."

"I trained in the great fencing academies in Italy. I know what I'm talking about."

"Surely you don't believe everything they teach? We only learn by mistrusting what others tell us. I mistrust everything and everyone. That's why I'm still alive. All right, I must admit I lost an arm, but I'm alive and strong. Whoever told you that you must keep calm in order to win a fight was teasing. If they were trying to turn fencing into an art, that scarcely justifies their hypocrisy. Besides, all teachers and scholars are hypocrites and the most dangerous of men. Illiterates are preferable, for at least they're aware of their ignorance. Those who possess a little knowledge, such as Padre Vieira, are worst of all, for they think they know everything. That goes for you, too, so take that smug expression off your face."

"When I fought Turkish pirates, I was merely protecting our granaries."

"No, you were protecting your feelings. If there's no fury, there must at least be anger. Anger at the rust on one's sword, anger at the rotten food, for all food is rotten in time of war, anger at having to wear shabby uniforms and to sleep on a hard pallet."

"If we can suppress our feelings in battle, we can see our opponent more clearly. If we show hatred, we only provoke hatred. We mustn't betray our feelings."

There were numerous guards standing around in the room, conversing at leisure. Some were practising with swords which resounded with a clash in mid-air.

"I agree to some extent," the Governor conceded, "but love makes us blind, coldness makes us slow; hatred, on the other hand, makes us alert. You are young and know little of the world."

"If we were to remain blind, we would be happier," answered

the fencing master, saluting with his sword and getting ready to
defend himself.

The Governor gazed at Serotino in surprise. He returned the
salute. The fencing commenced.

Antonio de Souza went to the dressing-room and removed his
damp clothes in front of a large mirror. He was painfully aware
of his physical ugliness. He was subject to fits of trembling and
dizzy spells during the night.

He tried to compensate for his missing arm with a Spartan
regime of regular fencing practice. Any improvement with his left
hand was slow and he alone noticed it. Not even Donato Serotino
bothered to follow his progress. Of course, the Governor mused,
Serotino must consider himself an Apollo with that perfect physique. How could he understand the feelings of a disabled old man?

De Souza still had political plans; confiding in no one, he said
very little and conducted his affairs with the utmost discretion.
He had never been interested in the opinions of others unless they
happened to coincide with his own. He had always tried to avoid
issues which might be troublesome and never involved himself in
unresolvable matters or those doomed to failure. And besides
being extremely adept at making deals, he found plenty of other
opportunities for getting rich. Yet despite his ever increasing possessions he had as much contempt for wealth as he had for the
human race. He disliked the Jesuits, especially their doddery old
preacher who was now quite senile. During his time in Portugal,
Padre Vieira had shown susceptibility to economic arguments,
which explained why he protected the Jews, who represented
wealth. He opposed the enslavement of the natives, but surely
there was some hidden motive on the part of the grasping Jesuits?
Perhaps it was a crisis of conscience or a tyrannical urge to catechize, since the rules of the Order were based on the teaching of
doctrine. The Jesuits did not withdraw from society, nor did they
live in the solitude of the cloister, walk in procession, recite litanies
or practise self-denial. They had transformed the medieval Church
to suit their own needs and, unlike Thomas à Kempis, were not
afraid of losing their integrity by setting foot outside the monastery. They interfered in worldly matters, alleging that they were

there not to save their own souls but those of others. But how can one save the souls of others without saving one's own? If a priest goes to hell, he takes the faithful with him. They wormed their way into the arena of power and influence – to save the souls of others? – they had embraced the doctrine of their own Padre Molina, opposed the Jansenists, been the confessors of kings and rulers which enabled them to voice their ideas, whether in an attempt to maintain the corrupt subservience of monarchies to the Church, or in an attempt to eradicate Protestantism. And here they were in Brazil defending the freedom of slaves so that they themselves could enslave them with their own ideas. And while claiming to oppose slavery, how could they justify their silence in the face of what was happening to the black slaves imported from Africa? Simple! Slave labour was essential if the colony was to become rich and prosperous. Those were the Jesuits for you, and especially Padre Vieira, because he was, without a shadow of doubt, a man of genius. Yes, he and Vieira had become enemies. At this very moment Antonio Vieira would be moving the pieces on his chessboard to overthrow the government. But he was no longer capable of this. Or was he? To seek out the Jesuit and try to persuade him to turn back would be a waste of time. The man took enormous pleasure in making enemies, in causing trouble. But it was he, Antonio de Souza, who was in control. He had nothing to lose. He had no further need of the Jesuits, he had the Archbishop on his side, although he didn't want to place all his trust in the prelate. No doubt Padre Vieira wanted to secure the post of governor-general for one of his protégés. Had he perhaps been foolish in turning against the Jesuits? Ah, the wretched humanity locked inside this mutilated body and troubled soul was making Antonio de Souza the martyr of his own mythology. His executioner was Antonio Vieira. He must get rid of him.

Once dressed, De Souza returned to the mirror. In the reflection he saw a shadowy form behind him.

He was startled.

"Who's there?"

Donato Serotino stepped forward. A ray of light coming through the window illuminated his face.

"Ah, it's you, Donato."

Donato slowly drew his sword from its scabbard. His eyes which were usually blue had turned almost black. The strange thought occurred to De Souza that he might be confronting the angel of death. He even had the vague image of two great black shadows hovering behind the fencing master.

"Don't you know it's forbidden to come in here, Donato? What do you want?" The governor glanced sideways. His weapons were on the bench. He reached out for them.

"Forgive me, Your Excellency, but what I'm about to do has to be done," Donato said. And with great agility he leapt at De Souza, bringing his sword down on his opponent. The Governor defended himself with his silver arm which rang out as it clashed with Serotino's sword. Antonio de Souza felt the most terrible pain in the neck muscles which supported the straps of his metal arm.

"Guards!" he called out. Those lazy good-for-nothings were never there when you needed them!

Donato returned to the attack, with greater force and speed. Again, De Souza fended off the blow with his metal arm. A third blow landed unexpectedly, tearing the metal limb from the Governor's body, and tossing it into the distance with a deafening clatter. De Souza instinctively raised his hand to his shoulder, and it was covered in blood. Donato looked at him, his sword raised, ready to strike the fatal blow. The Governor realized this could be his final moment. Whom should he be thinking of? The Prince? Padre Vieira? Why was Donato taking so long to bring his sword down on his head? Would he die with his body severed in two? Suddenly the door opened, soldiers rushed in, wrapped in towels, dripping water, some brandishing swords and shouting. Serotino ran towards them and, pushing past, made his escape. Barefoot, the men slipped on the wet floor. Pursued by the soldiers whose number multiplied at every door, Serotino fled through the palace corridors to his horse. He disappeared at a gallop down the streets, raising clouds of dust in his trail.

# VII

I T WAS IMPOSSIBLE to go on living in this house. If they
put up a search, they would find him immediately. Gregório
packed books and clothes in a bag and left.

He wandered through the city. Then he headed for the pond, a
natural lake formed from streams and water which flowed from
the vegetable gardens of the Benedictines. It was situated beyond
the church of the Carmelite Monastery, between the Palace and the
church of Our Lady of Salvation, encircled by forests. The Bel-
gians had increased the waters with dams.

On arriving, Gregório saw the patrols performing their rounds.
He hid and waited. Soldiers were chattering with women dressed
in brilliant white petticoats, soldiers were smoking and laughing
and running their hands over the women's breasts, arms, and
buttocks, as they embraced. One woman had her blouse pulled
down, exposing two enormous breasts. Washerwomen carried on
with their work, crouched by the waterside.

When the guards had gone, Gregório sat at the edge of the pond;
he threw stones into the water, watched the washerwomen, fresh
as daisies and so desirable. The mountain near the pond was also
shrouded in greenery. He wondered if the neighbour who was so
fond of cold mullet still lived here. With a twig he wrote on the
sand: ". . . *negresses laden with clothes which they wash in lye. Not
the loveliest of women, but surely the cleanest. Besotted with this one and
that one, whether washing or wringing out clothes.*"

He was reminded of Anica de Melo. He had known her soon
after his return from Portugal. She was a real beauty. She even
knew how to write her own name. What a pity she worked in a
brothel, and was white.

Anica had never treated Gregório like a client nor behaved like a prostitute, although at the time they met all the women in the place were whores and were pursued by every man in sight. To be a prostitute was no pleasure in a city of criminals and syphilitics. Gregório fell for Anica the moment he set eyes on her. She was vivacious, young, and covered in charms, and she doted on him.

Each room in the brothel possessed an altar with a holy statue surrounded by flowers. The rooms were spacious with tiny windows. In addition to a bed, there was a basin and a pitcher of fresh water, clean towels and embroidered sheets. Certain rooms were divided by black curtains and had two beds without sheets. Clients paid less for these. At the back of the house, a row of small cubicles had been made with black curtains. These were the *cabinets noirs*, and rented out to Indians and labourers at the lowest price. Anica had compassion for the poor and offered them her establishment, which was frequented by people from every social class. Only slaves were barred from the premises, for their presence would have discouraged the other clients even though the whores in greatest demand were black.

Anica lay naked on the bed. Enthralled, she listened to every word Gregório spoke.

"God is the witness of our innocence." He knew all too well that hell was full of men who thought they could improve the world and that intelligence was a gift bestowed by the devil. He reflected on the motives which had led to their involvement in conspiracies against the Governor-General. Not that life had much to offer these days, since they were living in a world indifferent to suffering and violence.

"If there's anything I asked of God," Gregório continued, "it hasn't been heaven or material wealth. I've asked God to bring some justice into this world."

"How did you come to know the Ravasco brothers?"

"I often heard people mention them and they were known to my family. Some years ago I came across a little pamphlet with the sermons of Antonio Vieira translated into Spanish. As a youth, I was full of ideals and the Jesuit's words made a deep impression."

That pamphlet had completely changed Gregório's life, in fact. Antonio Vieira was, at once, what everyone hoped he might be and what everyone was loath to think he might be. Everything he wrote or said immediately took on a wider dimension. He was formidable in debate, an able philosopher, a distinguished theologian; he had been court chaplain to the King of Portugal, minister at the Papal Curia in Rome and at other courts, confessor to His Highness the Infante, Superior and Visitor-General of the Jesuit missions in Maranhão, striking in appearance, physically well-proportioned, and witty as well as extremely learned. Everyone spoke about him with passion, no matter whether they were for or against him. He opened new horizons for the young Gregório. But as he later discovered, the pamphlet in Spanish had been published without Padre Vieira's permission and contained "as many mistakes as it did absurdities", which outraged the author. Gregório, influenced by his father, admired the Jesuit's character, his polemical spirit, his originality, and when he sailed for Portugal, he left with the intention of meeting Padre Vieira, and perhaps emulating and surpassing his achievements.

Gregório had studied with the Jesuits in Brazil. Well-versed in the humanities, he graduated with distinction. He had studied Horace, Cicero, Ovid, Virgil, the writings of Padre Cipriano Soares. He had been taught Latin, Grammar, Rhetoric, Humanities, the History of Greece, Rome and the Portuguese Empire, Geography, and even a little Greek. While still at school, he had already started to compose his first poems, to his father's dismay and alarm.

"What was your father like?" Anica asked.

"Thin, lame, with round shoulders and sad eyes. We lived here in Bahia between the monastery of the Reformed Friars of St Anthony, near the Franciscan convent with its frieze of Roman medallions, and close to the square opposite the Jesuit church. My father, who was also called Gregório, was a councillor, treasurer of the City Orphanage, Proctor of the Council. When he was at home he would shut himself away in his room and sing."

"Singing helps you to forget your worries. That's why the lower classes, poor, simple, hard-working men like my own father, sing and smile. But what was your father doing shut away in his room?"

"The old man had a telescope, he would remain there gazing at the stars. During the day, when he was out working, I would use it to spy on people, especially the women, as they walked along the streets or appeared at their windows," he replied, caressing Anica's legs.

At the time he enrolled at the Jesuit College, Gregório was already interested in women. Ever since boyhood, he had enjoyed looking at pictures of them in books; women saints, royal ladies charitably portrayed, who looked more beautiful than they ought to be, proud aristocrats, duchesses and princesses, and even witches condemned by the Holy Office of the Inquisition. In the streets, the young Gregório had stared in awe at women of flesh and blood, at their figures and complexions, pale as jasmine, ruddy, olive, or dark as night. The girls were pretty, the naked Indian women resembled pagan deities, the female slaves made him think of iron statues about to burst into flames. His sister, a chirpy little imp, possessed some mysterious force which Gregório regarded with quasi-mystical fervour. He felt himself attracted to all women like a bee to a garden of flowers. Their every gesture enchanted him, the slightest rustling of a skirt, the tiniest of details. Even ugly women intrigued him: a well-formed ear, a pair of firm ankles, healthy nails, abundant hair, a good bone structure, the calves of sturdy legs, round ample buttocks, a dreamy air, coy looks, a spark of intelligence or a nose that brought to mind an Egyptian princess. As he would often jest: "They may be ugly, but they are women."

"Ah, you're such a demon," Anica chided.

"No, no, on the contrary. You women are the demons."

He told her how he soon discovered that women were demons in disguise, treacherous sirens, wily Jezebels, with poisonous hearts and tongues, insatiable Messalinas; that to bugger a woman was tantamount to making a pact with the devil, that even fat and ugly women were sinners: those with angelic faces and feminine graces were the most dangerous of all. The sight of a woman's body aroused the most terrible, persistent cravings, leaving him distraught, frantic, feverish and close to madness. He was convinced they carried worms inside their bodies to devour men; that some even possessed fangs between their legs, capable of destroying men; that they brought shame and destruction, suffocated and enslaved their victims with their wiles and blandishments; that they were evil and possessed, capable of causing wars; that they did nothing but bicker and were only interested in trinkets, baubles, clothes and the arts of seduction; that they were false and drove men to the gates of hell. But such a blissful hell it was.

The books he read as a boy did not only describe women. They spoke of adventure. Gregório read them with some considerable effort for nearly all of them were written in Latin, French or Italian.

At one time he believed truly learned men, such as Padre Vieira, received their knowledge from heaven; little did he know that they got their answers from books. Things were very different from what he had imagined and his studies under the guidance of the Jesuits gave him self-assurance; he even became quite arrogant, in the moral sense of the word. That is where he acquired his early training as a scholar, considered essential in those days. He was preparing to become a Jesuit: every boy's dream.

The Company of Jesus spread from northern to southern Brazil, building churches, setting up missions to catechize the natives, and colleges for the evangelization of future generations. Throughout the world the Jesuits were creating settlements, populating lands, preaching the faith. They waged war, drew up armistices, conquered new territories, founded hospitals and seminaries. By 1626, there were approximately one hundred and twenty members of the Jesuit Order in the Brazilian colonies, including priests and spiritual coadjutors, with an additional fifty lay brothers and sixty-two students. They ran three colleges, six religious houses, thirteen annexed villages. In the College at Bahia there were no fewer than eighty fathers. Within fifty years the number of Jesuit priests and properties had increased substantially. They owned almost everything and Gregório wished to be one of them. Not because of the material wealth they controlled but because of their erudition. Whenever he saw a Jesuit father in the street it was as if he were seeing a walking book. And, in his youth, Gregório believed he had a strong religious vocation. But his experience of religious life would be brief and painful. His real goal, in truth, had always been to seek adventure. With time, he had come to the conclusion that the teachings of the Jesuits were tedious and fettered by religious and political bigotry. After mastering the principles of rhetoric, he began to find it boring and turned his mind to other things. It was during this period that he left for Portugal.

The ship took one hundred and twenty days to cross the ocean from Bahia to Lisbon. The voyage got off to a good start with a favourable southerly wind, but soon turned into a nightmare, with heavy storms day after day, pirate attacks, a voyage full of mishaps which could have been fatal for all the passengers – gentlemen and servants, slaves, aristocrats, priests, stowaways, horses, prostitutes and the mistresses of the officers – but for the hand of destiny. Gregório was fourteen years old and travelling alone. Fear mingled with fascination. He spent hour after hour watching the sea, one moment rough, the next calm; dolphins and whales, clouds in a thousand formations. He was assailed by the salty wind, insomnia, the chill in his bones. The food was inedible. He ate nothing but biscuits and drank water that tasted like vinegar. From below deck wafted the stench of human excrement and mould which, together with the swaying of the ship, made many of the passengers sick. There was baggage everywhere, lice and vermin, people huddled together sleeping among crates and cannons. Some passed their time frolicking, others playing at cards or reading obscene books. The world appeared to consist of nothing but towering waves. Gregório thought the ship would be dashed against the rocks at any moment and sink into the unknown. There were vast distances between the islands and long delays before the journey could be resumed. With his groin swollen and badly inflamed, Gregório felt ill. But he had a goal and he would soon reach it: the University of Coimbra.

It was as if the world were changing not only its outward appearance but to the very core. Gregório had never been away from Bahia and, like any inquisitive youth, he knew every nook and cranny. But he wanted to experience the great metropolis. How was he to know that all cities are alike?

From below, he suddenly heard the explosion of cannons and the clanging of bells. He ran up on to the deck. The grey ocean had given way to the blue waters of the Tagus. The square in front of the Palace of Ribeira was full of people awaiting the arrival of the fleet with the admiral's ship in front and the flagship behind, the tiny squadron sailing in formation ahead. From the palace windows, the armouries, and customs-house, people cheered, shouted, waved their handkerchiefs. Perhaps Dona Luiza de Gus-mão was among them, the wayward queen with rosebud lips and languorous eyes?

"And what were you doing in Portugal at such an early age? Surely you weren't old enough to study at the University of Coimbra?" Anica teased.

"For a while I lived with relatives, then with friends. I went to Vila de Guimarães to meet other distant relations, I spent many hours on the banks of the Tagus watching the ships, on the streets watching the people, learning how to chase women, chatting, watching the carriages and wagons."

Gregório was able to read books and texts before entering the University of Coimbra and that was an enormous privilege. Books were only to be found in convents, in colleges, and in a few private houses, and few copies were in circulation.

He took up residence in the parish of São Nicolau in Lisbon.

There Gregório continued to compose the verses he had exper-imented with in Bahia, but they now alternated between the religious poems of adolescence and ribald, defamatory satires in the manner of Martim Soares and other Portuguese minstrels. *"I frequent the beau monde causing rumpus and uproar; when bedlam breaks out I retreat to a whorehouse." "Maria Mateu, Maria Mateu, as greedy as me for cunt!"* (Afonso Eanes de Coton). *"Because I write verses mocking those whoremongers; one grabbed me and tried to debauch me, but missed and befouled me"* (Pero da Ponte). *"No need to ask why you're here, you're aching to know what's in Dom Goterre's cod-piece"* (Anrique de Almeida Pássaro). *"Such shapely ladies, how can I put it, all bum, tits and belly"* (Diogo Fogaça). *"My flower, they gave me your little bird with less plumage than this craving to possess you . . . Just to speak of it makes me despair and tremble from head to foot"* (Capitão Bonina). These salacious ballads would leave their per-manent mark on Gregório and his fellow-students at the Univer-sity, such as Estevam Nunes de Barros who had a weakness for nuns and had once written to one of them: *". . . This timid yet*

*constant admirer implores you, should you so desire, to treat him as your*
*servant or have him as your lover."*

But Gregório wrote little in Portugal. He had more important
things to do. A brilliant career as a magistrate awaited him.

He was respected, of good appearance, well-connected, came
from a good family entrusted with important offices, had no trace
of mixed blood, was endowed with impressive intellectual powers
and a remarkable flair in legal matters. Gregório's main ambition
in life was to graduate in canon law and make love to women. All
of them.

"You have all these whores flocking round you, all sorts of
women. Don't you ever think of marrying?" Anica asked.

"I'm a widower. I haven't found anyone suitable here. Well,
there was someone, but she didn't love me. But I know that
somewhere there is a woman for me. The princess of my dreams."

"In some convent perhaps," suggested Anica.

"Or in some kitchen. Or perhaps I'll find her here in a public
bath-house."

"Or in a procession."

"I love her as Jaufré de Rudel loved the Countess of Tripoli. In
*La leggenda dell'amore lontano.*" He had never seen her, yet he killed
himself for love of her.

"But suppose she turned out to be ugly?"

"I'd love her just the same."

"And if she turned out to be . . . a whore?"

"Even if she were to stink of onions, were toothless or had only
one eye," replied Gregório.

He was lying, thought Anica.

Gregório always drew a clear distinction between the women
one made love to and those one married. Between negresses and
the fair daughters of the aristocracy. Between harlots and respect-
able young ladies.

Anica got dressed. Her low-cut blouse partly exposed her
breasts. Her face was washed. She was not quite as common as
he would have liked. He embraced her tenderly.

"I'd love you even if you were a dwarf. Even if you didn't have
any legs. I like men who wear spectacles, they're more affectionate. I like men like you."

"Like what?" he asked.

"Who treat whores with respect. You're different from your friends."

"I don't have any friends," he replied.

"Yes, I know there's something troubling you and I know what it is."

"What's that?"

"There are things men don't know, but they're secrets that bring happiness. Do you want me to tell you or show you?"

"I want you to tell me and show me," he replied.

Gregório had a sad, vulnerable expression which aroused compassion. She allowed him to come into the nest between her legs, where something not unlike a mouth with parted lips, as he had once remarked, awaited him.


Wearing a little ribboned hat and wrapped in her cloak, Bernardina Ravasco was sitting beside her travelling-trunks. In one hand she held a tiny glass of liqueur, in the other a slice of cake.

Maria Berco was making the final preparations for her mistress's journey. She went back and forth, opening and closing chests, packing objects and clothes that would be needed on the plantation. She moved quietly, in her new leather shoes.

"And what about this?" she asked, holding up a corset. "Wouldn't it be better to take it?"

"What use should I have for a corset on the plantation? There will be nothing to consort with but cattle and farmhands."

Maria picked up a wide-brimmed hat.

"This is more like it, we must make sure you don't get sunburn."

Bernardina changed hats somewhat reluctantly. "I'm a little worried about my travelling companion. He's the poet Gregório de Matos. I'm aware he's a judge and about to take holy orders, but he has such a reputation . . ."

"What kind of reputation, madam?"

"I'll begin at the beginning: loquacious, seductive, a man of law. One minute he's kneeling before the Virgin Mary and the next he's buried in the lap of a common whore. A master in the art of lechery, which is a savage art. And he makes no attempt to hide anything . . ."

"You have no attachments, madam. What harm would there be in having a little affair?"

"True. What harm would there be? He's extremely dashing. If he hadn't written all those insulting verses and been less indiscreet . . . Have you ever heard any of his satires?"

"No, madam, I haven't. What are they about?"

"Sleepless nights, hallucinations; he openly admits the number of times he has slept with this or that woman. He bluntly criticizes the degenerate settlers, forgetting the virtuous ones. He's outrageous."

Maria found herself wondering what he looked like. Was he handsome? Did he have a fine moustache or pale hands? Was he gangling? Stocky? Slim?

"He believes the world has gone to the dogs and in his efforts to put it right, he makes it sound even more debauched."

At the sound of knocking Maria rushed to answer the door. Standing there, hat in hand, was a tall, lean man with a pale complexion and a dreamy expression. Maria felt her heart leap and found herself tongue-tied. He waited, gazing at her.

"Dona Bernardina?" he asked.

"One moment, sir . . ."

"Gregório de Matos e Guerra."

"Senhor Gregório de Matos e Guerra."

She ran inside and announced the arrival of her mistress's travelling companion.

"Come, girl, show him in at once and bring some glasses and a liqueur, unless you can find something better."

Maria ushered him in. She could feel his eyes following her. She went to the wine cellar and chose the best of the liqueurs. When she returned to the room, the visitor and Dona Bernardina were engaged in conversation, sitting face to face, apparently ill at ease. She poured the liqueur, put the glasses on a tray and served the visitor.

He raised his glass.

"Good health."

"To a safe journey."

Considering his reputation, he was very well-mannered. Maria stationed herself in a corner of the room and remained there observing him.

"Bring some of those nice biscuits," said Bernardina.

"Not for me, thank you," he insisted.

"You must eat something, the journey takes hours."

Maria disappeared and returned once more with the biscuits.

"Is there news of my father, Doctor Gregório?"

"No one is allowed to visit him in his cell, Your Ladyship."

"In his cell? My father in a cell? But he set out for the estate of the Jesuit fathers . . . Good heavens! What are you saying?"

"Forgive me, Your Ladyship, I thought you knew."

"Sir, I beseech you," Maria called out, "my mistress is delicate and shouldn't be upset." She put her hand to her breast, indicating her mistress's illness.

White as a ghost, Bernardina took a handkerchief from her sleeve and dabbed her eye.

"My poor father," she said.

Gregório hastened to apologize, and began at once to discuss the political aims of the Liberals. He spoke in a low voice.

"Sir, I won't be going to the plantation after all," Bernardina announced.

"But it is what your father wishes," he reminded her.

"No, no, I can't go. I'd be much too anxious without any news."

"Will you be annoyed if I insist?"

"It's no use," Maria said. "My mistress has made up her mind."

"I hope you will keep me informed of any developments, Doctor Gregório."

Anxious to reassure her, he promised her the whole business would shortly be resolved and they would soon be joking about it. Padre Vieira was already taking measures. Gonçalo would go in person to inform the Prince's advisers of their troubles. Everything would be over within a week, perhaps sooner.

He then began reminiscing about Góngora y Argote and how he recited his poems in Spanish. One minute his eyes were fixed on Bernardina, the next on Maria. The two women listened to him in rapturous silence. His words rang out clearly, full of emotion. In her confusion, Maria was aware that she was blushing. She was overcome by the feeling that, in some mysterious way, the man before her was to be trusted.

When Gregório de Matos left, Maria lingered for some time in the doorway. When the sun's golden rays were fading he headed off into the distance. Maria drew her jacket tightly around her.

She prepared her mistress's bed and, after making certain that she was asleep, Maria locked the front door of the Ravasco mansion and went home.

She kissed her husband tenderly on the forehead, checked the supper cooked by the negress whom they had hired the previous day, and went and sat on her bed. She was overcome with the most pleasing sentiments of tenderness and – she resisted the thought – of love for the poet whom she had just met.

Nor could Gregório de Matos stop thinking about her. The same old story. Ah, why did he waste so much time daydreaming? Why was he so soft-hearted and so susceptible, and so obsessed with sex?

# VIII

THE MAGISTER LUDI left the College. The building was silent and closed, the classes finished. They lasted for five hours daily in two equal sessions, one in the morning, the other in the afternoon. Only in the Jesuit library, where several *alphabetarii* were preparing their lectures and correcting essays for the elementary course in humanities, was there a light.

Two priests, their hoods drawn over their heads, left the stone building. They crossed the square, watched by the Governor's guards who bowed to receive their blessing.

The priests moved quickly, making for an alleyway. On reaching the streets in the lower part of the city, they exchanged a sigh of relief.

The pair entered the brothel and made straight for the *cabinets noirs*. You could hear people moaning, laughing, crying out in pleasure or pain. It was a warm evening. Gregório de Matos stood at the window, beside a tiny altar with a baldacchino. The sun still cast a soft reddish glow over the outline of the city. The dark forms of pack-horses swayed from side to side. Gregório saw the two priests enter the brothel. He waited for them. The door presently opened and the men came into the room. They were Gonçalo Ravasco and Donato Serotino.

Gregório told the Secretary's son of his visit to Bernardina Ravasco and of her refusal to seek refuge on the plantation.

"She must go," said Gonçalo. "Things here can only get worse."

He told the poet of Donato's failure to assassinate the Governor and about the situation inside the College.

"He found my father's papers and has confiscated them," Gonçalo told him.

"But where's the harm in that? These things rarely survive. They're fated to go up in smoke and vanish into thin air," Gregório told him.

Gonçalo sighed. "My father would be deeply distressed if he knew they had been lost. Poor man. For years he has been editing them, making corrections, redrafting them, analysing and discussing extracts; he's interested in nothing else. He reads passages to his friends time and time again, takes advice, makes modifications. For him, they are as valuable as his benefices and honours, his possessions, his women, his children. To lose his writings would be worse than the prison in which he's been confined. He wants them to be published either in Portugal or Holland."

"What are they?"

"They're descriptive essays about Brazil; the country's topography, her clergy, the civilian population and the military. There are also his poems, and these he treasures most of all. They are his best poems, though he continues to refer to them as pale imitations."

"In that case, it's essential they be rescued."

"I agree. I myself would like to put my father's mind at rest, but he and my uncle insist that I shouldn't venture into the palace. So everything will have to be carried out in secret. It would be quite impossible for either Donato or me to gain entry to the Governor's palace. It's true that we've managed to go around in this disguise, but there are guards posted at every door and on every street corner, and they won't allow anyone to pass without identifying himself."

"Then how are we to rescue Dom Bernardo's papers?"

"There is one solution," said Donato.

"What's that?"

The judges would be meeting the next day at the palace. The ministers of the Tribunal and High Court of Appeals had also been invited. It wouldn't be difficult, only a little risky, for Gonçalo to appear at the meeting with the ministers from the High Court. The poet would have to use his influence to obtain the necessary credentials. And once inside the palace, Gonçalo could try to retrieve the writings.

"If that's all you want from me," rejoined Gregório, "I'll do my best to get the papers you need. I hope your courage won't fail you, for it's a risky business."

"It won't fail me," Gonçalo assured him. "We're fighting for our ideals and our lives. Why don't you come with us to Portugal?"

"Stowing away is for young heroes like yourselves, not for a bag of bones like me."

"You must be on your guard, poet. I don't trust Braço de Prata," said Gonçalo. "Not even Donato Serotino, our finest swordsman, indeed one of the finest in Europe, succeeded in getting the better of him. I doubt whether I'd have had Donato's courage."

"You've never wavered, Gonçalo."

"Of course, I've wavered. I've wavered many times, however prepared for setbacks, privation and adversity. Despite being a Ravasco, I've lived on the streets. I've gone around with a dagger in my belt, challenged anyone who tried to abuse me. You know very well what life was like at university."

"Well, speaking for myself," Gregório rejoined, "the only thing I was any good at was a lively debate. I felt awkward, inferior and delicate. Even at that age I needed spectacles. But thank God, my arse was the wrong shape, and nobody interfered with me. My pride was as stiff as a corn cob from morning till night and all I could think about was black women. That's how I got my reputation. And you, Gonçalo, when did you get your fearsome reputation?"

"One day I had to fight off a bunch of students," Gonçalo said. "They were armed but I managed to knock all of them to the ground, don't ask me how. I also took up fencing, but for pleasure. My father kept on reminding me that true strength lay in reasoning things out, in expressing ideas and provoking discussion. My uncle believed that the real struggle lay in training one's memory according to the methods of Quintilianus and Cicero. That victory lay in persuasive conversation and the ability to develop an argument."

"Ovid also wrote about the flea, Lucan about the mosquito and Homer about frogs. But they wrote works of greater substance than my trivial verses. But none of this is important. What matters now is to protect our lives and honour. So you really mean to seek an audience with the Prince?"

"Indeed," said Gonçalo without hesitation. "I shall do whatever is necessary to get my father released and to clear my uncle's name."

"Believe me, my friend," said Gregório, "the glorious day will dawn when your father's name will be so renowned that his enemies will see it engraved among the stars."

Mata crossed the patio behind the Governor's palace, stepping over heaps of dung. Grooms and coachmen were hanging around while the harnessed horses stood in front of the carts, waiting to depart.

Some women servants were seated on the staircase, smoking, others chatted to male slaves and guards. Only the kitchen hands were working at full tilt. Black smoke billowed from the chimney, carrying with it the smell of roasting meat, oil and pepper.

Mata went into the palace and straight to Antonio de Souza's study, using the entrance reserved for the Governor and trusted footmen. He knocked gently. Finally the major-domo opened the door and signalled him to enter and wait.

Mata snatched another glance at the leather folder of papers. He was afraid to show them to De Souza. Perhaps he should lie, and say he had found nothing. But the Governor would be furious and whenever he lost his temper, he couldn't bear to think about it. He heard the Governor approach.

"Well then, Mata?"

Mata looked at him, open-mouthed, hesitant.

"Let's go through here," said De Souza, "I want to speak to you alone. Make sure we're not disturbed."

Mata passed on these instructions to the major-domo. He returned and stood beside De Souza.

"Have you brought what I asked for?" asked the Governor.

"Well, no, sir, that's to say, yes, sir."

"Good. Sit down . . . then. Sit down there and read it to me."

"Well . . . it's just that . . . I don't think I should, Your Excellency."

"Why not?"

"It's much too slanderous to repeat. Base, despicable, malicious, if Your Excellency gets my meaning."

Antonio de Souza sat with his feet resting on the opposite chair. He glared at Mata who was trembling.

"I'm waiting," he said.

Mata slowly assembled the papers and placed them on the table. He struggled to arrange them in sequence, but the sheets kept falling to the floor, and he realized that he could not procrastinate any longer. "Dear God," he thought, "he's sure to take his anger out on me. I'll be blamed for all the insults Gregório de Matos has addressed to the Governor in his satires." But he had to go through with it.

The silence that filled the palace seemed to extend all the way from the street. Mata picked up the first sheet, took a deep breath and started reading: *"Don't be alarmed, Dom Antonio, that Bahia should venture with plaintive voice and narrow plectrum, to sing your praises, for eloquent poets"* and at this point Mata shrugged his shoulders almost as if to excuse himself, *"are wont to indulge in such perversities."* He glanced at the Governor. "At least the poet confesses his perversity."

As Mata read on, the Governor began to pace up and down, shaking his head.

*"That lank moustache curled with tongs droops there in exile, each sparse hair so remote from your face; as for your wig, blind men swear you bought it in the Arco dos Pregos. Your eyes . . . your eyes . . ."*

"Why have you stopped, Mata? Continue."

*"Your eyes . . . liverish eyes dripping rheum, the eyes of a twisted soul, especially when seen through those horn-rimmed spectacles: luminous pebbles set in frames. Poor sight rather than reluctance prevents you from seeing anyone, so blind you fail to see your own prejudice, for that requires judgment, you are blinder than I who whisper in your ear, who see you as nothing but a jackass.* He now goes on to describe your nose, Your Excellency. Should I continue?"

"Yes."

Mata cleared his throat, his voice almost reduced to a whisper.

*"A flat, fleshy nose covers your whole face: down on all fours, you. Search for some hole where they won't know you by your navel; until I see you no more as I run from the stench of your breath."*

The satire went on to describe Antonio de Souza's mouth, his legs and feet, his jacket, his wineskin, and the walking-stick he always carried under his arm; there were insinuations of theft, tyranny and corruption. Other satirical verses made similar allegations. The Governor insisted on hearing them all, and listened patiently. On finishing, Mata handed the material to the Governor, expecting him to explode. But De Souza surprised Mata for he sat down with the utmost composure, locked the papers away in a chest. He ordered Mata to withdraw.

As he was about to close the door, Mata heard the Governor call.

"Yes, Your Excellency?"

"Those satires are damn clever. Had they not been written about me, I might well have thought them amusing. He could do me a great favour by using that sharp tongue of his against certain other individuals."

The following morning, the city was still in a commotion. It was rumoured that the new Captain-General would be Antonio de Teles de Menezes, the brother of the murdered Francisco.

Gregório told Anica that he would have to leave shortly.

"You're out a great deal. Isn't it dangerous?" she asked.

Yes, but he had to locate some papers. And he had no wish to stay cooped up in his room, uninformed. In fact, this had not been the case at all. He had wandered the streets the day before and had received a visit from Gonçalo Ravasco and Donato Serotino that night. For the moment, his life was not as grim as he had imagined. But he knew this situation could not last. Things would get worse.

Anica seemed happy. She had woken up smiling, and was humming to herself. She would willingly spend hours on end conversing and fornicating with her guest.

He read her extracts from books, told her the strangest things. He would declaim verses like an actor in a play and move her to tears. He showed her engravings of Portugal and eagerly pointed out places from his childhood. Gregório seemed to have forgotten his meeting with Maria Berco, to have erased the deep impression the girl had made.

The Governor told the Archbishop João da Madre de Deus about his haunting dream. He nearly always dreamt about Padre Vieira. Indeed he thought about the old Jesuit more often than he cared to acknowledge. In this dream he had encountered Vieira near the windlass. Padre Vieira looked even older than when De Souza had last seen him; the priest's hands were shaking, and he had a sickly pallor and appeared frail. They fought a duel. Antonio de Souza won. When he saw the priest's decrepit body stretched out, he prepared to plunge the sword into his heart. But he could not see his own hands. He asked: "Why am I unable to kill you? Have you robbed me of my hands?"

His dreams were like this. Always about something he was unable to carry out. And it was always Vieira who was to blame.

João da Madre de Deus was concerned. "You should try to suppress these feelings, Dom Antonio. To live with so much hatred isn't good."

"I was thinking," the Governor continued, "how Dom João III believed himself to be haunted by the ghost of the Duke of Bragança whom he had ordered to be executed at Évora. And the Duke Dom Jaime could hear the wailing soul of his wife, Dona Leonor de Gusmão, who was accused of adultery and put to death."

"But Your Excellency has done no harm to Padre Vieira," said the Archbishop.

"But I intend to. I can see his image now. He appears before me with his white, dishevelled hair and mocks me. I loathe the man."

João da Madre de Deus looked at him with his pale blue eyes. He was wearing a biretta like a red onion sliced through the middle and the smell was just as pungent. He had a tuft of hairs on his upper lip, which he continually stroked with the tip of one finger.

"How strange," said the Archbishop, "that Your Excellency should see Padre Vieira's ghost. Ghosts are usually people who are dead and buried and he is alive!"

"Yes, but his final agony has already begun," snarled De Souza. "A sage in a kingdom of fools who babbles in Chinese where everybody else speaks Latin. There's his punishment."

The women in the brothel were making an incredible din. They were laughing, talking about clothes, recipes, their rag dolls. Many were mere girls.

"Be silent," snapped Anica de Melo. "The poet is trying to talk with the two priests who called yesterday; he wants some peace and quiet."

The women lowered their voices, twittering on like little birds.

Leaning up against a window, Gregório de Matos watched a negress pass along the street, head held high, semi-naked, descending the slope with a swaying of hips that reminded him of Galileo's famous words: *eppur si muove*. A priest accompanied her.

"There goes the lecherous friar," said Gregório. "Discalced friars, preaching in socks. They're nothing but a bunch of rakes. They bring whores into their monasteries, go out at night to seek their pleasure, sometimes in disguise, turn churches into brothels. And next day the hypocrites are walking in procession, flagellating themselves before all and smelling of the wine and sperm from the previous night's orgy. And then in their sermons they offer us platitudes about wearing hairshirts and doing penance. Spiritual values are dead and buried. This distresses me."

"I have other worries on my mind," said Gonçalo Ravasco. "Did you get what I asked you for?"

"Yes." Gregório handed Gonçalo the necessary credentials to gain entry to the palace. "Once you're inside, you must get into the Governor's study. I surveyed it myself."

"The problem is how to get out," said Donato Serotino.

Gregório picked up his quill, dipped it into the inkwell and drew a square on the sheet of paper. "Here is the Governor's palace. Here is his study. You know where it's situated, don't you, Gonçalo? After all, your father's study was only down the corridor."

"I'm afraid I don't. My father never showed me his study."

"Well, the entrances are here."

The three men discussed at length the most effective way of

getting into the Governor's study, of searching his desk and locating the papers, of how best to conceal them and leave the palace unseen. Finally, a plan was drawn up.

"Padre Vieira fears they may force their way into the College. What do you think, Gregório?" asked Gonçalo.

"I think it's unlikely, but not impossible. There is less to lose by upsetting the Church than there is to gain by invading the College. If I were in Braço de Prata's position, I'd force my way in. The Archbishop doesn't strike me as being a very decisive man. I was with him this morning, to obtain the credentials you requested."

"How much influence do you have in the Ecclesiastical Court these days?" inquired Gonçalo.

Gregório pursed his lips and shook his head. "Not much. But we'll know soon enough. If João da Madre de Deus follows tradition, he'll oppose Braço de Prata. For the last hundred years, every bishop has quarrelled with the governor of the day, and I don't believe he'll have the courage to remove me from the Ecclesiastical Court and risk making enemies of the Ravascos. It wouldn't make sense."

"I no longer put much faith in logic," said Gonçalo.

"I'm not so concerned about remaining under episcopal jurisdiction. The place is a den of thieves. But if they should get rid of me, you'll be to blame, along with Tomás Pinto Brandão and the other scoundrels in my coterie. If you hadn't kept going there to say such awful things about Quevedo and Góngora y Argote, I wouldn't have accumulated quite so much paper on my desk."

"You know I can't stand those poets," said Gonçalo. "They have what Lope de Vega describes as the worst possible style. Their poems are all over the place and remind one of those ghastly women who make up their faces with rouge on their nose and ears, instead of on their cheeks."

"Bah, Dom Luiz de Góngora's ballads and *letrillas* are every bit as popular as those of Lope de Vega, and only his *canciones* and sonnets were *strictly withheld from the man in the street.*"

"How pretentious, spouting Spanish words where people don't even know how to recite a playful pun addressed to a nun."

"You know perfectly well that Spanish is as much our language as Portuguese."

"Portuguese? But you're a Brazilian poet and here the language is quite different."

The fact that he was a Brazilian poet made Gregório de Matos feel like an idiot. He was living remote from the metropolis and often lapsed into confused thoughts about himself. He believed he had nothing more to lose now than when he was back in his native land, widowed and on his own. He did not give a damn whether he substituted Jesus for arse, God for atheist, church for envy, Jesuit for pimp, judge for swindler, poet for fool, St Anthony for Satan, writing for masturbating, history for chicory. And he felt just the same when he composed poems about a mulatta or love, a muleteer or a penis, a parrot or a governor, a monarch or Almighty God. And all the women pursued him with such speed and fervour it made even Gonçalo turn pale.

"How right you are, my friend," said the poet. "These women are all so eager for sex. It must be the heat."

"We might as well blame them."

Again, they could hear the women inside the brothel.

"I was thinking of having a competition to find the best whore," said Gregório. "Prostitutes, married women, repentant virgins, women who are highly strung, lonely, desperate, out for a quick profit, women married to cuckolds, dissatisfied with their situation. They can all take part. Then we shall crown the queen of all whores. The one who fornicates best. I'll inspect all the prostitutes, hussies and harlots myself, examine their bosoms, their waistlines and their thighs. I shall write a poem about this one day. Carnal pleasure is the only theme worthy of the true poet."

"That's outrageous, you can't be serious!" shrieked Gonçalo.

"That's what you think? Then read this." Gregório took a sheet of paper from his pocket.

Gonçalo read it.

"Good heavens," Gonçalo Ravasco said, "so many years of study to write *this*?"

"Too true. My studies have taught me how to go straight to hell," replied the poet. "I forgot, you don't believe in hell. That'll take you in the end to the same place as me."

"There is no hell *after* life," Gonçalo insisted.

# IX

THE INVASION OF the College began with the arrival of army officers. Antonio de Souza divided the men into two groups. One would enter the building, the other would surround the College to ensure no one escaped. In this way, anyone trying to get away would fall down the ravine and meet certain death. They went into action, their weapons ready, swift, keen, and alert.

Passers-by gathered round to watch.

Faces, both white and Indian, appeared at the windows of the main building. Some were priests but most were students and children.

The Governor stopped at the entrance. He raised his left hand and the soldiers came to a halt.

"Padre Vieira," he called out.

The crowd fell to whispering.

The door remained closed.

De Souza called out the Jesuit's name again. After several minutes, the College door opened and an elderly priest emerged with dishevelled hair. There was a hush. The priest wore a tranquil expression. Padre Vieira was not there, he said. De Souza looked contemptuously at the tiny priest who could scarcely be heard. He warned him that he was looking for possible criminals and wished to search the College. They would do better not to offer resistance. The priest insisted there was no one there who could be involved in crime. The Governor made it clear that he would prefer to make certain for himself.

"I cannot allow you to enter, Your Excellency," the priest replied. "The College is a sacred place in the eyes of God and the Supreme Pontiff."

De Souza dismounted from his horse and confronted the elderly priest. He glared, forcing the old man to lower his eyes. Fear was written on the old man's face. The priest raised his eyes.

Leaning forward, De Souza muttered between his teeth that his word was law in the colony. He pushed the old Jesuit aside and entered the College.

The Governor was followed inside by officers. Shots could be heard. Outside the building mothers cried out, fearing for their children trapped within. Some fell to their knees, pulling their hair. Frantic parents tore at their clothes, shouting hysterically, slapping their own faces. Soldiers formed a barricade in front of the main entrance.

Moments later soldiers re-emerged with the prisoners. They had arrested Antonio de Brito, João de Couros, Francisco Dias do Amaral, Barros de França, Antonio Rolim, along with some Jesuits and students. The captains of the garrison, Diogo de Souza, nicknamed O Torto or Crooked One, and José Sanches del Poços, had also been detained.

Gonçalo Ravasco escaped. When the invasion took place he was in the brothel wearing the Jesuit habit and plotting with Gregório. One of the girls from the brothel had run in with news of the invasion, and Gregório and Gonçalo left to mingle with the crowd and watch the activities of the troops. They looked on with bitter resentment, as their friends were led away.

The palace gates were open. The garrison was parading and exercising in brown uniforms in the great square before the Governor's residence, as gaping bystanders looked on. The soldiers belonged to the permanent garrison which consisted of two infantry divisions, known as the Old and the New, each with a nominal force of eight hundred men. The infantry regiments never reached this number because few able-bodied men in the colony wished to serve. They disliked the discipline, were afraid of catching disease and were discouraged by the low wages, which were nearly always paid in arrears. In both divisions, white, black and half-caste soldiers served side by side. But the militias were organized according to the colour of skin, each regiment commanded by an officer of the same colour as his troops.

People came in and out of the palace, litters and carriages stopped and moved on. At five o'clock in the afternoon the judges arrived, dressed in their formal robes.

Gonçalo, disguised in the black tunic of an ecclesiastical judge, which Gregório always wore when carrying out his duties at the Curia, headed for the main door and entered with the retinue accompanying the Archbishop, his face concealed beneath his hood.

Gonçalo remained with the retinue until they reached the great hall where guests were assembled, drinking from goblets served by male slaves with enormous bows tied round their necks. Some of the judges gathered round the Archbishop. Others were dispersed throughout the great hall. They were laughing, conversing, some in loud voices, others whispering in their neighbour's ear. Young Gonçalo moved among them, listening attentively to their conversations. He recognized some of the judges. Dom Francisco de Pugas e Antas, wearing his cross as a Knight of the Order of Christ; Sottomayor; Sepúlveda, son of the market inspector; Banha, a former magistrate; the sinister Palma and Gois. What were they doing here? Why had the meeting been called? He moved closer.

The conversation was about the criminal assault on the Captain-General, about the standard of living and earnings of magistrates, about the Code of Law promulgated by Dom Felipe, about the latest decrees issued by the Crown, and other such matters. Gonçalo kept his head lowered. But he could not linger. Otherwise someone was sure to become suspicious and arrest him.

He saw there was an open door. No one was watching him. He slipped through the door into a large, darkened room containing nothing but a table and two large pictures on the wall. He moved closer. They were portraits of João IV and Luiza Francisca de Gusmão. The King had a rather long face of irregular proportions. Nonetheless, he had shown a considerable flair for politics during his reign. Gonçalo noted the queen's wilful expression, her complexion, her nose, the black gloves she wore. He thought it strange that the portraits of past monarchs should be hanging there. Yet there was no portrait of Pedro the Peace-maker, the regent who had married his sister-in-law while his demented brother rotted away in the squalid dungeons of Vila de Angra, in the Palace of Sintra, items of news which reached the colony through being reported in *Mercúrio*, the Portuguese newspaper.

Gonçalo heard voices and footsteps. There was a door in one corner of the room, concealed by a curtain. He stepped behind it and into a tiny alcove with no windows and only a bench and chair. On a table behind a screen stood an empty chamber-pot, a large basin, a pitcher, and folded towels and linen. The alcove gave off a slight odour of flowers and urine. Gonçalo hid behind the screen and waited.

Lowered voices came from the portrait gallery where lamps had been lit: the voices of men having a heated discussion. But it was difficult to make out much more than an odd word here and there: payment, revenge, everything turning out all right. The judges' meeting was getting under way. Eventually, they withdrew from the portrait gallery. But the muffled sounds of feasting, of speeches, clinking goblets, doors banging, bursts of laughter could still be heard from the room next door. Little by little, the sounds faded away until everything remained perfectly still.

Gonçalo heard footsteps in the next room. It was a man all alone. A man heavy on his feet. The lamps were again lit. Then came the footsteps of a second man.

"Mata?" someone asked. Gonçalo recognized Antonio de Souza's voice.

"Yes, Your Excellency." Mata's voice was shrill and tremulous.

"Give me a hand."

The sound of metal.

"What have you discovered, Mata?" said De Souza.

"Everything has gone according to plan, Your Excellency. The judges were worried about what you said."

"They're a bunch of idiots. They've all been in Brazil far too long for their own good. I wonder if I'll ever get any of them into the Misericórdia Alms-house. If I do, that'll be another favour they owe me."

"Give them a few crates of sugar, some barrels of good wine, and they'll support you."

"I'm not so sure, Mata. Don't forget that these pedants are educated men who've been trained to examine matters carefully and ponder them at length before reaching any decision. But everybody knows how much corruption there is in the Court of Appeals. The enormous amount of paperwork, the duties and powers of the judges, have given them endless opportunities and encouraged practices which, although not exactly illegal, are nevertheless immoral."

The footsteps came closer. The door opened. The weak flame of an oil-lamp cast a faint light. The footsteps halted. Gonçalo tried to breathe without making a sound. He could hear his heart beat, feel the beads of perspiration break out on his forehead. The Governor was there, alone, his back turned, and he was unarmed, perhaps even without his metal arm to defend him. This was the moment Gonçalo had waited for. He placed his hand on the dagger in his belt. Perspiration ran down his face. Any minute now he could pounce on De Souza and stab him to death.

Water trickled into the chamber-pot. The Governor was urinating. Gonçalo could easily have jumped on him and cut off his genitals. Would he perhaps lose his nerve deprived of his penis? He had not lost it when left without his right arm. Clearly he found it difficult to urinate, to eat, to write. To fornicate. How did he manage to keep his balance with only one arm when lying on top of a woman?

More footsteps, then the door closed. Gonçalo kept still, once more in darkness, inhaling the sour smell. Then he heard further footsteps, voices, doors slamming, and finally complete silence.

When he was certain that everyone had gone, he left the alcove and went back into the portrait gallery. On the table stood a casket overlaid with gold and secured with two locks. Gonçalo broke it open with his dagger. He heard footsteps and rushed back to his hiding-place. The footsteps crossed the room. It must be one of the guards. Mata. The door of the alcove was ajar, allowing a little light to filter through. Gonçalo's heart was pounding, his hand firmly gripping the handle of his dagger. Moments later the footsteps retreated. The door slammed. Gonçalo returned to the casket and opened it. The documents on the top were letters from the Governor, still unsigned, reporting details of the crime to the Crown and accusing Antonio Vieira of being the true culprit. There was a memorandum of the lawsuit written in much the same vein. To his surprise, he also found satires composed by Gregório and addressed to Braço de Prata. There were documents referring to a public auction. And at the bottom of the casket, among Antonio de Souza's private papers, were the writings of Bernardo Ravasco. Delighted, Gonçalo tucked them into his shirt and closed the casket.

He fled, dagger in hand, along the deserted corridors, following the plan Gregório had drawn for him, until he reached a back room without guards. He lifted the heavy crossbar. The room, with a canopied bed, was empty. He went to the window, opened it, and jumped out. There was no one in sight.

"Poor Bahia! *What change is wrought since days of yore, neither you nor I are as we were before,*" mused Gregório. He went to the window. He drank another goblet of wine. The keg was almost empty. *"I see you impoverished, you see me in debt, now I see you enriched, while you see me quenched."* Cargo ships were anchored in the estuary. Casting his eyes over the city, Gregório recognized that the merchants were the root of its economic ruin, fostered by worthless and fake merchandise. *"Ships laden with cargo have sailed up your broad straits; while I've bartered and been sold short by shady deals on every hand."* He remained at the window in silence.

"Have you decided to go to Praia Grande after all?" Anica asked.

"I doubt it. Who wants to be hidden away in Praia Grande? I couldn't bear the solitude. I prefer the island of Itaparica, white sands, wonderful beaches, clean and inviting, tasty octopus, delicious lobster, plenty of whales and all the whores you could wish for."

"They'd find you at once on Itaparica. I think you should go to Praia Grande, or anywhere so long as it's far away. You're in danger with all these soldiers on the alert. They're rounding up any men capable of wielding a pole-axe. They torture them before setting them free, some are left crippled, others blind or even impotent."

"I don't want to go away. But I must leave with Gonçalo to speak to the Archbishop."

"What do you want to tell him? Can you really trust him? He's only just arrived."

"We won't say too much. He can help us. After all, the College has been invaded and is still surrounded. It's an outrage. We're determined that the ecclesiastical authorities in Europe should learn about the invasion through the right channels, then Braço de Prata will be discredited. But it isn't only the Governor we need to report. They ought to be told about the colony."

"What will you tell them?"

"In my opinion, this city could be summed up with a double 'l': one for larceny – the other for lechery."

"You wouldn't dare."

"Why don't you come with me to celebrate the feast?"

"I can't. On feast days there's plenty of work to be done. Come back soon. Promise? I love you so dearly," she said.

Gregório kissed her on the cheek.

"Can I call you my own?"

"Yes."

"All mine?"

"All yours," she said.

"Forever?"

"Forever."

She smiled.

Gregório arrived in the Rua Debaixo, with its imposing houses and uninterrupted views of the sea; attractive little harbours and landing-places. The fire crackled, casting a reddish glow over the bodies of the black women who were dancing, their hips wiggling suggestively, their feet tapping, their petticoats swirling. Some moved in wild contortions, their skirts gathered at the waist. Drums beat. Street-urchins let off rockets and fire-crackers.

"How well these mulatto women dance, how well they dance the *paturi*," the poet muttered. Some people came up to greet him, raising their hats, trying to persuade him to recite some verses.

Gonçalo was sitting on the stairs. Gregório joined him.

"Just look at those lovely negro women, Gonçalo!"

"Recite one of your satires, poet."

"*Catona, Ginga and Babu, with another little negress, went into the palm-groves and began wiggling their bottoms: when Jesus saw them he said, how well they shake those hips! But if Angola produces such lovely violets, I'll explode if I don't bed those four black beauties before the day is out."*

Gonçalo held out a mug of rum to the poet.

"Just what I need," said Gregório.

The concoction they served there was a mixture of raw spirits and molasses which sent heads spinning within seconds. The music was deafening.

Gregório took the mug and drank the lot. He wiped his mouth with the back of his hand. "Ha, it's like swallowing fire. As warm and sweet as any whore." He whispered into Gonçalo's ear: "Did you get the papers?"

"They're here," Gonçalo assured him, half-opening his jacket. "Braço de Prata was within reach. That's the second time he's escaped death. Or the third? Or for the thousandth time? But I suddenly felt sorry for the man, one arm missing, standing there struggling to piss. I read the lawsuit to be brought against Padre Vieira. I also read the letter Braço de Prata has written to the Prince, incriminating my uncle and mentioning the meeting held in the cell of O *Torto*. And other accusing letters. He is already well informed. It won't be long before he discovers the identity of the hooded men who killed the Captain-General. Here are my father's papers. It might be safer if you were to look after them. Take them to Dom Samuel da Fonseca, the Rabbi at the Synagogue of Matoim, on the plantation near the river. He's a friend of my father and is able to publish manuscripts in Amsterdam where they have a printing press. And there's something else you ought to know. Braço de Prata keeps the satires you wrote about him in that same casket."

"Are you serious? If he's read them, I'm in trouble."

"Are you suggesting he can read?"

Gregório howled with laughter.

"Are you drunk already?" teased Gonçalo, refilling his tankard.

"Drunk, my ass," answered Gregório. They lingered for a moment, watching the fire.

"They've all been arrested, Gonçalo. That crippled bastard detained all those inside the College. You escaped because luck was on your side. The others have taken refuge in the cellars beneath the Council chambers or on the plantations of relatives. Sanches del Poços and Diogo de Souza have been dismissed as leaders of their regiments and the posts have been given to protégés of Teles de Menezes. The Captain-General's successor has been nominated: Antonio Teles. A swine just like his brother Francisco, and with the same black blood in his veins."

A chaise came to a halt in the Rua Debaixo; a young woman and a man with a walking-stick alighted. He walked slowly, groping his way forward. She wore a dark dress of cheap cloth. As she guided her blind husband, the girl glanced in their direction. Gregório followed their movements. Noting his friend's interest, Gonçalo whispered in his ear: "Have you met Dona Maria Berco, my sister's companion?"

*"Who could gaze on such a flower without wishing to pluck its petals?"*

Gregório stood transfixed. What made her so attractive? Could it be that repulsive husband at her side? *How can such a tiny sphere hold so much sunlight?*

"Do you remember the sonnet Felipe IV wrote to his mistress?" asked Gregório. *"To compare you with snowdrops and roses would be to exalt the flowers and diminish your beauty. Why describe your eyes as sapphires when your eyes are the brighter gems?* Such a beautiful girl, such natural grace."

"Time to go," said Gonçalo. "Let's join the procession."

They conversed on the way to the Archbishop's new palace.

"So that blind old man is married to . . . Dona Maria Berco?" asked Gregório.

"You're interested in that girl, eh? A real beauty! But strange."

"Strange? How?"

"I can't really say," Gonçalo told him. "They tell me she's trying to learn to read."

"Is that all?"

"My sister pampers her, gives in to her every whim. Where would you find a lady's companion so well treated by her mistress? She's beautiful, but tied to that blind man to whom she's apparently devoted. When any man tries to pinch her bottom she fights him off like a wild cat."

"If only I could have one night with that flighty little madam, I'd teach her a lesson. There's nothing I like better than a challenge," boasted Gregório.

"But the women have to play their part," Gonçalo added.

"Oh to fornicate, to fornicate, to fornicate day and night."

"You're mad. Women should be skittish, gay and demure. You must never allow a woman to get the upper hand. They have to be kept in their place, treated harshly with the odd caress and many a threat, according to the precepts of Tiraqueau."

"I'm at the mercy of women, I tremble just to see them go by. Can you see this scar on my forehead? I became so infatuated with a negress I saw walking along the street, I banged my head against a wall," said Gregório.

"But you only satisfy their lust."

"What more do they want? Well, I must admit that I've also experienced some lyrical moments. And I'd honestly like to fall deeply in love with some woman I could marry." For Gregório it had been quite a pleasant day despite their anxiety about the fate of those in custody and those responsible for Teles' death. He had spent the entire afternoon with the girls in the brothel, not enjoying their favours as one might expect, but playing games and amusing himself by helping them to apply silk patches to their faces.

He powdered their hair as if they were French courtesans preening themselves before the mirror. They adored Gregório and his escapades.

"I'm going to give you a beauty spot," he had said cutting tiny circles from a piece of black taffeta – an embellishment devised by human vanity to highlight female beauty, to emphasize the paleness of their complexion, to disguise any imperfections, and to convey different messages, depending on where the patch was applied.

"Near the eye," recalled Gregório from what he had learned at Court, "signifies":

"Passion."

"On the forehead."

"Majesty."

"On the nose."

"A challenge."

"The cheek."

"Flirtation."

"Near the mouth."

"A kiss naturally."

The poet explored other parts of the girls' bodies where they might be applied and they invented suitable messages. Worn on the nape of the neck, they might convey temptation, and when Gregório stuck a patch on one girl's breast with a little saliva and felt his penis swell, they labelled it madness.

All the whores longed to be in bed with Gregório. He would tell them amusing stories and they would gather in a circle, enthralled. Some were madly in love with him, as if he were a prince, and they dreamed of marrying him and of abandoning the brothel forever.

Gregório told Gonçalo about the silk patches and the youth assured him he needed his head examined, wasting his time on such innocent pastimes with so many obliging women around.

"In three days," said the poet, "I could have satisfied every whore in the place."

Gonçalo roared with laughter. He was beginning to relax.

Gregório, on the other hand, was as caustic as ever. As they strolled he spoke of a thousand enemies who were waiting to see him crushed. And Gonçalo knew immediately what was on his mind and where the conversation was heading.

The poet enjoyed conversing with his young friend because Gonçalo knew how to counter his remarks, often diverting the conversation to less intimate matters, such as politics or poetry. But without discouraging the poet from indulging in obscenities. Ah, thought Gregório to himself, here was a fellow who had not been tainted by Jesuitical hypocrisy. And once he got started, he did not need much encouragement to carry on. He criticized Antonio Vieira, discussed the horrors of syphilis which he himself was in danger of catching, he praised the wonders of Gomorrah and cursed the inconvenience of menstruation (there were times when he couldn't fornicate because all the women were menstruating, in a universal conspiracy against him); he berated the debauched clergy and ridiculed one friar in particular whom he had nicknamed Foederibus Mulieribus, then the petty-minded bailiffs and a dim-witted captain. As usual, no one was spared. And these outbursts were invariably accompanied by biting wit and sharp criticism. Indeed it was not by chance that so many men and women had become his sworn enemies.

The countryside was bathed in moonlight and with his hair in ringlets and his shoulders silhouetted against the light Gregório looked quite angelic, even as he stood conjuring up the horrors of hell and spouting obscenities, a fine figure of a man, yet so miserable. That was Gregório de Matos. His face quite pale, wide forehead, arched eyebrows, gesturing with his hands, his nimble feet scarcely touching the ground as he moved.

# X

JOÃO DA MADRE DE DEUS had only one good eye and kept
it wide open. His blind eye could scarcely be seen for he
tended to keep it lowered as if constantly at prayer, as befitted
his priestly vocation. The eye was watery with a discoloured
blue spot which never moved and made him look quite terrifying.
The very fact that he was blind in one eye enhanced his role
as God's representative. He was different from other priests and
therefore more trustworthy. Because he had only one eye, the
King had chosen him as one of his confessors and had bestowed
numerous favours on him. Having only one eye, he could only
see venial sins. This defect also accounted in part for his success
throughout Portugal as Father Provincial, as a preacher of distinction, and as Inspector of Military Orders.

During dinner, he thought about the matter that Judge Gregório
de Matos, an incorrigible wit, wanted to discuss with him. The
company of such people brought back pleasant memories of
Coimbra. Also present were the treasurer of the episcopal see and
young Gonçalo, one of the most courageous and able members of
the Ravasco clan, famous even in Portugal, despite the fact that
he was a conspirator in hiding. The poet and his young friend
had been instructed in the teachings of St Ignatius, which the
Archbishop, who belonged to the Seraphic Order of St Francis,
viewed with reservation. But every Order had its merits.

The Archbishop's palace was vast and empty. João da Madre
de Deus had only recently taken up residence and the rooms had
still to be furnished and the walls and ceilings decorated. The only
furniture was a table and two long rough wooden benches. A cross
in the same wood, inlaid with silver, hung on the wall above
the Archbishop's head. There were packing-cases everywhere,

stacked one on top of the other. A painter on the scaffolding was decorating the ceiling with angels and other religious images.

Supper was laid out on the table: beef, chicken, fish, lobster, preserves. The food gave off a pungent odour mingled with the sweet smell of wine made from cashew juice.

Gregório and Gonçalo waited in the antechamber, glimpsing the Archbishop through the open door.

A slave passed by with a large platter of roast meats, which he gripped with two cloths. João da Madre de Deus was seated at the head of the table from where he could observe every corner of the room. He downed his goblet of wine in one gulp and ordered it to be refilled with a discreet gesture. His manners were impeccable although he looked more like a forester than a prelate, with his one eye and huge beefy hands. He laboured over the food on his plate, cutting it into little pieces; his expression was serious, sombre, and betrayed irritation. He lifted the food to his mouth in rapid movements. He munched and chewed, and then put his hands to his forehead, leaning over his plate, lost in thought. Then he made another furious attack on his food, chewing it with the same glum expression.

Another bottle of wine was served. Having finally finished his dinner, the Archbishop had the men shown in.

Gregório entered. Gonçalo followed him, filled with curiosity. The poet glanced round the room, trying to appear nonchalant, but not convincingly, because no man, least of all a poet with a flair for satire, could ignore the grotesque sight of João da Madre de Deus, white above and dark below, and surrounded by packing-cases.

"Sit down," said the Archbishop, pointing to the chairs. "What brings you here?"

Gregório straightened his collar: "First of all, I've brought you this sonnet which I composed in Your Grace's honour."

The Archbishop read it with a smile.

"Your Grace must be aware of the turmoil raging in the city," said the poet.

"I've been informed. I understand there is tension between the Menezes and the Ravasco factions. How did this quarrelling start?"

"After bribing his way into office, the Captain-General started abusing his position and, with a viper's tongue, began slandering prominent public figures, including the Ravascos, who had dared to criticize his excesses. Then last year, when Antonio de Souza arrived to govern the colony, the Captain-General, confident of being protected, began to take revenge on his opponents. Those allied to his enemies were threatened. Finding themselves persecuted, they were forced to seek refuge, many of them in the Jesuit College. On Christmas Eve, Padre Vieira paid the Governor a visit in an attempt to intercede on their behalf. Antonio de Souza turned him away with insults. The quarrel then moved to the streets. One of the Captain-General's young nephews set up an ambush for the De Brito brothers, Antonio and André, near the Carmelite Church, on the road descending the Pelourinho. The youth and his friends fired arquebuses at the two brothers from one of the houses; they almost killed Antonio. Nothing but a bunch of cowards. The purveyor, André de Brito, seeing his brother lying on the ground, attacked the assailants in their hiding-place and chased them off single-handed. They escaped by leaping over the barrier around the College grounds. The rest Your Grace already knows."

"So, Bahia has turned into a battlefield, with families feuding and the bitter taste of blood on everyone's lips."

*"Oh Holy Shepherd of fair America, how I lament these dark deeds,"* recited the poet. "Antonio de Souza considers himself King. He has become reckless. He exploits disputes about honour to discredit the Liberal faction. He relies on the collusion of judges and officials to persecute his opponents. And the judges," continued Gregório, clenching his fists, "are drawn into this vortex of intrigues and quarrels between the factions."

"Surely the Ravasco clan is capable of defending itself?"

"True," replied Gregório. "The Ravasco family have ties with the Court of Appeals. But their greatest defence is their own personal integrity."

"Yes," conceded João da Madre de Deus, "I need no convincing. But certain acquaintances and ties do help. The Ravasco brothers have connections with the Costa Dorea family, not to mention the Sodré Pereiras and Carvalho Pinheiros."

"Yes, the Vieira Ravasco family has a lot of influence," admitted Gregório.

"They also have links with other factions," the Archbishop went on. "The father of the Vieira Ravasco brothers, and grandfather of this brave young man here, was extremely powerful. Not to mention the influential role played by Antonio Vieira in Portugal."

"But this isn't making the slightest difference," Gregório reminded him, "the Governor's brutality knows no bounds. Judge João de Gois, who is a native of Bahia, and his ally Judge Palma are unscrupulous. Gois is a tyrant and related to all the powerful families in São Paulo."

"I can see that this could turn into a war between North and South," said the Archbishop, fixing his one eye on the visitors.

"There's another judge mixed up in this affair," the poet said. "Cristóvão de Burgos, who helped his stepson Francisco Teles buy the office of Captain-General in Bahia from Anrique Anriques, that infamous pimp at the Court of Afonso VI. He bought the title so that he could thieve and murder to his heart's content. Tyranny on a grand scale. The powerful protect each other while the vipers devour each other. Ever since Braço de Prata arrived here, our lives have been in peril. The Captain-General used the Governor's power to sanction the enmities he cultivated with his sword, certain he would never be brought to justice. Take the case of the judge João Couto de Andrade. He was beyond reproach, yet when he denounced the Captain-General's abuses, he was forced to seek refuge in the Jesuit College to escape being killed. My cousin Antonio Rolim was brought to court on trumped-up charges. João de Couros and Francisco Dias do Amaral were removed from office, only to be replaced by the Governor's appointees who were prepared to pander to the Captain-General. He filled other minor offices in similar fashion by unjustly imprisoning the incumbents and nominating his friends. He publicly abuses and insults military officers and government aides until they retaliate with disloyalty; he speaks contemptuously of the city of Bahia, invades private homes and sanctions night patrols, which are becoming more frequent. Innocent people are arrested and imprisoned. Few public figures are shown respect. André de Brito had to submit to a full inquiry into the affairs of the Judiciary and Treasury instigated by Judge Palma, noted for his mistrust and suspicions. Alleging that a conspirary against the government was being hatched inside the College, the Captain-General and Antonio de Souza ordered patrols to keep it under surveillance and look out for men wanting to seek refuge there. Finally they forced their way into the College, ignoring its sacred right to offer sanctuary. They might as well have trampled on Papal Authority. And on yours too, Your Grace, if you'll pardon my frankness."

"As you are well aware, Doctor de Matos, I publicly censured Antonio de Souza's decision to invade the College. I lost no time in reminding him that the Government Statutes, drawn up by Roque da Costa Barreto, guarantee the protection of the Indians and Jesuits, alms-houses and hospitals. They also specify that all vacant government posts should be filled."

"Yes. But this isn't good enough. The Secretary has been unjustly arrested. Men of honour seeking shelter in the College have been thrown into jail. Their only crime is to have been friendly with the Ravasco family. Your Grace, there is no longer any truth, dignity or honour in this city."

"I dare say you're right. But what can I do? Politics are not within my jurisdiction. In truth, I'm only a suffragan bishop." He spoke with his face half turned, so that his one eye was in the centre.

"There is one thing, Your Grace," said Gregório. "Have a word in the Governor's ear. It's important that the soldiers stop besieging the College and the fugitives be freed. And there's something else you should know: Antonio de Souza has written to His Royal Highness accusing Padre Vieira of being responsible for the crime."

The Archbishop looked at him with surprise.

"Padre Vieira?"

"Vieira and his brother Bernardo. The Governor has fabricated a string of lies. Surely Your Grace believes in Padre Vieira's innocence? Nothing could be clearer."

The Archbishop's brow furrowed, his two fingers pressed to his nostrils, his ring gleaming. "Yes, I believe you. Well . . . I must think about this before cautioning the Governor. Don't forget, my first duty is to the Church and not to the government. This is a delicate matter and I must think things over carefully before reaching any decision, I might even consult the Cardinal d'Este."

"Your Grace, there is no time. As a judge of the Ecclesiastical Court, that is my opinion. We cannot allow the Governor to go unpunished, for that would prejudice the right to sanctuary. Your Grace must trust me. Do you still not know what kind of man Antonio de Souza is? Even after all those visits to the Governor's palace? *For the well-being of your flock, forge your crook from good example.*"

João da Madre de Deus was pale. He rose to his feet, held out his hand and they kissed his ring.

"Doctor Gregório, you judge me unfairly. I have heard the views of other ministers at the Court. Not all of them share your opinion. I am a prudent man and I did not come to this colony to get involved in quarrels. I'm also asking you to trust me. I, too, have a right to expect loyalty. I shall carefully consider this matter and then I will make up my own mind."

He withdrew to his private apartments, followed by a retinue of clerics and guards. A priest accompanied the visitors to the door.

"What a swine!" exclaimed Gregório as they descended the hill.

"Keep your voice down," said Gonçalo. "You're to blame. There are certain things one doesn't say. You didn't show much tact. If only you'd kept your mouth shut."

"What good would that have done? Can't a man speak his mind? People say I have a wicked tongue and that I'm mad, they accuse me of being malicious and evil, but those who don't bite have no teeth. Those who live in glass houses don't throw stones. Playing dumb sanctifies these imbeciles. They're a degenerate lot. Did you recognize the priest who showed us out?"

"The dean, Dom André Gomes."

"Yes. He's known as the Skull. He and the Archbishop are always plotting against me. He's in the background, hoping to be appointed bishop. But who will have faith in a prattling skull?"

"What happened between you and the chaplain from Marapé?" asked Gonçalo.

"One night, after leaving the Council chambers, I was walking along the street when, for no good reason, a boy at a window threw a stone and hit me on the head, drawing blood. I fell to the ground and a friend called out to me: 'You've just been purged and you're trying to get up?' I swore I'd give the boy a good kick up the backside. And guess what the chaplain had the nerve to write to me? That I should write a satire about the stoning instead of mocking the clergy from Portugal. I wrote back, telling him to mind his own business. But he took no heed until I wrote so many satires about the sanctimonious villain that he was beside himself with rage. But he was a poor target. An ignorant fool, a dim-wit of a priest, and such a prude."

"Nobody escapes you, do they?"

"Just wait till it's your turn."

Gonçalo smiled and crossed himself.

"On one occasion," continued Gregório, "a nun was surprised that I should have poured scorn on Padre Damaso, protesting he was such a worthy clergyman and that she'd already given birth to his child."

"Gregório, for heaven's sake! You're impossible!"

*"Sor Madama de Jesus confesses,"* he recited, *"that after nine months abed with X, she conceived with the help of Padre Y. She finally gave birth to Z, sired by an Irish priest with a mouth like a bucket of shit."*

Gonçalo's laughter echoed through the deserted street.

"Another of these scoundrels I lampooned was Padre Manuel Loureiro, who arrived from Vila do Conde. He refused to accept the chaplaincy in Angola. He was arrested and tortured for having disobeyed the Bishop's orders. He refused to embark and was pushed on board the ship with his hands tied, ranting and raving, shouting that he preferred to spew in the galley rather than shit in the prow. They wanted to send him to Lisbon but the priest, drunk as usual, only wanted to sail in a sea of wine. You can imagine what I wrote about him. Then there's the sodomite Friar Joanico, the gluttonous Padre Perico and Friar Tomás who despised you for spewing in the presence of his lady nun and then covering it over with a hat."

"You ridiculed him? Recite it for me!"

"I mocked him, saying Friar Tomás made everyone sick when they thought of him stinking like a lecherous goat, pot-bellied, po-faced, and hollow as can be. Friar Tomás knew how to wear out a nun, before crawling off in a state of exhaustion."

"I'll bet your days are numbered in the Ecclesiastical Court," Gonçalo laughed.

"That remains to be seen. I'll try sending flattering verses to the Archbishop. I'll make him the eternal temple of my muse and sing his praises for evermore," recited Gregório, miming as he spoke.

"Such pithy eloquence!"

"It's a great virtue. Yes, I'm convinced certain vices can become virtues. Everything depends upon when, how, and why."

"For you everything is a vice, which explains why you're obsessed with hell."

"But nowadays there's nothing but vices. And they often pass for virtues."

"Nowadays, Francesca da Rimini would be sent to heaven instead of hell."

"And where else should she go?" asked Gregório indignantly.

"All women should be sent to hell. Let me tell you what happened to me: I fell madly in love with a young girl and wooed her respectfully, hoping she would marry me. She refused. I asked her why she would not have me and she replied: 'You're ardent and considerate, you court and love me with devotion. But one evening, as you were sitting and conversing with your dog, I stole upon you quietly and you went on speaking, oblivious to my presence. How could I love a man who fails to notice me even when I'm standing right behind him?' I could have strangled her."

"My dear Gonçalo, men always feel like strangling the woman who gets the better of them. I'll have to give you a few lessons in the art of seduction. For every lady you need a different approach. Whores like a touch of romance. Young ladies love speeches that bring blushes to their cheeks. There are few women in the world who are likely to turn crimson at the sight of an erection. It's simply a question of knowing how to show it to them."

Sometimes even Gregório found his theories on this subject rather coarse, but he was always right about women.

It was humid, oppressive. A fiddler played in the distance. The two men walked in silence, listening to the music.

"I wish I understood the spells women cast," mused Gregório. "As for Dona Maria Berco, there's a creature who still manages to look pretty, even in a dowdy old dress. How gracefully she moves . . . I feel so wretched! She's driving me out of my wits and she alone holds the cure. *In the serpent's tongue you'll find both the poison and the remedy.*"

"That's what you want her to do," said Gonçalo.

"What?"

"Bite you."

The moon was high in the heavens and had never shone more brightly. Gregório was silent and pensive. His former companions at the University of Coimbra and the Jesuit College in Bahia, most of them mediocre students, were now successful; they were men of wealth and influence; they owned plantations, had wives and children. And yet he, the most brilliant scholar, was a mere bohemian, who whiled away his afternoons in a brothel playing games with the girls, spent his mornings reading rubbish, and his nights fantasizing about women who did not exist. Or did they?

For all his boasting, the poet was not the greatest whoremonger in the city of Bahia. He would often go for days, even weeks, without a woman. He did not feel that he was to blame for his sins. There was no lack of available women. Gregório used to say they were all available, especially the widows, the women abandoned by their husbands, the unfortunate women with "impotent or castrated" husbands, who could not satisfy them or couldn't get an erection however hard they tried. Older women were the easiest catch of all.

Gregório lay naked on his bed, admiring his prick. Women assured him black men had penises as hard as the wood of the jacaranda; that white men's were as soft as cork. Rubbish!

But what good was an erection to him as he thought of Maria? This was a moment when he could have done without it. It was agonizing, left him hopelessly frustrated.

The previous day he had watched one of the girls in the brothel casting a spell to make her husband impotent by putting the wretch's sperm beneath a large pitcher of water. Since the classical age of Ovid, such spells have proved ineffectual, for the earth continues to be populated with unwanted children. Besides, a man could get an erection using a lemon. But *"To push a lemon up one's arse, without feeling a thing, was something for the perverts, solace for pansies rather than pussies."* If it were left to them, women would make all men impotent. His feelings towards women were ambivalent. Love mingled with hatred.

"You're dreaming. What's the matter?" asked Anica, interrupting her kisses.

"Nothing. I'm thinking. I once knew someone . . ."

Anica sat up on the bed.

"A woman?"

"Yes, a young woman."

Anica got up.

He felt repentant: *Which of them will be so foolish as to resign herself to the misfortune of having to share sorrows, caresses, worries and torments with the other, since women are not worn like shoes in pairs? Sweet love, if I must choose, let me have both. I won't abandon the one for the other, or show either any preference; for they're both women to my liking, and unless death intervenes, they'll both be mine. They could become good friends, share the weeks between them, the one leaving as the other arrives; and I'll share my money, my favours and affection, for let it be known, that while it may defy logic, favours can be divided in the arithmetic of love.*

Anica was at a loss for words. The poet's silence bothered her. She knew he was thinking of the girl he had met. She knew that one day he would leave her for another woman. But it saddened her to think about it.

"I've bought a length of silk and had a skirt made. And a blouse. I went to Simão, the cloth-merchant, the blue shop-front third along the street and bought some ivory-coloured silk. Should I try them on?"

"Anica," sighed Gregório, sitting up in bed and taking her by the shoulders. "Don't expect too much of me, can't you understand? I've never given women anything but trouble."

"That doesn't bother me."

Anica left the room.

Gregório thought about Góngora y Argote. Don Luis was walking along a street ankle deep in mud. He came face to face with some women. They stopped and told him to go first, for there was not enough room for all of them to pass at once. They could not help laughing at the poet's enormous nose. Góngora turned, waving them on: *After you, rude wenches.* Gregório smiled quietly. *"Where are the Spanish gallants of yore?"*

Gregório felt weary and no longer wanted to think about Anica or Góngora, about Braço de Prata and the crime, about his late father, and Antonio Vieira, about the little games he played in bed. Filled with desire for Maria, he shut his eyes.

He could feel his penis swell between his fingers. Had he any right to cherish such feelings for Maria? What did he want from her?

*Vengeance*

A COCK CROWED. The pale light of morning penetrated a horizontal slit up on the cell wall of the conspirators. The light did not reach the floor and the men who were sitting there could scarcely see each other. The meagre ration of oil never lasted all night and the glazed, earthenware bowl with a spout, which served as an oil-lamp, had been put out.

Along with the conspirators there were four more prisoners, one murderer, two thieves, and a heretic. And rats. The men's appearance betrayed how long they had spent behind bars; those who had served most time looked thinner and more ashen, their hair and nails now long and filthy.

The men shared a damp straw mattress. On warm nights, they used it in turn; come the cold weather, they used it together, sleeping back to back.

Antonio de Brito sat and watched the light on the wall. He fingered his torn, bloodied clothing, inhaled the stench of excrement and urine from the buckets distributed throughout the cell. In the distance, the Cathedral bells rang, summoning the faithful to early Mass. De Brito could not get up or walk even as far as the bed. Someone lit the lamp and approached him. De Brito saw João de Couros' face. Others also gathered round. They examined his blood-stained hands, the soles of his lacerated feet, the scars where his skin had been scorched. De Brito felt the most terrible pain going through his body and his head began to spin. He raised a hand to his mouth and realized several teeth were missing.

Diogo de Souza, known as the Crooked One, said something. De Brito could not make it out but was relieved to find that he was no longer in the torture chamber.

# I

THE WHITE FULL MOON cast its rays through the
window-panes of the Governor's palace.

Reclining in a comfortable chair with his feet resting on
a cushion, Antonio de Souza watched the reflections on his silver
hand. Mata was reading aloud.

"And here we are, saddened by so many misfortunes. The aforesaid assassination had been planned the previous evening
in the College and Antonio Vieira was one of the participants
along with other Jesuit fathers; his brother was also there with
several laymen. This can be easily proved by reliable witnesses.
Gonçalo Ravasco helped Antonio de Brito carry out the
murder, because he was in the College at the time, having taken
refuge there when I ordered his arrest." Mata looked at the
Governor.

"Does that sound all right, sir?"

"Yes, it's fine," replied the Governor. "You may continue."

Mata's voice was lost in that vast, sparsely furnished room. He
finished reading the letter. The Governor signed it.

"Ah, such trouble. Nothing but intrigues, everywhere you
look." He remained thoughtful.

"Would Your Excellency like me to read it once more?"

"No. That's enough. Antonio Teles will be here soon. When
he arrives, leave us alone. I hope he won't be late. I feel very tired
after a sleepless night."

They heard knocking.

"The Captain-General," announced the major-domo.

Sitting upright in his chair, De Souza adjusted his metal arm,
to strike the right pose.

The Captain-General entered with a fatuous smile.

"I've brought you some good news, Antonio," he said. "We've succeeded."

"The door," said the Governor. Mata went out and closed the door behind him.

The Captain-General removed the coat draped over his shoulders and sat down beside the Governor.

"Now then," continued the Captain-General, "De Brito didn't flinch when we tortured him, but he lost his nerve when we threatened to kill Bernardo Ravasco, and told us everything he knew."

"Indeed?" There was a glint in De Souza's eye. "Were our suspicions correct?"

"Some of them. The Secretary didn't stain his own hands with blood. But everything was planned in his presence and with the connivance of the Jesuit Fathers. Ravasco attended the meeting in the College immediately following the crime. The old man went at once to the College chapel to join his brother, and they left for the Jesuits' estate after calling at the Secretariat to collect his papers. You know the rest."

"Well, in any case, the Ravascos are mixed up in this."

"De Brito stabbed my brother, just as we suspected. And now I will surprise you, Antonio: Luiz Bonicho was one of the eight hooded men, also the blond fencing-master."

"The councillor? I'm not surprised in the least. He only pretended to be on our side. He has never sided with anyone except Old Nick. Pederast that he is, going around with a fan! He ignores the rules of etiquette which forbid men to use fans and he minces around like a courtesan. In Portugal he'd already have been behind bars. And there's no doubt that it was Luiz Bonicho who told the fencing master to finish me off."

"João de Couros was another. So was Diogo de Souza, better known as the Crooked One. It was Diogo who removed the ruby cross from Francisco's chest. Apparently the cross once belonged to his old father, who must have gambled it away. The other assassin is the notary Manuel Dias. And finally, Moura Rolim, the cousin of the poet Gregório de Matos."

"So, the picture is nearly complete: Antonio de Brito, Luiz Bonicho, Donato Serotino and João de Couros."

"Four."

"Diogo, the Crooked One."

"Five."

"Manuel Dias."

"Six."

"Moura Rolim."

"Seven."

"Seven, well then? . . ."

"Well, there's one missing," said the Captain-General.

"De Brito will tell us who. Torture him harder."

"I suspect Gonçalo Ravasco. No doubt De Brito is protecting him. We might even catch a bigwig there, like Ravasco."

"It's going to be difficult, Teles. The rich are well protected. A real aristocrat never removes his gloves and hires henchmen to do his dirty work. Neither Gonçalo nor his father would allow themselves to be caught ambushing someone on the street. They have enough prestige – and money – to convince – or to bribe – others. A Ravasco sits in his study or spends the summer on his country estate. A Ravasco whiles away his afternoons at the gaming tables or goes hunting in the countryside, or amuses himself playing the guitar or lute; a Ravasco does not conduct his own defence, he engages a lawyer. The Ravasco clan don't utter obscenities, they don't whip their slaves; they wear silk stockings, shirts of the finest linen and they employ a secretary. Even their dogs travel in a palanquin. Padre Vieira never involves himself in violence, has probably never as much as killed a fly. He simply gives the orders. But we'll catch him, however long it takes."

"But how, Antonio?"

"We'll issue a warrant for the arrest of those conspirators who are still free and set up a judicial enquiry to prove their guilt," answered the Governor.

The Captain-General rose abruptly, interrupting the Governor. He took a few steps, raising his hands to his head, lost in thought. He sat down again and spoke:

"As you yourself said, Antonio, they're all men of considerable standing. They'll have their alibis well-rehearsed. They have powerful friends at Court and, unless we can offer substantial proof, they'll be pardoned at once. As usual. You don't need me to tell you how justice works here. Besides, the Court of Appeals is divided. There are those who are prepared to take sides with the Ravascos, simply to oppose you."

"But we have Palma and Gois in the Courts. They're influential and will do as I say."

"Is that sufficient guarantee?"

The Governor reflected.

"No, Teles, I suppose not. Nor do I trust the judges. But how is one to control their activities within the Tribunal? The judges are only interested in the Royal Councils, Brazil is merely one stage in advancing their career, so it doesn't matter whether they're on one side today and on the other tomorrow, so long as they achieve their ambitions. The requirements for promotion and recognition are seniority, merit and precedence, and, of course, we mustn't forget patronage. What is merit? Simply that the judges mustn't create problems or cause trouble. Seniority may also take into account the years of service given by proxy. And the most important factor of all in a magistrate's career is the date on which he took the oath, an issue which often provokes heated discussion and unseemly exchanges or even fisticuffs. Precedence simply confers greater power on those magistrates who have retained their seals of office from a previous appointment. Call for Mata."

The Captain-General rang the bell.

Mata entered.

"Mata, how much do the judges earn?"

"Almost six hundred thousand réis, Your Excellency, without gratuities. Their profits exceed a hundred thousand réis but they expect gratuities for the Feast-day of the Eleven Thousand Virgins and other solemnities. Without counting the taxes they impose for special services and their fees for commissions and inspections, which could amount to another one thousand, two hundred réis. They believe they are entitled to the same salary as the judges in the Royal Judiciary in Lisbon. But the Prince has refused their demands."

"Let's grant them an additional sum for the Feast-day of St Anthony. Draft a letter to the Prince Regent petitioning an increase in salary for the judges. And send a copy of the letter to each of them."

"Yes, Your Excellency."

"You may leave now, Mata."

"Thank you, Your Excellency."

"Antonio de Brito will be sentenced after lengthy proceedings," said the Captain-General. "He can expect to spend considerable time in prison, and even that will be a lesser sentence than he deserves. But it is difficult to have him hanged. The office of almoner is a profitable one and André de Brito must be a rich man and capable of buying a release both for himself and his brother. João de Couros, too, is wealthy. These criminals are from good families; to be sent to the gallows is considered dishonourable. They can also escape the executioner's axe if they hire a good defence lawyer. And we can do nothing about it."

"Then what do you suggest, Teles?"

"I can think of nothing through legal channels," he replied.

"I don't understand."

"I'd like to allot them the same treatment they gave my brother Francisco."

The Governor nodded. Then he said: "No. I want no more deaths. We mustn't sink as low as the Ravascos. We have more effective means at our disposal; we have an army and the forces of law and order. I've no desire to be implicated in any crimes. I have my position to consider. I'm in good standing with the Court, I cannot afford to take risks. Under no circumstances must you kill any of the prisoners for any such move would be held against me, and you. Besides, it won't be easy to track down the fugitives. Gonçalo Ravasco, Luiz Bonicho, Manuel de Barros, and Donato Serotino may already be located outside of our jurisdiction."

"I doubt it, Antonio. They're almost certainly in hiding and intend to join the fleet when it sails for Portugal in early July. Unless we act quickly, they'll fly off like paper kites."

"I'd be more than satisfied if you were to arrest Gonçalo Ravasco and Luiz Bonicho. I detest them. And they despise me, exposing me to ridicule and failing to show respect."

"If we were to arrest close relatives of these criminals, let's say a father or a brother, they could be kept as hostages."

"But not all of them have a close relative."

"But young Ravasco has a sister," said the Captain-General. "Which reminds me, I have another interesting piece of news for you. A Jewish diamond merchant has been arrested after being found wearing my brother's ring. The one he was wearing when they cut his hand off. The jeweller confessed that the gem had been pawned by a certain Maria Berco. I made some inquiries and discovered that the same Maria is the companion of Dona Bernardina Ravasco, the Secretary's daughter. That's enough to incriminate him."

"Is the girl from a good family?"

"She's the wife of João Berco, an old blind man who is the biggest miser you've ever met. He's not short of money but lives like a pauper, forcing his wife to work when there's no necessity. He obviously intends to leave his gold for the rats to devour."

"He'll protest if we throw his wife into prison."

"If he protests, we can offer him money. I'll pay him out of the funds I administer. And besides Dona Bernardina, we can detain the sisters and wives of the De Brito brothers as hostages. They're still in the city and have been seen at the market. Ravasco himself will be a useful hostage until we can find his son," added the Captain-General.

"Send for his daughter, Dona Bernardina Ravasco. She will reveal her brother's whereabouts in exchange for her father's release. But we won't be making an exchange. The Secretary can rot in prison or perhaps I might send him into exile. I'm prepared to give you all the assistance you need to track down these conspirators and murderers. I can provide you with men, money, resources . . . It's in my interest, too, that they should be outlawed, imprisoned, deported, banished. But remember, no deaths."

"But Antonio, don't forget the councillor tried to take your life by using his fencing master to do his dirty work. No one will miss that traitor Serotino, he's merely a pawn. Don't you long for revenge?"

"No. Serotino did a good job training our soldiers. You might even say I've forgiven him. When he drew his sword he showed compassion. He was merely obeying orders. But I loathe that viper, Bonicho."

"The councillor knows certain things he could use against us."

"If he has any proof, make sure it's removed. Arrest him and he'll keep his mouth shut. That's all the satisfaction I need."

"But it won't satisfy me, Antonio. I want blood."

"No!" said De Souza. "Carry out my orders or suffer the consequences. We must act within the law if we hope to gain the upper hand. We can always resort to imprisonment, exile, torture, legal proceedings, judicial inquiries, persecution. I've had plenty of enemies in my time and I've never been outwitted. Thefts, foolish acts of revenge, crimes, breaches of the peace, these are for novices. My position as Governor no longer permits me such behaviour. You will obey my orders."

"You may count on it," said the Captain-General.

"Find out if there are others involved in the conspiracy. That fair Italian Jesuit, for example, who stands as tall as a church spire and goes around taking notes for some curious reason. Or that Jewish friend of Ravasco. Or that so-called poet Tomás Pinto Brandão. Then there's Pedro de Matos and Pedro Gomes. I want all the associates of the Ravascos to be tracked down and interrogated. We must incriminate one of these Ravascos with reliable evidence. Arrest her companion who pawned the ring. Bring Gonçalo in for questioning. Torture him until he reveals everything he knows. Then I'll dispatch his confession to the Prince. My one hope is that Gonçalo took part in the crime and that we can prove it. Then I'll be able to bring these troublesome Ravascos to heel. They reek of corruption. God will assist us in this mission of justice. How I'd love to strangle the lot of them with my own two hands." Antonio de Souza paused. "With my one hand, I should say. Unlike Padre Vieira, I'm no coward. I'm a soldier, even if I'm getting old for such adventures. I'll expect news. I want results. And without delay. Do you have reliable men to make the arrests?"

"I'll see to it myself, Antonio," the Captain-General replied. "I'll take a few men with me. I've chosen the captain of the garrison, João Lobato, known as the Bull, and his henchmen. The Bull worked a confession out of De Brito. The men under his command are well-trained in trailing suspects and torturing them."

"Fine. Pay them well and make it clear that they mustn't fail."

The Governor stroked his thin moustache. "You're quite certain they're the right men for the job?"

"The best, Antonio. They're loyal, upright men."

"Is this João Lobato married?"

"No."

"Does he keep company with whores?"

"No. He's a God-fearing man and, as his nickname suggests, his main weakness is food."

"Just as well. In Bahia, affairs are settled and secrets cease to be secrets once people fall into bed. Speaking of which, I think you ought to add the ecclesiastical judge to your list of wanted men, the notorious Gregório de Matos, who keeps on writing those offensive satires. He's sure to be involved in this affair – he's a close ally of the Ravascos. You yourself told me that his cousin took part in the ambush. Besides, he has mocked and taunted me with his obscene lampoons. He was recognized coming out of the Jesuit College on the morning of the crime. Track him down. And if he refuses to mend his ways, throw him into prison or deport him to Angola, or São Tomé or anywhere that is far from here. He won't be missed. As His Royal Highness wisely observed, we have far too many scholars here in the colony."

De Souza dismissed the Captain-General abruptly.

Alone in the great hall, he looked at the moon through the window. He ran his finger over the hard muscle at the base of his neck, chafed by the strap supporting his silver arm.

## II

"YOU CAN PUT OUT the oil-lamp," ordered the Captain-General looking serious.

The Bull, captain of the garrison, weighing a ton and built like his namesake, went up to the stone wall and removed the oil-lamp. He blew out the flame. The acrid smoke made Bernardo Ravasco cough. He was sitting on the damp floor in a corner of the cell. He tried to get up but was prevented by Teles. A grating voice called out:

"Saints and Demons!"

"It's the Blasphemer," explained Teles. "He's in the cell next door. He was once human, but no longer. Now he's nothing but a dried-up old stick covered in vermin, without a tooth in his ugly mouth and with a mop of hair which is neither combed nor washed. That's the fate of everyone who spends any length of time in this place." Teles bent over the prisoner: "It's you I'm talking about."

Ravasco was in good health, his skin was clear and well-preserved. He had enjoyed a happy life, but now, confined to a cell, happiness had deserted him. Perhaps forever, the Secretary thought to himself.

"You're in luck, Ravasco. I've been given orders to spare your life. At least, for the present."

"It's illegal to keep me here, no criminal charges have been proven," Ravasco protested.

"That's not up to us, Lord High and Mighty. Here we make other decisions," said Teles, pointing to the iron spikes in the Bull's hands. The Blasphemer's voice rang out once more.

"Throw salt on Caiaphas, salt on Pilate, salt on Herod and on the Devil."

126

"Hold your tongue, Ravasco. You're no longer Secretary. Here you're a prisoner and you have no rights, and this is a miserable place, even more miserable than those streets above us. Nothing but a slag-heap. Up above us," he continued, "there's no sky, only filth trampled on by all who pass by." He stopped, drew out a snuff-box from his pocket, opened it, took a pinch between his fingers and inhaled. The Blasphemer was still shouting.

"These blasphemers . . . ," muttered Teles.

He sneezed six times in succession, then sighed. A few more sneezes. He inhaled vigorously, and slowly breathed out, his eyes turning red. He tapped his nose with one finger, as if to reassure himself it was still there.

"These miserable blasphemers . . . ," repeated Teles. "More than half of Paris and its rural outskirts are inhabited by starving beggars. The same is true of Holland and England . . . In Switzerland, wealthy landowners have become so exasperated with the mobs who ransack their property, rob them on highways and burn down their forests that they've set up militia to exterminate these . . . what are they called?"

Ravasco remained silent.

"*The Homeless Ones*. It's a nice solution, don't you think? Perhaps we should do the same here."

Ravasco looked at him, his eyes almost hidden beneath his bushy eyebrows.

On a stool the Bull sat eating.

The Blasphemer called out again.

"Bull," ordered Teles, "tell that heretic to shut his mouth."

The Bull went to the cell next door, muttered something to the Blasphemer, who began shouting then fell silent.

"Poor fool. Tomorrow I'll set him free."

"Most compassionate," Bernardo remarked.

"As I was saying, Bernardo Ravasco, the law permits me to use, how shall I put it . . . cruel methods to obtain a confession. But, fortunately for you, I already know everything."

"You've never shown much respect for the law, Teles. This would be the first time."

"I know the whole affair was planned by you and that brother of yours, an atheist masquerading as a Jesuit."

"My brother is not an atheist."

"The hypocrite calls himself a priest, but he's nothing but a heretic."

"And who's the Christian? What do you think you're achieving here? Ridding the colony of corruption? Turning Bahia into some place of pilgrimage?"

"I'm simply taking my revenge, Ravasco. Even if I have to spend all I possess, everything I've acquired and inherited, even if I have to shed my own blood, I'll make certain there isn't a Ravasco left in this world, that the entire clan is wiped out. Nothing will stop me. I serve the Prince and Almighty God. I'm not afraid of hell. Nor am I afraid of Antonio Vieira. Not even of the Bull here, isn't that so?"

The captain of the garrison grunted.

"The Bull is fearless. He's seen the devil, haven't you, Bull? Tell us."

"That's right, I've seen the devil," murmured the Bull.

The Captain-General continued: "The devil said his name was Asmodeus and that he wanted the Bull's blood or the blood of anyone who would make a pact with him to indulge in certain perversions with young virgins. He appeared in the guise of a man, a woman, a serpent . . ."

"But I renounced him," the Bull interjected, "and now I see no one but God."

"That's enough," said Bernardo Rasvasco. "No more."

"Vieira has always been very clever, secretly plotting one ambush after another," said the Captain-General. "So be careful, Ravasco. Mind what you say and watch your step. I'll be waiting for you. You killed my brother."


Distressed and anxious for her father's safety, Bernardina Ravasco waited to be received by the Governor.

Maria waited out on the street, sitting beside the coachman. She wrung her hands, terrified that the summons from Braço de Prata might have something to do with the Captain-General's ring. She pulled her veil down over her face. If only she hadn't given her name to the jeweller! If they found out, all would be lost.

The hollow sound of the guard's lance striking the stone flags in the Governor's palace roused Bernardina.

"The Governor is ready to see you, madam," said the major-domo.

Bernardina rose to her feet and passed into the Governor's study.

Antonio de Souza was sitting at his desk and made no attempt to get up as she entered. He stared at her.

Bernardina felt a shiver run down her spine. Yet there was something about De Souza's tortured expression which intrigued her and she couldn't take her eyes off him.

"Do take a chair," he said.

Bernardina sat down.

"Now let me get straight to the point," he said. "I'm interested in having a chat with Gonçalo. Do you know where he is?"

"No."

The Governor stroked his dark moustache. He thought to himself how proud these Ravascos were, even the women.

"We could strike a bargain," the Governor offered.

Bernardina waited.

"If your brother gave himself up, I would release your father."

"Is that all you wished to say?"

"Yes."

"I must think it over. Is my father all right?"

"As well as can be expected, given the conditions."

"The prison is damp and his lungs are very weak."

"It's for you to save him. I hope you'll be a dutiful daughter."

"And a treacherous sister?"

"And a kind sister."


Bernardina was dressed in black. Despite her youth, her face was marked with tiny lines around the eyes and mouth. She greeted her uncle.

"Decent women shouldn't be seen on the street unless attending a baptism, weddings or funerals. You know how I disapprove of women visiting this estate," Padre Vieira admonished her.

"I'm your own niece."

They sat down on a bench on the verandah. There was a mist

over the hilltops. Water could be heard pouring into a trough.

"What do you want?" asked Padre Vieira. One foot tapped on the ground.

"I've spoken to Braço de Prata."

He looked at her in surprise and his foot stopped.

"He summoned me to his residence."

"You shouldn't have gone there. This doesn't concern you."

"Perhaps not, but I went."

"And what did the Governor want?"

Bernardina fingered her pearl necklace.

"What did he want?" he repeated.

"He told me he would release my father if I were to hand over Gonçalo."

Padre Vieira rose to his feet, visibly annoyed.

"The man is an arrogant fool. Forever interfering. What did you say?"

"Nothing. I don't know where to find Gonçalo. I came to ask your advice, uncle."

"My advice? Would you be capable of betraying your own brother?"

"It was Gonçalo and not my father who got mixed up in this feud. He was the one who took part in ambushes and sword-fights, and now my father is paying for his crimes."

"Listen carefully, my child, your father would be in prison even if Gonçalo didn't exist. It's me Braço de Prata really wants to throw into prison. I'm the one he's anxious to see out of the way. He won't put up with anyone who shows more mettle than himself, even if that person is a frail, old priest like me. Human hearts can be stubborn and vices difficult to eradicate. Conflict of opinion creates confusion in men's minds. They don't know whom to heed, and whether, in life or death, they follow those who tell them what they want to hear. The solution is not simple or easy. There's no point in handing over one Ravasco in exchange for another. Antonio de Souza will hold on to both. For the more Ravascos in his grasp, the better. Kings are the servants of God, and if Kings don't punish the vassals who disobey them, God will punish them in turn for disobeying His commands."

*

"A mathematician!" exclaimed Antonio Vieira. "That's what I should have been. Only mathematicians are capable of finding proof and coming up with sound theories and convincing arguments to contradict what is in fact self-explanatory."

Padre José Soares listened. Antonio Vieira's niece had just left the villa which the old priest used as a retreat. The clattering of hooves could be heard as the coach journeyed back to the city.

"A mathematician," he repeated. "Just think how I've spent my life, my friend. I spent so much time abroad in foreign kingdoms that I ended up a stranger everywhere. There was a time when I had a country to call my own, but now I no longer know what country that might be, the country where I was born, where I lived, or where I wandered in my imagination. Now I'm the prisoner of my own conscience, a broken old man. In my time I've settled wars between nations, resolved conflicts between armies, arbitrated in rifts between popes and kings, even in disputes of a divine nature. And now I'm having difficulty in persuading a one-armed colonial governor to stop waging his campaign of hatred."

"But Padre Vieira, there must be lots of things you can still do."

"Indeed, my friend, there are still lots of things for me to do. But I'm old and tired."

"It's true, we've suffered so many setbacks and disappointments. Things seem to have become much more difficult."

"Well, if they're determined to fight, I'll retaliate. My brother is in prison and my nephew sentenced to exile. Now that they've declared war on us, I will fight one more battle."

"What will you do, Padre?"

"I'll send a messenger to Portugal. He'll deliver letters to powerful allies."

"What messenger?"

"Alderman Luiz Bonicho."

"But how can the councillor leave for Lisbon when he daren't venture out in public for fear of arrest?"

"He'll slip aboard the flagship. Gonçalo will accompany him and plead our cause before His Royal Highness. And something else: I shall go and see one of my brother's closest friends who is influential in Court circles. He's a rich man with considerable power. Perhaps he'll be able to help us, despite being Jewish."

"Jewish!" exclaimed Padre Soares. "Is it wise to become involved with Jews again?"

"I will write to Roque da Costa Barreto. He was governor in Brazil and he knows how the internal affairs of the colony are managed. He's a man of authority and is much respected at Court. Need I explain why I cannot draft all the copies in my own handwriting, now that it looks like the scrawl of some novice learning to write?"

"I don't think that will be necessary, Padre."

"My Lord," wrote Antonio Vieira, reading aloud as he put quill to paper, "I thank Your Excellency for the honour you have bestowed on my brother and nephew in all your dispatches. I doubt whether my brother will be able to write to you personally because of the conditions in prison; as for my nephew, he will seek an audience with Your Excellency in Portugal unless he is prevented from embarking; and since I, too, have been removed and banned from the Governor's palace and have been accused of criminal offences, leaving the general grievances to those who are returning for good, I hereby wish, for my own satisfaction, to give you a full account of the injustices done to me so that Your Excellency may be apprised of the matter with all due formality. Since it was the intention of Your Excellency's successor to sell offices and supplies for personal gain and to ensure that this illegal bartering should be handled solely by him and his intimates, his first concern was to dismiss the Secretary, Bernardo Vieira Ravasco. Encouraged by the Captain-General, he accused the Secretary of forging a letter from Your Excellency in favour of Sebastião de Araújo; and since it was not sufficient to produce the aforesaid letter, the Secretary had to appear in person, and all the Governor gained from this proof of the honesty of the one and the deceit of the other, was a closer alliance with the Captain-General and implacable hatred towards the Secretary. The Governor dismissed my brother from office and, so that all future supplies might be bartered without any interference from the Secretariat, he no longer used legal channels, saying to all traders or bidders: *Why bother with the Secretary?* If a transaction had to be made through the Secretariat (it being for some reason unavoidable) and then failed to make a profit, the Secretary was ordered to reimburse all losses without delay. And so the Governor declared that the ships from Boipeba, Cairu, were not from the coast, and therefore need not pay. Finally, he decreed that the codes of practice Your Excellency established for the Secretariat should be replaced with the legislation drawn up by the Conde de Óbidos, thus rendering your own decrees null and void." Padre Vieira paused to collect his thoughts. He continued:

"This deprived the Secretary of any rights or funds and exposed him to great hardship. The Jesuit Fathers were adamant that it would be scandalous to ignore my brother's plight, so I went to speak to the Governor two days before Christmas, and here is a faithful account of our conversation. *I've come to offer Your Lordship Christmas Greetings before the festivities begin and I'd also like to ask a favour of Your Lordship; somewhat reluctantly I must admit, but this is a matter of conscience and justice, as I'm sure Your Lordship will agree.* He realized immediately what I was about to say, and losing his temper, he assured me that while he may not be a priest in the Jesuit Order, his conscience was as clear as mine, and that he was more familiar with God's commandments than I was. He lost all patience; but it was God's will that I should speak my mind and I told him that he owed it to his conscience to uphold the original legislation in my brother's Secretariat, as approved by the Prince. He continued his ranting. Shall I write down the word shouting, Padre?" asked Antonio Vieira.

"Ranting sounds better."

"Ranting. *Do they think they're entitled to greater powers than mine?* Whereupon I insisted that it was precisely because His Lordship was so powerful that I had felt emboldened to ask such a favour, while reminding him that I myself had always served His Lordship whenever possible. Here I was referring to my intercession with the Duke, which the Governor had asked of me at Santo Antão, on the only occasion I ever met him in Portugal. With this he rose to his feet, shouting that he had never asked me for any favour whatsoever. But I told him: *Yes, you most certainly did. There's no reason to doubt my word because at that time all sorts of people asked me* to intercede on their behalf with the great and powerful, with the exception of the Prince. He retorted that no one was greater than he. *I'm not referring to qualities*, I replied, *but to status and titles*. And with this he screamed: *Get out and don't show your face again here in the palace.* Mata and another valet were in the room at this point and, defying them, I told him: *As one who has frequented the palaces of all the kings and princes of Europe I shall be only too pleased to avoid this palace of shame*. He turned his back on me saying: *I'm fully aware of the places you frequent, Jew. I'm well informed of the places you frequent, Jew.* And here our conversation ended. Your Lordship will observe that, when he refused to respect me as a priest, I forgot to address him as Governor. This is something I've had cause to regret and repent after examining my conscience, which is more guilt-ridden than that of the Governor."

Vieira paused and thought for a moment.

"Should I mention the Captain-General's death, Padre Soares?"

"Yes, I think you should."

Vieira continued to write. Once he had finished, he asked Padre Soares to make copies in time for the fleet's departure.

"Bahia, June 1683. Chaplain and loyal servant to Your Lordship. Antonio Vieira."

Vieira opened a parchment book. He read the exhortation: "When you sit to dine with a governor, carefully examine what is set before you. Do not covet the delicacies set before him, for they are deceiving." He turned to José Soares. "There's no time to sleep or doze, or even fold one's arms. Warn the poet, Gregório de Matos, of the Governor's intentions. Tell him to warn Gonçalo. We'll see who suffers most in this contest," Vieira muttered to himself.

# III

THE BLASPHEMER was released from his cell. The blinding
daylight forced him to close his eyes. Wraith-like, he wandered through the streets, and it was already dark when he
remembered his important mission.

He dragged himself up the steep roads of the city, lantern in
hand, searching for the house.

The wind shook the trees and caused the flame of the lantern to
flicker.

Finally, he caught sight of it. The house was large, standing on
its own, and situated east of the main port, close to the shore. On
the front, there was a great wooden door and two small balconies
on the first floor. To one side there was a great furnace. Along the
edge of the roof there were statuettes, eroded beyond recognition.

The Blasphemer knocked. No one appeared. The house was
dark, with only a glimmer of light in one of the upper windows.

"Luiz Bonicho, you smelly, old hunchback with that big nose
of yours," called the Blasphemer. "Bonicho, Bonicho, you foul-
beaked toucan, open this door before the devil blasts it to pieces."

A shadow appeared at a window.

Eventually the door opened.

Donato Serotino appeared, the barrel of his gun pointing at the
Blasphemer.

"What are you doing here at this hour, Blasphemer? I told you
to stay away from here. I thought you were in prison?"

"I prefer tramping the streets."

Serotino lowered his weapon. Bonicho appeared behind him.

"Let the wretch in, he's as good a fellow as you'll find on this
earth, if you ignore the vermin," quipped Bonicho.

"What do you want, Blasphemer?" asked Donato.

"You will tell me all you know, give me all you possess, and shun all men for love of me."

"Just listen to him, Donato," said Bonicho. "Isn't he a wise old bird? Sit down, my friend, sit you down, won't you have something to eat? Give those feet of yours a rest. Some soup, Donato, give the poor devil a little soup, that's if you still know how to light a fire. Otherwise you'd better wake up that bloated slut and tell her to prepare some broth, this old rascal deserves a little warmth. Sit at the head of the table where I eat, Blasphemer; your nickname's as good as a passport. Here the barns and pigsties are reserved for governors, captains-general, priests, soldiers and for those who consider themselves wholesome. They in fact are the ones who are sick. The whole human race is sick, we're a festering sore inherited from our parents. To be born is to grow sick. 'Life's one continuous sickness', wrote Democritus. Isn't that so, Blasphemer?"

The Blasphemer smiled and nodded. An enormous negress appeared with a steaming plate which she set down on the table.

"Eat up and then away with you," Donato ordered the old man.

"Wait, Donato, be patient, perhaps he has something to tell us."

The Blasphemer dipped bread in his soup and ate it noisily.

"Wine, you stupid bitch, bring some wine for this old donkey rustler. These slaves are getting lazier every day, they live in dirt and disorder and do nothing but fuck from morning till night," muttered Bonicho.

The slave brought a bowl of wine.

When he had finished his soup, the Blasphemer peered at Bonicho. "You're the donkey and a stupid one at that, to go on living here when the search is on to track you down and kill you," the Blasphemer said, eyeing Bonicho. He champed the bread with his gums.

Bonicho watched, puzzled.

"Kill me?"

Bonicho and Serotino looked at each other.

"They've loosened De Brito's tongue, he's told them everything," the Blasphemer cackled. "Good riddance to that groveller," he laughed.

"Come on, speak up, you old rascal, or I'll thrash the daylights out of you," said Luiz Bonicho.

"They know everything," said the Blasphemer. "The names of the hooded men. Seven switches of the devil's penis, seven lashes of the whip."

"Ah, now we know," said Bonicho.

Serotino turned pale.

"Their names? Our names? Damn!" cursed Bonicho.

"We must warn the others," said Serotino.

"We'll do no such thing," retorted Bonicho. "We have to hide. It's every man for himself. We mustn't go near the College, or the Jesuits, or any of the Ravascos. It's too risky."

"But it's our duty as honourable men. I'll find some way of warning the others," Serotino insisted.

Rewarded with a coin, the Blasphemer left.

"May this face bring you light, this body stars, heed no evil spoken by my enemies," the Blasphemer sang to himself as he walked away.

Night was approaching as the Mass ended. Maria made her way home lost in thought. Clutching his Bible, the priest had fulminated from the pulpit: "Honey flows from the lips of the adulterous woman and her words are smoother than oil; but in the end she is more bitter than wormwood, more deadly than a double-edged sword. Her footsteps lead to death, descend into hell. She does not pause to think where she is heading; she wanders at random, unaware of danger."

Maria kept on walking, repeating one name under her breath: Gregório, Gregório de Matos. A name sweeter than honey. If she could tear her lips from her face and discard them, then perhaps she might be able to save the rest of her body from ending up in hell. But there was only one man she longed to touch. If only she could cut off her hand and throw it away. Far better that she should lose a hand than see her whole body rot in hell. If only she could firmly reproach herself, as Jesus had rebuked the wind and the sea! What had she done with her serpent-like cunning and dove-like simplicity? She was not even worthy of being received into her master's house for she had stolen.

"Who shall have fire in their breast without setting their clothes alight? Who can tread upon live coals without burning the soles of their feet?" The priest's voice rumbled in her head like thunder. She had stolen, yes, that's what she had done. She no longer deserved anything other than hell. And now her body throbbed with desire, anxious to plunge her into the chasm of adultery. She could no longer bear to stay indoors. She roamed the streets, hovering around public squares, searching every nook and cranny in the hope of seeing Gregório de Matos again. God had willed that she should attend that Mass and hear the priest condemn the adulterous woman. She must try to forget him. But where could he be at this hour? Perhaps walking along the street on the corner of her house, making his way to the tavern, concealed by the shadows of night. Were she to see him, she would run up and kiss him on the cheek, and brazenly tempt him: "I've prepared my bedchamber, perfumed my couch with myrrh, aloes and cinnamon. Come, let us become inebriated with the joys of love, indulge our passion till dawn." Surely one reads that in the Bible? The priest's voice had proclaimed: "The virtuous woman is the jewel in her husband's crown. But the sinful woman is like decay in his bones."

Maria opened her eyes. She was standing before a mirror. She saw herself mounted on a beast with seven heads and ten horns. She was arrayed in hues of purple and scarlet, bedecked with gold and precious stones and pearls, a golden chalice in one hand. Upon her forehead was written: *Babylon the Great, the mother of harlots and the earth's abominations.* She tried to get down but could not. She was inebriated. She looked up. She realized that she was at the bottom of an abyss, engulfed by stagnant water. Birds swooped, howling like dogs. She gulped a mouthful of wine and spat it out: it was blood. Her body began to change into wood and burst into flames. She awoke in a fever. She rose from her bed and went to the mirror. Her face had not changed.

She lit a candle and went into the other room. Fetching a whip, she returned to her bedroom. Years had passed since she last spent the night making love; her aged husband no longer took her to bed. She undid her blouse and skirt in front of the mirror. The garments dropped to her feet. She removed her under-garments. She saw herself naked, her image diffused and distorted in the glass. Her skin was the colour of marble. She moved closer to the mirror. Her mouth, the upper lip firmly outlined, appeared to be coming away from her face. She examined her teeth, and the pointed canine-teeth made her look like a savage beast. Her tongue was bright red and quivering. Her small, round breasts began at her collar-bones. A dark line divided the white curves of her waist-line and hips before opening out into a tuft of pubic hair. Her breathing became heavier, her heart was ready to burst. Gregório de Matos. She had never before stripped in the presence of a man. And rarely in front of her own reflection. Nudity was sinful. She was falling into that abyss she had dreamed of. She had heard people say that in the churches in Rome you could see statues of naked men. She kissed her own lips in the mirror. She felt possessed by demons. Her fate would be as bitter as absinthe. She picked up the whip and lashed herself like the penitents she had seen in Lenten processions, walking behind the litters carrying religious images, barefoot, crawling on their knees, chastising their bodies with lashes, leaving bloodstains on the cobblestones. She must return that ring, she must put Gregório de Matos out of her thoughts.

"Gregório!" a husky female voice rose above the uproar in the brothel.

She was bedecked in earrings, necklaces and bracelets. Pregnant, she walked with her legs forced slightly apart under the weight of her belly.

"Gregório," the girl called out, "Anica de Melo is looking for you; she needs to talk to you."

"Where is she then?"

The girl pointed upwards.

Visibly agitated, Anica appeared at the top of a narrow staircase. On seeing Gregório, she opened her arms. She was wearing a floral dress in muted shades edged with brightly coloured embroidery, and she had a red flower stuck behind one ear.

She waved to Gregório, indicating that she was about to come down.

He waited for her.

"In there, quickly," she said.

Gregório glanced round the room. The Governor's soldiers were slouched over a table, drunk. A young girl was twisting her hair into a coil on the top of her head. For an instant, her hairless armpits blurred Gregório's vision. The men sitting beside her went on drinking and gambling, indifferent to the girl's sensuous gesture.

An amber glow pervaded the room; people's clothing, faces, hair, seemed to absorb the light.

Near a door, screened by a curtain, a man with huge hands and crimson ears was writing on a piece of paper which he rested on one thigh.

Gregório and Anica went into the kitchen. He had been to bed with all these women, except for the negro woman who was combing her hair and showing her armpits. She had not been here long enough.

In the spacious kitchen, lit by the flames from the burning logs, a girl, surrounded by huge pots and pans in burnished copper, was sitting by the hearth drinking a bowl of steaming broth.

Seeing them enter, she got up. Her feet were clad in velvet slippers.

"Heat up some food and set the table for the gentleman," Anica instructed her.

The girl laid aside her bowl of soup, wiped her hands on her apron and began transferring some food from various large pans into smaller ones which she then set over the flames.

"They've been here," said Anica.

"Who?"

"You know who I mean. Braço de Prata's henchmen."

"Were they looking for me?"

"They ransacked your room."

"They've also been looking for me at the Court of Appeals. I wonder what they want?" he mused, without looking at her.

"They mentioned some writings. What are they? You've gone quite pale."

"How the devil did they discover my whereabouts? What does Brazil want of me, persecuting me like this? What does that swine hope to gain with so much hatred? Here only the mean are honoured while the generous are hated."

The slave put a full plate in front of Gregório. The food smelled good. Anica filled two goblets with wine. He ate ravenously while she looked on.

"Have they abused any women? The girls? You?" he asked.

The girl returned to the hearth and sat down to finish her soup, looking at them warily.

"Get out, Jerônima," commanded Anica. The girl got up, taking her soup with her. In a whisper Anica said: "I'm frightened."

"Well, *I'm* not. They'll never be able to prove anything against me since I haven't committed any crime."

"They don't need proof to arrest you. You only have to arouse suspicion."

Anica continued to watch him. She refilled his plate.

"There was a woman here."

"A woman?"

"Yes. A certain Maria Berco. She said you knew her."

"And what did she want?"

"To speak to you. She wants you to meet her tonight in the Rua Debaixo. She says it's urgent. She was an odd-looking creature, but the hussy kept staring at me as if she'd seen a ghost."

Gregório closed his eyes and took a deep breath.

"Who is this girl?" asked Anica.

"Well . . . she's employed by the Ravascos."

"You're deceiving me. Do you think I don't know about your little adventures? Is she your mistress?"

"No. She's married."

"Don't forget that I caught you fondling Córdula's breasts, that slut who goes around with Padre Simão Ferreira. And right under my very nose."

"But Padre Simão isn't married to Córdula."

"Are you in love with the hussy?"

"No."

He ate a few more spoonfuls.

Anica sighed, regaining her composure.

"Thank heaven you've still got some sense left. If you abandon me for some other woman, I'll murder you."

Gregório thought of the negro girl and those armpits. He could feel Anica's breath on his face. She smelled of mint like the peasant-women from the Alto da Panaventosa, where her father used to plant vines. Or was it the smell of grapes? A smell capable of making a man feel drunk. Anica was warm and affectionate. All women possessed such warmth and affection. He recited: *"Sweet ladies, I implore you, show me a little love, or at least allow me to love you. My heart-beat races just to watch you go past with such airs and graces, and then my soul is lost; why wound me with death when you can give me life?"*

Jerônima was singing in the backyard. There was the faint buzz of people chatting in the next room.

"More wine," he demanded.

Anica refilled the poet's goblet.

"I want to drink until I drown in rum, I want to get drunk. Ah, the tyranny of love! But why live a life of boredom?"

He could feel Anica's hand touch his penis.

"Will you abandon me because I'm ugly?"

He reassured her that he would not, told her she was the goddess of whores, the perfect mistress whom he'd never abandon. How did such a lovely whore from the provinces ever come to lose herself in this colonial wasteland?

"You're a lying fool," said Anica. She laughed, revealing a full row of sparkling teeth. "At the age of seven I was a skinny little thing. I used to lift up my skirts and stare at my long, thin legs which came out at the knees and tapered in down to my feet. Within a few years, I had suddenly grown up, but my feet remained small. I was forever tripping and bumping into everything: furniture, doors, strings of onions. Do you see this scar? Just like yours." She showed him a tiny mark at the roots of her hair. "Then my body filled out, especially my breasts and hips, and the youths who lived on the Alto began chasing me, and I don't need to tell you what they were after. I was forever falling in love. But all they wanted was a quick fuck and to disappear."

"They were a disgusting bunch, those louts."

"Then I went to Lisbon. In the street, youths used to call me a country bumpkin. I was ashamed of my rosy peasant cheeks and my runny nose. How I longed to be pale like a fine young lady."

"That's face-powder, you ninny."

"I'm fated to be alone."

Gregório looked at her. For the first time he noticed that her face was beginning to age, there were delicate lines etched around her mouth, a slight roughness in her complexion, a certain look of weariness in her eyes.

"Have you never been married?"

"No. I dearly wanted to marry and raise a family. But I haven't much patience with children. Men and children make me sick. I could never be the sort of wife a man would be proud of. Men prefer being with whores who know their place."

"Men aren't all alike."

"The world's much the same everywhere. The world and human nature."

Anica remained serious, her eyes vacant. "Being the daughter of peasants also embarrasses me. I'm sure that's why I left Portugal. I decided to come here because in Brazil everybody feels like a peasant. But I dream of leaving one day for some nice place."

"Perhaps Abyssinia," he suggested. "You'll find the fabulous Kingdom of Prester John."

"Do you want to go there?"

"I keep on trying. But I always end up staying here."

"And what's to be found there?"

"A blue river."

"Is that all?"

"That's all."

"There are plenty of blue rivers here."

When Gregório entered his room he realized they had rummaged through his books. This was not a case of someone looking for something. The books had been thrown on to the floor, some had their pages torn: everything had been vandalized.

Gregório was shocked, believing as he did that even the most crass and wicked of men would respect books. But people hated what they did not understand, and Braço de Prata's henchmen were a bunch of numbskulls.

The girls occupying the adjacent rooms felt sorry for him. Some came to tidy things up and repair the damage. One of the girls brought a pot of glue to mend the torn pages. It was the young negro girl, the new arrival. Gregório pushed the other girls outside. He was alone in the room with the girl. Without a word, without as much as asking her name, he removed the girl's clothes and, throwing the books to the floor, laid her on the bed. She was magnificent and as mysterious as night. He held her body with passion and possessed her over and over again, without uttering a single word. Then he picked up one of the books and began reading from Góngora as she dressed in a daze.

"Who will gaze on the Andalusian without showing compassion? Who will deny him their favours?"

# IV

GARMENTS MADE OF VELVET, silk and linen were scattered over the bed. Maria helped her mistress to remove her dress. As she dismantled the pear-shaped wire hoop, it collapsed onto the floor. Standing with her legs apart, she held her steady by the hips to loosen the laces of her corset. Then she crouched down to remove her stockings by untying the garters below the knees; finally, she put on her nightdress.

"Ah, that's much better," said Bernardina. "I feel trapped in those clothes."

"But they're so beautiful, madam."

Bernardina looked at her young companion.

"Tell me, Maria, are you certain you want to go?"

"Yes, madam, I'd do anything for you."

"If something should happen to you, at least my conscience would be at peace. For you yourself offered to go and look for my brother."

"There's no danger, madam."

"Just to stay alive in this country requires facing risks. I know you've no fear of danger. Where will you look? In the brothels? The taverns? In those dark, polluted alleyways? He might be far away on some plantation. And suppose they arrest you on the road?"

"They won't catch me."

"You mustn't tell anyone of my meeting with Braço de Prata. I hope to persuade Gonçalo to give himself up in order to secure my father's release. His friends won't like it. They're heartless. My own uncle, a Jesuit, a man of God, refused to hear of any such exchange. He would prefer to see his own brother die. Gonçalo is young and strong; besides, he was the one who got us into this mess refusing to heed my father's warnings. But he's a good boy and once he hears what's happening, he'll agree to surrender."

"Don't worry, madam, things will sort themselves out."

"Off you go, Maria, go. Who knows if I shall ever see my father again. This could be another of Antonio de Souza's dirty tricks. The man is unscrupulous and capable of anything. But I'm prepared to take that risk. Be careful, Maria."

"Yes, madam."

Bernardina fetched a pistol, loaded it and put it into a leather bag and handed it to Maria.

"You might need this," she said.

"God forbid!"

"Our men are dead, imprisoned, or in hiding, and we must take their places. Let's show that all the Ravascos are courageous. Even the women."

Gregório was back in the Rua Debaixo, but there were no festivities, no negro women dancing. Still feeling the effects of the wine, he waited for Maria.

It was a quiet, chilly night. The stench of dead whale filled the air. Gregório could see the outline of a woman approaching. It was Maria. He was almost trembling as he watched her draw near. He went to her. He looked at her face and remembered Padre Vieira's words: "One love is paid by another, one love suppressed by another. There was never an ailing heart without some weakening of judgment."

"Sir, I've come on behalf of my mistress who is in great distress. Dom Bernardo once told us that we could trust you. We need your help and hope Dom Bernardo was right. As you know, the Ravascos are in trouble, and unless I can speak to Dom Gonçalo, it is likely to get worse. I've searched for him without success. They assured me at the College that he's no longer hiding there. Can you tell me where to find him?"

Gregório stared at her in silence.

"Well?" she asked.

"I don't know where the boy is hiding."

"I beseech you, sir."

"I honestly don't know."

"I implore you."

"I've already told you, I don't know where Gonçalo is hiding, but even if I did, I wouldn't betray him. I know why you want to speak to him. Before coming here I received a visit from . . . a friend, who told me about Dona Bernardina's meeting with Braço de Prata. They want Gonçalo to surrender in exchange for the Secretary."

"It's not that simple," said Maria.

"I'd do anything for you. Anything except betray a friend. Friendship is more sacred than love."

"I doubt if you know what love means." She clasped her hand over her mouth.

"What are you trying to tell me? What do you know of my feelings? Let me tell you: *My soul is restless, my heart aflame. I roam the streets, shivering, but not from cold. I scarcely sleep. For the wings of desire are swifter than those of time. When your message reached me, the clouds and stars stood still, clocks remained silent, hours seemed eternal.*"

"What are you saying, sir? I'm a married woman and I love my husband. No heart can embrace two loves."

"*I hope to persuade you, and I will, that my love is stronger than your desire to escape,*" he said.

"Sir, I've come here to talk about the Ravascos."

"I feared as much. Especially since you women are allowing yourselves to be duped by Braço de Prata. He'll never release Bernardo Ravasco. He'll end up by throwing both father and son into prison, for that's his intention. Unless he murders Gonçalo first. Dom Bernardo will be freed from prison, but by other means. We are fighting reckless men, Dona Maria Berco, we are living in a society plagued by ignorance and corruption where no one is respected. Here dog scratches cat, not because the dog has more courage, but simply because dogs always run to each other's assistance. Dom Gonçalo is in safe hiding. That's what his father wants and we'll obey his wishes."

"Tell me where I can find him, sir. His family can decide what should be done."

"His family? What family? Dona Bernardina? These feminine intuitions are fevers that pass like malaria," said Gregório.

"Please!"

"Very well. Your pleading has touched my heart. I promise to speak to Gonçalo and to try and persuade him to talk to his sister. But I must warn you, it won't be easy to convince him. Not because he does not love his father, but because he has got common sense."

The two-storey house was dark when Maria returned. As usual she went to the kitchen and began preparing something to eat. For weeks now there had been no shortage of anything in the house. She took a purse of coins from her belt and counted them. There were not many left. How was she to raise the money to redeem the ring? A lady's companion earned a meagre monthly wage and she spent most of it on food. Even if she were to take up an evening job sewing it would take at least a year to earn that amount of money. Why hadn't she thought of this before?

Maria tiptoed upstairs with a lighted candle. She pushed open the door of João Berco's room. He had fallen asleep in his arm-chair. The female slave stretched out at his feet opened her eyes. Maria signalled her to go back to sleep. She went to her room.

"Ah, the things that happen to me," she sighed. "I'm so foolish." She recalled her meeting with Gregório. He loved her. How she longed to see him again. She put on her long nightdress, lay down and prayed to God that the night would pass quickly.

The next morning, Gregório departed for Recôncavo. The scorching sun beat down on him and sweat trickled down his forehead, his hair, his neck. He passed through a region of steep slopes covered with sand and rocks.

Gonçalo Ravasco was not hard to find.

"Some hiding place," said Gregório. "Anyone could track you down here. And I know you walk the streets of Bahia at night as if you'd nothing to fear."

"To hell with the lot of them," said Gonçalo. "At this hour Braço de Prata must be preparing for bed."

"Don't you think they'll come after you? Donato Serotino told me to warn you that Teles has all the names."

"Yours too, I imagine."

"They ransacked my room, destroyed my books. They have told the Archbishop outrageous lies in a plot against me. The swine have set everyone against me. Hypocrites, meddlers, chatterboxes, sly politicians, fawning good-for-nothings, they all seek me out to be amused by my satires. These fools think I'm a jackass. In Portugal I was a man of discretion, wisdom and judgment. A better poet than most, and as scholarly as the next man. Once I arrived in Bahia I became a heretic, an idiot, a poor Christian, and an even worse clergyman."

"Stop moaning, poet, we all have troubles. What's the latest news?"

"The judge in charge of the case is none other than Palma himself, De Souza's right-hand man. Together with Gois, he has accused Padre Vieira of the Captain-General's murder."

"Another innocent victim. Is my uncle going to pay for all of us?"

"That would be no bad thing," said Gregório. "He's a priest. He has immunity, he enjoys the friendship of kings. Besides, he's the real target."

"It wouldn't be just. I'd rather die. Padre Vieira is too good a man for this world. He's a philosopher, a saint. That is why he's become so anxious and embittered."

"And why should God protect philosophers and saints from suffering? They're only human. Don't they need their morning shit like the rest of us? Shitting and suffering were created for poets and saints. The rest of mankind is unworthy of such relief. I sleep with a woman who likes watching me piss. I piss on her and she pisses on me. Nobody gets out of shitting and pissing. Not even God. And He shits right on top of our heads. *Blessed be The Lord's prick as He pisses all over me.*" The poet appeared to be enjoying himself. "Did you know Jesus was a sodomite?"

"What I don't understand is why the Holy Inquisition hasn't already burned you at the stake. That's the greatest miracle of all."

"God's on my side. We have friendly little chats together and he knows I'm no hypocrite."

"You're more fortunate than me, poet," Gonçalo said, "for I can no longer believe in His existence."

"Such blasphemy, such blasphemy!" shrieked Gregório, cross-ing himself. "But what really brought me here was a message from Padre Vieira warning you to be on your guard. Braço de Prata is spreading the rumour that he'll release Dom Bernardo in exchange for news of your whereabouts."

"And what do you think? Should I give myself up?"

"Under no circumstances!" said Gregório. "I received a visit from your sister's companion. The poor girl is longing for a night of passion. Dona Bernardina fell right into that villain's snare. They'd be wise to stay out of this affair. The Captain-General wants to get rid of you. But he'll gain nothing by killing Bernardo Ravasco."

"I'm not so sure, poet. You know what conditions are like in prison. My father's an old man and he won't last much longer."

"He'll survive."

"Women are ingenuous and far too sentimental. Braço de Prata is a swine."

"What shall I tell them?"

"Say you couldn't find me."

"Maria Berco is spirited and obstinate. She'll insist. But I wouldn't mind seeing her again. I know what I want from her. Besides, no virtuous woman walks the streets in this country. Women who value their reputation have enough sense to stay indoors."

Maria awoke to loud knocking. Unafraid, she ran downstairs. The slave had already opened the door and was talking to men in brown uniforms. Maria paused.

João Berco appeared, leaning on his walking-stick.

"Who's there?" he asked, in a gruff voice, groping his way forward.

"We have a warrant for the arrest of Dona Maria Berco," said one of the soldiers.

Maria remained frozen at the foot of the stairs.

"There must be some mistake," said the blind man. "Get out of here!"

"There's been no mistake," the soldier replied and stepped

inside, brushing the slave aside. He came to a halt before the pale young woman near the stairs.

"Is it you?"

"Is it me?" echoed Maria in a whisper.

"Go! Leave here at once!" bellowed João Berco.

Maria stared, wide-eyed and confused. What should she do?

"I'm not leaving here without the girl," the soldier said.

"My pistol," shouted João Berco. "Somebody get my pistol! I'll despatch this fool to hell."

Maria went to her husband. "I knew this would happen, João. I knew it."

"What have you done, you shameless bitch? What have you been up to?"

"I intended to tell you everything."

The soldiers grabbed her by the arm.

"At least allow me to put on some clothes," Maria asked.

The soldiers let go of her and she went upstairs. Once dressed, she was led away through the buzzing crowd of busybodies who had gathered outside.

"Good riddance, slut!" yelled João Berco, brandishing his stick.

# V

IEIRA SET OUT FOR Matoim accompanied by José
Soares. They skirted the river until they reached a small
village. They followed a narrow path through the woods
and stopped at an abandoned sugar-mill. Hidden among the trees
and almost in ruins, the mill was situated on the river bank and
supported by enormous brick pillars. The tiled roof was set on
wooden beams with wall-plates and joists. Adjacent to it were
two tall, spacious buildings, one which had housed the plantation
owner and his family, the other the furnace.

The Jesuits came to a great iron door at the far end of the storage
shed. Padre Soares knocked. They could see a shadow behind a
tiny aperture. Seconds later, a voice came from within.

"What do you want?"

Vieira gave his name.

The two priests waited for a long time, while scraggy oxen
grazed nearby. There were shafts, pipes and wheels scattered
throughout the undergrowth; ox-goads, metal rings and axle-pins
were lying on the ground.

The Jesuits could hear heavy footsteps and clanking swords
from behind the door. They eyed each other anxiously and as the
door opened, José Soares drew back. Five armed men appeared.

Antonio Vieira held out a letter which the oldest of the men
took and read. The letter passed from hand to hand and was read
carefully. The visitors were allowed to enter.

The men escorted the priests through a yard into a large room
which contained a burning lamp and a long table with a basin.
High-backed chairs stood in a row beneath a canopy with column
supports. Light filtered between the broken roof-tiles.

They went into another room which had a wooden ceiling. It

was darker than the previous one and smelled musty. There was an enormous table surrounded by sturdy chairs. Amidst shadows Vieira could discern the Rabbi at the other end of the room. He was wearing a white tunic. His bald head was oval-shaped, the bridge of his nose marked with two creases from the tiny spectacles held in the hand he rested on a book. The Rabbi bade the priests to be seated.

"Welcome," he said, in a hoarse but friendly voice as he put on his spectacles, enlarging his dark eyes and causing the wrinkled pouches beneath them to bulge more. He removed the yarmulke from his head, scratched his pointed ears, settled in his chair at the head of the table and stared at Vieira.

"Samuel da Fonseca?" asked Vieira.

"Yes, Padre, that's me. So, you're the famous Jesuit whom I've heard so much about from my dear friend Bernardo Ravasco, your brother. Despite the great difference between our faiths, you have shown none of the repressive instincts or greed of many of your people. The Jewish community owes you a debt of gratitude. I dare say you don't remember me but we met some years ago in Rouen, when you travelled there to meet Portuguese Jews fleeing the Inquisition. You were staying in the house of the poet Antonio Anrique Gomes, the protégé of Cardinal Richelieu. It must be twenty years ago, in 1664, when I, too, was passing through. In those days I lived with an uncle in Amsterdam."

"Yes, I vaguely remember. For I'm now so old that to talk of twenty years ago is like referring to last night."

"In Amsterdam," continued the Rabbi, "I had the pleasure of hearing the sermon by the famous Manasseh Ben Israel which you yourself heard out of friendship. When he was told of your presence in the congregation, Manasseh wanted to make a good impression and tried to justify his preference for the Old Testament. I was told later that you were waiting for Hakham Manasseh as he left and that you both launched into a lengthy discussion which unfortunately I missed. Two incomparable theologians, two highly respected scholars. Both of you persuasive orators, both of you fond of reasoned argument, both well versed in Holy Scripture, but after debating for hours on end, you both went your separate ways without successfully convincing the other."

"Yes, I remember. That was a difficult period in my life," reflected Vieira. "I was sorry to have missed the opportunity of meeting your uncle Isaac Aboab da Fonseca in Amsterdam. What a distinguished grammarian and poet he was! As you know, he was Brazil's first Rabbi, and he founded the first synagogue in Recife. But the intolerance in Brazil made his life impossible. Hundreds of Jews accompanied him into exile in Amsterdam. Many others headed for New Amsterdam in Guyana. A great loss . . . a shameful loss . . ."

"No matter," said Samuel da Fonseca. "The Phoenix is consumed by fire and is reborn from its own ashes. The Phoenix is also the emblem of the Neweh Shalom. The Inquisition may burn us at the stake but it cannot destroy us. Love is as powerful as death."

"Is your uncle alive?"

"I don't know. When I last received news about a year ago, he was still alive. He was teaching in the rabbinical academies of Torah Or and Yeshiva de los Pintos. He might still be there. His first wife died and he married again."

"I've happy memories of Holland," said Vieira.

"You were a different person then."

"Yes," agreed Vieira, holding his hand to his mouth as he smiled. Now that he no longer had teeth, he smiled with his mouth shut or covered it with one hand. Most of the time he tried to avoid smiling. "I was different I must admit. Such are the sacrifices a soldier must make. Calvinist intolerance didn't permit me to be seen in my Jesuit habit. I was obliged to wear a bright red woollen tunic and to carry a sword, to keep my hair long without a tonsure and grow a horrid moustache. I can now say honestly, and from having experienced it, that the life of a layman is not for me. I feel much better in this old cassock. It protects me from the company of men and women, from frivolous social gatherings, from idle gossip after dinner, from trifling pleasantries and witty repartee. But then, a layman's life was hard in Holland, however lucrative. After spending time there, I was able to write passionate satirical verses about human vices and wanton pleasures."

José Soares, who had kept to the background, was eyeing the

Jew warily. He had never seen a Rabbi before and this holy man did not look in the least like someone who would crucify children and drink their blood or take a whip to crucifixes and desecrate sacred hosts; he didn't have Satan's hooves or wear horns, nor did he look like a heathen or heretic. He had the face of a wise and learned man and his expression betrayed suffering and sadness. Despite all the persecutions, these Jews had preserved their individuality as a people and kept their faith.

"It's clear from your letter," said the Rabbi, "that we have some important matters to discuss."

"Yes," answered Vieira. He told the old man about the conflict between his friends and the Governor, about the ambushes, the spectacular sword-fights between the two factions in the streets of Bahia, about the persecutions, murders and arrests, about the torture suffered by Bernardo Ravasco in prison, about the death threat hanging over those men who had been accused of assassinating the Captain-General. And finally about the legal proceedings pending in the Tribunal which incriminated the Ravascos. Palma, the judge in charge of the case, had ordered detentions and postponed court hearings; the new Captain-General was tracking down suspects and promising to make an example of the culprits with harsh sentences.

"This is truly lamentable, Padre Vieira. One would never have imagined that a man chosen by the Prince for this enviable appointment could stoop to such conduct. I believe you should use your influence with His Royal Highness to have the tyrant removed from office."

"No, dear friend," replied Vieira, shaking his head, "there's no more to be done. I no longer enjoy the favours once shown me by ministers and men of influence, such as the Marquês de Gouveia. In Portugal, everybody knows I believed King Dom Afonso to be more popular than his brother, and rightly so. And for this reason I was persecuted and humiliated because I am no longer powerful. I cannot think I've deserved the Prince's disapproval, remembering the happy relationship I enjoyed with his late father, whom I served for so many years despite all the trials and dangers. You can well imagine my sadness and surprise now that everything has changed. I feel as if my hands and feet are in chains."

"In Portugal your achievements have not been forgotten. The Duke of Cadaval is still willing to offer you protection in the Royal Judiciary and you will find the same old friends in the house of Dom Teodósio. You will be shown the respect you deserve."

"I'm not so sure."

"Perhaps I can help. After all, I'm impartial and, like you, I have friends in the government, despite being a Jew under threat of persecution, or perhaps for this very reason. I shall never forget how indebted we are to you. Thanks to your efforts and skilful negotiations, the General Trading Company of Brazil was established. This was a great benefit to the Jewish community and, more important still, it dealt a severe blow to the Inquisition, our old enemy. They could no longer confiscate our possessions in order to burn us at the stake with spectacular *autos-da-fé* paid for with our own money. Indeed, the entire Jewish community is grateful to you."

"No," said Vieira, "you owe me nothing, but if you're offering to help me I shall humbly accept. The death sentences passed by the Captain-General are simply an excuse to eliminate those who oppose the present government. And Palma, in connivance with Braço de Prata, has been the principal agent of these abuses. I have no objections to a criminal inquiry so long as it is executed with justice. An impartial judge would be more acceptable."

"Yes, I agree. But who?"

"The only man to be trusted in the Court of Appeals is João da Rocha Pita. He'll tell the truth, no matter whom it may offend."

"Perhaps I can find a way to ensure that Rocha Pita is appointed presiding judge and put in charge of any inquiry. Your attorneys must swear on oath that Palma is suspect, and then leave it to me to persuade the Chancellor to heed your complaint."

The Rabbi opened the great tome, the Torah or Book of Holy Law, brought from Portugal by Heitor Antunes in 1557. He leafed through its pages and removed a handwritten note.

"Here are some lines my uncle wrote, perhaps the first poem ever to be written in the colony: *"My Lord God,"* translated the Rabbi, *"Rejoicing, I shall sing Thy name in the assembly. My sins led to my exile in a distant land. I fell from heaven into an abyss, my head sank beneath the waves. In the year 5405, the King of Portugal decided*

*to destroy what remained of Israel. He hired a wicked man, mothered by*
*a black slave and ignorant of his father's name. This fellow amassed much*
*gold and silver and headed the revolt. He cunningly plotted to overthrow*
*the Dutch government, but his plans were discovered. He lost no time in*
*persecuting the Jews. The revolt led to the besieging of cities by land and*
*sea. I begged the people to fast for the redemption of their sins. The sword*
*wrought havoc without and fear within. There was no bread. Beleaguered*
*Recife suffered famine. People ate fish instead of bread. On the ninth day*
*of Tammuz, two ships arrived bringing aid to my people. 'Who among*
*the gods can equal you, oh Lord?' Those ships were the Valk and the*
*Elizabeth."*

Samuel da Fonseca held out his hand to Vieira and showed him
the gold medallion set in his ring with the inscription *Door de Valk*
*en Elizabeth is het Recief ontzet.*

Vieira ran his fingers over the medallion, looked at it closely
but could not read the couplet.

"Recife was saved by the *Valk* and the *Elizabeth*," said the Rabbi.

"And who will save us now?"

"Padre Vieira, I feel confident that Rocha Pita will succeed in
deposing De Souza."

"I'm not as hopeful. I'd be satisfied if I could prove my innocence. But with De Souza deposed, the people of this city could
breathe more easily."

"But there's something we can do in the meantime. I'd like to
put my plantation at your disposal. The place is remote and protected. I can offer your friends sanctuary."

"Again I'm indebted to you. There aren't many with enough
courage to defy the Governor."

"I hope nothing we may decide here will prove to be a two-
edged sword. Trust me, Padre Vieira."

"I do, Fonseca, I know I can rely on you."


"Why do people call Padre Vieira *the Brazilian Jew*?" asked Anica
de Melo.

"For slaughtering birds and livestock in a certain way,"
Gregório answered. "Testing the blade of a sword with one's
thumbnail, abstaining from game, pork, conger eel, ray; the
height of one's dining table, washing the dead, cleaning oil-lamps,

changing one's undergarments and eating plaited loaves on Saturdays are considered crimes worthy of excommunication and death. They are the unmistakable signs of Judaism."

Anica made the sign of the cross and kissed the scapular pinned to her bosom. She was God-fearing and believed in sin with all her heart. She believed herself to be plagued by demons which she must somehow exorcize, though she had grown used to them. Notwithstanding her success, the fact that she ran a brothel often left Anica downhearted and she prayed that God would give her the strength to get out. Sometimes, while the other whores were entertaining their clients, she would lock herself away in her room and weep. But most days she was happy and tranquil.

"The persecutions dating from the reign of Dom João III, who was noted for his stupidity, fanaticism and ineptitude," Gregório continued, "drove the Jews from Portugal to trading centres such as Flanders, Leghorn, Bordeaux, Antwerp and Amsterdam, where they found sanctuary and even protection. Once Dom João IV came to power, Antonio Vieira suggested to the monarch that he should create two trading companies, one for the East, the other for the West, so that without draining the resources of the Royal Treasury, Portugal's trade with the Indies and Brazil could be protected."

"Like the Dutch trading companies?"

"Yes, something very similar. Any money invested in these trading companies would be exempt from levies in order to attract both Jewish and Christian merchants from abroad, as well as merchants of the realm."

In the proposal put forward by Vieira, the Jews would no longer have their property confiscated by the Holy Inquisition. But, Gregório went on to explain, the Inquisition refused to accept this proposal. Nevertheless, the need for trading companies had become urgent and a company for the West was established. Soon the Company's business far exceeded its own commercial obligations, and helped to finance the war against Castile, to preserve the realm, and even to restore Pernambuco. Antonio Vieira became an influential aide and trusted adviser to the King. He was sent on delicate diplomatic missions, often in secret. Some years later, Vieira suggested to the King that one way of dealing with Portugal's poverty would be to offer certain guarantees to the Jews if they were to return from Europe where they had sought refuge, taking their trading skills and considerable wealth and possessions with them. This would require amending the statutes of the Inquisition and Treasury regulations. Vieira's idea was that "not only would merchants who are at present settled in Holland and Castile come to this realm, but also merchants from France, Italy, Germany, Venice, the West Indies and many other regions, whereby the Portuguese empire would become all-powerful and the levies charged by the customs-houses would bring in enough revenue to sustain Portugal's wars, without any further need to tax or oppress her people. Public demands and protests would be silenced. The levies would also pay the interest rates, pensions and salaries which the royal revenues could no longer meet, thus ensuring loyal service from her subjects. The population would increase, creating greater strength, and the realm would become resourceful and prosperous. The King would have a vast number of powerful ships owned by his subjects, without having to buy or hire them from foreigners or to equip them whenever he needed a fleet or reinforcements for some new expedition. His Majesty would also be able to exploit the intelligence and expertise of the Jews, for not only could they buy the necessary arms for any wars from foreign nations at a favourable price but, through their secret intelligence, Portugal would be able to learn of their plans and gather news from foreign kingdoms, without which no monarch can hope to rule his own kingdom efficiently."

The Jews were not strangers. The apostles had been Jews, Mary had been a Jew, even Jesus, as Vieira had reminded his critics. In Rome there were public synagogues where they professed the law of Moses. And why should heretics from Holland, France and England be allowed into Portugal when Portuguese merchants were being expelled simply because they were Jewish? The Jews were leaving while Lutherans and Calvinists from foreign countries were allowed to stay. Vieira had suggested that there were lessons to be learned from the Jews who had conquered the Promised Land taking the Egyptian treasures with them. The ideas Vieira preached disturbed complacent minds. Religious fanaticism and bigotry had destroyed philosophers such as Giordano Bruno, archbishops like Spalatro, scientists like Marco Antonio de Dominis, even kings such as Charles I of England. But Antonio Vieira was not intimidated by tyranny and confronted the Inquisition, causing a fellow Jesuit, Padre Cristóvão Soares, to comment that he might not be allowed to die in the Company of Jesus. It was more likely that he would end up at the mercy of the Holy Inquisition. And so Vieira became the most hated man in Portugal. And the more he was hated by the Inquisition, the more he condemned its conduct. He accused its officers of cloistering themselves in the Rocio where their treachery could not be seen; of presuming to assist God in ruling the universe; of professing religion while exploiting it for other ends.

"But where did you get to know each other?" asked Anica.

"The first time we met was in Lisbon, during my vacation as a student at Coimbra. I was eighteen years old and Vieira had just arrived from the Jesuit missions in Maranhão. He was attending Court and the Judiciary in order to secure laws guaranteeing freedom for the Indians. I had already seen him once or twice in the Judiciary, but I had never dared to approach him. One afternoon he sat down beside me, took my hand and said something I shall never forget: 'You're staring at me like one of Athanasius Kircher's chickens.'"

Anica smiled.

Gregório later discovered that Kircher was a Jesuit priest, an expert in the occult and physical sciences, a native of Geisa near Fulda in Germany but now living in Rome, and that he had invented, among other unusual contraptions, a magic lantern and a machine for writing. He carried out interesting experiments with chickens, sending them to sleep by swinging a pendulum before their eyes and then awakening them with a gentle slap on the neck. Gregório became tongue-tied in the presence of Vieira. He had discovered that Vieira spoke like a prophet. Not that he could divine the future or guess what others were thinking, but the priest had a gift for attracting people and taking them into his confidence, and he could assemble the pawns in any game with remarkable judgment.

"There was another important facet to the old Jesuit's character," observed the poet. "His foul temper."

"Ah, old men are always bad-tempered. They know too much about the world and its ways to maintain their patience."

"True, but when Padre Vieira lost his temper he went into a complete frenzy."

In 1661, the Jesuit and the poet met again, in Lisbon. Gregório had just graduated in Canon Law and had married Dona Michaela de Andrade. Vieira had been expelled along with other Jesuits from Maranhão and was bitter. The poet had offered to stay and be his assistant but Vieira did not need anyone. Padre José Soares had attended to all his needs for years with a devotion bordering on idolatry. They had worked together in the missions at Maranhão. Padre Soares removed the old Jesuit's boots, took dictation, made copies of his letters and never sat in his presence, an act of reverence which Antonio Vieira described as heretical. Nevertheless, Gregório remained at Vieira's side for some time and when the old priest was not denouncing the abuses of those in government or the vices of the inhabitants of Lisbon, he would turn his wrath on Gregório, and often gave vent to his temper by upbraiding him. He accused him of conniving with those guilty of corruption, of having married out of self-interest, of not having done enough to oppose the enslavement of the Indians and defend Christian converts against the Inquisition; he called Gregório a Brazilian 'Kaffir from Europe' and unleashed even more bitter and unjust criticisms, insisting that the poet would gladly have him burned at the stake as a heretic, a witch-doctor or Jew. Gregório listened patiently to it all.

But apart from these sudden tirades, Antonio Vieira was a tranquil and agreeable person. He would often recall happy times at the French Court, canoe trips up the Amazon, the missions in Maranhão, his friendships with royalty, meetings in Amsterdam. Gregório tried to arrest these moments when Vieira revealed his inner self, confided his dreams and memories. The poet tried to penetrate his soul and to absorb – even capture – some of his knowledge and wisdom. On one occasion, the old priest even suggested that the poet had achieved more with his satires than he had with his missions. But when Gregório tried to press further, the Jesuit denied that he had said any such thing, that the poet would do well to hold his tongue rather than talk about things he did not understand and which he would later regret.

Gregório de Matos had graduated in Coimbra, receiving the

biretta and being sworn in before the open book. He was intelligent and eloquent in debate, but had little experience of life. He could think of nothing but valour and passion.

After the palace revolution of 1662, Antonio was exiled to Oporto and shortly afterwards Gregório was appointed magistrate and procurator, representing Bahia at Court. João IV had protected Vieira from the Inquisition. But when the King died, Queen Luiza de Gusmão revoked the measures adopted in favour of the Jews and suppressed the Trading Company. The Inquisition excommunicated the King posthumously and began investigating Antonio Vieira's orthodoxy. They suspected he was of Jewish descent but a meticulous examination of his ancestry revealed that his paternal grandmother was a mulatto woman in the service of the Count of Unhão. She had come from Africa and was probably Arab. What Vieira did for the Jews was not a question of blood but of conviction. Abandoned by those in power, the Jesuit began to suffer every manner of persecution. The accusations against him were endless. Chaplains, judges, Dominicans, priests of other Orders, even Jesuits and several Jews, went before the Holy Inquisition to give evidence against Antonio Vieira; they accused him of preaching heresy, swore he believed in the supernatural; that he had criticized the Pope for canonizing certain saints, smuggled forbidden books into Portugal, married a wealthy Jewess in Amsterdam, and treated God as if He were an ordinary mortal given to jealousy, envy and wrath. None of these accusations could be proved, but Vieira was thrown into prison on the pretext that he had uttered prophecies.

"I tried to speak to lawyers and judges about Vieira," continued Gregório, "but no one was prepared to talk about him. They were frightened. There were spies everywhere. I was fond of Antonio Vieira but could do nothing to help him. Not even mention his name. I had terrible nightmares, I felt so helpless and disloyal. In truth, *I* feared the Holy Inquisition."

"What sort of nightmares?" asked Anica.

"I remember one of them clearly. Vieira was kneeling before the Inquisitors. The Grand Inquisitor looked like the devil with claws, tail, horns, blazing eyes, the ears of a monkey. He was holding a whip and lashing Vieira as he demanded the names of

his accusers. Vieira replied that Portugal accused him: the Dominicans, the King's minions, the Prince and the Queen; those who
felt they had been stripped of their privileges because of him; those
who had asked for favours he could not grant. All the ambassadors
and ministers whose expenditure he controlled; all the enemies of
his relatives; all the opponents of the Jesuit Order; the governors
and ministers of Maranhão; those who had enslaved the native
population and were in favour of keeping them as serfs; those
who were unable or unwilling to make impartial judgments. The
mediocre preachers and the illiterates who thought themselves
educated. The cowardly, the ignorant and the envious. All those
canonists who refused to acknowledge his existence. Then,
pointing at me he shouted: 'All you craven youths who love and
respect me yet do nothing to defend me. A villain who robbed
me. A thief! He stole my sermons! He copied my style of writing.
Gregório de Matos e Guerra!' I looked at the Grand Inquisitor and
could not believe my eyes: it was me! I would awaken from these
nightmares bathed in perspiration. My drawers bloodstained.
Fleas had bitten me all over."

"But how dare they throw a saint into prison?"

"Many saints have been thrown into prison. And Antonio
Vieira was demoralized. Not only on account of the King's death
but also because his prophecy that Dom João IV would come back
to life and create the Fifth Empire in 1655 had not been fulfilled."

"Ah, just like the followers of the Sebastian Movement."

The year had passed uneventfully except for the publication of
La Rochefoucauld's *Reflexions ou sentences et maximes morales*, the
appointment of Juan Cabanilles as organist in the Cathdral of
Valencia, the death of the Flemish painter Pieter Jansz Saenredam,
the great plague in London and the sighting of several comets in
the sky.

"Suffering in silence in a cell no bigger than fifteen spans, lit
during the day by a chink of light coming through the door, and
at night by a tiny earthenware oil-lamp; surrounded by rats
and vermin, with nothing but common criminals for company
and unable to write or converse, Antonio Vieira tormented my
soul like a demon."

# VI

AT SUNRISE LUIZ BONICHO was already awake. "Pernambuco? Rio de Janeiro? Lisbon? Paris? Ah, dear old Paris. A false name and a good disguise will solve all our problems, at least for now. Then we can return."

Bonicho was alone and talking to himself in front of the mirror.

"Where shall we go, sir?" Bonicho asked his reflection.

Fearing the Governor's reprisals, he had sold all of his possessions except the jewels and money. These would be enough to live on for the next few years, in either Portugal or Paris.

"Ah, Paris! A city of crystal palaces and polluted streets."

Bonicho had taken refuge in a squalid wreck of a house in the lower part of the city. Through the window he could see ships being loaded and unloaded.

"Dried olives, Cordovan leather. There I go, escaping once more, like a bit of old cod in the hold, fit only for bait to lure sharks and pirates."

Armed men guarded the entrance to his hiding-place. Donato Serotino, foolish and irresponsible and oblivious to the world around him, was probably roaming the streets as if nothing was wrong. Why couldn't he stay indoors? He might easily arouse the suspicions of the Captain-General and the Bull, and lead them back to this miserable slum.

The door opened. A stocky man entered, wearing a hat pulled down over his head, a long coat and dark boots.

"What kept you? It's already night. Do you honestly think that no one will recognize you in that disguise?" said Bonicho.

Donato Serotino, the fencing master, removed his big hat and smiled. Such teeth! thought Bonicho. They gleamed even by

candle-light, white, even teeth, enhancing a face as perfectly pro-
portioned as a Greek statue. His physique, too, was impressive;
his movements harmonious. Indeed Serotino was the very image
of perfection, more handsome than any effigy of a Roman athlete,
or male nude painted on a church fresco.

"My disguise is a great success. I've walked the streets without
attracting any attention," said Serotino. "I've been through side-
streets and alleyways, amused myself chatting to acquaintances
who mistook me for a rich Venetian merchant and greeted me
most respectfully. The city is calm. There are more soldiers than
usual in the streets, probably about fifty. They're on the alert
but didn't suspect me. They seemed to be more concerned about
arresting a group of students who had the nerve to appear on the
streets wearing hoods in defiance of Braço de Prata's prohibition.
Gonçalo was with me."

"That Gonçalo is a great arse-hole," scowled Bonicho. "If he
hadn't been such a coward he could easily have killed Braço de
Prata."

"He must have had good reason."

"There's no reason on earth why anyone should hesitate to
finish off that swine. But why bother discussing it, since neither
we nor Gonçalo managed to kill him. While we're waiting for his
rule to end, we can enjoy ourselves in fair Europe. Once removed
from office, he'll be nothing but a miserable cripple. The Prince
will have paid his debt and Braco de Prata will be dispatched to
some miserable hole in Africa, even worse than this *culis mundi*
we've got here. I don't really care whether I'm in Brazil or Portugal. France, though, is different. Life is good there. You must be
wondering what I've been doing here all these years. It's simple,
here I've been able to enjoy power and fame. Among the three
thousand rich men in Bahia, I'm probably the only hunchback. In
Paris there are more than a hundred of them. You need only count
the hunchbacks in the *Comédie Française*. There you have to fight
to get attention and there's always someone trying to steal it away
from you. Here I can live with greater freedom and I feel more at
ease, because every inhabitant of this damn colony has some
greater deformity than mine. But never mind, we'll spend a few
years in Lisbon and Paris and then we'll come back, having buried

all our woes. Who knows, I might even come back as Governor. Have you brought me any news?"

"Well . . . I . . ."

"You roam the city and discover nothing. While I sit, trapped in this stinking den. But in fact I've some news for you."

"What?" asked Serotino, sitting down beside Bonicho.

"They've found a rotting corpse, floating like a drowned cat in the Rio Vermelho."

Serotino turned pale.

"It was the Blasphemer," said the councillor. "They killed him when they discovered he wasn't actually mad and was working for me. Those bastards are not playing games. They're deadly serious. Who could trust that pompous madman Braço de Prata? He's got a fistful of stones. He was on target with the first one, and he'll be on target with the rest. He must not find us."

A light drizzle fell over the Tanque countryside. The house with its clay tiles and the trees on the hillside were cast in a dark hue. Water overflowed from the stone tanks. Antonio Vieira watched the water trickling down the window-panes.

Years ago, a solemn Te Deum was sung in the royal chapel at the Ribeira Palace in Lisbon. Antonio Vieira arrived after the ceremony, while presidents and ministers were kissing the King's hand as they filed out of the gallery. He remarked:

"I understand, Your Majesty, that they're all kissing your hand to mark the capture of Dunkirk. For my part, I offer you my condolences."

The King asked him to explain, whereupon Vieira told him that the Dutch were maintaining a fleet facing Dunkirk to ensure their ships safe passage through the channel; now that they were allied with France, this threat no longer existed. Now they could remove the warships from there and send them to Brazil, which, as Padre Vieira had learned in Amsterdam, was what the Dutch were hoping for. Sigismund, who was governing Pernambuco for a second term, would now do as he had promised in the time of Diogo Luiz de Oliveira: take possession of Bahia without any bloodshed, by using his fleet to block the entry of the Portuguese supply ships.

"So what do you think we should do?" the King asked.

In Amsterdam a wealthy Dutchman had offered to sell Portugal fifteen thirty-gun frigates with all the necessary equipment, and these would be delivered at Lisbon for three hundred thousand cruzados. The money could easily be raised by levying a tax on the rich fleet which had just arrived with more than forty thousand crates of sugar bought for a pittance in Brazil in order to be sold at the highest price in Lisbon. By charging one *tostão* or six *vinténs* for every *arroba*, they would soon raise the three hundred thousand cruzados. Once the frigates arrived from Holland, Portugal would have two fleets: one in Lisbon and the other assisting Bahia.

The King asked Vieira to write his plan "without trying to be clever", and, once furnished with the document, he consulted his ministers.

Initially they deemed Vieira's proposal "somewhat premature".

But six months had not elapsed before he received a summons asking him to appear before the King at Carcavelos early next morning.

"You're a prophet," said the King. For the previous evening a caravel had arrived from Bahia with a Jesuit priest on board, bringing the news that General Schkoppe was garrisoned in Itaparica.

"What do you suggest we do?"

"The solution is obvious, Your Majesty," replied Vieira. "Did your ministers not tell Your Majesty that my proposal was somewhat premature?"

"They did."

"Well, let those who found it so now make it mature."

Yes, there were good reasons why they should resent Antonio Vieira. For in the end, the Jesuit obtained the money to purchase the armada from the Jews.

There was no longer any gratitude or loyalty. After taking so many risks out of allegiance to the Crown, Vieira now found himself banished as if in exile. He was even forbidden to continue peacefully with the writing of his sermons and commentaries on the Holy Scriptures.

As a young man, Antonio Vieira believed in words, especially those spoken in good faith. Yet all the words he had spoken – from pulpits, in lecture halls, at meetings, in catechism classes, in the corridors of power, in the hearing of kings, clerics, inquisitors, dukes, marquises, judges, governors, ministers, presidents, queens, princes, the natives – of all those millions of words spoken after much reflection, few or none had produced any effect. The world carried on as before.

He thought of all the times he had moved his lips, of the thousands of times he had opened and closed his mouth and now all that remained was a terrifying sense of emptiness. And the certainty of not being understood. How could he have been so long-winded? He was reminded of the parable of the barren fig-tree.

His written commentaries on the Holy Scriptures had been interrupted, for Vieira had more pressing matters on his mind. But at least he felt alive, as he found himself treading once more the familiar terrain of politics. Yes, this was his destiny and this was the soul he possessed. The soul of a Jesuit. Were Ignatius of Loyola still alive, he would be congratulating this soldier and offering his support.

Burying her head in her arms, Bernardina Ravasco wept. Gregório tried to console her.

"Poor Maria," sobbed Bernardina. "First my father and now her. I'm so afraid of what might happen."

"You still have your uncle, your brother, your friends, who are all capable of putting a stop to these abuses."

"If Gonçalo hasn't appeared by tomorrow, I shall take measures."

"Why don't you let the men deal with this matter, my lady?" said Gregório.

A lapdog settled on Bernardina's lap. She put it down onto the floor and the dog curled up at her feet.

"I must think of something because the men aren't doing anything. They'll end up letting my father die in prison," she reflected. "Do you believe that Maria actually removed the ring from the Captain-General's finger?"

"The girl is poor, perhaps she needed the money. We mustn't judge her."

"Well, I don't believe it for a moment," said Bernardina. "I don't want to believe it. But how could they have invented such a thing? What can we do for her, Doctor de Matos? As a lawyer, you must know of some solution. Otherwise, they'll almost certainly hang her."

"I've been outlawed by Braço de Prata, otherwise I'd defend the girl myself. Perhaps I can find another lawyer to fight her case."

"Money is no problem. Find a good lawyer to defend her. Her blind husband has no financial resources despite what people say. I will pay for it. After all, none of this would have happened had Maria refused to help my father. Poor Maria! She spent her childhood being ill-treated by her own father, then she was sent to a miserable orphanage, then married off to a bad-tempered old man. She found no happiness in marriage or in life. Such a lovely girl, even dumb animals adored her, licking her feet and rubbing up against her legs. Men followed her everywhere but Maria has remained faithful to her husband. She's the soul of virtue. I don't know how she puts up with the wretch."

No sooner had Gregório departed than someone knocked at the door.

"Who can that be?" Bernardina wondered. "Gonçalo?"

The maid answered the door. A stout fellow stood in the doorway wearing a brown uniform with gilt buttons and a cap. The house was surrounded by the Governor's soldiers.

Bernardina was arrested and taken to prison. On arrival, she was pushed into a cell where she found the wives and sisters of the De Brito brothers.

# VII

THE WHEELS OF the old carriage wobbled. The horse, accustomed to roaming freely through the grounds of the estate, shook its head impatiently, trying to free itself from its trappings.

As he got into the carriage, Vieira was reminded of an exhausted deer being cornered during a hunt at Sintra. He wondered whether he should follow the advice of his friends and leave Brazil. Perhaps he should have accepted Queen Christina's invitation to go to Sweden and become her confessor. His health was much worse than when the Father General of the Jesuit Order had relieved him of his administrative duties at the Professed House. He was now in his seventies. He had lost the sight in one eye and the other was weakening every day; his memory was no longer reliable; his right leg still suffered from the effects of a previous illness. The climate in Rome was cold and damp, and his present state of health would not enable him to endure another winter in Europe.

Lisbon was out of the question because of the Inquisition. His former enemies still lived there, scheming and spreading gossip. For all its disadvantages, Bahia was the one place where he could write his sermons undisturbed. These anxious times would not last forever.

"What's troubling you, Padre?" asked José Soares.

"Last year there was a street brawl in Coimbra, where a group of students and ruffians staged a mock auto-da-fé and burned my effigy. What more can they do to me? Burn me alive? Honourable funeral rites. Meanwhile, in the University of Mexico tributes have been paid to me in the Faculty of Theology. I pay little heed to the praise of others. Yet I can't help feeling sad that, while they insult me in a university in Portugal, and here in Brazil, a colonial university in Mexico decides to honour my name. I deserve neither abuse nor adulation. But were I Swedish or Spanish, people here wouldn't be treating me so badly."

"Not true," José Soares said. "In this colony they don't even respect God."

"Abducting women! This is what the Governor's hatred and wrath has come to. All those who can should leave this place. The government, or what passes for one, has been entrusted to this tyrant; property, honour, freedom and the lives of so many loyal subjects are under his control. It's only out of respect and obedience to His Majesty, who is so ill-served by this villain, that we tolerate his behaviour. Throwing women into prison indeed!"

After half an hour, their carriage reached the cobbled streets of the city. They travelled along a busy road flanked on either side by tall houses with pointed gables, shuttered windows, doorways bedecked with merchandise. They crossed the square where itinerant clerks drafted petitions in exchange for modest fees. In this bustling market-place, merchants traded sugar and tobacco from Brazil, cinnamon from Ceylon and an infinite variety of other goods. The aroma of spices overcame the stench of the polluted streets.

Evening was drawing in. Vieira saw fishermen selling their catch of lobsters, crayfish and shellfish; Benedictine monks were selling vegetables from the saddle-bags on their donkeys; housewives were selling their needlework, embroidered table-cloths they displayed over railings, small objects made of wood or silver.

There was a procession that day. Some people were wearing their Sunday best, neatly turned out with boots highly polished except for the soles which sank into the mud. The poorest of them walked barefoot, but their hairstyles and clothes, like those of the better off, imitated the French fashions favoured by the aristocracy.

Girls passed lifting their full skirts lest they should trail on the ground; some of the women wore black hoods. Others remained at their windows, displaying their jewels. The poor mingled with the rich, mendicant friars made their rounds among the students; fine gentlemen stumbled over stray dogs.

Vieira passed other carriages clattering loudly through the streets. Palanquins, sulkies and litters transported rich merchants, politicians, Crown officials, elegant courtesans, plantation owners. The wheels ploughed through the mud on the ground, trappings jingled, harnessed horses neighed and stamped their hooves in the quagmire, spraying mud on to the breeches of litter-bearers, coachmen, ostlers, slaves, urchins, bystanders, tramps and other onlookers.

The sea turned red in the sunlight, the shadows of houses extended over the assembled crowd. When Vieira alighted at the College gates, a voice called out:

"Death to that Jew, Vieira!"

Escorted by his personal guard, the Rabbi Samuel da Fonseca looked nervously at the mob from his carriage. As they approached the square, he could hear a tirade of insults, threats and obscenities. He pursed his lips, closed his eyes, and took a deep breath. When would it all end?

They stopped in front of the prison. Remaining inside the carriage, he exchanged a few brief words with the guard at the gates, handed him something, and departed.

An assembly of judges, flanked by military escort, entered the gates of the Governor's palace. The carriages bearing Palma and Gois headed the procession. The horses neighed, straining at their bridles; their harnesses jingled. Immediately behind came the palanquin bearing the Captain-General. He looked pale.

They gathered in the Governor's audience chamber.

"Bad news," said Palma.

"Palma's findings were accepted by the Court," added Gois.

De Souza paused.

"We must do something," Teles insisted.

"Vieira must be rejoicing," said Palma.

"He is somewhat premature," said the Governor.

"He's here in the city," continued Palma. "Parading the streets like a mighty emperor."

"This is the man who claims to live in seclusion," said the Governor. "Yet he's forever making public appearances. Could he have come to celebrate the feast? His next celebration will be a visit to the Holy Ghost, by order of His Royal Highness the

Prince. That's one feast he won't be in a hurry to attend. I've shown him leniency by asking His Majesty to deliver him to the Holy Ghost rather than back to Portugal where the Inquisition is awaiting him."

"I'd be delighted to see him burn at the stake," said the Captain-General.

"Our preacher isn't as moribund as you suggest," retorted De Souza. "You don't need a pulpit to spread propaganda. We've got to shut him up, to silence him once and for all." He turned to the Captain-General. "No letters written by Vieira are to be dispatched with the fleet. Tell the head courier I want to see him."

The Captain-General eyed De Souza. He was not satisifed with the Governor's ruse to deceive his enemy. De Souza seemed aloof and indifferent, concerned only about Padre Vieira. Because of the Governor's perversity they were losing the war, not like the Dutch who had withdrawn to Bahia leaving bloodshed behind them, but dishonourably in a slow and prolonged defeat. Stubborn as a mule, De Souza protested his political integrity. But they would all pay the price if things turned out badly.

"The accused are always condemned unless they speak up," said Palma. "Padre Vieira was getting quieter with old age, but now he's started speaking again to ease his conscience."

"His conscience must be more than tolerant not to cause him any remorse," said De Souza. "He knows full well that his nephew killed the Governor-General, yet he's prepared to do everything in his power to secure Gonçalo Ravasco's freedom. He fears neither hell nor God's punishment."

"And now that he's scored his first victory, no doubt he'll spread the word as if he were preaching the parable about the oil-lamps," answered Palma. "Do men light a candle and put it under a bushel?"

"He'd do better to read a parable about the wickedness of murdering honourable men," snarled De Souza. "Now Vieira is in need of favours. He's as dishonest in his dealings as any scoundrel. But he'll find I'm no servile footman. I drink at the same table as Kings. My father was major-domo to the Royal Household, captain-in-chief of the guard and commendator. He waited on three Kings. No half-baked priest will get the better of me."

"The charges brought against the Ravascos are serious and His Majesty cannot ignore them," agreed Palma.

"The Ravascos won't give in until they're well and truly beaten," replied Teles. "It's up to us."

"It's unlikely that Antonio Vieira has come to the feast. Why is he here?" asked Palma.

"Follow him and find out," De Souza ordered the Captain-General.

Teles remained in the room after the judges had left.

"I must warn you," he told the Governor, "that your intransigence is not only doing us a great deal of harm but will almost certainly ruin us. We've given so little thought to the future that we're now facing what Vieira prophesied."

Antonio de Souza remained silent.

"But there's still hope," continued the Captain-General, "if you'll allow me to deal with this."

"How?"

"In my own way, Antonio, and I'll answer for my actions without incriminating you. The Tribunal is letting you down by showing that it lacks the power to confront Padre Vieira. Military force is the answer."

"Are you asking me to wash my hands of him?" De Souza asked him.

"You're no Pilate, nor could Vieira be mistaken for Jesus. I'm after the hooded assassins. I won't harm that so-called priest you protect though you claim to despise him."

"Very well," agreed De Souza. "But you'll take all the blame should anything go wrong. I'll want nothing to do with it. You're on your own."

The sun had disappeared. There was a cold wind blowing. The crowd had dispersed from the square in the same manner it had gathered, little by little, in tiny groups, leaving a ground of trampled mud.

Vieira went directly from the College to the prison. Bernardo, his velvet garments soiled and his hair dishevelled, was overjoyed to see his brother. He seemed overwhelmed by fear. The solitary confinement of prison tormented him, the dampness made him cough and he felt pains in his chest.

"How is my daughter?" he asked.

"Don't worry, she's safe on the plantation," his brother answered, ashamed at the lie. But to mention her imprisonment would only make matters worse.

"I'm worried about her health."

"I've brought you news," Vieira told him, handing Ravasco a chest containing a blanket, books, paper, a quill and inkwell.

"Good news?"

Vieira told him about events which transpired after the Secretary's arrest. "And do you remember Palma, the steersman's son?"

"Yes, of course I do: he was the scoundrel who created difficulties about the fees for judicial inquiries when he was in Paraíba. A thousand cruzados each month. He fawns on the Governor. Those in power are constantly surrounded by cretins and sycophants. We're at his mercy."

"No longer. Palma has been removed from the case."

"Removed? I don't believe it," exclaimed Ravasco.

"We made several appeals to the Judiciary. Then the people began rioting in Bahia. Everybody knows that the judge is in league with the Menezes. There were many false witnesses and the Chancellor had no alternative but to appoint another judge to proceed with the inquiry."

"And who'll replace Palma?"

"Rocha Pita, born and bred in Bahia."

Rocha Pita had always distanced himself from the sordid intrigues of local politics. He had refused to become involved with coteries of self-serving groups. He was known for his honesty. He conducted dangerous inquiries. Fearlessly he investigated the haunts of thieves, moved among the fugitive slaves, vagrants and assassins who infested the city and countryside. He confronted the sugar barons, tobacco planters, cattle-ranchers, and refused to be intimidated by criminals, even in the hinterland, where the protection of a rich landowner and his henchmen was worth more than any Crown decree.

"Let's see if Rocha Pita can survive this inquiry," said Ravasco.

"The charges against me have divided the Tribunal judges down the middle. And who would ever have thought that our greatest enemy in the Tribunal is none other than Gois, our sister's brother-in-law. Our own kinsman you might say. Banha is going to Luanda to administer the Governor's residence and that should help. Some of the military support us. And the clergy's been on our side ever since the College was invaded. The Archbishop . . . I'm not so sure about. He made a favourable impression on everyone when he first arrived in Bahia, but he does not speak out against corruption. Some noblemen and merchants have also expressed their goodwill. You'll be out of here soon, I promise. I'm old and weary, a sick man, but I intend to fight."

For several moments neither of them spoke.

"But tell me, Antonio, how did you manage to get in here?"

"Through Samuel da Fonseca. He has done everything possible to help us."

"Ah, that holy man is considered a true Christian," remarked Ravasco. "My daughter's companion is also here in the prison and she's being ill-treated. I can't understand it. What crime has the girl committed to be locked up and tortured?"

Padre Vieira told him about the theft and the pawning of the Captain-General's ring.

"But how disloyal," exclaimed Ravasco, "how could she have done such a thing! She's getting what she deserves. It only goes to show what one can expect of a woman. Betrayal, infidelity, self-conceit."

"An order passed by the Court authorized the use of judicial torture to extract a confession, even though it's discouraged by the regulations. Any use of torture should be carried out in the presence of a doctor, a priest and a lay brother from the Almshouse. The defendant could appeal to the Judiciary to have the order revoked, but this has seldom happened."

"Here, too, the innocent suffer cruel injustices," said Ravasco, his thoughts elsewhere. "I hear people moaning all night long."

"Poor flock, abandoned and persecuted. I wonder if God is even aware of this colony's existence."

*

Water seeped through the stone walls of the underground cellar. The dim light cast reflections on the metal bowl sitting on the table. The Bull was eating at his leisure. The Captain-General was listening attentively but he couldn't make out what the two brothers were saying in the adjacent cell. Nervous and agile, he paced up and down. He dipped his fingertips into his snuff-box and brought them to his nostrils which soon set him sneezing.

Covered in sweat, the Bull looked grubby. Bristling hairs sprouted from his ears.

The silence from Bernardo Ravasco's cell worried the Captain-General. He went up close to the iron door of the cell where Vieira was chatting with his brother.

"I say, Bull, what do you think's going on in there?" asked Teles. "I can't hear a thing."

The Bull went on gorging himself as he looked at the Captain-General.

When Vieira made to leave Ravasco's cell, Teles signalled to the Bull and concealed himself.

The Jesuit left after blessing the jailor. Love your enemies and pray for those who persecute you, Vieira thought to himself. How difficult to observe Christian precepts. The service of God certainly demanded self-abnegation.


Venturing out of his hiding-place under cover of darkness, the notary Manuel Dias had gone to visit his mistress, the negro slave, Ursula do Congo.

"It's almost morning, shouldn't you be going?" Ursula asked.

The notary clasped his arms round her waist and rested his head on her ample breasts which strained against her blouse.

"I've had a terrible dream," he said.

"Then don't tell me." She freed herself from his embrace. Dias, as usual, ignored what she had said.

"In my dream you were devouring me. You had the body of a woman and the wings of a bat and you were sucking my blood. Guess from where?"

"From your bollocks."

"No such luck. That at least would have given me some pleasure. You know my little vices. Your teeth were ever so dainty and you were licking them with your tongue."

"Let me show you."

He put out his long, red tongue and Ursula sucked it. Then they burst out laughing.

"And what is the meaning of this dream?" she asked.

"It's a game. Just a game."

Manuel Dias was handsome and charming. And Ursula loved him, although no deep understanding existed between them.

"I haven't got the money for us to elope, but Padre Vieira has promised to get me some. I must go to Lisbon."

"Are you going to leave me here on my own?"

Lost in thought, they remained silent.

"I earn forty thousand réis," he said. "It isn't enough to take you with me. But I'll be back just as soon as things quieten down."

"I've never seen that much money."

"Indeed. A salary as good as mine means that others are after my job and there's endless intrigue and blackmail to do so."

"How did you manage to secure it?"

"I have nice handwriting."

"And what about your other little jobs?"

"They don't bring in much. And I'm overworked. Sometimes I even have to hire an assistant. My work as a notary doesn't leave much time for anything else. All Court matters are dealt with in writing, especially those concerning the Crown, which is four thousand leagues away from here. I do so much work that I suffer from writer's cramp, a common complaint among notaries. There are times when I can't even bend my thumb. Dancers get a cramp in their legs, and musicians in their finger-joints. But pain or not, I have to get on with all the declarations, testimonies, question-naires and statements which make my job so important. We also act as intermediaries between judges and litigants, and can hasten or prolong a lawsuit at will. That brings in a little more money, but not enough to escape to Portugal."

"Quite the spendthrift, aren't you? How many whores do you get through in a night?"

"All my money's spent on you. I'm bored with my wife. I'm sick and tired of being in hiding. I'm tired of being poor."

"And what about me, stuck in this place, with madmen raving all night long? I told you not to get involved in this crime," said Ursula, lowering her voice.

"One more makes no difference. And this crime even deserves praise. Besides, I've every reason to want Teles de Menezes out of the way. After he discovered I was friendly with the Ravascos, he started hounding me and did his best to deprive me of work. I detest the man. And he loathes me."

Manuel Dias went up to the tiny window and saw soldiers posted at the College gates.

"Suppose they catch you leaving?" Ursula asked.

"Anything might happen. But if they should arrest you, promise me you'll never mention my name."

"I promise."

Dias embraced her.

"I love you," he said. "You've bewitched me. I haven't slept with my wife in a long time, not that she's not pretty or good in bed for all her prudery and that *chemise cagoule* she insists on wearing. I'm making her unhappy because of you. I've lost my desire for her."

"That's all I ever listen to. Stories from men who leave their families to live with a negro woman. Why do you stay with her?"

"I don't know. Some scruple or other my mother must have instilled in me as a child."

"I'm going," said Ursula.

"I love you," he pleaded.

"Yet you won't leave that pampered ninny. She's a living scarecrow. Stretched out all day on a mat with her slaves, telling her children stories like some fairy godmother."

"I wish you wouldn't repeat the things I've told you."

"It's for your own good."

Yes, he loved Ursula, but best to leave things as they stood. He departed with a kiss and rushed back to the little house on the outskirts of the city where he had found refuge.

When Vieira emerged from the prison, the Bull was waiting and followed him through the streets. The carriage carrying the Jesuit stopped a number of times to allow the occupants to alight so that the horse could get up the slope. Wherever they stopped, passers-by gathered to greet Padre Vieira and to ask his blessing.

Occasionally someone hidden in the background would call out: "Jew!"

The Bull stalked him, keeping his distance. He felt hungry. He was in the habit of buying whole bunches of sweet bananas and eating them on the way to or from work.

He put his hand into his knapsack, brought out a huge lump of unrefined sugar and ate it, nibbling the pieces with his small, round teeth, all crooked and blackened. Then he took out an orange and using a dagger, peeled it without removing the pith. He then ate the segments and spat out the pips. He always carried a supply of cold roast beef dipped in cassava flour and wrapped in paper bags. Whenever he felt hungry he stuffed pieces of the meat into his mouth. He devoured the lot as the day wore on, and once the bags were empty the Bull threw them away. An interested party could easily have picked up his trail simply by following the litter he scattered along the street: crushed sesame seeds, the shells of Pachira nuts, palm-kernels, fish-bones, the stalks of capsicums, the backbones of small animals, the tendons of boiled goatsmeat, discarded paper, leaves that had been stuffed with a mixture of flour and butter. This litter could bring on evil if it fell into the wrong hands, especially hands skilled in the art of witchcraft; but, when warned, the Bull declared he was not superstitious. He would lunch on fish, goat, cow, lamb, chicken, pheasant or other game, on anything. He never felt full, he was never troubled by his kidneys or bowels, or suffered from colic or other stomach upsets. He looked the picture of rude health. He never suffered from itching, hot palpitations, prickly heat, liver attacks, diarrhoea, skin disorders, coughing or indigestion. He ignored the usual warnings about bathing after a heavy meal. He drank milk with crushed mango, water after coffee, ate cake fresh from the oven, fruit in season, hot water-melon, unripe breadfruit, catfish, lemon-peel, food which had been reheated, beef dripping, the skin of roast chicken. And he claimed that the secret was to wash everything down with a mug of rum. He feared no one except God and the Saints. And Old Nick.

After travelling a distance, Vieira came to a country estate where the land had dried up. He stopped at the little house where Manuel

Dias was hiding. The notary was sitting at a table in the company of a buxom young woman. Their young children were being fed on the laps of slaves. The negro women took food from the gourds, kneaded it into tiny balls and popped them into the children's mouths, telling them stories all the while.

When he saw the priest, Dias asked his wife to leave the room and take the children with her.

From outside, the Bull could spy through the window. He watched the men as they sat at the table and conversed in whispers. The sight of all that food made his mouth water.

Their conversation was brief. Vieira handed the notary a small parcel, got up, blessed him and left.

The Bull made a mental note of the house's location as he followed Antonio Vieira back to the city. They went down the street below the Governor's palace, parallel to the windlass hoisting merchandise, down to the lower part of the city. They entered a side-street on the corner of the Rua da Praia. There was not a living soul in sight except the two men who were heading in the same direction. Mules were eating mangoes that had fallen to the ground.

Antonio Vieira's carriage came to a halt before a dilapidated house. Two heavily armed men opened the door and let him in. The Jesuit was carrying the parcel under one arm. The men prevented the Bull from getting any closer. He carefully noted the street and the location of the house and waited.

An urchin passed with a basket of coconuts and the Bull bought some. After picking out the heaviest, he paid the boy and sauntered back to the house. But the carriage was gone. This had been a shorter visit than the previous one.

The Bull had no choice but to return to the prison. But no matter, he had two good pieces of news.

Sitting on a high stool and dressed in a long threadbare cassock which trailed on the floor, Luiz Bonicho looked into a small mirror.

Holding scissors in one hand and a comb in the other, Donato Serotino was tonsuring Bonicho's hair.

"What are those papers Padre Vieira gave you to take to Portugal?"

"They're letters addressed to certain noblemen, ministers and protégés who are plotting against Braço de Prata and Captain-General Teles. Vieira should ask himself what the Prince must be thinking. It must be: If they're conspiring against my government, they're conspiring against me. And if they're conspiring against me, how can they expect me to show them consideration or mercy? Are they asking me to disregard the Governor I myself appointed? Make no mistake, Donato, the Regent isn't that stupid. Unlike you, he's no dim-witted commoner. He's of royal descent, and educated by advisers, tutors, musicians, poets, philosophers and masters of rhetoric. His Royal Highness has been trained to think, and you can be sure that he won't trust conspirators. These letters will only convince the Prince that he must track down these trouble-makers and have them arrested. And that includes us. Can't Vieira see this? He's not being very intelligent and this is one battle he's sure to lose. No one is likely to get the better of Braço de Prata. But how can I refuse him? He'd get rid of me at once. I'll take the letters."

"It's dangerous. Suppose they catch you? Aren't you afraid, Luiz?"

"Yes. I'm ashamed to admit it," replied Bonicho. "Braço de Prata's men are making inquiries, working in secret, burrowing underground like moles, getting closer and closer, I can feel it in my bones. It petrifies me. The world deserves something better. But you can't change the government in the colony. After two hundred years, the wickedness and injustice are entrenched. Money, power, barter, dishonesty, the illegal sale of appointments; fortunes acquired by robbing others; the widespread corruption of rich and poor which has turned the colony into a cesspool of depravity. The Court of Appeal presides over this chaos, but it isn't Justice that worries me, that can be bought at no great cost: what frightens me is the treacherous soul of Antonio de Souza. His long, sharp claws never miss their prey. I can sense him getting ready to pounce, getting closer, and I'll wager I'm the next victim on his list. The Blasphemer was the first to die; scarcely human, he didn't really count. Did you know that the Romans burned their dead on a funeral pyre, and that the Inquisitors burn the living on that very same pyre? At least I'm not a Jew, so there's no fear of me finishing up on a bonfire in Portugal."

# VIII

T HE WHARF WAS CRAMMED with sugar crates. Giving off
a musty smell, and grunting like an animal, the foreman went
up and down shouting orders to the stevedores.

Gregório de Matos looked around. People were strolling about
in front of the warehouses, stores and smaller commercial instal-
lations. Not very far off, the ramparts of the fortress penetrated
the blue waters of the sea.

Large ships lay anchored in the bay. Fishermen's huts, bundles
of sails, and old ropes were scattered on the shore. In the main
port stood barrels of pitch, oil, and rum, and packing-cases,
stacked one on top of the other.

Wagon-wheels creaked, timbers collided, furnaces crackled. An
aroma of tobacco mingled in the air with the smell of smoke and
leather.

People seemed to have forgotten the former Captain-General's
assassination and, with no other interest in mind, they returned
to a humdrum existence within the city's thirteen churches and
chapels, the taverns and brothels, the streets. At the gaming tables,
they argued and quarrelled.

The continuous rivalry between the merchants on the sugar-
growing islands of the Caribbean and the plantation owners, who
were facing hardship as the price of sugar fell, had precipitated a
crisis which led many into bankruptcy.

The sugar barons found themselves competing with tobacco
growers, who generally produced on a smaller scale and did not
require huge investments to trade. As a result, men of humble
background suddenly grew prosperous. A new group of rural
aristocrats emerged to join the sugar barons and the cattle breed-
ers. In the city, from where the agricultural produce was exported,

wealthy merchants and traders expanded their business, enlarged their holdings and vied among themselves for influential appointments. In 1683, there were approximately a hundred wealthy merchants in Bahia and they controlled all commercial activity between Portugal and Africa. Trade had increased with the Gold Coast, where rum and tobacco from Bahia competed with European products. From the port of Whydah alone, some eight thousand slaves were shipped each year to Bahia, which was becoming more African by the minute. The colony's agriculture and commerce were totally dependent on the labour of slaves whose lives, both on the plantations and in the towns, were shortened by misery and hardship. "Without Angola," declared colonial advisers, "Brazil would be lost unless she fought another war. Without African slaves, there could be no Bahia. Without Angola there could be no Brazil."

Meanwhile, despite the apparent prosperity, the impoverished populace was exposed to even greater famine and privation. The poor prayed each day that God would work a miracle to ease their suffering. Surely God must know they were worthy of something better.

Two carriages came to a halt at the wharf. Armed men jumped out and began patrolling the docks and the surrounding area. They entered the warehouse and carried out a careful search. One of them signalled and then a coach appeared with two coachmen, elegantly attired in red velvet, occupying the driver's seat. Samuel da Fonseca sat inside.

Gregório watched the Rabbi's arrival. A white-haired slave helped the old man to alight.

With effort, Fonseca crossed the tiny yard which led to the warehouse and finally came up to Gregório. They embraced each other. The wheels of an ox-cart transporting wooden crates to the warehouse could be heard grinding round laboriously.

Fonseca and the poet entered the warehouse by a winding path cluttered with piles of timbers and came to a great staircase. The warehouse was dark and hollow, like the shell of an abandoned construction. They climbed up the stairs one by one.

"Ah, I'm getting so old and heavy," complained Fonseca, as he struggled to the top. A female slave kept close behind him. Young and pretty, she was dressed in white satin petticoats and a blue linen blouse. She wore earrings and bracelets made of coloured beads; chains supported a cross which rested between her breasts.

"You must forgive the attire of my personal guard but times being what they are," apologized Fonseca, pausing to regain his breath. "The Jewish community has had to put up with the most terrible injustices. And now it's the Ravascos' turn."

Finally they reached the top floor. They ducked through a low doorway into a comfortable room with a large window looking out on the wharf. Below, stevedores were busy stacking crates.

"This warehouse belongs to a friend. But it's as good as mine. Make yourself at home."

Gregório sat down. The slave girl left, giving the stranger an appraising look on her way out. Gregório returned her glance.

The men were now alone.

"A slave from the Gold Coast," Fonseca said, noting the poet's interest. All his slaves were *Agoins*, an African tribe settled in the region near São Jorge da Mina. The slaves of this particular group were also known as *Fantees*. The men were experienced fishermen and the women famous for their cooking. These women were perhaps the most beautiful of all the slaves, with their delicate complexions the colour of golden olives. The Rabbi whispered into Gregório's ear: "These women are known for their voluptuousness," and he smiled with his beady eyes, lifting a glass of liqueur from a tray and offering it to his visitor. "That explains why the Portuguese and French find them so appealing. I prefer them for other reasons. I like to eat well." He patted his protruding belly.

"For the plantation," said the Rabbi, "I buy *Hausa* slaves. They're very strong and hardy, good workers, and nearly all Mohammedans. But I'm sure you haven't come here to talk about slaves."

They heard light footsteps and a boy appeared. His clothes were colourful.

"This is my son Gaspar," said the Rabbi. "He greatly admires you."

"And how are you, Gaspar?" Gregório asked. The boy blushed.

"I named him Gaspar in memory of the first Jew to set foot on this Land of Parrots. He led a squadron under the command of Sabayo, the Arab Governor of Goa. Anchored off the Island of Angediva, the Jew sighted the fleet of Vasco da Gama. He set off to greet him and was welcomed aboard by the Portuguese. But Vasco da Gama accused him of spying, and ordered that he be arrested and tied up. The Jew was stripped, tortured, and locked in a cell. They refused to release him because he could speak many languages and had visited India, Turkey, Mecca and many other remote kingdoms. They took him back to Portugal and forced him to be baptized with the name Gaspar da Gama. He was a handsome fellow with long, golden locks. Intelligent and educated, he ingratiated himself with King Dom Manuel I, who gave him his freedom, clothes from his own wardrobe, horses from his stables, servants and money. Gaspar da Gama had won over the King by recounting his travels. The King appointed him adviser and interpreter to Admiral Pedro Alvares Cabral whose expedition brought him to the shores of Brazil. It is rumoured in *Legends of the Indies* that Gaspar da Gama's parents were Jews from Bosna, who were banished to Jerusalem, then to Alexandria where Gaspar was born. These stories about Jews do not differ much from one century to the next."

Gregório squinted from behind his spectacles.

"Timid as he looks, my boy is very bright."

Gaspar blushed, shrugging his shoulders.

"I withdrew from the city with my family soon after arriving from Holland. I wanted to get away from all the worries, distractions and hostility of city life. It's not easy to conceal things here, as you know, and almost everyone knows we're Jews. Or Yids, as they refer to us: dirty Yids. But my son Gaspar stayed behind in the city and continued with his studies of the Talmud Torah. Next year, he'll return to Europe – to Holland, naturally, where Jews are welcome. But never to Portugal. You might as well throw yourself onto the bonfire of the Inquisition." The Rabbi poured his visitor another glass of liqueur. "I don't want him to forget his religion, to turn to vice and be stricken with that shameful disease which spreads among the young. Gaspar lives in the city with relatives who are strict and curtail his freedom; they make sure that he takes his studies seriously, leads a disciplined life with little money to spend. Nevertheless, like all boys of his age, he manages to find the time now and then to frequent the taverns. Isn't that so, my boy?"

Gaspar was blushing again.

"And although he keeps it quiet, I'm well aware that he participates in political discussions and naively plots to overthrow the Portuguese government in Brazil. The boy's getting a good education," continued Fonseca. "But I'm talking too much. I am here to listen."

Gregório took a sheaf of papers from his pocket.

"These belong to Bernardo Ravasco. They were confiscated by the Governor and, at great risk, his son Gonçalo rescued them. They can't be published in Portugal and the Ravascos fear they will be destroyed. I've been asked to entrust them to you."

Samuel da Fonseca readily agreed and, putting on his spectacles, began to examine the papers one by one. "Good heavens!" he exclaimed. "These papers are more valuable than the dowry of a rich bride from Rouen. How could anyone wish to destroy them! I'll dispatch them to Amsterdam."

"I'm certain Dom Bernardo would be delighted if you were to publish them in his name. This is the last remaining copy. The originals were delivered by His Highness to the Grand Inquisitor on the understanding that they should be returned. But this never happened. The originals were taken for lost."

"Doctor de Matos, the papers will be quite safe," Fonseca assured him, "and your wishes will be carried out. I have another offer to make which should also give you cheer."

"But nothing of late has brought me much cheer."

"This is something I've always wanted to do. I'd like to publish a fine edition of your poems with no expense spared. You know I have a printing house in Amsterdam. Revise the originals and we shall send them with Gaspar to Holland along with Ravasco's manuscripts. You can rely on them to do a good job."

To the Rabbi's disappointment, Gregório did not seem enthusiastic.

"I don't have a single poem in my keeping," said the poet. "The ones in circulation are false and rife with mistakes, unauthorized changes, cuts, addenda, and corruptions, to quote Padre Vieira.''

"We could make a list of the poems which have been corrected or amend them to conform in every detail with the originals."

"Nearly all of them are unsuitable for publication. They're intended for people to recite rather than for scholars to pore over and criticize. They're really not worthy."

"I don't understand," said Fonseca.

"Let me explain. I'm aware that people are greatly amused by my satires, but they're even more amused by my fall from grace."

Poets who were reckless, mad, disheartened and homicidal could be influential in a city. But Gregório had his doubts. To have graduated in Canon Law and be qualified *de genere* for a Bachelor's degree gave him little satisfaction. As a young man, he had devoted himself to writing verse and dreamed of becoming a great poet. His ear was not good enough to realize his dream of becoming a fine musician and he could not compete with his brother Eusébio when it came to playing the viol or composing music. Gregório composed ballads merely for his own amusement. He considered his lyrical poems quite inferior, even fatuous, compared to Góngora's. He would sit at his desk full of good intentions, only to concede, in the end, that all he had achieved were bawdy verses about knavery, theft and fornication in a language which was unmistakably colloquial. It caused him great anguish. He loathed his work as a judge in the Ecclesiastical Court and was all too familiar with the corruption and hypocrisy of the clergy. He had persevered with these duties only because of the benefices and immunities he received. And to be sure of the Archbishop's goodwill, although he might well have lost that by now. He was spending more time in the low quarters of Bahia and was rarely sober. And now he was no longer certain why he was running away. He would go to Recôncavo and, from there, perhaps travel further afield.

"I no longer have a profession," he confided.

"Come now, you're an ecclesiastical judge and a poet."

"Being a poet isn't a profession: it's like being a widow. A poet's a poet, just as a horse is a horse. Horses are useful beasts. But as for me, Gregório de Matos e Guerra, widower, poet, born in Brazil, I'm less than useless. What do others think of me? I feel more hated than loved."

But the world had always been full of poets like him: Afonso Eanes de Coton was never away from the gaming houses and brothels; the Galician Pero da Ponte, a pot-bellied rogue, had composed outrageous lampoons condemning the sodomites who had abused him; Padre Martim Moxa had written verses extolling carnal delights; Chiado had exchanged life in the monastery for drink and debauchery, living on the immoral earnings of male prostitutes and whores; the aristocratic Tomás de Noronha had slept in common lodging-houses and squandered his entire fortune on wanton pleasure; Francisco Manuel de Melo had taken part in a murder and been exiled to Bahia. Gregório was by no means the worst. There was even some justification for his behaviour. Poets like him were loved by the people, not simply because of what they wrote but because of the sins they committed. The divine aura of poetry did not mean they were no longer men of flesh and blood. Saints were much more troublesome.

Beneath the philosophical veils of chastity even Camoens had allowed the stirrings of sensous love to surface: *"Delicate robes and silken skin are the greatest incitement to love. In the forest, eager kisses, soft caresses and joyful smiles."* Gregório knew precisely what Camoens was suggesting in those lines. For such was human nature. Góngora had written: *"My philosophy is to live well and drink to my heart's content."*

"I'm tired of trying to imitate Góngora," said Gregório. "My verses are more sensual. The truth is, I'm terrified of the Inquisition."

"It's your lyrical poems that interest me," said the Rabbi. "And they're not likely to give offence."

Seeing how it distressed the poet even to talk about his work, Gaspar came to his assistance. He took a book from his satchel.

"Have you read this marvellous book?" he asked.

"I have nearly a hundred books here on the plantation," Fonseca added with some pride, "I brought many of them from Amsterdam where they're easier to find. Others I had sent from Spain or purchased in Portugal. Some I published myself, mostly about religion. Do you know *Arnalte y Lucenda* by Diego de San Pedro?"

"Yes, of course, the Jewish writer."

"We Jews are in the habit of underestimating our own people. Without wishing to sound boastful, I must say that some excellent works have been written by Jews. Take Bento Teixeira's *Prosopopéia*. He's a Jew. And the *Diálogo das grandezas do Brasil* by Ambrósio Fernandes Brandão. Another Jewish writer. I could spend my entire life reading books. My modest library is at your disposal. I treasure many of these books and I suspect they're completely unknown here in the colony. You're a well-read man. That makes me happy. I spend day after day trying to find time to read difficult texts and I always end up feeling depressed, defeated by this world around me which thinks of nothing but commerce and religion. I admire poets like yourself, who have the courage to devote their lives to literature."

"I'm no poet. At least, not the poet I'd hoped to be."

"There's a great deal of poetry in your writings, just as there's poetry in the eyes of a woman, whether Jew or Gentile. Don't you agree?"

"I do," replied Gregório.

"Yet who can deny the evil caused by women," continued the Rabbi, "ever since Eve or Lilith, the Queen of Demons."

"I'm only trying to be fair, dear philosopher," answered the poet. "Not to myself but to the people who are dying of hunger and ignorance. I write my verses for those who cannot read."

# IX

PELTS PILED ON STRAW served as a bed. And resting on it were the notary Manuel Dias with his wife. They lay side by side, sweating and motionless. He was thinking about Ursula do Congo. After a while, Aldonça turned and gazed at her husband. She examined his profile, his pale face and sad expression.

"What's wrong, Manuel? What news did Padre Vieira bring?"

"Nothing, nothing."

Bats hung from the wooden beams roofed with dark clay tiles. One flapped its wings gently in a wheezing sound. Aldonça was startled.

"They're just like flying mice," he said. He recalled his dream in which Ursula had appeared.

"Bats, priests, people arriving. Secret conversations. It's all rather unnerving. And now this old house with a sapodilla tree outside."

"What's wrong with a sapodilla tree?"

"Bats tend to lurk in them. It also explains those ominous shadows and why children are not allowed to play there."

"Old wives' tales. But you're right. Lots of people seem to be turning up. What kind of refuge is this? First thing in the morning, I'll look for another place."

"How long can we expect to live in hiding?" his wife asked.

"Not for long, don't worry."

They heard a child crying. Aldonça was about to get up but her husband held her arm.

"Leave him, the slaves will look after the child."

They embraced.

"You haven't shown me so much affection in ages," she chided.

"I've had a lot on my mind lately."

"More than you have now?"

He looked at her and smiled.

Two horses were concealed among the trees a short distance away.

In the kitchen, the Bull had his dagger pressed to the throat of a woman slave who sat gasping in terror and holding a child in her lap.

"Silence that brat or I'll murder the lot of you," threatened the Bull. The other slave gave the child some milk from a gourd and he fell silent.

"What now?" the Bull asked the Captain-General, who was standing beside him. "They've seen our faces."

"We won't say a word, Captain, not a word," cried the slave. "Take anything you want. We're poor folk with nothing to offer you."

"Ha! they've nothing to offer. Did you hear that? There's nothing here," said Teles.

The slave was silent. They guessed what the men were looking for.

"Where's your master?"

"He's upstairs," answered one of the women.

"He's out," said the other, almost in the same breath.

"Put the child on the floor," he ordered. The woman obeyed. She was the first to die. Quick as a flash, the Bull lunged forward and stabbed her in the breast. The woman fell to the ground, the blood spurting from her wound like water. The child started crying again.

"I hear a noise below," said Manuel Dias jumping up at once.

"Stay with me," pleaded Aldonca. "I'm frightened."

Opening the door, Dias came face to face with two men. Their hands and clothes were stained with blood. Their shirt-sleeves were rolled up.

Aldonça shrieked. The notary clasped the gold chain round his neck.

Teles closed the door behind him.

"We've brought you a souvenir from a friend," he said raising his dagger.

Dias drew back.

The Bull rushed forward and thrust the dagger into the notary's heart. The impact of his body crashing to the floor was muffled by Aldonça's cries. Shocked into silence, she fell to her knees beside her husband's corpse. The Bull stabbed her. She writhed on the floor, bleeding and choking.

Teles ordered the Bull to deal another blow. "She shouldn't suffer more than him."

The Bull then cut off Dias' right hand, wrapped it in rags and took it with him.

The men returned to the ground floor and headed for the door, passing the child playing on the floor alongside the dead slaves. His tears had turned to whimpering.

The fierce, southerly winds sent the waves crashing against the rocks. Thick clouds began to gather in the grey sky.

As he walked on, Gregório thought about Maria Berco. The longing he felt for her seemed to spur him on. It was a mistake to have blurted out his feelings. He should have kept his thoughts to himself rather than risk losing all hope by saying too much. He was hopelessly infatuated and could see no way of ever winning her. Now she was in prison, and for all he knew she might have been hanged.

Anica was overjoyed when she set eyes on the poet standing there in the middle of the brothel.

"Let's go to bed, darling," he said.

They pushed their way past whores combing their long hair by the light of an open window, and headed straight for Anica's room.

Once inside, Anica vanished through a narrow door and re-appeared in a silken, almost transparent nightdress with flounces.

"I thought you'd left me," she said.

"Suppose I'd died?"

"Don't say such things. I love you. I want to hear you say you love me."

"Stop this silliness. I don't want to hurt your feelings."

He sat down.

She sat down beside him.

"I know you're deceiving me. That's why you didn't sleep here."

"You're wrong," he said. "I spent last night in the cellars of the Council Chambers having a meeting with friends. Manuel Dias has been killed. He's the notary who was involved in the Captain-General's assassination."

"Do you think it was Braço de Prata?"

"Him or the Captain-General. I'm being followed by guards. I don't know what to do, but I can't stay here any longer."

"For God's sake don't leave now. Where will you go? And your work? You can't just abandon everything."

"I've only been going to the Curia to collect my wages."

"I'll find you a place to hide."

"Where?"

"In Vicente Laso's warehouse. Would that do?"

"I suppose so."

"When all this is over, will you marry me?"

"I'm not interested in getting married."

Anica got up and went to fetch something from a chest. "I've got a present for you." She brought out a wooden dummy head with a wig. "Do you like it?"

"Won't people laugh at me?" he asked, trying it on. He admired himself in the mirror. "Has my hair become so thin?"

Anica stretched out on the bed. Gregório lay down beside her. He lay quite still, staring at the ceiling. She stroked his penis.

"What's the matter?" she asked.

"I'm not in the mood."

"Then why did you come? Why did you call me? Don't try to fool me. I know you're in love with someone else. A woman can always tell when a man's thinking of another woman."

"I'm not thinking about anyone. I've already said so."

"Then you're tired of me. How stupid I've been to imagine that you were any different from the rest."

"Nothing has changed, Anica. I still feel the same about you. But you can't expect a man to make love every five minutes. Be fair, for heaven's sake! You're so demanding. You used to be so considerate but lately you've become possessive. What's wrong with you women? You all talk of love but persecute a man until you wear him down. Life's short and there's a lot of loving to be done."

Anica began to weep, covering her face with her hands. This was too much. He couldn't bear to watch a woman crying. He threw himself on top of her, pulled up her nightdress and penetrated her, uncertain whether he was experiencing ecstasy or rage.

The heat was unbearable outside, but Anica was wearing a cloak with a rabbit-fur collar dyed bright red. It looked splendid if somewhat odd. Absurdly overdressed, she looked ready to burst out of her clothes. There were dark circles under her eyes and her face appeared pale against the red of her collar. Her lips were tinged with crimson. She and Gregório were heading for Vicente Laso's warehouse, located on the outskirts of the city.

"How quiet, and not a woman in sight," he observed.

"It's not that bad. You'll get used to it."

They walked in the shade, watching out for patrols and soldiers on guard. Wealthy citizens, haughty and elegantly attired, passed in their litters. Street-vendors bustled through their daily rounds, calling out their wares. Their clothes looked as if they had been dipped in a vat of grease and reeked of spirits even from a distance, the result of having to wade through the mire of this dirtiest of cities. They turned into a filthy street. There was cracked plaster and rolling timbers on the buildings, and everything was coated with a thin layer of salt and dust. It was one of Gregório's favourite streets, for it overlooked the beach where the sea sent its spray over the black rocks. Going there with Anica, now the picture of misery, was depressing.

Gregório was overcome with melancholy. He looked unwashed and dishevelled, and felt awkward in his newly-acquired wig. Reassured that there were no soldiers around, he invited Anica to sit on the rocks by the sea, in the shade of the pink-leaved mango trees.

The wind carried the stench of urine from the city. Indeed that foul place appeared to breed people with their guts turned inside out, allowing their secretions to flow as freely as their emotions. Anica's love for the poet was stronger than ever. But this was the last thing Gregório wanted, now that he was infatuated with Maria. He was ashamed of his need to possess her but could not control himself; and he clung to Anica in an effort to forget Maria. Adopting a girlish tone, Anica became coy and flirtatious. They embraced and Gregório inhaled the odour of Anica's skin mingled with the pungent smell of her collar: dyed fabric and cheap perfume.

Why was he behaving like this? The more he returned to Anica, the more he would hurt her, until finally he would abandon her. But he had always felt indebted to those who loved him and showed him affection, even though his debts to women and money-lenders might never be paid.

# X

"YOUNG GONÇALO HAS COME to say goodbye before he leaves for Portugal," announced José Soares.

"Then why keep him standing at the door?" said Padre Vieira. "Surely you realize his life's at risk? Show him in at once, for this might be the last time I'll see him."

The old Jesuit stroked his chin. He had only two nephews still alive and he dearly loved them: Gonçalo Ravasco and Francisco Dorea. Gonçalo's mother Filipa was the sister of the ravishingly beautiful Maria, who had bewitched Francisco Manuel de Melo during his period of exile in Bahia. On returning to Europe with the fleet that sailed in 1681, Vieira had discovered that many of his relatives and friends were dead. The most bitter loss of all was that of his favourite nephew, Captain Cristóvão Ravasco, who had sacrificed his young life for King and country; yet another service rendered by the Ravascos which had gone unrewarded. Nearly all of Padre Vieira's brothers and sisters had passed on.

Gonçalo entered Vieira's cell. He knelt beside his uncle's pallet and kissed his hand.

"It is good to see you, my boy," said Vieira.

"Has everything been arranged, uncle?"

"I've given a lot of thought, Gonçalo . . . to this visit of yours to Portugal. The voyage is likely to be hazardous, with storms and calms, pirates and buccaneers. Just think of all the uncles and cousins you've lost in shipwrecks and volleys of cannonfire. And the journey itself is risky for anyone, and especially so for a stowaway. Gonçalo, I've considered the matter carefully and I don't think you should go."

"I must. The future of our family depends on it. Our good name! Our integrity! Remaining here could be even more dangerous. Braço de Prata is waiting, ready to strike at any moment."

"With his good hand or his bad one?" asked Vieira.

"The swine has no good hand."

"Everybody has both good and bad. Look at yours. Look at mine. Dom João III was known as Pious João, yet he sent thousands of Jews to their death to uphold the faith. He, too, was a good Christian. Don't be foolhardy, my boy, this is a time for extreme caution."

"Nothing will dissuade me, uncle. I'm sorry, but I've made up my mind."

"Very well, Gonçalo. But be careful. Remind his Royal Highness of the words I spoke on the third Sunday of Lent in 1655, when I preached in the Royal Chapel in the presence of Dom João IV. Those words are just as important today. Tell the Prince that the Portuguese colonies, because of their diversity and remoteness, need viceroys, governors, generals, captains, judges, bishops and archbishops. But they should be chosen and posted with wisdom and discernment. If the Prince should send a greedy man to a colony where there is every opportunity to thieve, or a weak man to a colony where strength is needed, a disloyal man to a place where he may commit treason, a pauper to a place where he might get rich, such appointments will soon destroy Portugal's empire and undo all the achievements of those who make her great. We need men worthy of their ancestors," he said. "The colonies must be given enough soldiers to fight, defend, and conquer in the name of justice." He paused, then, lowering his voice, he said, "And not men who will exploit and ruin us. Who are intent on getting rich while bleeding the State. Not men who retreat from battles laden with spoils. And, Gonçalo, tell Dom Pedro that the more remote the colony, the more trustworthy and honest the men appointed must be. Convince him that anyone entrusted to govern four thousand leagues away from Portugal, and whose administration can only be investigated every three years, must be a zealous man who respects truth, justice and religion!"

Gonçalo listened patiently. Tension made the veins stand out on the old priest's neck. He fidgeted with his gloves. Then, with some effort he sat up on his pallet.

"In Brazil, Angola and Goa," he continued, "in Malacca and

Macao, where the Prince is known and obeyed only in name, men of experience and proven loyalty are desperately needed. Explain this to His Royal Highness, Gonçalo. If high-ranking officers neglect their duties in Lisbon where the Prince is visible and heard, what is one to expect of these far flung regions where the Prince, and even God, seem all too remote?"

José Soares looked apprehensive. Vieira was losing his temper, his hair tousled, beads of perspiration covering his forehead.

"How did Habakkuk reach Babylon? An angel lifted him by the hair and carried him by force. So let men come from Portugal to govern the colonies, but let angels lift them by the hair and bring them by force. Angels who will guide, enlighten and protect them. For imagine what will happen if, instead of being brought by force, they come for their own selfish ends . . . and are prepared to cheat and bribe until they succeed? And suppose they're dragged here not by an angel but by the twin demons of ambition and greed? And if these two infernal spirits drag them everywhere, surely they will eventually drag them into hell?"

As he spoke, Vieira became transformed. He was no longer an old man prone to fits and weakened by the lingering effects of malaria, bronchial infections and attacks of coughing. It was feared he might be suffering from tuberculosis, a common disease in the Jesuit Order and caused by polluted drinking water and insanitary latrines.

"Why all this greed and corruption? What are the causes, the motives?" Vieira shouted. "There is nothing in this world, Gonçalo, that drags a man to hell for no good reason. The whys and wherefores blind, deceive and destroy the greatest of men."

"Surely, it's the money, uncle."

"I don't deny the power of money. But I'm less worried by what is stolen than by what is not stolen. There are many Crown officials in this realm who have never allowed themselves to be corrupted by money. But they allow themselves to be corrupted by friendship and patronage, and though these have nothing to do with gold or silver, they are the real cause of injustice in this world. Seeking favours is more insidious than pursuing wealth, and is also more advantageous. Favours granted as a token of esteem go unnoticed; they're neither flaunted, paraded, nor jingled in one's pocket. Should you ever decide to barter your soul or your friends, let it be for money rather than favours."

"I shall never barter either," Gonçalo replied.

Vieira beckoned José Soares, then placed a scapular round his nephew's neck.

"This will protect you, Gonçalo. I want Luiz Bonicho to deliver some letters because the mail bags are being searched. I've written a letter to Roque da Costa Barreto, another to the Duque de Cadaval, and two more: to the Marquês de Gouveia and Diogo Marchão Temudo. You will plead our cause to Dom Pedro, but I'm more confident that these letters will win us support. If any harm should befall the councillor, you must take charge of them. If anything should befall you . . ."

"I won't go alone. Barros de França, one of Bahia's first noblemen, has been dismissed as councillor and he'll travel with me. Diogo de Souza and José Sanches del Poços have been removed from their posts as captains of the garrison by the insatiable Menezes faction, and will accompany me too."

"God bless you," said Vieira, making the sign of the cross. Then Soares assisted him back to bed.

Gonçalo departed.

Luiz Bonicho was wearing a Jesuit habit.

Donato Serotino was dressed in a jacket trimmed with lace.

They made sure they had not forgotten anything, checked their trunks and documents carefully. Padre Vieira's letters were stored in one of the trunks. The luggage was then taken away to be loaded on board. The fleet was due to set sail in an hour's time; but Bonicho and Serotino would only embark at the last minute.

Two armed men guarded the door and a third was posted at the docks.

"Paris. I can scarcely believe it," said Bonicho.

"Time to go," said Donato. "Our man at the docks has just reported. Our ship is ready to sail."

Bonicho and Serotino left, accompanied by the armed men. They were carrying a small chest containing their jewels and money.

They had taken the coastal road and were approaching the docks when two mounted guards halted in front of a shed where a blacksmith was vigorously striking his anvil. The rhythmical banging echoed through the air. Sparks flew everywhere lighting up the horsemen.

The guards, armed with pistols and swords, dismounted. It was the Bull and his adjutant.

Bonicho spotted them first and looked at Donato. The soldiers were scrutinizing every passer-by and all those embarking. They appeared nervous and alert; even at a distance you could see their sweating red faces. More soldiers were posted at the gangway, checking the passengers' papers.

Bonicho went pale.

On recognizing the councillor, the two men on horseback eyed each other. They exchanged words and galloped towards them.

Bonicho whispered into Serotino's ear. Clasping their swords, the fencing master and his men formed a barrier around Bonicho. Unsuspecting pedestrians pushed past them.

The Governor's men stopped and watched the men trying to protect the fugitive. The Bull looked to both sides, then behind him.

"They're about to charge into us," Bonicho warned.

"There are five of us and two of them," replied Donato.

The Bull seemed hesitant, and looked again to left and right. Suddenly soldiers appeared on both sides of the street. They jumped from their horses and advanced on Bonicho and Serotino.

"'We're four and a half, and they were two. Now they have ten. Two sad hyenas, a ravenous pack of hounds. What shall we do?''

"We'll lure them into a side-street while you run to the ship," said Serotino.

"Good idea," said Bonicho. "Speed isn't exactly my strong point, but I'll try. Damn this heavy chest. I'll meet you on the flagship or in Paris."

Serotino and the slaves headed for the nearest alleyway. The Bull ordered several soldiers to chase them on horseback.

Bonicho ran as fast as he could to the ship. He saw the Bull running behind him, aiming a pistol. He could have shot me by now if he'd wanted to, Bonicho thought. Obviously the Bull meant to take him alive. Why?

Concerned pedestrians darted into nearby workshops. Eyes peeped through cracks and chinks at every door and window. The blacksmith's anvil had stopped striking.

Bonicho was now alone with the Bull on the waterfront in full view of a ship crammed with startled passengers.

"Come with me," the Bull ordered, pointing his weapon.

They entered a squalid alleyway.

Bonicho surrendered the chest.

"You might as well have this. It weighs more than a miserable corpse without any value. It holds the greatest fortune that you have ever seen or touched."

The Bull smirked.

"I know what you're thinking," Bonicho said.

"A treasure-chest and a corpse are worth more than a treasure-chest and no corpse."

"Keep going, wretch," threatened the Bull.

"Where are you taking me, Bull? To the palace? In that case I can go alone. I know the way. Is the Governor expecting me for tea?"

"Shut your trap, you filthy sodomite. I don't find you funny and if I did start laughing, my finger might slip and, boom . . . I'll fire at anyone who gets in my way."

For the first time in his life Bonicho chose to keep quiet.

"Get in," ordered the Bull, pointing to the charred door of a burned-out house. Only the façade remained standing.

There was nothing inside but weeds and rubble.

The Captain bolted the door.

"Move," he ordered.

Bonicho trampled through the undergrowth.

"Suppose there are snakes in here?"

"There are," the Bull replied.

"Two," retorted Bonicho. "You and I. You're the snake that swallowed the rhinoceros."

The Bull gave Bonicho a hard shove and turned him round so that they were face to face. He pushed him up against the blackened wall.

"Keep quiet and don't move." He took a few paces, untied his breeches and began pissing.

His urine splashed on to Bonicho's habit and gave off a bitter smell. Bits of twisted iron, splinters of wood, discarded shoes, and yellowed papers lay scattered on the ground.

"Put that loot down," said the Bull, still pissing. Bonicho put the chest on the ground.

The Bull laced up his breeches. A round, damp stain appeared on the crotch. He told Bonicho to raise his arms. He then began searching him. "Ugh," he exclaimed. "Fancy having to soil my hands touching this ugly, hunchbacked ape."

"The hazards of your profession," said Bonicho. "Did you know Silenus was a hunchback?"

"You don't say."

"The Phrygian sprite of fountains and rivers, father of the satyrs. Hunchbacked and tenebrous. Scaramuccio, too, that splendid harlequin of the Italian theatre in Paris. Piero della Francesca had a nose that curved like a staircase. Louise de la Vallière was crippled but she danced divinely and stole King Louis XIV from the Duchess of Orleans. You're as repulsive as Satan, with that paunch and those bandy legs, yet you've just landed yourself a fortune. You can say goodbye to all the bullying from your master, that bastard Braço de Prata, eh?"

The Bull looked puzzled.

"Would you like to borrow a handkerchief to wave farewell to misery?" Bonicho asked.

"Shut your mouth! Turn around, scum!"

"You're not going to shoot a poor hunchback in the back?"

The Bull didn't answer.

Bonicho faced the wall.

"Put your hands up."

He obeyed.

The Bull crouched down to open the chest. It was locked. He shot the catch. He opened the lid under the watchful eye of Bonicho, who had turned his head. The captain stuffed his pockets with jewels and money.

"Turn your face to the wall," growled the Bull. "There's something missing here. Where is it?"

"Back on the ship. Wait here while I go and get it for you."

"Enough of your sarcasm." The Bull got up and pushed his pistol into Bonicho's face. "Do you want me to blast a bit off your snout?"

"That might be an improvement. What do you think?"

"Where are the papers?"

"What papers? The ones with the printers, in the library, in the Judiciary?"

"You know which ones I'm after."

"State papers? Newspapers? Paper money? Note-paper? Crepe-paper? Blotting-paper? *Papier mâché? Papenbroek?*"

The Bull struck Bonicho on the mouth with the butt of his pistol. A trickle of blood appeared and his lip began to swell and turn purple. He spat out blood and several broken teeth.

"Pope, Papist, Parrot, Pomegranate, Pimp, Parasite, Palsy and Pox to you."

He received another blow, this time in the stomach.

"I want Vieira's letters, you filthy bastard." The captain gave him a hard kick. "Speak up or else!"

"I don't know of any letters."

Bonicho took two more punches and slumped to the ground.

"Coward," he moaned.

"Speak up, you miserable wretch."

"I don't know of any letters."

There was a loud knock. The Bull went to one of the front windows, pushed it open and looked out on to the street. He opened the door and in walked Captain-General Teles. This was it, Bonicho thought. His heart froze.

"Well done, Bull, well done. A bird in the hand is worth two in the bush," said Teles. "The fencing master is dead. Stretched out on the road. He tried to resist arrest. Has the hunchback got the papers?"

"I've found nothing, sir."

Teles drew his sword.

"Hold out your right hand, Bonicho."

"What for?"

"Have you forgotten that morning? There were eight of you.

Eight cowards. Hold it out Bonicho. The same one you chopped off my brother Francisco."

"No! No! I didn't chop off anybody's hand," shrieked Bonicho.

The Bull overpowered him, forcing his arm down on to a boulder.

"Wait, wait, this is a . . ."

With his great paw, the Bull covered Bonicho's mouth.

The Captain-General raised his sword above his head with both hands. He held it there for an instant, aiming at the alderman's thin wrist, drained of blood.

"Reminds me of a bare twig," thought Teles.

Bonicho's screams were muffled by the Bull's fist. He struggled, trying to break free.

The sword came whistling down, cleaving bones and stone. Bonicho's hand rolled to the ground. He fainted within seconds.

"Finish him off," said Teles.

He then left, without looking back.

# XI

"ELEVEN O'CLOCK," whispered the staff-officer to the major-domo. Responding to the Governor's nod, he opened the door and invited the Archbishop, João da Madre de Deus, to enter.

"I'm grateful to you, Antonio, for seeing me without delay," said the Archbishop.

"Be seated, Your Grace," said the Governor, after kissing the prelate's outstretched hand.

They faced each other. Antonio de Souza studied his visitor. Over his cassock the prelate was wearing a purple cloak with lace cuffs and collar.

"Despite the official mourning," said De Souza, "there's been so much to do that I have had scarcely any time to myself."

"May the Captain-General's soul rest in peace. And how are legal proceedings coming along?"

"Legal proceedings, Your Grace?"

"Yes, legal proceedings. That's what I've come to discuss with you. Most of the clergy in Portugal and Rome are critical of you and their displeasure is justified, for despite any minor differences between one religious order and another, we're all members of God's Church. The Pope is certain to hear of the persecution being waged against Antonio Vieira. This matter will cause grave concern to Innocent XI, not to mention the Grand Duke of Tuscany and Cardinal d'Este. So, on behalf of the Church and the Holy Father, and as the Pope's representative, I beseech you, De Souza, to put an end to this conflict. Forget the past and withdraw your accusations against Vieira. He's an old man. None of us believes he was guilty of this crime, even while acknowledging his active interest in secular affairs such as diplomacy, patriotism and military strategy."

"Even conceding that he denounces the ill-gotten wealth of the aristocracy," the Governor interjected. "Even if we know he uses the pulpit to spread propaganda, preaches tolerance towards the Jews as a means of restoring Portugal's fortunes, advocates freedom of conscience for the Jews and the abolition of the Holy Inquisition. Even if we know he has harshly criticized the Dominicans in his defence of the Nheengaiba tribes and the Jesuit missions. Even if we know he was expelled from Maranhão for his opposition to slavery, for having concocted his own theory about race, and pointed out the limitations of divine omnipotence. Even if he has shown greater concern about comets, theories about the vacuum, mothers-in-law, and wars than about Christian souls and their religious obligations. Even if he has been suspected of having written anonymous pamphlets against the Holy Inquisition. And so on. And with so many 'even ifs', is it not just possible that he was involved in committing this crime? After all, he has been involved in warfare in the past. A thorough investigation will be carried out. For the moment, everyone is under suspicion. If the Jesuit is innocent, he'll have the opportunity to prove it. After all, isn't he renowned for his eloquence at the pulpit?"

"I'd like you to consider this as a plea not only from me, but from the entire Church. You will be rewarded if you show more tolerance. Invisible rewards, of course. Spiritual. I'd also like to mention that our treasurer, Gregório de Matos, has told me certain things which, if true, bode evil times ahead in the realm. I hope you can reassure me he's exaggerating. The Judge tells me he's being persecuted. For what reason?"

"Gregório de Matos? No one is persecuting him!"

"Yet he's in hiding because he's afraid he'll be arrrested."

"Arrested! By me? There must be some mistake, Your Grace. Doctor de Matos is clearly exploiting the present situation to shirk his obligations. A disciplined life isn't to his liking. The fellow is a scandalmonger. He spends his time spreading lies."

"Not all of his time, Dom Antonio. He's composed some fine verses in my honour."

"That's his cunning little game. He composes flowery poems

of tribute, then pleads for favours, nearly always in the form of money. He panders to archbishops, infantes, kings, almoners, magistrates and judges. And when he doesn't achieve his objective, he wags that biting tongue of his. He protests his contempt for hierarchies, but continues to grovel and pay them homage. Your Grace, beware of flattering words from false poets. And what he writes about the men of the Church is not merely wordplay. His verse is overpowering, designed to destroy everyone."

"That's nothing new. Countless poets have written diatribes about the clergy."

"True, but with a certain decorum you won't find coming from Mouth of Hell. A suitable nickname for Bahia's Gregório de Matos, don't you think? Your Grace, this country is full of perils. You haven't been here very long, so be careful about the people you consort with."

"Good heavens, De Souza, I'm not a politician, nor am I aware of having enemies. Nobody would have anything to gain by harming me."

"In Bahia everyone's a potential enemy. Anyone in high office is considered a person of privilege and influence. Another reason why Gregório de Matos should be kept at bay. He's ambitious, anxious to further his career in the Church, and he'd stoop to anything in order to become a bishop or archbishop. That's the only reason why he stays in the Church. Surely you don't believe he has a genuine vocation? A man with his . . . how can I put it? . . . depraved nature."

"Depraved? Ambitious?"

"Much worse, Your Grace. When he's not conspiring, our poet is getting drunk and brawling in taverns."

"Gregório de Matos is not the only one who creates such problems in the diocese. If we were to banish all sinners, we'd be left without a single priest in nearly every parish; there would be no treasurers, deans or missionaries. In truth, I don't know what is to become of the Church. And the problem, dear Antonio, isn't only in Bahia. Men no longer join the priesthood because they truly feel they have a religious vocation. Nowadays, especially here in the colony, we have to make do with men who are anything but virtuous. Our main concern is to ensure that those of us who lead good lives should try to avoid those who sin and offend God. Gregório de Matos vigorously upholds our interests and he has never been defeated in any public debate. Besides, he doesn't wear a religious habit, so he isn't likely to compromise us with his childish behaviour."

"Childish? The day adolescents and children start to behave like him, we can expect the Apocalypse. It's common knowledge that he works for the diocese."

"I agree, it isn't all in the wearing of a habit," said the Archbishop.

"And Gregório de Matos forgets his unfortunate frolics with whores. If Your Grace were to suspend him from his ecclesiastical functions, you would assist His Royal Highness, the Prince Regent, in his efforts to regenerate the Church. The name of João da Madre de Deus will resound like the pealing of bells throughout the land. For there is nothing that would give His Royal Highness and the Supreme Pontiff more satisfaction than to see the Church spiritually reborn."

The Archbishop considered De Souza's words. "My predecessor, Dom Gaspar Barata, God rest his soul, was favourably disposed towards Doctor de Matos," he said. "And Padre Vieira holds him in high esteem."

"They're all tarred with the same brush, Your Grace. We mustn't be ingenuous. After all, whose side is Vieira on?"

"On God's side, Dom Antonio."

"My dear Archbishop, we're not living in a fairy tale. You'll soon discover for yourself that the poet and his accomplices are not to be trusted."

"Your weapon is daring," said the prelate. "Mine is compassion."

The Archbishop's palanquin proceeded up the steep slopes of the city. The slaves toiled and sweated, their faces strained.

Pedestrians removed their hats and knelt, only to find that their knees were covered in mud when they got up again.

In former times, when the nobility were remote from the people, it was left to the Archbishop to summon provincial councils, to elect and consecrate the suffragan bishops, from whom

they received an oath of obedience: they supervised the administration of their dioceses, replaced them in the event of absence or
negligence; made the necessary arrangements to fill any vacancies
when deemed appropriate.

Popes had elevated and deposed kings. And just as popes held
greater power than monarchs, bishops were more important than
governors.

After Pope Julius III established a bishopric in Bahia with the
Bull *Specula Militantis Ecclesia,* bishops were expected to address
the governors as Your Lordship; they in turn were addressed as
Your Excellency. The Governor treated the Archbishop just as he
would any other member of the nobility. Those were happier
times. The cape, the pectoral cross and the coat of arms with
three tassels on either side of the prelate's hat had become mere
ornaments. The Judiciary and Municipal Council, acting on behalf
of the Prince, had done everything possible to limit the Church's
powers.

The world was different; men of stature had gradually disappeared. And the Archbishop now found himself on remote
slopes, covered in filth and squalor, moving among the most vile
people, mestizos, ruffians, Jews, and riff-raff, and being drawn
into quarrels which were as petty as they were meaningless. He
had ended up in this hell, which had nothing to do with streets or
houses, or even nature. This was the hell of men.

After descending another slope, the palanquin halted in front of
a dilapidated warehouse. Plaster peeling from its walls. Worm-
eaten shutters. All of it cold and depressing. This was where Gregório was hiding.

He sent one of the slaves to knock on the door. It was eleven
in the morning.

Gregório opened the spy-hole. His face looked crumpled as if
he had been asleep.

"Your Grace!" exclaimed the poet. He ran his fingers through
his hair and tucked his shirt into his trousers.

"I'd like to have a word with you, Judge."

Gregório opened the door. Inside were plants in stoppered glass
jars imported from Holland. In the light they appeared like a dense
woodland. The jars of ingredients were lined up in sequence, from

left to right, ready to be transformed into herbal remedies and essences. The odour was overpowering. The living-quarters were in the central part of the warehouse: two large rooms separated by a patio with a Moorish fountain, and a kitchen with an open fire. A neglected garden lay at the back. Withered twigs were a reminder of the days when it had been full of flowers and shrubs.

Gregório fetched two stools from the kitchen and they sat in the room facing the patio.

"I'm afraid it's rather Spartan," he apologized.

"Austerity is less offensive than ostentation. We mustn't forget the words of the Son of God when he warned us that *It is easier for a camel to go through the eye of a needle . . .*"

"*Than for a rich man to enter into the Kingdom of God,*" Gregório finished.

"It's the Kingdom of God I've come to discuss," said the Archbishop. "Today, you must decide your future. I've been informed of your misconduct which is scarcely edifying in someone who serves the Church. People have complained of your refusal to wear a religious habit, expressed their concern at the places you frequent and people you associate with. Giving a bad example won't improve your reputation. *A man is known by the company . . .*" he paused. Gregório lowered his eyes and made no attempt to complete the proverb.

"In the diocese they tell me you only turn up to receive your salary, while neglecting to carry out your duties; that papers and documents lie piled up on your desk. What is happening, Gregório?"

"Your Grace, I have no excuses for my behaviour other than my weak nature. But the difficulties created by Braço de Prata have made matters much worse, as I've already explained. I daren't walk the streets unless accompanied by friends who know how to use a sword and keep their weapons at the ready. My life is at risk. Braço de Prata has me followed by his thugs. The new Captain-General is eager for blood. How can I perform my work under those conditions? I am trapped in this hole, running for my life every time I see a soldier in the street. Whenever I close my eyes, I'm in danger of waking up in my grave."

"If you were to take holy orders, as I've frequently suggested, you would be entitled to certain immunities. No one would be able to lay a finger on you."

The poet remained silent.

"You would prosper," the Archbishop continued.

"Since when has prosperity enriched a poet's soul?"

"Spirituality and poetry go hand in hand. In a monastic cell you would find the right atmosphere in which to compose verses equal to those of your admirable Góngora."

"But, Your Grace, if all I ever write about – or care to write about – are homosexuals, pederasts, vagrants, perverts and thieves . . ."

"You can write about whomsoever you choose. But in a spiritual manner, extolling their virtues instead of their vices."

"Poetry finds its inspiration in human weakness."

"Who taught you such nonsense, Gregório? Some of the greatest poets of all time were deeply religious: Cynewulf, Einhard, Eckhart, Peter Damian, Andreas Capellanus, St Francis of Assisi, St Thomas Aquinas, Bishop Thomas Simonsson . . . even I find time to write sonnets despite my poor eyesight."

"To be a bad layman is not nearly as reprehensible as being a bad priest. I cannot pledge to God what weak nature makes me incapable of fulfilling."

"My son, only by taking holy orders can you hope to remain in office."

"I'd prefer to lose all the wealth and honours of this world," replied Gregório, "than resort to lies."

"Is that your final word?" said the Archbishop.

"Yes, Your Grace."

Gregório stood in a large tub, throwing water over his head. Without clothes, he looked even thinner.

"Ah," he muttered to himself, "I must find myself a woman to wash me, to prepare my food, make preserves, cheese, liqueur . . . to fetch and carry my correspondence."

He dried himself and lay down, still undressed, on top of the mats which served as a bed. The floor was covered with blobs of candle grease.

He was still thinking about the Archbishop's words.

He heard a knock at the door. He went down wrapped in a towel.

He opened the door and found himself face to face with Anica. She glanced anxiously around.

"What's wrong?"

Breathlessly Anica told him about Donato Serotino's death and Luiz Bonicho's attempt to escape.

"They cut off Bonicho's right hand. He fainted and that thug, the Bull, who was about to kill him, went off to find a pouch for the councillor's jewels, and when he returned, Bonicho had regained consciousness and shot him dead. Then Bonicho fled to the docks where he found a boat to ferry him out to the flagship. His bleeding wrist was bandaged with a handkerchief. If there's a surgeon on board, and he's not the usual drunkard, Bonicho's life might be saved."

"And Gonçalo Ravasco? Did he manage to get away?"

"Yes. While they were chasing the councillor and the Italian, Gonçalo slipped aboard the flagship. You must be next on their list."

Gregório went to the kitchen and prepared a bowl of milk. He wasn't much good in the kitchen and had great difficulty lighting the fire. Anica went to his assistance. Gregório drank the warm milk in sips, savouring every drop.

"Can you cook?" he asked.

"No."

The milk left a ring round Gregório's mouth.

"Didn't you hear what I said? You'll be next. The wives and sisters of the De Brito brothers are still in prison, as is Dona Bernardina. And that girl you're infatuated with, Maria Berco, is to be hanged for stealing the ring. The whore is nothing but a common thief. The Ravascos are being rounded up. Those who haven't escaped are already under arrest."

Gregório said nothing, busying himself in the kitchen.

"Why don't we leave together for Portugal like Bonicho and Gonçalo Ravasco?" asked Anica.

"I haven't got the money. I'm the latest vagrant to roam this city. The Archbishop has just been to see me."

"I thought so. Can't your family give you money to escape?"

Reminiscing about his family, Gregório, with Anica close on his heels, went back into the room. They originated from the wine-growing region of Vila de Guimarães in Northern Portugal, colonizers who had helped to enrich Brazil. They had purchased the hoist which transported merchandise between the upper and lower parts of the city, cattle ranches in the interior, vast sugar plantations and the mill at Sergipe do Conde, which had once belonged to the Governor-General Mem de Sá. They owned almost one hundred and thirty slaves. His father, who owned a sugar plantation at Patatiba in Recôncavo, had been an alderman and inspector of weights and taxes on foodstuffs. His brother Eusébio was famous for his sermons and the size of his prick which, as the poet was wont to comment, had serviced many a nun, whore and virgin. His other brother Pedro, a sugar planter, worked day and night cultivating their father's lands, and had the same reputation as his brothers when it came to women.

His grandfather used to take him for walks around the barracks, show him the fountains and squares he was building, share the secrets of his trade, drawing up plans and working out measurements, perhaps in the hope that the boy would follow in his footsteps one day. But Gregório only had eyes for the girls whom he chased at every opportunity. He eventually married a woman whose family was influential in legal circles. She was nineteen with "a nose the colour of buttermilk and lips as red as the earthenware from Estremoz". She had never attached much importance to her husband's poems. When she married Gregório, Dona Michaela had no idea what married life with the poet would be like. He squandered most of his time – and money – in the brothels, where the prostitutes adored him, in the bedchambers of virgins, in the convents where pretty nuns offered him every consolation. He loved all women: young and old, serving-maids and duchesses, white, mulatto, or Jewish. At the same time he showed a certain contempt for men of mixed blood or of Jewish descent – loose women on the Rua Nova who were easy prey for Franciscan friars, peasant girls in hoods, low women, vagrants and gypsies from the countryside around Coimbra. Dona Michaela spent her nights waiting for him to come home. Women who married poets had no right to expect a conventional husband like any other.

Husbands were husbands. Poets were poets. No wife would succeed in changing Gregório de Matos's nature. He was being devoured by some hidden monster, being swallowed up in the chaotic city, caught between his fertile imagination and his embittered soul. The pleasures of the underworld earned him the nickname: Mouth of Hell. But Gregório was not the Mouth of Hell. It was the city of Bahia. It was the colony.

He had been given his share of his father's property two or three years previously while in Portugal. But he had squandered almost everything. He did not have the courage to ask for any more help from his family. Nor did he have the courage to escape.

"If I must die, let it be here. And I pray to God that I'll die inside a wench rather than being riddled by gunfire."

Back in the palace, Captain-General Teles raised the glass of wine the Governor had just served him and proposed a toast:

"Victory at last, Antonio," he stated in an even voice.

"Victory?"

"The alderman has escaped, unless he's died on board the flagship after losing his hand. Donato Serotino's out of the way. Gregório de Matos no longer has any immunities or official functions. Vieira's worn out. Bernardo Ravasco's locked up. They're the real culprits. The Ravasco faction has lost its ringleader. They're finished."

"Finished? Then where are Vieira's letters? Where are Bernardo Ravasco's writings? What will happen when Rocha Pita arrives? Bonicho might still reach Lisbon, minus his right hand, but furnished with a list of complaints and incriminating evidence against us. Gonçalo Ravasco has escaped along with the noble alderman and the captains of the garrison. The executions you've ordered won't do us much good. A mad blasphemer, a harmless notary, a stupid fencing master, an innocent woman and a few slaves. While we've lost poor old Bull, who did an excellent job as captain of the garrison. I don't know what I was thinking of when I agreed to allow you to do things your way. You've made nothing but blunders. From now on, I'm in charge here."

"You're mistaken, Antonio. *Finis coronat opus*," said Teles.

# *Judicial Inquiry*

THE CODE GOVERNING legal procedures in the colony, like that of Portugal, was based on the *Leis extravagantes* of Canon Law and the *Ordinances* ratified by Afonso V and Manuel I. These were incorporated into the *Philippine Ordinances* because they were promulgated during the reign of Filipe the First of Portugal – and Third of Spain.

In Brazil, jurists, magistrates, attorneys, procurators, lawyers, judges and arbiters worked in a backward and depressing environment. They were saddled with an incomprehensible mishmash of rudimentary principles of Roman, barbarian and canonical origin. The law fluctuated between norms of social behaviour and the definition of sin.

The Court of Appeals conducted its affairs in an impressive building. From the windows, one could see litters and palanquins pass amidst the crowds and pack-animals. Inside, the walls were dingy and in need of repair, the floors were pitted and worn and covered with debris. The waiting-rooms and audience chamber were situated on the ground floor. The conference room with its Great Table and the judges' rooms were located on the somewhat tidier first floor. Legal documents were on the second floor, piled high and covered in dust; cobwebs with trapped insects swayed from every corner in the cool breeze.

When he was not out conducting investigations, this was where Rocha Pita could be found, working at his desk. He worked extremely hard.

# I

FROM HIS CARRIAGE WINDOW Antonio de Souza watched
people milling around the vast square which opened onto
the port. Crates were piled up everywhere: huge consignments
of coarse and fine cloves, sarsaparilla, balsam, crates of sugar,
cotton yarn, anatto for making dye, turtle shells, and hides.

"Rocha Pita should be here soon," said De Souza. Wringing his
hands, Mata hovered at his side. "He's going to make us work,
Mata. He'll be much more troublesome than the others. But we'll
manage. The Ravascos are mistaken if they think Rocha Pita can
help them. As for the Chancellor," the Governor continued seemingly to himself, "his powers are no greater than mine and I can
always allege that he, too, was involved in the assassination of
Teles de Menezes. It was that Rabbi who persuaded the Chancellor
to heed Palma's suspicions. But if the Rabbi thinks he can also
win over Rocha Pita, he'll find he's too late. We'll get him first;
he's certain to have a weak spot. Show me a man who has none.
Rocha Pita thinks he's all-powerful. Certain people will try to set
him against me. One false move and I could lose everything. We'll
have to take precautions. When the Crown Judge was our ally,
things were different. We had a mutual understanding, to protect
each other's interests. Any power judges hold over the governor
is diminished by the governor's right to control and supervise the
affairs of the Tribunal. As Governor, I'm entitled to admonish
them. But I refrain. There's no tension between the two organs
of government. But with Rocha Pita the situation is different. I
don't believe he'll be easily influenced. We must be careful."

"Perhaps he's ambitious? Or has a weakness for the ladies?"
suggested Mata.

"Rocha Pita is as morose and stubborn as a mule. The man has never been married, ignores his relatives, possesses no property. He lives on his salary and is considered honest. He shows no interest in money or drink, feasting or gambling. I knew someone just like him. A sworn enemy whose integrity seemed beyond question until I discovered his weakness for women with blonde hair. The fairer they were, the more he liked them. Especially if they were Polish."

"I see," was all Mata could say.

"Has Teles suspended those abitrary sentences?"

"Yes, my Lord."

"I want no further action for a day or two."

"Should we release Bernardo Ravasco?"

"Let's wait. We might be surprised."

A boat rowed by scruffy-looking sailors drew alongside the quay. Two men dressed in black disembarked. The one in front was tall and stocky. He wore an expression of disdain.

"Is that Rocha Pita?" asked Mata.

"That's him."

"He's terrifying. Look at the size of those hands. And those feet. You wouldn't think he'd just sailed upriver, he looks so fresh and relaxed. Such energy! But he doesn't strike me as being very clever."

"The big fellow isn't Rocha Pita. He's the other one."

Behind the tall man, who was the bailiff, followed a smaller one, hunched and frail, his hair dishevelled. He was wearing an enormous white ruff which concealed his neck and part of his jaws and chin. In one hand he carried a horn ear-trumpet, which he put to his ear whenever anyone addressed him.

"Is the Judge deaf?"

Antonio de Souza did not answer.

The din of the soldiers' drums filled the square. Judge Rocha Pita, the son of a lawyer, forty-six years of age, with fifteen years of service to the Crown, five in the Court of Appeals, was unsteady on his feet and kept on tripping. Under one arm, he carried a book that looked larger than he was. It was continually slipping toward the ground.

Rocha Pita's eyes wandered without taking much in. He looked up and down, right and left, and appeared to be completely distraught. Now and then, he would put the trumpet to his ear with the open end pointing nowhere in particular. And onlookers, quick to notice the stranger's odd behaviour, commented and joked amongst themselves.

The bailiff, dressed in a long, dark tunic with gold buttons and apparently indifferent to ridicule, untied a scroll. The soldiers stopped beating their drums.

"By royal decree," the bailiff read out, "the Chancellor has ordered that a full judicial inquiry be carried out here in the Captaincy of Bahia, to investigate the circumstances of Francisco de Teles de Menezes' assassination and to bring the guilty parties to justice."

Complete silence fell over the crowd. In ringing tones, the bailiff read out the Chancellor's statement, which provoked as much fear as curiosity.

"Complying with this order," the bailiff continued, "the Crown Judge, João da Rocha Pita, wishes to inform the public that he will question reliable witnesses in private, treat their statements as confidential and examine all the affidavits submitted in order to ascertain the facts of the case."

Anyone in possession of any proof or evidence would be obliged to come forward or incur severe penalties. No one would be forced to testify in court, but should anyone wish to make a statement, he or she would be under oath to speak the truth, or face the consequences.

Rocha Pita appeared oblivious. From time to time he would glance at someone in the crowd, then quickly avert his gaze and stare at someone else. He sighed, shaking his head, almost as if he were talking to himself. Several bystanders moved away, convinced that the Crown Judge was a madman.

Others jibed that a deaf judge was a clear sign that the Court of Appeals had no intention of listening to any criticism of the Governor, and that Rocha Pita had been chosen to make a mockery of the Ravascos. The Prince's hostility towards Padre Vieira was common knowledge. To have sent this particular judge was further proof of His Majesty's contempt for the Jesuit. It could not have been more obvious.

Rocha Pita sat at the desk in his room at the Court of Appeals. He spread his hands out on the wooden surface and breathed deeply.

"This inquiry," he said to Manuel do Porto, the bailiff, "isn't a matter of justice. Perhaps the stronger man will win and not the one who's innocent. We can't waste time."


Judge Manuel da Costa Palma was the first to testify. He arrived in his long, black robes, his neck was bare and red, his expression sinister.

"The witness has arrived," announced the bailiff.

"Although he's better qualified than most," observed Rocha Pita, "our witness is no more interested in spiritual matters than his fellow judges and magistrates."

Manuel do Porto smiled.

Rocha Pita motioned him to show the Judge in. No sooner had the bailiff gone out than Rocha Pita heard the footsteps of two men in the corridor.

Palma entered, followed by the bailiff, who asked him to be seated.

Judges in the colony presided over the election of magistrates, the registration of births and adoptions, bequests and inheritances; they dealt with benefices and concessions, arbitrated in matters concerning legitimacy and libel damages, and checked all legal procedures and formalities. They were all too familiar with the vagaries of the law and the need to enforce it – just or otherwise – and they were more than mere observers in the commercial and political affairs of the colony.

Once seated, Palma waited for Rocha Pita to speak.

"You've come here willingly, Judge?" began Rocha Pita, his voice tremulous.

"Yes," replied Palma, tapping his fingers on the desk. Rocha Pita continued to take notes without once looking at Palma. He always made a point of jotting down his own impressions of statements. He was left-handed. Using his right hand, he held the trumpet to his ear and pointed it at the witness. Palma could not help being reminded of the jokes he'd heard about the deaf Crown Judge.

"There's nothing wrong with my eyes," said Rocha Pita, as if guessing Palma's thoughts. "Words can be so deceptive." As he spoke, the Crown Judge waved his quill like a schoolmaster. Then he leaned over his book and wrote in a minute, painstaking hand, periodically dipping his quill into the inkwell without spilling a drop. He wore a disconcerting smile.

Rocha Pita had prepared a list of questions. Establishing the ties between Antonio de Souza and Manuel de Palma and the Governor and the Tribunal was essential to the inquiry. It was not simply a case of solving a crime, but of knowing to what extent the plaintiffs were politically involved in the affair, and whether those under suspicion were being persecuted. The Crown Inspector took a long, hard look at his fellow judge.

"Did the Governor attempt to persuade you," asked Rocha Pita, "that witnesses for Antonio Vieira shouldn't be allowed to appear before the Tribunal?"

"Certainly not," snapped Manuel de Palma.

"Did the Governor become involved in these proceedings with a special interest in the outcome?"

"No."

Rocha Pita went on writing.

"Surely the Governor must have been an interested party since the victim was none other than his own Captain-General?"

Palma appeared to waver. Then replied: "No."

"Who is the interested party then?" he asked, poking the tip of the trumpet even more vigorously into his ear.

"It's a question of justice. Criminals must be punished. Not as an act of revenge, but as an example to the people."

"An example to the people . . . I see . . ."

He leaned forward and wrote more. He looked again at the Judge. Palma's forehead was covered in perspiration. He was wringing his hands. The outline of a pistol was visible under his robes.

"Palma, are you in the habit of going around armed?"

"It's common knowledge that everyone goes around armed in the colony because of violence."

"Not everyone, Palma. Many judges have their personal guards. Isn't that so?"

"Yes."

"I didn't hear you," said Rocha Pita, bringing his ear-trumpet closer to Palma's face.

"Yes," shouted Palma.

Rocha Pita paused. He coughed. The bailiff brought him a glass of water. He took a sip. "How many?" he continued.

"How many what?" said Palma, trying not to appear nervous.

"How many personal guards?"

"A few. What does it matter?"

"Three?"

"Well . . . in some cases . . ."

"I see that you yourself have a fair number of personal guards. Eight? Ten?"

"They're not all mine. Some of them serve the Governor and they've escorted me here to ensure that I'm allowed to testify in safety."

"Is there some risk in testifying?"

"One makes many enemies here. The Ravascos have a great deal of power and influence."

"Do the Ravascos oppose you?"

"Well . . . so I'm led to believe . . ."

"And for what reason?"

"I don't know."

"You don't know?"

"No."

Rocha Pita looked puzzled. He shook his head, thought for a few moments and then went on.

"Do the Ravascos oppose the Governor?"

"I really don't know."

Clearly annoyed, the bailiff tapped his foot on the ground, and fidgeted in his chair, standing up and sitting down. Rocha Pita lost none of his composure. Patiently, and sounding almost benevolent, he asked Palma:

"Coming back to De Souza. Did the Governor-General assist the magistrates and other ministers with their inquiries or did he try to interfere?"

"He did not interfere."

The bailiff's foot tapped in the background.

"Did the Governor-General ever veto any sentence or insist that it be passed?"

"Never."

Rocha Pita paused. "These are somewhat unusual charges which have been brought against Padre Vieira. Everybody seems to fear him as if he were the Devil incarnate."

Palma affirmed that the Governor was the victim of an infamous and slanderous campaign instigated by Padre Vieira and his brother Bernardo Ravasco.

"They're harmless, my dear Palma. They have neither power nor money."

"But there's something else you ought to know," insisted Palma. "The Ravascos are in league with the Sephardim."

"You mean the Jews," said the Crown Judge.

Palma smiled. He then began to go through the names of all the influential Jews he knew, pronouncing each name slowly so that Rocha Pita could write them down.

Attired in crimson livery and pumps, the major-domo entered, followed by a footman carrying a tray of tea and cakes flavoured with lemon peel.

From his armchair, De Souza poured tea into one of the cups and selected a cake and then passed these to his valet who sampled them for poison. Then the Governor was served.

Once he had finished his tea, he moved to his desk. Using his good arm, he pushed aside the papers in front of him and ordered Mata to be seated.

"Now then?" asked De Souza.

"Apparently he's incorruptible. And well informed."

"Apparently?"

"Those were Judge Palma's very words. I've brought you the names of some of the people who have testified. The public treasurer, some merchants, several sugar planters, a number of Jews, artisans, even a prostitute. The Crown Judge is taking statements from people of every social class. Nearly all of them have testified in your favour."

"That could change everything."

"Who knows, my Lord? Ravasco's manservant, Strong Arm, has been arrested as you ordered."

"Good, that's one less busybody to worry about."

"They tell me he calls out all day long from his cell that the man who denounced him as a thief was none other than the man who gave him orders. That ten birds of prey sent him out to steal. That he was simply the middle-man in all their shady dealings."

"Have him gagged."

"I've one last piece of news: Padre Vieira has dispatched defence lawyers to the Tribunal."

"Do you think that's good or bad, Mata?"

Mata thought.

"I'm not sure, my Lord. The fox may change its coat, but it goes on devouring chickens."

## II

WHEN HE WAS SPEAKING to the bailiff, Rocha Pita did not use his ear trumpet. After working together for so many years, the Judge could read Manuel do Porto's thoughts and feelings simply by watching his eyes and reading his lips. Moreover, the bailiff had developed an unusually powerful voice through reading in public.

"What would you do if you were in my shoes?" asked Rocha Pita.

"I don't know, sir. Probably what most judges do. Close the proceedings. Release the prisoners. Pardon those accused of the crime."

"When I walk through the streets I can hear voices hurling abuse at the Governor from behind closed doors and windows."

"I've had much the same experience," agreed the bailiff. "People refuse to come forward."

"Hmm."

Manuel do Porto waited.

"Let things blow over and not get to the bottom of this affair? Certainly not! I shall pursue this inquiry for as long as it takes, even if it means knocking down walls to get at the truth. I must have a word with De Souza."

"With Braço de Prata?"

"Arrange an appointment for me, Manuel. In the meantime, I have another task for you."

The Governor-General smiled when he received Rocha Pita's request for an audience at the palace. He had predicted this. The Governor knew that ministers and others in power would close ranks and protect their peers.

"He's getting nowhere," said De Souza. "This is why he wants to see me."

It was raining, and Rocha Pita got drenched as he climbed the stairs to the palace. His wig was of inferior quality, his robes made of coarse material. His leather sandals, tied with cords, were like those of friars.

When working in the palace, the Governor, too, wore simple garments. Neither his buttons, sword nor inkstand were made of gold. On his desk he kept a few objects of polished metal but they were of no great value: bronze, copper, tin-plate. The paintings hanging on the walls had been acquired by his predecessors, and the furnishings were sparse and plain. The Governor's private study was not so very different from the others in the palace. Nor could it be compared with the sumptuous apartments of most merchants and traders.

Rocha Pita glanced around the room.

"Forgive me if I seem a little apprehensive," said De Souza. "Anything I might say could be used against me, isn't that right? You rarely pay me a visit and the only occasion we see each other is at a meeting or around the Great Table. How should I interpret your presence here today? Am I being honoured or censured?"

"Neither. I merely wish to clarify a few facts," Rocha Pita replied.

"What facts might those be?"

Rocha Pita was about to answer but changed his mind and smiled. He looked into De Souza's eyes. The two men remained motionless, staring at each other. De Souza knew that any hint of emotion in one's enemies could be interpreted as a sign of weakness. The Judge had lost none of his composure, and sat with one elbow on the table, holding the trumpet to his ear. For his part, the Governor felt in perfect control, both physically and mentally, part of the discipline he had acquired during military service. His training in the cavalry and at the helm of a ship had proved the best school for developing self-control. And for learning to control others.

"Despite the unusual nature of this case," said De Souza, "I'm delighted that someone of your integrity – as many influential

friends both here in the colony and in Lisbon would acknowledge
– should have been chosen by the Prince Regent to condemn the
wicked conspiracy instigated by the treacherous Ravascos, and I
know that I can rely on you to attest to the honesty of my conduct
in this whole affair. People love to gossip. And anyone in government soon finds himself exposed to malice and envy, slander and
effrontery, ridicule and abuse. Our enemies vent all the frustrations caused by their own ineptitude and ignorance on the government. They even slander the Prince himself."

As he said this, De Souza turned to the large portrait of Dom
João IV.

"I've commissioned a painter born in the colony, a most gifted
young man, to paint Dom Pedro's portrait. He's already in Portugal to start work on the commission. But, as you know, people
born here in the colony are unreliable, and our painter is taking
his time. I intend to turn one of the rooms into a portrait gallery
in memory of our past sovereigns, God rest their souls."

Rocha Pita knew what he was implying. The dead King had
bestowed favours on Padre Vieira. As a precaution, the portrait
of Dom Afonso had been withdrawn from the room. De Souza
was tactfully warning the Crown Judge that he might incur the
Prince's anger if he were to show any leniency towards the Ravasco faction.

"Well, what can I do for you?"

"I've been informed that the dead man's relatives, led by
Captain-General Teles, have persuaded you to arrest Colonel
Pedro Gomes, who pioneered a number of notable expeditions in
the North-East, and Colonel Álvaro de Azevedo whose favourite
pastime is hunting wild boars. I understand Teles asked you to
authorize the detention of the De Brito brothers' wives and Dona
Bernardina Ravasco. This sounds more like a personal vendetta
than lawful punishment, and it provokes unrest and rebellion
among the infantry and nobility. Which is precisely what has
happened, and I'm convinced that this rebellion is not in your best
interests. My job is to solve the mystery of the Captain-General's
assassination, and I can see no reason why all his enemies should
be arrested for the crime, simply because you and Judges Gois and
Palma think so. No governor or judge has the right to meddle

with my inquiry. I shall decide what legal steps are to be taken. To arrest suspects before their guilt has been established cannot be justified. If the assassins have been identified and there is no lack of witnesses, on no account should innocent women be arrested and thrown into prison just to take revenge on their husbands, fathers and brothers."

"As soon as I learned of their imprisonment," said the Governor turning pale, "I ordered their immediate release. If you wish to examine all the relevant documents, this is an open house. We have nothing to hide. I shall ask one of my secretaries to put all the papers at your disposal. And I trust Your Lordship will inform the Crown authorities of my readiness to cooperate. As you can see, my integrity is beyond question. I have hardly accumulated wealth in the colony, only problems and worries. I have gained nothing. If the truth be told, I've lost any assets I ever possessed," said De Souza.

Rocha Pita caught sight of his artificial limb, something he'd been trying to avoid.

"Believe me, De Souza, I deeply regret the Captain-General's death."

"I only hope you'll get to the bottom of this ordeal, Your Lordship."

The Governor believed that by making Rocha Pita express regret, he had scored another victory. He sent for Mata, who appeared, obsequious as ever.

"Accompany the Judge and show His Lordship all the documents he may wish to examine without any restrictions. Hand over any papers His Lordship may wish to retain."

De Souza rose to his feet. His impressive build made him seem even more intimidating.

Guided by Mata, Rocha Pita shuffled out of the room.

Early next morning Rocha Pita awoke to the clatter of a horse approaching. He stole out of bed and went to the window.

Manuel do Porto was standing at the front door with bundles of paper under his arms. The Judge staggered downstairs, carrying a candle in one hand.

"Good, very good. I can see you've been working well into the night. What have you brought me?" Rocha Pita asked.

"Your Lordship was right. I've confirmed what you suspected. They made me most welcome at the Secretariat. I was shown secret archives by a notary who begged me not to reveal his name because the Governor ordered him to destroy all the files. I was allowed to see everything I wanted. I've brought you the documents."

Rocha Pita and Manuel do Porto went to the upstairs room. The old Judge was wearing a long, white nightshirt and velvet slippers, a starched nightcap on his head. He sat down and started poring over the papers.

"Hmm, hmm," he muttered.

Manuel do Porto waited, a gleam in his eye.

"Just what I wanted. A list of the properties owned by people related to the Governor and Captain-General, acquired through Luiz Bonicho during their time in office, and most of them sold to third parties. Let's see now: on the hill going down from the Carmelite convent, two one-storey houses; near the Monastery of the Antonine friars, a one-storey house; another one-storey house facing the prison; in the vicinity of Nazaré and Fort Barbalho, a plot of land; and in the Rua do Paço, yet another house; in the Rua da Poyeira, a plot of land; a butcher's shop on the corner of the Rua do Peixe, another opposite the pharmacy of the Public Alms-house, and a fishmonger's shop behind the jail; a house in the Rua do Ximenes, another in the Rua da Montanha opposite the fountain of the Jesuit Church, and a tavern in Taboão. A sugar plantation in the district of Santo Amaro; two thousand spans of land in Jequitaia; an estate some one thousand six hundred spans wide along the River Paraguaçu and stretching one thousand six hundred spans into the hinterland, and some land on the sand-bar of the River Curumatai. A mining site in Itapicuru, and a spring. Two houses in Ilhéus, various plots of land near the River Missão and extending into the marshlands, an estate in the Sertão do Tucano, farmlands in Lima Ventura and Matança, the sugar mill at Pitinga, with factories, houses and slaves, cattle and lands. In Porto Seguro, two leagues of land at Cape Tapera. Two caravels, a Dutch pinnace, a small sailing boat and various canoes. Horses and stables in Itapicuru and Piquaraçá. Almost everything bought at auctions and re-sold at much higher prices. The profits were then invested in Portugal. Slaves were bought in the port of Ajudá." Rocha Pita read no further.

"What did Your Lordship find in the palace?"

"Me? Oh, nothing, nothing at all. Apart from . . . one little discovery of no great importance," replied Rocha Pita.

"What was that, my Lord?"

"It was all too easy."

# III

GREGÓRIO WENT TO the Court of Appeals. By displaying his canonist's ring and distributing a few coins he was allowed to enter the room where the legal records were kept. From a huge pile of documents he fished out Maria Berco's file.

It consisted of four pages of objective statements without one word of defence. He examined it carefully. Then he checked the ledger of pardons and sureties. He took notes on a piece of paper and slipped it into his pocket. There had to be at least three votes in cases involving capital punishment.

Legal proceedings could drag on for two to four years. Yet Maria's case had been settled within a matter of days. A verdict had been reached by means of a secret ballot. Each of the judges, after reading the relevant documents, had written down his conclusions in Latin, and these were then passed on, together with the appropriate documents, to the next member of the Tribunal. The verdict was not signed, no details of the voting had been put on file. The stilted prose of one dissenting judge made it easy for Gregório to identify him: it was Gois. Grammatical errors revealed another: namely Palma. Why so harsh? Profession of the accused: prostitute. Not true. Crime: theft and aiding and abetting an act of murder. Not true.

The bureaucracy of the legal system in colonial Brazil was extremely complicated. Regulations were established by legal clauses and letters-patent, court orders and decrees, bye-laws, statutes, official protocol, land rights, concordats, privileges, edicts, council decisions, judicial directives and procedures, which constituted a baffling conglomeration of rules, each with its own specific duration. The *Philippine Ordinances* on penal law were so exacting that in certain cases they could not be enforced.

Quarrels and crimes were a daily occurrence in Bahia. Gregório went through the list of cases for that year. Two hundred murders and criminal assaults; three hundred deportations, mostly involving negroes and mulattos; nearly a thousand pardons and sureties; one thousand six hundred minor offences; one thousand seven hundred civil disputes regarding inheritance and treasury matters; one thousand seven hundred or so criminal actions. For a population of approximately one hundred thousand people that was excessive.

The problems handled by the Tribunal summed up the city's image. Power was in the hands of a tiny minority who were nearly always immune from punishment; but if the lower orders disobeyed the codes of social conduct they were punished with penalties which could range from fines to exile, from enforced labour to branding, from flogging to the gallows, or beheading.

All the other Captaincies were under the jurisdiction of the Court of Appeals in Bahia. The Crown resisted any suggestion that separate tribunals should be established in other regions, insisting that it lacked the funds to pay more magistrates. In Portugal it was generally felt that the number of lawyers in Brazil should be reduced. The colony was "in much greater need of soldiers". There were, in fact, few trained lawyers in the city. Sham courts abounded, "brass rings set with false gems". Nevertheless, there were some very able jurists in the colony who served important clients. The *Ordinances* stipulated fees and honorariums but reputable lawyers could charge what they liked.

The Tribunal was only allowed eight magistrates. Legal proceedings were cumbersome and slow. Magistrates complained of being overworked. Crimes often went unpunished because the obligatory quorum could not be reached.

The rota of court hearings was strictly observed: civil cases were dealt with first; criminal cases next, and finally matters of interest to the Crown. There were so many civil cases that there was never time to hear the rest. Consequently, prisoners due to appear on criminal charges were left to languish in their cells, many of them dying of disease and hunger.

Helping Maria would require a great deal of planning and effort.

"What can one hope for in this madhouse where so-called men of law revel in intrigue and corruption?" Gregório muttered.


Locked away in his study, Rocha Pita had sat up all night leafing through affidavits and annotating points of interest. He had read the papers relating to the Captain-General's death many times and found numerous problems: discrepancies, incoherent statements, blatant lies, vague and ambiguous phrases; there were frequent contradictions, evasive phrases and dubious facts. How could these discrepancies have escaped the attention of a jurist as experienced and knowledgeable as Palma?


At the home of Rocha Pita, Gregório was admiring the five beautifully bound volumes from the Monastery of São Vicente de Fora – the only press authorized to publish the *Ordinances*. There were many other important works which brought judges and magistrates to this library. Rocha Pita still had a lot of reading to do before he died, Gregório thought.

The Crown Judge raised his eyes from the papers on his desk and stared at the lawyer standing before him.

"Matos e Guerra, Gregório de Matos e Guerra . . . that was also your father's name. I'm told you're in a difficult situation?"

"Your Lordship, I haven't come here to intercede on my own behalf. Nothing could be further from my thoughts, knowing how you respect integrity and justice. Nor have I come to intercede on behalf of Padre Vieira, who has his own attorneys."

"A man of your education and talents should have greater regard for your profession and reputation. It's a great pity that someone with your gift for satire should be so neglectful of your duties. In Lisbon I once read of a civil dispute over an inheritance which a colleague of mine was handling: a lawsuit involving so much clerical work that the papers had to be carried around by several porters. The litigant had no hope of winning the lawsuit and sent it to you as a last resort; he had heard of your wit and perspicacity. The papers were delivered to your house. Some days later, the litigant saw you at your window admiring the landscape, and complained that you had neglected his case. But there was no need, was there?"

"True," replied Gregório, "I found good grounds for annulling the case even before reading the documents, for that same year, Filipe IV had passed a decree invalidating all legal proceedings written on paper which hadn't been sealed with the coat of arms of Castile. Those voluminous papers bore no such seal. The case was annulled."

"Very clever indeed. Your intelligence and cunning had everyone talking in Lisbon. An ingenious move on your part. Now tell me: why did you refuse to investigate the crimes of Salvador Correia Benevides in exchange for a place in the Court of Appeal? Were you afraid the accused would protest? Or was it because you didn't trust the promise, however genuine?"

"For neither reason," replied Gregório.

"Why then?"

"It's a long story. I'll tell you one day."

Rocha Pita did not insist. "Haven't we seen each other before in the Tribunal?"

"Yes, I used to go there to represent the Ecclesiastical Court." Gregório fell silent.

"Now then!" said the Crown Inspector. "How can I help you?"

"I wanted to speak to you about a woman who's been sentenced to the gallows. Dona Maria Berco."

"Ah yes, I've been informed. What is your interest in this matter?"

"I've no personal interest, Your Lordship. I only know that it would be a grave injustice if she were to hang."

"Surely that's only your opinion. You can't expect the judges to act on opinions. Can you produce evidence?"

"I know what I'm talking about, Your Lordship," insisted Gregório. "I also know that the Court of Appeals, at the request of certain influential parties, is quite capable of imposing a far harsher sentence than her offence justifies."

"You mean her crime."

"All right then, her crime. Nevertheless, the powers of the courts often overstep the force of law. Miscarriages of justice are not redressed. At every level of the judicial hierarchy: magistrates, lawyers, clerks and notaries, one finds the same crass bureaucracy."

"That's quite enough," interrupted Rocha Pita. "Don't forget that I've read your satires and malicious jibes, especially against the legal profession here in Brazil. I'm prepared to concede that there are some grounds for criticism but I'm not convinced that the entire Judiciary is as 'corrupt, unjust and contaminated' as you claim. You can't denounce every lawyer in the colony because of a disreputable minority."

"Equal justice for all is an unquestionable right. I examined the files on this woman in the Court of Appeals and confirmed that any possibility of bail had been ruled out. Why? In other cases, women who committed similar offences were released on bail, having been granted letters of safe-conduct, permission to go free, or even a pardon. Their husband, father or brother had only to intercede on their behalf. But no such opportunity has been allowed Maria Berco. Her only crime was in foolishly agreeing to dispose of the Captain-General's hand. Who can prove that she even knew it was his hand?"

"A severed hand should have aroused her suspicions. Besides, she stole the ring without thought to the consequences."

"She wasn't to know. Nor could she have known."

"She was an accomplice. She aided and abetted the assassins. She played her part in this sad affair and she must bear some of the guilt."

"But Antonio de Brito hasn't been sentenced. Would you say Maria Berco had committed the greater crime?"

"Antonio de Brito will face trial in good time."

"And receive a pardon."

"What makes you so certain? You're merely speculating."

"This woman's offence is in no sense serious. She was only carrying out orders."

"What are you trying to say?"

"I could insist that she discovered that gory hand among the garbage dumped on the street, if all other arguments should fail. But I'll be frank with you, Your Lordship. Dona Maria Berco was the companion of Bernardo Ravasco's daughter. He ordered her to conceal the hand. He took it upon himself to see that it was quietly disposed of to avoid any retaliation by the assassins. The Secretary, who is innocent, is rotting away in prison. Luiz Bonicho may already be dead. Serotino, the fencing master, is in his grave. As is the notary, Manuel Dias. All these crimes have been committed by one man, the Governor's right-hand man, Teles, who is out to avenge his brother's death. The Governor is using this unscrupulous man to punish and eliminate all those who oppose his regime. Wouldn't you agree Braço de Prata has played a part in these crimes? Wouldn't you say he's condoned them? Yet he's allowed to go free, to give orders and preside over the Court of Appeals, to govern the Captaincy and the entire colony. Anyone who criticizes him is removed by legal and illegal means, regardless of the judges' consent."

"I see you know your Seneca and that's to your credit. But I'm afraid there is nothing I can do to help this unfortunate woman."

"Surely there must be something?"

"Justice takes its course along paths which often run into contradictions and absurdities. Why should I believe you? Tell me!"

"Because I'm telling the truth."

Rocha Pita half closed his eyes and studied the poet.

"In treating illness, there's nothing more harmful than prescribing the wrong medicine," said Gregório.

"We're not talking about illness. This is a trial. But go on!"

"A trial not unlike the judgment of Tiberius Claudius in the Tribunal of Aeacus. Worse," said Gregório. "Governors, too, are susceptible to love and hatred. But there's no reason why that hatred should be turned on Maria Berco."

"I see." There was a long pause while Rocha Pita paced up and down the room. "Is the woman's husband willing to plead on her behalf and put up bail?" he asked, turning to Gregório.

"Your Lordship, give me a few days to raise the money for bail and obtain her husband's consent."

"Two days."

"I'm deeply grateful. It's well known that you've never condemned anyone unless they've been proved guilty."

"Don't flatter me. I'm just an ordinary citizen trying to do an honest job."

\*

Gregório had knocked several times. Through the crack in the door he could see a little man in rags, pointing a rusty old pistol.

"I must talk to you. It's about Dona Maria Berco," shouted Gregório.

"That whoring slut doesn't live here any more."

Gregório waited.

"I'm a friend, sir. You can lower your gun."

He continued waiting.

João Berco stood behind the door. Eventually he decided to let him in.

"Sir? You called me sir? One gets nothing but abuse in this city, nobody addresses anyone respectfully, educated people are a thing of the past. But I can see you're different. Come in, young man. This gun no longer works. Besides, I'm blind."

Gregório entered the room which was crammed with the most hideous bric-à-brac.

A thin negro girl without a blouse or shoes stood at the old man's side, her breasts just beginning to form.

"Go and fetch some fresh water," the old man told her, as she helped him sit down. He sank into an old, worn armchair covered in Burgundy velvet. He continued to lean on his walking-stick.

"Sit down, my friend," he said.

Gregório settled on a bench, facing the old man.

"You're Dona Maria Berco's husband?"

"That's right. You could say I bought her from her father. She was living as an orphan in the Misericórdia Alms-house. I'd have done better to sell her as a maid or whore. Just think how I've lost out! That bitch was worth a lot of money. Gold. Precious money. Silver coins. And here I am, a poor, old man. But what did you want to tell me?"

"There is one way we could save her from the gallows."

"We?"

"Would you sign a surety? Would you be willing to ask the Governor to show clemency?"

"How much would the surety cost?"

"The surety together with other expenses would come to around six hundred thousand réis."

"For that amount of money I could buy myself a fine mulatto

woman and a negro slave who speaks Portuguese. Or three sturdy negro lads. Or a trumpeter and three horses. Or a young thirteen-year-old virgin. And I'd still get some change back. Besides, what do I get out of this?"

"But . . ." Gregório began when João Berco interrupted.

"A hundred pairs of good breeches made of fine cloth. Fifty silk shirts. Three hundred pairs of linen drawers. Eighty hats in fine beaver. Four hundred and fifty pen-knives. What would I gain from this? She must be in a bad way. No longer worth having. You know what soldiers do to women once they get them into the cells. They soon catch the pox. She must be a sorry sight by now."

"Would you plead for clemency if I paid the surety?"

"Yes, so long as she comes back to me," he replied. Then he appeared to have second thoughts. He tapped his stick nervously on the floor.

"Won't this be a bit risky?" he asked. "I don't want any trouble. I know what she's like, I know her little game. It's a bad business, no good can come of it, there are too many important people involved, and God forbid that I should get mixed up with that lot."

"You're in no danger, João Berco. Husbands are always pleading for their wives before the Tribunal. They form part of their patrimony. You won't get involved in anything. Besides, what could they posssibly do? Why should they harm you? How could they? You don't hold an appointment or enjoy any privileges, you possess nothing of interest. Please don't refuse. You can only benefit by doing me this favour."

João Berco thought a while. "All right," he said.

Gregório stood up.

"Wouldn't you like a glass of water?" the old man asked.

The slave girl returned with fresh water. Gregório drank some.

"Why are you doing this for my wife?"

"Because I know she's innocent."

"Nothing else?"

"For no other reason," Gregório replied.

*

The chairs were occupied by the nobility, court officials, judges, lawyers, and several priests. Standing at the back of the room were members of the public, some very poor, but all wearing their Sunday best. Beggars and paupers were kept outside.

João Berco, led by the slave girl, pushed his way through the crowd with his walking-stick. He passed between rows of footmen and soldiers standing on guard.

At the other end of the room, the Governor's empty chair was raised on a carpeted dais. They had been awaiting his arrival. Those assembled then yawned and whispered among themselves while officials took notes or read the papers on their laps. People were careful to speak in a low voice. Antonio de Souza would make his entrance along a carpeted corridor. In the chair to the right of the place of honour sat the Archbishop with folded hands, rubbing his ring and staring at the floor with his one eye. He wore a tiny skull-cap made of crimson silk, from which a few straggling white hairs emerged. His expression was solemn.

Antonio de Souza swept into the room. Some people rose to their feet, others scarcely moved and remained seated. Making no attempt to conceal his irritation, the Governor began his Audience.

The Archbishop was the first to speak. It was a matter connected with the ecclesiastical definition of usury, which fixed the rate of interest at six and a quarter per cent, the highest rate permitted. Then they discussed the chaplain who said Mass before each session of the Court of Appeals, and views were exchanged about what he should preach. These discussions went on at great length.

The Audience proceeded.

Next to speak was a judge who waxed lyrical about his own virtues, boasting grandly that he had "served with an authority and justice which even the most experienced of his peers might envy."

He was followed by a Jesuit who proposed that new methods of studying should be adopted in the colony.

There were further interventions by jurists, clerics, noblemen and representatives of the middle classes. Those who were poor or shy had to be patient.

If the speeches dragged on, De Souza would periodically doze off, especially when the topic was of no real interest to him; sometimes he would tap his foot on the floor, thus dismissing the current speaker. He promised to pursue all the matters raised and to reach a decision as soon as possible.

With every window shut, the Great Hall reeked of body odour.

After allowing one or two people to voice the standard complaints about high prices, to plead for favours or denounce an injustice, De Souza signalled to Mata, thus closing the session.

João Berco walked along the carpeted corridor to the Governor's dais, guided by the slave girl. He stopped when at the two steps and several guards rushed forward to prevent him from advancing any further.

"Your Excellency," he growled in a deep voice. "My name is João Berco and I beg of you to heed the pleas of an old man. I can no longer walk without assistance and I'm completely blind."

On hearing the name Berco, De Souza stopped. He looked at the old man and gestured to the guards to allow him to draw nearer.

João Berco made no attempt to mount the dais, afraid he might trip and fall.

"Speak from where you're standing," said the Governor and returned to his chair.

"I've come here, Your Excellency, not to ask for any favours but to plead for justice. Justice for my wife, Dona Maria Berco. She's been sentenced to hang, but has done nothing to deserve such cruel punishment. She's been accused of helping to murder the Captain-General, God rest his soul, but I can prove her innocence. On the day of the crime she never left the house. I had agreed to let her work for the Secretary of State and she looked after his daughter, a young woman of excellent character. My wife is a hard-working girl who had a brush and bucket in her hand when they came to arrest her."

De Souza tried to conceal his impatience. "They tell me she's even good at digging graves," he said.

"Digging graves? She couldn't handle a spade if she tried."

People chuckled.

"I can't live without her, Your Excellency, blind and destitute as I am. This is destroying both of us."

One of the Governor's aides came and whispered in his ear. De Souza smiled.

"Am I not correct in thinking that you possess slaves?"

"I have only one female slave who's no damn good. She's brainless and diseased. All she ever does is to steal from me, gorge herself like a fat friar and sleep all day long."

"And what does she do at night?" someone cried out, whereupon the crowd burst out laughing. João Berco flew into a rage. Waving his stick in the air, he bellowed: "Curse the lot of you. She sleeps all night as well. And it's none of your business. Dona Maria Berco is innocent. I beseech Your Excellency to pardon her."

"To pardon someone who's innocent would be like pouring water into the sea," joked De Souza.

This brought more jeering from those standing nearby.

"Cuckold," someone shouted.

Further hoots of laughter.

"One of our judges has already interceded on behalf of this prisoner," the Governor told João Berco. "He recommended that she be released on bail. Are you willing to put up the money?"

João Berco stuttered and stammered, before finally saying he would. "I beg of you, Your Excellency," he said, falling to his knees and slapping himself in the face. "I'm a poor old man."

"Have you no relations?" the Governor asked.

"No . . . no one, Your Excellency," he replied, without understanding why he was being asked such a question. Every word spoken within these walls had a hidden meaning.

"Very well," said the Governor, "leave it to me. I shall order this woman's file to be re-examined."

De Souza rose to his feet and departed. As he passed, people fell to their knees or tried to kiss his hand.

João Berco was then escorted by soldiers to the main doors of the palace. They helped him down the steps and he left, supported by his walking-stick and slave. His expression was one of utter relief.

# IV

*NIHIL EST IN INTELLECTU, quod non prius fuerit in sensu, nisi intellectus ipse.* Surely it was Padre Vieira himself who said that there is nothing in the mind which has not already been intuited, unless it be the mind itself? mused Gregório de Matos. He felt he must be going mad to think about Aristotle and Leibniz at a time like this. Everything goes badly in the real world.

Illness confined Bernardina Ravasco to bed where she lay surrounded by maids, basins and compresses. The barber-surgeon at her bedside was letting blood. Tiny crimson drops trickled over her white skin.

"Stop," Bernardina cried out, "I can't bear this torture any longer!"

The barber-surgeon held her foot and lowered it into a basin of cold water. He then requested smelling-salts.

Gregório waited anxiously in the other room. Finally the barber-surgeon emerged, greeted the poet and left. Gregório was taken in to see the patient.

He entered her bedroom on tiptoe, carrying a small bunch of flowers he had removed from the vase in the drawing-room. Bernardina looked paler and more delicate than ever, her eyes red, her white hands resting on her bosom.

"Forgive me, Your Ladyship, for disturbing you when you are ill. I've brought you some flowers."

"I feel better already. The days in prison have left me weak. That horrid place is only fit for rogues and criminals. Braço de Prata, hypocrite that he is, sent us food from his own table, candles to light our cells and clean sheets for our pallets; but nothing could relieve our sufferings. I didn't even have the consolation of seeing

my father. It isn't easy living among madmen. But I want to
forget the experience, never to speak of it again. What brings you
here? Have you brought me good news?"

"Alas, no, I've come to seek your help."

Gregório told her about Maria Berco's trial. "So as you can see,
I must raise the money for bail. The money-lenders have refused
me. And I've had no better success with wealthy relatives I've
contacted."

"How much do you need?" she asked.

"Six hundred thousand réis. And I need it by tomorrow."

Bernardina removed the cushion under her feet and stood up
with some effort. There were trays and tea-cups scattered over
the bed, plates with crumbs, goblets; on the bedside table there
were dishes with remains of food.

"Six hundred thousand!" she exclaimed.

"Only by paying this sum shall we secure Maria's release."

"How can they ask for such an exorbitant bail?"

"They can ask what they like."

"I can't bear to think of poor Maria with iron fetters round her
neck, locked up with all those dreadful people. But with my father
in prison and everything we possess inaccessible, I simply cannot
raise that amount of money. The only solution I can think of is
to turn to Samuel da Fonseca."

"Borrow money from a Jew? That'll mean interest at twelve
per cent."

"Not when you're dealing with Dom Samuel. He's as honest
as any Christian."

"Where can I find him?"

"Perhaps in Matoim, where they recite the Torah. I don't think
he'll have that sum of money in his coffers, but there is a fund to
help ransom Jews from pirates."

"Where does the money come from?"

"From the taxes all Jews pay on merchandise; on the gold,
silver, precious stones and amber sent abroad; from the duty
on all the sugar shipped out, on all trading profits, on slaves, on
house sales, on all captured pirate ships. They're a closely united
race."

"You don't need to tell me, Dona Bernardina. You've no idea

the trouble I've had trying to get a Jew to give evidence against another Jew."

"They simply won't testify against each other."

"This clandestine synagogue of theirs . . . Aren't they afraid of being burnt at the stake?"

"Of course they're afraid. But, as my father told me, since Isaac de Castro was sentenced to death around 1646, no Jew in Brazil has been burnt at the stake by the Holy Inquisition. Or as those pious Inquisitors would say when referring to their victims, 'mercifully burnt at the stake for the good of their souls'. The synagogue in Matoim is a solid stone building concealed in the forest. I'll take you there."

"I don't think you should leave your room, in your condition."

"Take Gaspar da Fonseca with you. He'll show you the way and introduce you."

They travelled in a coach. Gregório de Matos was carrying a small barrel of rum which was almost empty.

"I'm nothing but a drunkard, a miserable vagabond," the poet confided. "I'm no fit company for anyone. I've started avoiding everyone. The only company I crave is that of black women. I'm like a dog on constant heat. Take a good look at me. My hair hasn't been cut since I took refuge in that warehouse and how long ago was that?"

"How should I know?"

"I gambled away my velvet cloak and now I wear this cheap rag. The bold Braço de Prata even had the wearing of cloaks banned. The man is a fool and who knows what he'll ban next! My feet are covered in blisters, my face is ashen and my hair is getting whiter by the minute."

"But you chose this life," said Gaspar.

"Sometimes I'm not sure whether I chose it or if I was driven to it. But by whom? In truth, I feel fine. It's women who want to see us dressed like fops. And they can't keep their mouths shut after fornicating. They chatter their heads off. Sometimes I get the impression women don't really enjoy sex. They only endure it for the sake of having a good chat afterwards. By the way, how's Teresa? Have you seen her?"

"I saw her on the street the other day. I was with Tomás Pinto Brandão. She looked as if she wanted to stop and ask after you."

"Ah, Teresa, that dusky woman," said Gregório. "Strolling the streets with men staring at her, I lost her because of my silence. But I'll find her again and tell her how much I love her. And what about Maria João?"

"Who's she?"

"Isabel's daughter."

"Ah yes, I haven't seen her."

"And that little nun?"

"Are you still pursuing nuns, poet?"

"That's one game I haven't given up. I'm always on the prowl for an attractive woman, whether she sits behind a screen or grille. Such a pleasant pastime! The Abbess Dona Maria! The mother superior, the sweet little nun at the convent gate in Odivelas. You've never experienced such passionate women. They were game for anything, my friend. More versatile than any whore. Who could forget them?"

Gaspar laughed.

"In Odivelas, I wooed a nun whose name I can't remember, and just as we were about to reach a climax, the bed caught fire. The place went up in flames. Just imagine! There was another nun called Armida, who used to receive me swathed in precious furs. Russian squirrel, ermine, I'm not lying! Then there was a nun called Dona Mariana do Desterro who whimsically called herself Urtiga. When she sang my heart would stop from sheer excitement. *Ah, dear lady,*" he declaimed, "*if from the cloisters you send such tempting delicacies to someone as sweet-toothed as me, why complain if I reciprocate with honeyed words?*" He fell silent, watching the forest and river. "A nun once tried to make me a present of a red snapper, but was dissuaded by another nun who said I would only mock the fish. So do you know what I did?"

"You mocked the nun who dissuaded her."

"That's exactly right. Fancy leaving a poor, starving man to die of hunger! Another nun, Dona Fábia Carrilhos, sent me a blood sausage. Ah, such happy memories. And those young girls. Did you see Ana Maria?"

"The one from India?"

"That's the one. A thousand days living with the hope of gazing on her for a single day. And pale Brites with her doe-eyes and raven hair, who almost blinded me when I first set eyes on her. I couldn't even begin to describe her waist, so neat and dainty. And Betica? Our lips pressing, blood surging through our veins, our limbs writhing in passion."

"Is Betica the one from São Francisco?"

"No, that's Beleta. Betica asked me for a hundred thousand réis. She must have thought I was an apprentice sailor newly arrived from Angola! I had to work all night long just to earn a few coins. And that harpy asked me for a hundred thousand réis! From me, a poor apprentice, surviving on my wits! Who was going to pay all that money just to take a look up her skirts?"

"So you didn't seduce her, poet?"

"You're damn right I didn't. I wouldn't pay up, so I was rebuffed."

Gaspar smiled.

Gregório suddenly looked sad.

"What are you thinking about?" asked Gaspar.

"I'm thinking about a woman."

"Who?"

"Someone I love in secret, someone I even hide from myself. Don't let's talk about it, my boy," said Gregório. "Let's talk about Joana, the one and only Joana. Heavenly. Teeth like pearls, dressed in her fine linen blouse with lace frills. Do you know Anica de Melo?"

"Who doesn't know Anica?"

"Ah, all these women are as much a part of me as my own blood. Time's marching on. Thank God I can still fuck pretty women, sweet-smelling black girls. I can go on drinking, gambling, strumming my guitar, trying to lure a fair-skinned temptress into bed." Gregório passed his hand over his perspiring brow. "How's my friend, the poet Tomás Pinto Brandão? I'm prattling on, am I not, my friend?"

"I enjoy it. A pity we're almost there."

"Didn't I tell you so? We've arrived safe and sound," said Gregório. "It's Vieira they're after. Why should anyone want to arrest me?"

249

"They're afraid of what you might write. The people enjoy your satires. They take notice of what you have to say."

The trees seemed even greener and more luminous in the clear air.

"I dreamt of women," said Gregório. "Their heads were facing back to front and because they were unable to look forward, they walked backwards. I'm forty-seven years of age. Is this a proper life for a man of my age?"

They walked in silence. A village lay in the distance. Horses could be heard plodding on the hard soil.

"Do you still know how to fight a duel?" asked Gaspar, after looking over his shoulder.

"Certainly," Gregório replied. "Why do you ask?"

"We're being followed."

Gregório turned round and saw two men on horseback at the end of the highway.

"I can recite odes, dirges and anthems. But I don't think they'll be of much help. Wouldn't you agree?" Gregório joked.

"Good God!"

"Which god? Pious thoughts? Spiritual priesthood? Ecclesiastical devotion? Certain impulses? Jesuit rhetoric?"

"We must pick up the pace," said Gaspar and cracked his whip over the horse's rump.

There was an explosion of gunfire. The Rabbi's son jumped from the coach, dragging Gregório with him. They crawled away and hid among the bushes.

The shooting had stopped.

"Bloody hell," muttered Gregório. "Prepare yourself for death, my friend. Pray after me, I fucked, you fucked, Hail Mary, full of Grace. My God, I've sinned, I didn't doff my cap when the procession passed, forgive me, Lord."

Gaspar took a gun and pouch of ammunition from his belt. He untied the knot, removed a bullet and loaded his weapon. He fired.

The men dismounted and took cover on the other side of the road, a little further ahead. More shots rang out, the bullets whistled through the leaves.

"Hand me another bullet!"

Gregório obliged. "There's only one left."

"What shall we do?"

Gregório looked back. The River Matoim was only a few metres away. "Can you swim?"

"Yes," replied Gaspar.

Gregório pointed to the river.

"And what about you?" the youth asked.

Another bullet whizzed past them, skimming the undergrowth.

Gaspar aimed one last shot.

"I can't swim," the poet confessed. "But I'm eager to learn."

They removed their shoes and jackets and ran, heads down, to the river bank. They threw themselves into the icy currents.

Exhausted and with a stomach full of water, Gregório lay stretched out at the river's edge. With his eyes closed, he tried to recall Maria's face. There was only a glimpse, fleeting and blurred, amidst gleaming bottles, metal goblets, sensuous female forms, which moved to and fro in the waning light. How could he have forgotten that familiar face? Nor could he remember Anica's face. He no longer loved her. Yet just to think of Maria made him feel as if he were being sucked into a vortex. So why couldn't he remember her face? Good heavens, was her face about to disappear like water from a leaking tub? He could hear the sound of rushing water. He opened his eyes. What was he doing beside the river? Then he remembered the soldiers. How had he managed to escape drowning? Had God protected him? He tried to remember his age. To recall his life. Who was he?

Shaking him vigorously, Gaspar tried to rouse the poet. Until finally Gregório opened his eyes.

For a moment they remained there, staring at each other, gasping for breath.

"What a relief," whispered Gaspar. He stretched out on the grass beside the poet.

"Bloody bastards!" cursed Gregório.

"Who were those men? Were they brigands?" asked Gaspar, sitting up. "Why were they firing at us?"

"What do you think? Could they have been students from the

college? Turks or Persians from the market-place? Mongols, Armenians, or Greeks from the plantations, or Myrmidons from the workshops?"

Gaspar looked puzzled.

"Now then? Do you think they were black slaves from the galleys? Mulatto workers? Street-sweepers? Fruit-pickers? No, my friend! They're the Governor's boot-lickers!"

Gaspar smiled and got to his feet. He then helped Gregório. "Is it safe to go?"

"I think so."

"Should we keep to the forest or follow the highway?"

"The highway. Then you'll know how it feels to walk the road to heaven."

They began walking over the surface of sand and stones.

Samuel da Fonseca was circumcising little Israel, the son of Abrão do Sal, the spice-merchant.

He was the best *mohel* in the city. Not that there were many Jews left in Bahia. Since the signing of the 1645 Treaty between the Dutch and Portuguese, the Jewish population had been decreasing throughout Brazil, especially in Pernambuco, where one thousand five hundred Jewish people had once lived. After the capitulation in 1654, more than six hundred Jews from Pernambuco fled to Amsterdam where there was a large Jewish community.

The ceremony was attended by a number of Jews from Bahia. The Bravos, the provincial magistrate D'Albuquerque, the lawyer Lopes Brandão, the magistrate's son-in-law, Moniz Teles, Serpa the book-keeper and several plantation owners. In one corner stood the sailor Estevão Rodrigues Ayres, a native of Vila dos Redondos, who lived in Assumpaco. Many of them carried Bibles translated into Spanish and printed in Amsterdam or Leyden.

The Jews of Bahia were generally merchants, farmers, landowners or administrators of estates and plantations, exporters or importers, bricklayers, teachers, writers, or poets. Some of them had suffered torture at the hands of the Inquisition. All of them had relatives who had spent time in prison and been ordered to wear the degrading yellow habits for the rest of their lives, or were burnt at the stake. Many had all their possessions confiscated. That same year, Jews were being arrested and imprisoned in other Captaincies. Those detained were soon released but a decree was expected at any moment ordering Jews to be sent back to Portugal to appear before the Inquisition. They feared for their lives, for the sudden arrival of an inspector from the Holy Inquisition to investigate their activities. They were constantly watched, and denounced.

The child began to howl as blood trickled into the basin. And Samuel da Fonseca had not fully completed the ceremony when a skinny lad came up to him and whispered in his ear. The Rabbi excused himself and rushed out.

In wet clothes and covered in dust, Gregório and Gaspar sat in a room at the back of the mansion of the estate where the synagogue was housed.

Gregório examined the dark outlines of the furniture made of precious wood and covered in rich fabrics, the objects in shades of amethyst set out on the table, the slats of the shutters which allowed a white light to filter through.

Samuel da Fonseca entered. His son told him about the attempt on their lives and of their escape across the River Matoim, and explained the reason for this visit. As father and son chatted, Gregório reflected that many of the silver and gold objects in the dark room would fetch enough money to secure Maria Berco's release. He felt powerless and dejected; the situation was becoming unbearable.

"How much money do you need?"

Gregório tried to speak, but almost choked. He toyed with a button on his shirt. He then told him the sum.

"I suppose you both realize that Antonio de Souza won't allow the condemned woman to go free just like that."

"I'm afraid you're right," replied Gregório.

The Rabbi supported his paunch with both hands, and took a good, deep breath.

"Rocha Pita isn't an easy man to deal with. These legal proceedings have been a costly affair and I fear that any plea on behalf of Dona Bernardina's companion might upset our plans. I don't think we should count on too many concessions from Rocha Pita. He's much too interested in preserving his good name. Any favour he might grant us simply means that he'll be much more favourably disposed towards our enemies next time. And I can understand him, for that's how it should be. The law *de favorabelste conditien.* This may bring us some of the advantages I was hoping for. A lawyer knows how these things work, isn't that so, Doctor Gregório? But tell me, who persuaded Rocha Pita to add the condemned woman's name to the list of sureties?"

"I did," said Gregório.

"No small feat. Rocha Pita criticizes the Tribunal's readiness to grant pardons and allow bail. Along with Cristóvão de Burgos, he continually points out the abuses which have been allowed to go on for years. The list has grown longer and longer. And they never cease to wonder where all the money paid in sureties ends up."

"I knew nothing of this," said Gregório.

"When is the hearing?"

"Tomorrow."

Samuel da Fonseca got up and went to the metal casket resting on the table. He counted out the money and handed it over to Gregório, bidding him farewell. Then placing his hands on his son's head, he gave him his blessing.


Everything happened so quickly that Gregório could scarcely remember the details. He walked along the corridor leading to the magistrate's room. In his satchel he carried the six hundred thousand réis along with the necessary documents and affidavits.

He was made to wait a considerable time. Judges meandered round in their robes. People sat silently on benches. Others chatted amongst themselves as if eagerly anticipating the arrival of a scandalous court case.

Gregório turned round as each person came in, looking for João Berco. Voices trailed out from the courtroom. Perodically the chancellor's bell would ring.

There were only thirty minutes left before they were due to appear. Had João Berco refused to sign? Gregório decided to find him before it was too late. If necessary, he would drag him here by force.

He raced through the streets like a madman and found a crowd gathered at the front door of João Berco's house, chatting excitedly and peering through the windows.

Gregório pushed his way through. There were guards inside the house. The slave girl was seated on a stool beside the armchair where João Berco had received him. She was pale, eyes wide open, hugging herself across the chest as if she were cold. The room had been turned upside down.

A soldier tried to prevent Gregório from going upstairs.

"Are you related to the old man?"

"Yes," replied Gregório. He entered the room. João Berco's body was stretched out on the floor and covered with a filthy, blood-stained sheet. His mouth gaped in terror. The poet crouched down and closed the dead man's eyes.

A soldier approached.

"Whoever killed him made sure he did the job properly. They stabbed him in the chest and heart, then slit his throat. Was he rich?"

"I couldn't tell you," answered Gregório.

"Come with me, sir," said an elderly man wearing a hat and holding a walking-stick. He introduced himself as an official from the Judiciary.

The attic had been ransacked. Inside, a leather chest lay open and empty. Coins were scattered all over the floor. There were rugs rolled up, fine items of furniture, damask tapestries. In the corners there were pictures propped up against the wall. Gregório turned some of them over.

"Portraits, miniatures, illuminated manuscripts. A painting in the Gothic style. A man of property," commented the official. His young assistant was drawing up a list of all the items. "As you can see, the money is gone and it's impossible to say how much was stolen. But, judging from the coins scattered on the floor, we can safely assume there was a tidy fortune in that coffer. There is also this casket which the thieves didn't find." The official opened it. The chest was full of precious stones. "Had he any family or children?"

"A wife. She's called Maria Berco. I'm looking after her affairs and I'd like to sign the inventory of everything you've found. Nothing is to be auctioned. His wife will claim what is legally hers."

"There's something very strange going on here," said the lawyer. "The murderers have cut off the victim's right hand."

"Why would they do such a thing?" asked the clerk.

"Perhaps witchcraft?"

They made the sign of the cross and muttered, "Begone Satan!"

# V

ANICA DE MELO'S BROTHEL was closed. One of the Governor's men guarded the door. Gregório waited on the street-corner out of sight. After a while, one of the bawds appeared. He grabbed her by the arm. Startled, she was about to scream when she suddenly recognized him.

"Good heavens, what are you doing here? The soldiers are looking for you."

"Tell Anica I'm waiting for her in the Rua Debaixo."

The girl vanished into the brothel.


A while later Anica turned up at the tavern. She could smell the alcohol on Gregório's breath.

"What kept you so long?" he asked, grabbing her by the waist. She drew away.

"I almost didn't come," she told him. And then burst into tears.

"What's the matter?" he asked.

She pursed her lips, stifling herself, and wiped her face.

"They've taken everything. They've shut down the brothel, left me with nothing," she told him between sobs.

"Bring some rum," Gregório ordered the landlord. "Pull yourself together, Anica. Tell me what happened."

"The guards forced their way into the house and asked for you. I told them I hadn't seen you for ages. They started tearing the place apart. They went into my bedroom, took the casket where I kept my money and jewels." The tears ran down her cheeks. "They insisted I'd helped you, said you were a criminal, that you'd killed the Captain-General, and that unless I told them where you were they would kill me. I said you were in Vicente's warehouse.

They marched me there and Vicente said you'd gone to Matoim. I wouldn't have told them a thing if they hadn't threatened me," she said, sobbing.

"Calm yourself. Here I am safe and sound."

"They burned your books and papers, took your clothes, smashed up everything inside the warehouse. Then they gave Vicente a beating and raped me."

"Filthy swine," shouted Gregório, banging the table with his fist.

The landlord filled a mug with rum, eyeing the couple.

They drank, and gradually Anica began to calm down.

"Cheer up," he said. "You did the right thing. They might have killed you had you not told them everything. And that would have been worse for me."

"Seriously?"

"Yes."

He held her hands.

"Did you manage to raise the bail?"

"Yes, but it didn't help." He told her about João Berco's death.

"Are you doing all this for her?"

"It's not for her."

"For whom, then?" Anica asked.

Gregório looked at Anica and was about to reply that he was doing it for himself, but said nothing.

"Did they catch up with you?" she asked him.

"They tried to kill me on the road from Matoim. Or to scare me off. And they almost succeeded."

"For heaven's sake, why don't you go immediately to Recôncavo? Or what about the kingdom of Prester John?"

"My place is here."

"In St Francis's vault?"

He did not reply, and kept on drinking. A lock of hair covered one eye. Anica tucked it behind his ear.

"Let's go away together," she said, "let's travel to the East. I left home at the age of thirteen, taking nothing but a kerchief, a skirt and a comb. And now, twenty years later, I'm as poor as ever. I have no horses, carriage, or jewels. God help me! Now I might even lose my home and end up on the streets."

Gregório said nothing. He watched her, biting his lip, shaking his head. And then lowered his eyes.

"You're always the same when you're drunk."

"I don't know why anyone should be born in this filthy hole."

"Have you been thinking about me?"

"I almost forgot your face. But not your body."

Gregório could not explain why he suddenly felt he must see Rocha Pita again. There was nothing more to be done for Maria Berco. Or for the Ravascos.

"Are the Ravascos capable of murder?" Rocha Pita asked. "Or let me put it another way, would they have any reason to kill someone?"

"No!" replied Gregório.

"It is just possible that Padre Vieira condoned the Captain-General's death, although I find it most unlikely. On the other hand, the crimes attributed to Antonio de Souza seem much more feasible: the imposition of additional taxes and the mysterious disappearances of revenues before they ever reached the public coffers; the charges now demanded for certain services previously provided free, and all the money going into his own pocket; his acquisition of farmland, houses, livestock, warehouses and commercial buildings. Taking every precaution to keep his affairs private. Nothing has been registered in his name, yet his family grows steadily richer. It would be difficult to trace the details of these transactions. It is clear that the Governor has used his power to enrich his friends but without ever becoming directly involved. Favours are bestowed to his advantage and that of his associates. He hounds his critics and enemies, shelters criminals in monasteries in exchange for concessions or offers protection to the clergy while intimidating them and threatening reprisals against those who refuse to obey his orders. But people are too cowardly to speak out against him. I invited certain parties to lodge formal complaints about his conduct. No one came forward. Suspicions vanished into thin air. Just as no one is prepared to defend the Ravascos in court."

"They've probably been scared off by Braço de Prata."

"Papers have disappeared from my office. I suspect De Souza

was responsible. But nothing has been found to implicate him. No one would be foolish enough to try and prove his misconduct. For it would be most unworthy of a man who had been appointed Governor of one of the largest and most important of the Portuguese colonies."

"But there is also no evidence to prove that the Ravascos were involved in the Captain-General's assassination."

"What more could I do, Doctor Gregório?" asked the Judge. "What? You know how I respect the truth." Rocha Pita pursed his lips, scratched his chin. "And what about the condemned woman, Dona Maria Berco?"

"There's no solution."

"There's always a solution. Do you still have the six hundred thousand réis?"

"I have them right here,"

"Then listen carefully to what I say."


Dressed in the red habit of the Confraternity which looked after the Misericórdia Alms-house, a group of lay-brothers arrived at the prison gates. They were carrying sacks and bundles and identified themselves to the guards.

"We've come to minister to the prisoners," one of them explained.

The guards allowed them to enter.

Maria Berco's cell was dark and narrow. She raised her eyes when she heard the lay-brothers arrive. She was manacled and chained, and filthy. Her head had been shaved, and her face and arms were badly scarred. She wore tattered clothes and nothing on her feet.

"Has my time come?" she asked, trembling.

"It has," replied one of the brothers. He turned to the jailor. "You may release her, my man."

"Where's the money we agreed on?" the jailor asked.

"First undo the manacles."

The jailor took the keys from his belt and, with reluctance, removed the manacles. Maria Berco rubbed her wrists.

One of the brothers removed a purse from his satchel and

handed it to the jailor who opened it and checked the amount inside. He gave a toothless grin.

They helped Maria to her feet, dressed her in a red habit and drew the hood over her head.

Another jailor was guarding the corridor, rattling his keys nervously. He gestured to the brothers and they fled.

Once darkness fell, Maria Berco was escorted to Samuel da Fonseca's plantation in Recôncavo by Tomás Pinto Brandão. She could scarcely believe what was happening and stared straight ahead.

Meanwhile, during a routine search of passengers' baggage aboard a merchant ship sailing for Holland, the customs officers found a sealed trunk in the possession of the student Gaspar da Fonseca, who had been under surveillance by the Governor's men. The trunk was confiscated and taken to the Governor for inspection. When he opened it, Antonio de Souza got an unexpected and agreeable surprise. Carefully tied up inside were the papers of Bernardo Ravasco.

Antonio de Souza destroyed the pages one by one with the flame of a burning taper.

Of Gaspar there was no trace. Thinking he was safely on his journey, the boy's father was unconcerned and received a devastating blow when Gaspar's corpse was washed up on the shore, the eyes and entrails already gnawed away.

In the great hall which was used as a refectory on the estate at Tanque, long trestles were set out in rows. Scores of famished men and women were already seated, waiting for the food to arrive.

Dressed in brown and black rags, their hair was matted and tousled. The sour stench of unwashed bodies filled the air.

The sacks and bundles at their feet looked just as filthy and untidy as their owners. The gathering included drunks, vagrants, cripples, tramps, ageing prostitutes and other social outcasts. Some of them were so weak they could scarcely sit upright, their heads resting on the tables. Few spoke. Some sat staring at the door where a lay-brother with rolled sleeves kept a watchful eye.

He had the brawny arms of a sailor and a mean expression.

The brothers circulated, carrying great pots which they placed on one of the tables. Nuns stood behind the piles of white crockery, ladling huge helpings of food. The food was all the same, a thick gruel with dark lumps of gristle. Milk was poured into two-handled tin mugs.

When Padre Vieira was carried in on a palanquin, followed by José Soares and a small retinue of priests, the paupers felt obliged to lower their heads and pray, and the old Jesuit blessed them with his scrawny hands. Then the meal began.

A nun cut slices from an enormous loaf of bread while another shared them out. The nuns spooned the food into the mouths of the disabled.

Padre Vieira was helped into his chair at one of the tables and ate with the paupers. He was as thin as a wraith and looked feverish. Everyone feared that he was close to death.

Padre Vieira turned to José Soares who was standing beside him.

"Let us be thankful to God that Rocha Pita is on our side," Vieira said. "Tell me what has happened, Padre Soares."

"At your insistence," Padre Soares informed him, "the Governor has ordered a judicial inquiry."

Padre Soares then explained the legal procedures conducted by Rocha Pita.

"And what about Bernardo?" Padre Vieira asked.

"In a moment, Father. The Governor conceded that Rocha Pita was right and assured him that he would suspend any sentences passed on the accused and hand over all the petitions relating to the trial. Contradicting the Governor for the first time, Captain-General Teles and his associates argued that Rocha Pita would let them down and said he wasn't to be trusted."

"Good heavens! So what did the Chancellor decide? Did he heed their suspicions?"

"The Teles faction failed to produce any convincing arguments and the inquiry was suspended."

"What a relief! God works in mysterious ways."

The paupers fell on their food like wolves. They would soon be back on the streets.

"The magistrate simplified proceedings by releasing some of the prisoners who had committed minor offences," rejoined Padre Soares.

"Who?"

"Quite a few. And here's the best news of all. Rocha Pita went in person to talk to Bernardo Ravasco in his cell and deliver the papers authorizing his release. Charges have been dropped in the absence of any incriminating evidence other than the fact that he was detained because his son had been involved in the crime."

"So my brother is free! And where is he?"

"Outraged as he was at the magistrate's benevolence, De Souza had Bernardo banished."

"Oh, no!"

"Steady, Padre Vieira! Bernardo is still in Bahia. Having no one to look after his property, he decided to seek refuge with the Discalced Carmelites in the convent of St Teresa."

"Very wise. The convent is near his estate on this side of Preguiça, and overlooks the harbour at Balthazar Ferraz where that fig-tree stands. From there he'll be able to write to me."

Captain-General Teles could hear the noise of the meeting taking place inside the Governor's palace. Armed soldiers guarded the main entrance and refused admittance to anyone without an official invitation.

An aristocrat, powdered and bewigged, minced in ahead of him, tossing coins to the crowd, who with much shouting and jostling struggled to catch them, throwing themselves to the ground and on top of each other.

"Such riff-raff!" Teles muttered.

People in the crowd were punching and kicking each other like a pack of wild beasts. "These are the castrated animals I'm supposed to govern," thought the Governor-General.

Slaves in velvet livery or long, white cotton tunics, parked the litters bearing their masters' coats of arms in the palace gardens. The nobility and gentry proceeded through the open doors to the great hall, its doors wide open. Everyone appeared agitated and flustered.

The slaves were hustled into a side courtyard where a serving-woman distributed food from the kitchen-door. Some stood around in groups, chatting.

Surrounded by the religious paintings decorating the great hall, the Governor's guests conversed uneasily. They formed circles, whispering and gesticulating. The men carried swords, some wore medals on their chests.

A judge fanned himself.

The clergy strolled up and down, rattling their rosary beads.

A little footman approached Teles.

"The Governor wishes to have a word with you, sir," the boy said politely, despite his disdainful glance at the Captain-General's modest attire. Teles was wearing his everyday uniform and had only changed from his old boots into pumps because his feet hurt.

Beckoning the Captain-General to follow him, the footman proceeded to the far end of the room where people had gathered.

"Your Excellency, Captain-General Antonio de Teles de Menezes," announced the page. The Captain-General spotted Antonio de Souza seated in the middle of the group, his gold-buckled boots gleaming, his wig arranged in ringlets.

"Just as well you've arrived!" said the Governor. The Captain-General approached. At Antonio de Souza's side, the Archbishop was holding a lorgnette to his empty eye-socket.

"Hypocrites and prevaricators," Teles thought.

The Archbishop extended a limp, pale hand which the Captain-General kissed. Flanking the Governor were representatives of the Church and Judiciary, men of wealth and political influence, members of the colonial oligarchy. Hostile factions momentarily united in mutual concern for their future.

Had they betrayed him? He tried to fathom why the Governor would invite the Archbishop, who had been favourably disposed towards the Ravascos. He believed De Souza was becoming senile and inept, and that he was to blame for the mess in which the Menezes faction now found itself. He's far too weak!

"Come and join us," De Souza called out. "Do sit down. We reserved this chair for you. After all, you're a key figure in this whole affair."

The Captain-General sat down, struggling to conceal his annoyance. Things were turning sour for him. He looked at Antonio de

Souza with his artificial arm, and wondered if he'd been bribed by the Ravascos. That might explain why the Governor had given in to Rocha Pita.

The meeting had been convened to examine the events of recent days. Those present also discussed what might happen next. Now that the Governor's authority had been weakened, members of his faction felt vulnerable.

"We were wrong to underestimate Vieira's influence over the Tribunal," remarked one.

"Rocha Pita has allowed himself to be bribed!" said another.

"If you'll allow me to speak," intervened De Souza, "this is not the end of the matter."

Within the next few months, another fleet was expected, bringing dispatches from Portugal. The Governor felt confident they would bring good news.

Teles did not wait for the meeting to end. The Governor accompanied him to the door.

"Thank you for coming," said De Souza. "I hope we're still friends."

"I know you didn't expect me to turn up, Antonio. I came here swearing revenge. We'll never forgive your betrayal."

"Don't talk such nonsense, Teles. You'll only regret it."

"His Majesty won't mete out justice."

"Don't make hasty judgments. We don't know what Dom Pedro thinks."

"You may not, but we do. The Teles de Menezes of this world know all too well. The Ravascos lost no time in acting, while we, or rather you, Antonio, who promised to resolve everything in our favour, have done nothing. Nothing! You'll soon see what's coming to us."

"You've no right to speak to me in this manner."

"Farewell, Antonio," replied Teles, leaving quickly by the garden patio. Water cascaded from a tiny fountain in its centre. Trees in bloom spread their fragrant branches.

"This is our last night together," said Gregório. "I can't stay here. I've been reduced to poverty, forced into hiding, refused any favours, provoked and persecuted. I've been dismissed from the Curia and am no longer allowed to practise law. I leave in the morning."

"Can't you take me with you?" pleaded Anica.

"How can I? I shall be wandering the Praia Grande."

"Won't you come back?"

"How could I ever stay away from this city? It is in my blood. I'll come back when I feel homesick. Blessed is the man who inhabits the wilderness. I shall awaken to the sweet songs of mating birds. At Court I had a secure appointment, but foolishly chose a wanton existence. Bahia is the rubbish dump of the Empire. Here there's nothing but theft, injustice and tyranny. The years soon pass in the palaces of kings and prelates. In the future I shall sing only of birds and flowers. I now realize that earthly goods are worthless and that the sun shines by day only to be followed by night's darkness. Beauty and light pass all too quickly. My soul was born to suffer. Tears will never quench the fires that consume me."

"Will you miss me?"

"Of course. I'll remember you with sadness."

"What will my life be without you?"

"You must make a new life. *Sail on and never look back.*"

Gregório waved goodbye. She threw him a kiss, touching her lips with her fingertips.

# Downfall

SETTLERS FOUND THE SUGAR-GROWING region of Recôn-cavo irresistible. It was a valley with rich, dark soil which extended to the coast where the air was pleasantly warm and invigorating. Over this wide expanse of black earth, alongside the clear waters of the ocean and criss-crossed by abundant rivers, the vast cane-brakes stretched into the distance in various shades of green, their swaying crests turning to gold. Hedgerows of dwarf-pines divided the land which stretched on forever, a picture of infinity.

Each large estate had its own water-mill and work-shops set alongside water drawn from a river or lake. Smoke billowed from the sheds around the clock and by nightfall the furnaces were aglow, casting fiery rays in every direction. Stacks of cut cane lay waiting to be transported to the roadsides.

But there was more than sugar-cane in Recôncavo. Lime, cotton and ginger were also produced in the region; fishing and horticulture; ships were built and a whaling industry yielded oil. Tobacco-growing in well-manured beds, or in forest clearings, fenced in or surrounded by walls, became increasingly common, resulting in long, dark green strips and yellow blotches gouged into the ground.

Sugar was planted in the rich, clay soil known as *massapê*. Where the soil was more sandy, manioc and vegetables were grown. Boats plied the rivers and sea, their paddle-wheels turned by poles instead of oars. Carts drawn by oxen went back and forth over dirt tracks, sometimes transporting faggots of cut cane or crates of sugar, other times empty.

Many forests had been reduced to half their former size or were felled completely. Some had been transformed into pastures for horses, cattle, sheep and goats. Turkeys, hens and ducks strutted around the huts where the slaves lived or near the houses of the chaplains, schoolmasters, foremen and other skilled workers in the mills.

The mansions of the sugar barons dominated the landscape. These provided the perfect setting for games and festivities, for sport and religious ceremonies over which the landowners presided with their families, local dignitaries, priests, chaplains and invited guests.

In the slave quarters, the black labourers lived out their lives amidst hardship and tyranny, accidents and disease, drunkenness and merry-making, marriages and abortions, suicide and death, sacred rituals and sexual orgies.

# I

O N ONE OF HIS JOURNEYS through Recôncavo, still hoping he would find Maria, Gregório de Matos decided to pay Samuel da Fonseca a visit.

Without being miserly like some landowners in the region or profligate like others who wished to pass for aristocrats, Fonseca managed his plantation efficiently. His estate was provided with all the essentials but he avoided any ostentation and kept few horses, musicians or footmen. Male slaves, dressed in coarse woollen tunics, served at table; comely women slaves prepared appetizing delicacies which were served on tin plates.

The place was gloomy. From the distance came the perpetual roar of blazing furnaces. They were in constant use for eight months of the year.

The Rabbi and the poet began discussing the serious difficulties facing plantation owners. Bahia produced between fourteen and fifteen thousand crates of sugar annually, each crate weighing thirty-five *arrobas*, and worth between one thousand and seven hundred and one thousand and eight hundred *contos*. In that year, 1684, a good harvest was expected, but increased production was forcing the planters to sell at lower prices and even to burn the refined sugar. As well as coping with the vagaries of nature and the inevitable problems in sugar production, the landowners were also at the mercy of inept policies authorized by the Crown.

"Plantation owners are on the brink of ruin," Fonseca explained. "If you want to make a profit nowadays the thing to grow is tobacco."

The demand for tobacco from Lisbon was increasing every year, and the large consignments of rolled tobacco carried by fleets could no longer supply a market which was expanding beyond Europe.

The profits from sugar and tobacco were a godsend after the evils caused by the Dutch War – for which they were still paying – with a tax known as the Dowry of England or Peace of Holland, introduced by Francisco Barreto de Menezes, the victorious general of the Pernambucan War. But the colony was shackled to Portugal. The bullion and wealth did not remain in Brazil. The economy progressed when it served the needs of the landed gentry in the metropolis.

They exchanged sugar for salt, tobacco for oil, rum for wine, and a system of barter was instituted whereby payment was made in sugar rather than money. Prices for merchandise in the colony were disastrously low. In Portugal they were exorbitant. People lined up outside the shops and markets to buy whatever was available. Some blamed the authorities for the city's misfortunes, others blamed the fleet which set off with a full cargo of meat, fish and beans, while people in the colony starved.

"Brazilians are fools to spend their lives toiling in order to support the idle rich in Portugal," declared Gregório, putting on his spectacles. He got up and began examining the books in Fonseca's study. A light breeze penetrated the open window. With it came the smell of cane, of sugar simmering in the cauldrons.

Fonseca stared out of the window which looked onto scorched fields; beyond them lay the sea. Slaves were lined up outside one of the storage sheds; a negro woman at the door of the mill was pouring off the scum from the boiling sugar cane into jugs which the slaves set down at their feet. They offered in exchange a chicken or a basket of cereals, a bunch of bananas, or vegetables from their kitchen-gardens. Slung over their shoulders, male slaves carried crabs, strung together and dripping mud, their claws still moving. Black children drank from earthenware mugs.

The mill was driven by water from the river. The wheels turned slowly. In one day, anything from twenty-five to thirty cartloads of cane could be milled. The quantity of sugar produced depended on the quality of the cane. Production could not be increased by the mill itself. Only a certain amount of cane could be fed into the press at a time to avoid breaking the spindle or a spoke. The speed of the rollers had to be kept steady by controlling the amount of water because the supply from the reservoir was limited, and the large cauldrons could only boil the quantity determined before-hand. Fonseca's plantation was somewhat primitive.

He commented that Europeans were becoming richer and more civilized by the day. They were inventing machines, introducing laws to protect merchants, improving their methods for manufac-turing goods. A Jew from Barbados had paid him a visit and shown him plans for a new type of mill which would produce greater quantities of sugar with less effort. But Dom Samuel did not have the capital to invest in such a project and he had tried to interest the Crown in setting up a similar invention in Bahia. This suggestion was met with scepticism and derision. Even the Jesuits were frustrated in their efforts to found a university in Brazil because of persistent refusals on the part of the King and his advisers. In France, a wonderful machine had been built at Marly to raise the water-level of the Seine. The English scientist Newton had made admirable discoveries. Papin had invented a safety-valve and introduced the theory of using steam for engines. People said he was a lunatic; they were all lunatics, but that is how the world progressed, driven on by prophetic minds.

"Knowledge can be deceptive," replied Gregório. "The people who know most about this world are the fishmongers in the market-place and the washer women by the stream."

"You're wrong, Gregório. As the philosopher Vieira once said, 'The ignorant man sees the moon and thinks it is bigger than the stars. The wise man knows how to distinguish the real from the imaginary.' It has to be proved that air exists even though we breathe it, one has to be able to calculate probabilities, and verify that there really is a circle of light around Saturn; one has to experience for oneself the poetic hemispheres of Magdeburg."

"And speaking of poetic experiences, how is Dona Maria Berco?" asked Gregório. "Has she found happiness now that she's rich?"

"She's still confined to bed and trying to recover. She's not like other young women who are never happier than when they can set out for church dressed up in finery and fluttering their fans. Money has not changed her. She can't help brooding on the past. I suppose she'll get married again and have children. She's an excellent cook and can weave better than most women. Yet she seems apprehensive . . . Not because she's frightened of giving birth to some monster with crooked horns and rabbit's paws, that's not what's worrying her. She finds life disturbing."

Gregório thought about his wife Michaela who had died in Portugal. She could not sew or embroider and burned whatever she tried to cook.

"Even God makes mistakes," the poet reflected. He departed, frustrated in his desire to see Maria.

His burning passion for Maria, his overwhelming desire to hold her in his arms, made life on the Praia Grande unbearable for Gregório. He played nothing but melancholy airs on his guitar. Invariably drunk, he composed and recited his satires. Now and then he met up with a negro woman who provided some comfort. He could not resist their charms; he would hold them in his arms, and at nightfall possess them on the beach, in the water that gathered between the reefs, or beside a bonfire.

Many friends came from Bahia to visit him; they showed him much kindness, but their warmth and affection did little to alleviate his boredom, or assuage his nostalgia for city life. He felt abandoned and rejected. He missed the women of Bahia, those winsome girls from Portugal, intriguing hussies who opened their fans to conceal their faces, throwing provocative glances. Widows, negro women, half-castes, white women from the lower classes, nuns, docile maidens, shrews, Portuguese ladies and painted whores. He missed his outings with friends to the Rio Vermelho, the merrymaking by the Dyke, the comedies played in the open air, hunting expeditions in the hamlet of São Francisco, the escapades on the island of Madre de Deus where Gregório and his friends used to stage mock bull-fights in the fields with a cow named Camisa; pleasant reunions with friends in the Caijus, solitary outings by boat, trips to the Island of Gonçalo Dias transporting bananas and flour. Sadly he recalled the riotous jousting in Cajaíba, the black magic of Madre Celestina, the festivities in honour of Our Lady of Perpetual Succour which attracted bevies of grand ladies full of airs and graces, banquets where the wine flowed and the women got hopelessly tipsy and started dancing, shaking their hips, playing tambourines, quarrelling, retching, swooning, feasting, going off with their lovers. What fun they had during the feast of the Virgin of Guadalupe when the mulatto women got drunk and bathed in rivers of wine, laughing, slurring their words, belching, panting for breath, shamelessly lifting their skirts, belly-dancing, stuffing themselves with bread dipped in broth, and downing wine from Oporto and the Canaries. Why had it taken him so long to realize just how much all of this had meant to him: those open-air jousts in honour of the eleven thousand virgins of Cologne, those quadrilles and games?

He had turned into an old sea-wolf, and thought it unlikely that women would give him a second glance were he to return to the city. He was penniless, possessed no land or property, no private income. He had squandered everything his father had left him. In his despair he drank more rum. He had become sarcastic and bitter; his lampoons became increasingly spiteful. He censured hypocrisy, and mocked virtue with defiant arrogance. He even came to loathe Góngora's poetry despite the Spaniard's lofty diction. As if to prove his contempt, he himself began adopting the ribald speech of the lower orders without discretion or restraint.

But he had not forgotten Góngora. And certain phrases ran through his mind: *The thieves I denounced while protecting the seducer.*

Tomás Pinto Brandão went to visit the poet. He found Gregório in his hut, pacing to and fro, stark naked, his penis shrivelled up. He went outside and relieved himself. Then he put on a pair of breeches.

"There's nothing more satisfying than having a good piss in one's own backyard. When I used to do it in the streets of Bahia, the negro women would watch me, then run off shrieking."

His friend smiled.

"I've lost any shame I ever had."

"You'd better watch out, Gregório."

Gregório sat on the mat which also served as a bed, and started juggling shells. The ground was strewn with debris washed up by the sea, dried star-fish, corals, shells of every size and shape, conches, burrs, oyster shells, molluscs, crabs' claws and fishbones.

"I've also lost some of my hopes and ambitions. I've even lost a toe-nail which I stubbed on a stone. I've lost my books, my wife, my appointments, and I've wasted my days wandering from one place to the next."

"That's no waste. Travelling broadens the mind, lets you see the world."

"And what is there in the world that's worth seeing?"

"Well . . ." Tomás Pinto Brandão began, "For you, there are women . . . music. I can't think of anything else. And for me, there's poetry and religion."

Tomás removed his pumps. They walked barefoot on the sand, conversing.

"I'm always pleased when you arrive, bringing me news from the city," said Gregório. "I spend my days writing satires. For there aren't many women around to distract me. Now and then a woman passes through accompanied by a female slave . . . or a negress from the sugar plantation . . . Or some wench who has heard of my reputation and decides to pay me a visit. I even had a visit from a slave who fancied I was black. Me, who's whiter than white. But she fell in love with me anyway, despite my colour and upbringing. When a woman catches my fancy, she knows I'll be her slave and do her bidding."

"Let me copy the poems you've written and take them back to Bahia. I'll make copies there and pass them around. Why don't you sign them?"

"To avoid being burned at the stake. To whom will you show them?"

"To everybody. Lovers read them in bed to excite their passion. They're read in taverns, brothels, in places of ill-repute, for they make people laugh. They're even read at the Jesuit College, in their library, at private gatherings. They're passed from hand to hand, mouth to mouth, ear to ear. People memorize, recite and paraphrase them, copy them into notebooks. The rabble amuses itself, jeering at the clergy, the magistrates, the gentry, the men of government, civil dignitaries, missionaries, women, thieves. No one escapes your mockery."

"Does Bahia deserve anything better?" asked Gregório de Matos. "You can't blame me, born and bred in Brazil, for the city's evils, its corrupt government, profligate clergy, dishonest merchants with their useless wares, grasping foreigners intent on getting rich, the endless thieving and violence, the clowning and buffoonery, the hordes of beggars and the swaggering aristocrats."

"Shall I tell you why the people like your verses? Because you don't give a damn whom you shock with your wicked jokes. You're as obscene as those ancient troubadours."

"What do you expect? There isn't much to amuse one here on the Praia Grande. I sit and stare into space all day long. Sometimes I feel as if I've been shut away in this solitary place for ages. Yet even here I can't resist putting my thoughts on paper. God help me! How I miss those negro women when I sing of love."

A few days later the poet received a visit from Samuel da Fonseca. The Rabbi alighted from his carriage assisted by a slave, who then lifted down a large trunk from the driver's seat.

"I've brought you gifts," Dom Samuel said. "Books, paper, ink, food, some fruit, preserves, flour, cheese and brown sugar. How are you faring?"

"Not too badly. Things could be worse."

Gregório sat down at a small table, took out some paper and began to write. He remained there for some time, scratching the paper with his quill which he kept dipping into the inkwell. He was breathing loudly, and tapped his fingers on the table. The Rabbi paced up and down, observing the room, staring out of the window, or watching the poet.

When he had finished the poem, Gregório read it to his friend. It was about his secret passion for Maria Berco.

"I long to see her again," he confessed.

"She's the person I've come to talk about. Dona Maria is on her feet again," the Rabbi said. "She has made a complete recovery. Poor girl, she had lost a lot of weight. They ill-treated her in prison. She was physically assaulted and raped. These things we must accept. Such are the misfortunes of war."

"Those bastards! The five most serious crimes have always been: murder, theft, armed robbery, forcing people to eat excrement and raping decent women. I'd love to get even with the Captain-General and Braço de Prata."

"Before leaving, Dona Maria asked me to convey her gratitude for all you did for her."

"Leaving? Why can't she remain on your plantation?"

"Because as you know, I intend to go back to Amsterdam to teach the Talmud in the Rabbinical colleges there. I'm about to sell the plantation to a friend of Dom Vasco de Paredes whom you probably know."

"Of course, he's Dona Angela's father!"

"Thanks to you, Dona Maria Berco has been recognized as the rightful heir to her late husband's fortune. The courts have upheld her claim and she has been granted a pardon through the good offices of Rocha Pita."

"Then I must also return to Bahia."

"I don't think this is the right time. Things are still volatile there. The repression has got worse. De Souza seems to have taken leave of his senses. He's stripping his enemies of all their rights; the men he consorts with are hateful, inept and unreliable. The evil prosper and the honest are persecuted."

There was no doubt in the Rabbi's mind that those appointed to high office overseas could get rich fast and abuse their powers. The Crown turned a blind eye to irregularities. Those who governed in the colonies were not playing games. They knew that they were sufficiently remote from Lisbon to do as they pleased without being censured or punished.

The Ravasco faction, like that of the Menezes, was apprehensive about what news the fleet would bring. What consideration would the King show them? The same as they had shown him? In the King's name, they had given sweat and blood.

"It's never easy to bring evil men to justice," said Gregório. "I'm pleased for Dona Maria's sake. Yet I can't help feeling anxious. Don't ask me why, but I'm afraid."

This was not a moment for explanations; but even to feel oneself in love was something of a triumph. Go on, go on, he thought to himself. It won't be long now. All he craved was one night in Maria's arms and he would have no further need of books, women, wine, Vieira, Góngora, a warm climate, travel, dreams. They would all become meaningless. But why, dear God? Why?

"She'll be waiting for you tonight in the chapel on my estate," the Rabbi told him. "Be there at seven."

Dusk began to fall. Gregório had dozed off. He woke up in a sweat, saw stars in the sky.

"Good heavens, Maria is expecting me!"

Overcome with emotion, his heart pounding, Gregório crossed the room, stepping over the clothes and food scattered across the floor, and dashed out of the door.

He rode as fast as he could to Fonseca's plantation.

The old goats and stray dogs were awake. There were tinkling bells on some of the animals. The gentle strumming of a guitar could be heard in the distance. A voice sang softly: "Where are the dead and dear departed . . .?" The landscape was washed in sombre tones.

The chapel was empty.

Gregório headed for the beach where a slave was singing and playing the guitar. The poet hovered nearby, listening.

The mill was working at full spate. Men were throwing great logs into the gaping furnaces. Some of the slaves worked in chains – syphilitics being purged of disease and criminals expiating their crimes. Smoke belched out and spread in the wind.

Thinking about Maria consoled Gregório. He had written poems and phrases he'd meant to show her, but had forgotten to bring them. Perhaps it was just as well. He felt a fool. How he longed to see her. How he had dreamed of this moment and had now ruined it by falling asleep like a lazy mule. *How to conquer hell with hell?* Góngora y Argote had once written.

He returned to the chapel and knelt before the altar. It saddened him to think of young Gaspar's death and of the departure of the Rabbi who, like a bird, suddenly felt the need to migrate. On the altar there was a statue of a saint with a sweet expression. He pondered Fonseca's reasons for preserving the chapel with its holy images and crucifixes after buying the plantation. Some men were capable of forgetting the past and forgiving. This was a Church which persecuted Jews. Perhaps Padre Vieira was right about the Jews being really good men. Samuel da Fonseca certainly was.

The sound of furnaces and cauldrons penetrated the deep silence of night. Gregório was still thinking about Padre Vieira when suddenly he heard a noise behind him. He turned round.

Someone was approaching, a woman, her face covered with a transparent black veil. It was Maria Berco.

"I thought you'd never arrive."

He was paralysed, staring at her in disbelief. Then recovering himself, he said:

"I rarely keep promises and I'm forever disappointing people. But believe me, I desperately wanted to see you again."

Maria was actually there. It was dark and they were alone, looking into each other's eyes.

"Don't worry. I often spend whole nights awake trying in vain to fall asleep," she replied.

The poet recalled how as a child he used to gaze in wonder at pictures of women in books. He had been a solemn and pensive little boy; perhaps manhood had brought on but few changes. For many years now, women had ceased to be remote images, mysterious and innocent. They had a distinct odour, form, will and determination. Yet Maria Berco seemed unreal beneath her veil.

They sat side by side in silence looking at the statue of the saint. Gregório wanted to speak but could not find anything to say. He felt tempted to stretch out on a bench and possess her in the darkness.

He waited.

"I prefer night to day," she said, rousing herself. Her voice seemed different.

"So do I."

Her long, shapely body had an almost noble dignity.

"Why are you wearing a veil? I want to see your face."

"No," she replied. "My face is not what it was. It is disfigured and ugly."

"Your beauty comes from those sparkling eyes, from those fair tresses falling in ringlets, from that sensitive soul which guides your every movement." He took her hand and kissed it, then put his arms around her. He tried to kiss her on the lips. She drew away.

"I'm thinking of going to Portugal," she said.

"Portugal?"

"Yes. Tell me about it."

He thought. "The place is ancient. Here everything is young and new."

"Is that what brought you back here?"

"Perhaps."

Maria smiled. She raised her hand to her mouth in a manner which reminded him of Padre Vieira. He caught a closer look at her face.

He could see the scars.

He loved her more than ever but he no longer desired to possess her.

"I love you," he said, "and it's too late to conceal it from you. I'm in the most awful chaos and confusion and in the throes of passion."

"You mustn't say such things."

"Why not? Are you in love with someone else?"

"No. There are no men in my life. And the few I've met are like animals. They repulse me."

They fell silent. Then he asked her: "Do you find me repulsive?"

"No," answered Maria, studying him.

"Do I remind you of a little grasshopper?"

"Not really. You're more like a hawk. And what about me? What do I remind you of?"

"The enchanted island of San Morondon."

She chuckled.

"The island no one ever reaches because it keeps moving away. And when you do finally get there, it's only to discover that it doesn't actually exist."

Maria replied: "But I do exist, and if I'm still alive I owe my life to you."

Gazing into her eyes, Gregório brought her hand to his lips and kissed it.

"This mouth people call the mouth of hell doesn't deserve to kiss you."

"I'm leaving for the city."

"Dom Samuel told me. I'll meet up with you there."

"Are you serious about going?"

"Yes."

"Can I wait for you?"

"Of course."

"What future is there for us?"

"We'll get married."

She remained silent, watching him.

"Goodbye," she said.

"Until soon," he answered.

She made her way home in the darkness.

Gregório lingered. Who is this woman, who is she? This woman called Maria Berco, who had won his heart from the moment he first set eyes on her, ever since that night of festivities in the Rua Debaixo. They had conversed so little. He did not want to know and felt ashamed for having posed such a question, especially since he had certain premonitions about Maria and felt that they would never be together again. What could she be thinking? She probably only knew two things about him: Gregório de Matos was a poet; he seduced women then vanished.

A tiny fleet of three vessels sailed quietly over the calm waters. Gregório sat alone on the stone wall. Once more he heard the strains of a guitar. Human forms began to appear on the shore and gathered round the slave who was playing. They lit a bonfire. There were drums, voices, women's laughter.

"What do I hear? Skirts rustling? Ah, those adorable negro women."

The poet dashed for the beach.

# II

I T WAS A BRIGHT MORNING in Bahia. The fresh mountain
breeze blew through the open windows of the palace.

After exchanging a few words with a skinny man carrying
a casket bearing the royal coat of arms, the major-domo opened
the door to the Governor's antechamber. The man entered and
informed Mata that he was a courier sent by His Majesty.

Several people were seated in the antechamber waiting to be
called.

Mata showed the royal courier into Antonio de Souza's study.

The Governor sat behind his desk. A halo of light outlined his
body against the open window. The sky was blue and clear.

"Your Excellency," said the man. "I've just arrived from Portugal with the fleet."

"Welcome to Bahia," De Souza replied.

"I've brought dispatches from the King."

De Souza looked at him uneasily.

The courier took out a sealed scroll from the casket.

De Souza smiled. He unrolled the scroll and began reading. He
began to turn pale.

"I'm deeply sorry, Your Excellency," the man continued. "The
Royal Council has ordered that the plaintiff, Bernardo Vieira
Ravasco, should be reinstated at once as Secretary of State and
War."

"But the man's a criminal!" the Governor exploded.

"The Council has decided that the Secretary should be allowed
to resume his duties and responsibilities without delay."

"So, Bernardo Ravasco is to resume his duties, favoured and protected by the Crown! And I am expected to reinstate him and to confront his guilty face every day in the corridor of my own palace!"

De Souza's eyes narrowed.

"I hope Your Excellency will bear with me while I read out the other dispatches," the courier said. "There is another document here from the King addressed to Your Excellency. A letter." He held it out to the Governor. "I also have a copy which I'm to deliver to the Chancellor. Its contents are to be made public."

De Souza read the King's letter. He leaned forward, resting his chin on one hand. So this is how it would all end.

Gregório had spent a troubled night, tossing and turning in his sleep. No sooner had he closed his eyes than he dreamt that Maria was at his side, but however hard he tried, he could not get an erection. A stranger appeared in his dream to taunt him: "Perhaps because she's an upright woman that prick of yours cannot perform."

The dream was still vivid in his mind when he was roused by knocking at the door. Half-dazed, he got out of bed. The sun had just risen.

"Did I get you out of bed?" asked Tomás Pinto Brandão.

"I haven't had much sleep, Tomás. I spent most of the night with a negro woman."

Gregório looked a fright. His hair was starting to thin rapidly. He put on his spectacles and peered at his friend. He sat down and stretched out his long legs, resting his feet on the table.

"Have you heard what's happening in the city?" Tomás asked.

"I haven't the faintest idea."

"Indeed! First of all, Dom Bernardo has come out of his retreat. He's going back to the Secretariat."

"Never!"

"And a Royal decree has been circulated in the city. My houseboy, Moçorongo, brought me a copy. Take a look."

Gregório read aloud:

"To Antonio de Souza de Menezes. Your King sends you cordial greetings. Having considered your advancing years and the long period of service you have rendered the Crown, I am sure you must be anxious to return to Portugal. Therefore I have appointed the Marquês de Minas as your successor, and hereby advise you of my decision. Written in Lisbon on the ninth day of March in the year 1684. The King.''

"From his sick-bed, at the other end of the world, Padre Vieira still has the power to topple governors. And within the space of nine months. Just as in the old days, when João IV entrusted him with the destiny of Portugal," said Pinto Brandão.

"I can't believe it!"

"I assure you it's true. The Marquis of Minas has been Padre Vieira's friend for many years. Moreover, he's related to close allies of the Ravasco family. Braço de Prata has already stated he'll seek compensation from the King if he's forced to accept early retirement."

"Is that so! I'm beginning to warm to the man. I've always been fond of losers."

Tomás Pinto Brandão smiled. He considered himself a loser.

A small cask of wine rested on the table, and debris still cluttered the floor. Gregório grabbed two tankards.

"A toast."

The poet declaimed: "Farewell meadows and pastures, farewell torrential falls, farewell rustic dwelling, farewell white sands bestrewn with tiny shells. Farewell dear servants and whoring housemaids, farewell my grooms and stable-lads. Farewell cool shadows where urchins romp and quarrel all day. Farewell sweet Recôncavo where loose women are all too scarce. How I'll miss you once I'm gone. But right now I must go and tell Dom Samuel what's happening."

Tomás sank onto a bench. "Can I ask you something?"

"Of course."

"What are you hoping to do once you return to Bahia?"

"I really don't know."

"Are you going to keep running away?"

"You asked if you could put one question. That's two."

"But you didn't answer the first one."

"One can't run away from . . ."

Gregório didn't finish the sentence.

"From one's destiny?" asked Tomás.

"From hell."

Gregório lay back and closed his eyes.

Pinto Brandão sat for several minutes, smiling. Then he asked: "And what about Braço de Prata?"

But Gregório was fast asleep.

On a wall in the chapel patio stood two bronze cannons made in Holland by Henrique Vestrink. They had been placed there to protect the plantation from Dutch corsairs whose ships periodically attacked, marauding and sacking the estates along the coast. The cannons were covered in verdigris and the reddish-gold patina of the metal had been completely eroded.

Arm in arm, Gregório and Fonseca emerged from the house and made their way to the patio. From there they could view the surrounding region and the entire bay, with the two extremities of land jutting out towards each other until they almost met on the horizon. It was a bright day, the sky and sea painted the same deep blue.

They sat on a wall built by slaves, the stones set one on top of the other with admirable skill. It surrounded the patio, then descended the mountain slopes, skirting the property parallel with the sea. To reach the shore one had to pass through narrow gaps.

Children played on the wall in the distance. Their shrill voices rang out, carried by the wind.

"I can just imagine what Braço de Prata is up to in the city, making good use of his last days in power: filling his coffers, overcrowding the prisons and cemeteries with all those who have opposed him, employing relatives, friends, and friends of friends to help him. A state of total chaos."

"It looks as if this nightmare is almost over."

"I'm sure you're right."

One of the urchins playing on the wall called out that people were coming. A ship was approaching, weaving through the water, veering away from the rocks, taking advantage of the gusts of wind. After some clever manoeuvring, it dropped anchor, not far beyond the docks.

A rowing boat was then lowered, with two oarsmen and two others: one in a cassock, the other of noble bearing, neatly attired and bewigged, and refined in his gestures.

"It's my brother," said Gregório.

"Yes, it's Padre Eusébio. And Bernardo Ravasco."

Gregório felt both happy and sad. How would his brother react upon seeing him like this, with a guitar slung over one shoulder, unshaven, scruffy and in rags? He ran his fingers through his hair, tucked his shirt inside his breeches. Rested his guitar against the wall.

A few minutes later the two men disembarked.

The brothers embraced each other.

Eusébio de Matos was the middle brother in the family and following tradition had studied for the priesthood. He was the author of poems and essays. Eusébio had joined the Jesuit Order and was highly esteemed especially by Padre Vieira. Possessed of a prodigious memory, he could debate in public without ever having to consult his sources to win his argument: he only had to study a theological matter for a few minutes in order to be able to elucidate it from the pulpit or in the presence of visiting Jesuits from Évora who had been sent by the Father General. He upheld that human happiness, so avidly pursued and desired by all, was found in simple things, such as stretching out on the grass and sleeping to one's heart's content, in full view of everyone who passed.

A brilliant preacher, he was often compared with Antonio Vieira and Francisco de Sá. He had been expelled from the Jesuit Order for advocating freedom, especially in his relationships with women who gave him a number of illegitimate children. He was appointed parish priest at the Carmelite church, and in this capacity he preached in the Cathedral. When Eusébio visited Portugal, Padre Vieira went to hear his venerable friend deliver his sermon. After the service, Vieira embraced him and expressed his personal regret that the Jesuit Order should have shown such intolerance by disowning one of its most courageous and outspoken members.

His hands worn, swollen and shaky, Bernardo Ravasco clutched a sheaf of papers. He was much thinner, and the suffering he had endured in prison had left its mark; his skin was in poor condition, his eyes rheumy and sad. Visibly moved, he announced the arrival of the new Governor, the Marquis of Minas. "We shall have peace restored at long last," he said.

Dom Antonio Luiz de Souza was forty years of age, the second Marquis of Minas, the fourth Count of Prado and Master of the Vilas de Guvari. He had started his miliary career at Elvas with his father, in the War of Restoration. After the signing of the Peace Treaty, he had been appointed army chief of the region between the Douro and Minho, and was subsequently nominated field-commander. He was reputed to be a kindly man, diligent in his duties as soldier and politician. Everyone knew the city's problems could not be attributed entirely to De Souza, yet people were convinced that things would improve under the Marquis of Minas. But the matter was not completely resolved. Bernardo Ravasco still had some revelations to make.

No one really knew what the King thought about the situation in the colony. For years now he had been fed the most damaging gossip about the Ravascos.

The flagship of the fleet had brought a letter addressed to Gonçalo Ravasco in which His Majesty expressed his extreme displeasure with Antonio Vieira for having undermined the Governor's authority.

The Ravascos had been hoping that the King would reprimand De Souza and order him to withdraw his allegations in public. After all, the old Jesuit had been publicly denounced as an accomplice in the crime. However, it had always been in Padre Vieira's nature to forgive rather than complain about a personal insult; he had been too slow in protesting his innocence. As a result of Vieira's generosity, or negligence or Christian piety, the King, who was ever wary, had drawn his own conclusions after listening to only the Governor's side of the argument. Antonio de Souza's excesses were only considered seriously by the King after different sources had lodged complaints. And even while deposing the Governor, Dom Pedro II had stripped Vieira of all privileges, communicating his decision, first through Gonçalo, and again through Francisco da Costa Pinto.

The King had secretly taken steps to ensure that Vieira was to be deprived of all benefices except those guaranteed by ecclesiastical immunity. And he issued other, more severe and rigorous penal-

ties, which were to be ratified in Portugal and then made public
in the colony.

Judge André de Moraes Sarmento arrived some weeks after the
flagship, to investigate the conduct of the deposed De Souza. The
Ravascos were under the impression that the Judge had been
chosen by the Marquis of Gouveia, who was well-disposed
towards Padre Vieira. But after Moraes Sarmento heard the people
offer more praise than criticism for De Souza, he appeared to
be wholly in favour of the ex-Governor. Many of De Souza's
enemies had refrained from testifying. They were content to see
Braço de Prata removed from power and recalled to Portugal
for good.

The Crown Inspector had been briefed by the King to establish
whether Bernardos Ravasco had really been removed from office
by Antonio de Souza without a formal hearing. The Inspectorate's
notary had also come empowered to assume Bernardo's duties,
should he be proved guilty.

During the inspection, the allies of the Ravasco faction faced
greater reprisals than those of the Menezes. The latter, who had
found refuge on the outskirts of the city, were now back home,
sleeping peacefully in their own beds. But friends of the Ravascos
against whom false evidence had been presented in Lisbon – either
by impartial witnesses who had been bribed to change their evidence or by enemies who spontaneously offered to testify – still
ran the risk of criminal charges. The Crown Inspector had the
power to pass sentence but not to release or pardon. Pity the poor
wretch who fell into his clutches.

His inquiry completed, Moraes Sarmento returned to Portugal
with affidavits to support De Souza, thus creating the impression
of an exemplary Governor.

Encouraged by the outcome of the inquiry, the Governor spent
his last days in office parading through the city streets, confident
that a favourable reception awaited him in Lisbon. He refused to
acknowledge defeat. He had even tried to bring the Chancellor
into disrepute by accusing him of also being involved in Teles de
Menezes' assassination.

A great many years before, the taciturn and deformed King of
Portugal, Dom Sebastião, known as the "King of Shadows", had

set out to fight the Battle of Alcácer-Quibir with a fleet of eight hundred warships, carrying large coaches, luxurious tents for the nobility, collapsible churches, and a retinue of thousands: chaplains, musicians, silversmiths, prostitutes, exotic birds, hounds, troubadours, poets, minstrels, chroniclers, choristers, and an infinite number of people without any specific function, one person assigned to look after each of the sixteen thousand soldiers who were ready to fight. And notwithstanding the vast number of attendants and warriors, or perhaps because they were so many, no one saw the King die. His corpse was never found.

Following the Portuguese tradition of large entourages, Braço de Prata took his leave with pomp and ceremony, laden with baggage and trophies: chests, boxes, parcels, horses, carriages, caskets. To mark his departure, a huge guard of honour was formed by the infantry, halberdiers and cavalry. Church bells were rung. Caparisoned horses with red velvet blankets, polished harnesses, reins, and jingling stirrups, startled by the shouting people who ran past with torches. Some of the onlookers cursed Braço de Prata, others praised him.

Some were even reciting lines from one of Gregório de Matos' satires: *"The man who ascends without merit takes office as a man, accepts it like a fool, and makes an ass of himself, for success often spells disaster. Perverse fortune often turns to farce, makes a hero of a worthless fool, and once the wheel of fortune stops turning, he's back to being a man, for fortune is discreet in her reversals. I know Your Lordship was a man when favoured by fortune, but an ass to assume high office. So call a halt! Go back to where you started. Far better to be an ordinary man than an exalted jackass."*

On taking his leave, Antonio de Souza assured the crowd that he would return to finish his term of office.

The King's decision to depose Antonio de Souza appeared to have been brought about by political pressures rather than his own inclination. Perhaps His Majesty felt it was preferable to recall a Governor with his reputation intact than leave him to suffer hardship in the colony. Another post could be found for Antonio de Souza in Portugal, or in some other colony.

As for Padre Vieira, the King remained intransigent, refused to show clemency and publicly censured him. Antonio Vieira was content to live out the last years of his life exiled in Brazil, but was saddened by the King's hostility.

In the end, it was far from clear who had emerged from this feud with shame or honour.

Bernardo concluded his story. His eyes were lifeless, his hands shaking. His last days in prison had been beset by misfortunes. A nervous wreck, he was often delirious.

Padre Vieira also became chronically ill. He spent night after night without sleep, he could no longer eat and became steadily weaker. Everyone feared that this relapse might prove fatal. He declared himself prepared for death and expressed his regret that the Ravascos were not being allowed to live or die in peace. It saddened him to think that his last years had been embittered by the offspring of a dynasty for which he had risked so much, rebuffed by the very same King for whom he had worked so hard. Despite his frailty and advanced years, Padre Vieira still observed an austere regime. He slept on a small, narrow pallet, his feet sticking out at one end, his head at the other. His sleep was troubled by nightmares and fits of shaking. He would wake up frequently, sweating profusely and muttering inaudible words. Though the causes of these disorders had long since gone, the effects persisted.

If the tidings brought by Bernardo from this world were bad, signs from the sky did not augur anything better. In May, two comets were sighted. Prophetic omens . . . The Jesuits had given instructions that drawings should be made of the meteors and dispatched to the King, to give him a clearer idea of this phenomenon. The first comet had been sighted in Pernambuco by a German priest, a famous mathematician. The second had appeared in the state of Rio de Janeiro, where it was seen by Indians and missionaries working in the region. The Pernambuco meteor had appeared during the day, dissecting the sun; the one in Rio appeared at night, trailed by three stars. All that was missing was a sign from the moon to confirm the adage: *Erunt signa in sole et luna et stellis.*

And thus ended the tyrannical rule of Braço de Prata.

EPILOGUE

# *Destiny*

G REGÓRIO DE MATOS stayed on in Recôncavo for some years. He forgot Maria Berco. Peace was restored under the governorship of the Marquês de Minas. Gregório went back to practising law. He fell madly in love with Maria de Povos, black, widowed and penniless, who became his wife. From this marriage, which brought a dowry provided by the bride's uncle, he had a son whom he christened Gonçalo in honour of Bernardo Ravasco's son. The poet celebrated his love for Maria de Povos in some of his finest verses.

But soon after marrying, Gregório went back to riotous living, carousing with his friends, riding or taking excursions, attending banquets on the outskirts of Bahia or in Recôncavo, and getting into bed with all the women he could find.

He could not resist negro women, fornicated with them all, and entertained them with his satires.

Eventually he abandoned his wife and spent his time wandering around Recôncavo, drinking heavily and writing some of his best work. It was during this period that Gregório penned some of his most outrageous and profound poems attacking immoral behaviour in the colony.

When the Marquês de Minas finished his term of office, Gregório found himself once more in conflict with the authorities. The new Governor of Bahia was Antonio Luiz da Câmara Coutinho, dubbed the Toucan because of his enormous nose and his hunched back. After refusing the poet several favours, the Toucan found himself being cruelly lampooned. Gregório called Câmara Coutinho a bastard, accused him of being a pederast, a charlatan, a hunchbacked monster with a nose like a fiddle stuck into a face like a mandolin, a hyena who squeaked like a whore, as dense and insensitive as a stone, as thick as a tree-trunk, a degenerate who kept his footmen shackled while he sexually abused them, a jackass with itchy hooves, a strumpet in breeches who preferred an arse-hole to a cunt any day, and on and on.

When the Toucan's term of office finished, one of his nephews stayed behind in Bahia with the intention of killing Gregório. João de Lencastre, who succeeded the Toucan and befriended Gregório, decided the poet should be taken into custody for his own safety.

The poet fled to the island of Madre de Deus, only to be betrayed by Gonçalo Ravasco, who sent him a letter arranging a meeting. At the appointed place, Gregório came face to face with Lencastre's guards who were there to arrest him.

Gregório was subsequently released from the prison at Lioneira and exiled to Angola, aboard a caravel transporting part of the King's cavalry to Benguela. Gregório bade one last farewell to the city he had so heartily loved and loathed. *Farewell shores, farewell city, farewell friends, farewell Bahia, farewell infernal rabble.*

In Luanda the exiled poet became involved in a military uprising provoked by excessive taxes and the widespread poverty and famine in the colony of Angola. In recompense for having collaborated with the Governor, Gregório was allowed to leave Angola provided he did not return to Bahia but settled in Pernambuco, a condition imposed by Lencastre who wanted him as far away as possible.

In Recife, the poet was forbidden to write satires. He practised law in an office decorated with bananas. He walked around stark naked, terrifying people. Struggling to survive and in poor health, he lived on until 1695, writing sonnets and his inevitable satires. He stuck to his beliefs and kept on intimate terms with women and God. Overcome by "a malignant fever which sent the strongest of men to their graves within seven days", Gregório de Matos died at the age of fifty-nine. He was buried in the chapel in the Hospice of Our Lady of Penha. The chapel was later demolished, leaving no trace of the poet's remains.

His poems were transcribed into a book at the request of João de Lencastre. The book lay open in a room at the palace and people would file past with satires and lyrics they had copied down, or they would recite them on the spot to be recorded for posterity.

No one could be certain that all these poems had been composed by Gregório de Matos, but he was to be remembered as the incomparable master of satire, verbal abuse, censure and ridicule; as a poet who feared neither man nor God; a master of ambivalence and innuendo, whose obscene and blasphemous verses recounted and invented scatological tales of lust and love. For years to come, any poems written in this genre continued to be associated with the name of Gregório de Matos.

ANTONIO VIEIRA, despite failing health, carried on writing and revising his sermons. He produced a volume of sermons every year, and thereafter one every other year until 1689. He painstakingly modified his notes and sketches and, although blind in one eye, he wrote everything down himself. Padre Soares, who remained at his side, assisted him.

But he felt the need to do more than simply write. From his sick-bed he continued to campaign for his ideals of justice and truth. He got involved in controversial issues concerning the government of the colony in which Bernardo Ravasco played a leading role as Secretary General. Then at the age of eighty, Padre Vieira was appointed Visitor General to the missions.

Severe flooding of the River São Francisco swept away houses and inundated the region. Two missionaries who were working among the Tapuya tribes in villages engulfed with water prayed in vain for the disaster to pass. When they saw that the Christian God was not so powerful after all, the Indians decided to create their own god. They chose the tallest man of their tribe, censed him with tobacco smoke, and began worshipping him in a thatched church. No sooner were the Portuguese authorities informed than they ordered the native god to be taken captive and the church burnt down. The Indians in their villages were then left to their fate. Padre Vieira interceded on their behalf. To relieve their famine, he sent them a generous sum of money, not from Jesuit funds, but from the profits earned from his own publications.

He waged a campaign to have black Jesuit priests instead of Italian missionaries posted to Palmares, in the Republic of Ganga Zumba along the River São Francisco.

He also took an interest in the devaluation of the currency.

There was a real danger of money disappearing altogether in Brazil because of the fleets. Merchants found it more profitable to send precious metals – on which they paid neither freight nor duty – than to export sugar. Those who were not merchants but who found it just as easy to send out gold and silver exploited this situation in order to purchase political power and influence, to secure ecclesiastical and secular appointments, or to pay the dowries of women destined for convents.

There were other reasons for the drain on money from Brazil. Merchants, ministers and other dignitaries who had made their fortune in the colony invariably returned to Portugal with more wealth than they had brought. The constant outflow of money gradually weakened the colony's economy. People living there could no longer find a market for their products, nor could they raise enough money to invest in manufacturing goods. Any cultural activities were fast disappearing. Potentially rich land was being neglected and abandoned. Padre Vieira had suggested to the King that the problem might be solved by creating a local currency with a stable value. But ministers in Brazil rejected this idea out of self-interest.

Padre Vieira also revived the Indian question. This time he angered the colonists in São Paulo who depended on Indian labour in the mines, now that gold had finally been discovered thanks to the pioneering efforts of explorers in Southern Brazil.

By 1696, Vieira was completely blind and partially deaf. Yet he continued to correspond by dictating his letters to José Soares. One addressed to Sebastião de Matos e Souza was about the endless conflict between merchants and plantation owners over the price of sugar. He argued that the price for sugar, still weighed by hand, should be lowered, so that the prices of other commodities could also come down. And he condemned the inflated prices of sugar in Portugal and Angola.

As a priest he knew that these matters were no concern of his, but Vieira believed that in moments of crisis and need, no one should remain indifferent and that everyone should help to remedy injustices.

He spent five years as a missionary in the Bahia region, and nine years in Maranhão, where he built sixteen churches and catechized the natives in seven different languages. In all, he made thirty-six sea voyages and visited France, England, Holland, Sweden, Italy and Brazil in the service of the Portuguese Crown.

He maintained a correspondence with friends in Portugal and other European countries, also with royal personages such as Queen Catherine of England. Sensing the approach of death, Padre Vieira sent a circular to the nobility of Portugal, bidding them farewell.

In response, an envoy from the fleet was dispatched at once to verify whether the old Jesuit was still alive so that word could be sent back to Lisbon. Almost to the end, the old man insisted on celebrating Mass every day.

Shortly after the envoy's departure, Antonio Vieira died. His final moments were witnessed by José Soares and the rector of the college in Bahia, Gianantonio Andreoni, an Italian Jesuit with whom he engaged in many a lively and heated discussion. Padre Andreoni was reluctant to condemn the slavery of the Indians and had translated an antisemitic work work entitled *The Disenchanted Synagogue* into Italian. Andreoni also felt that Italian and German priests should be appointed to all the important posts in the Jesuit hierarchy. This annoyed Padre Vieira, a rabid patriot who did everything in his power to advance the careers of his fellow Portuguese. He died soon after completing the writing of his *Clavis prophetarum.*

The ship which sailed for Lisbon in the summer of 1697 with the news of his death also carried a number of his letters.

BERNARDO RAVASCO died two days after his brother. Gravely ill, he knew nothing of Antonio Vieira's death. In 1687, he, along with his brother, had been cleared of plotting the death of the Captain-General.

His book, *A Topographical Description of Civic and Military Institutions in Brazil*, vanished without trace. Five years before his death, he wrote *A Political Appraisal of Portugal's Role within the present conflict between the Crowns of Europe, and the damaging consequences for the Portuguese monarchy should it declare itself neutral.*

He left behind a large output of poetry in Portuguese and

Spanish. But he never realized his dream of entering the Jesuit Order. Padre Vieira discouraged any such idea, for he believed that his brother could do more for the colony in his capacity as Secretary of State.

After Dom Bernardo's death, his son, Gonçalo Cavalcanti de Albuquerque, was appointed to replace him as Secretary. The nomination was officially ratified on 13 July, 1663.

Having betrayed his good friend Gregório de Matos, Gonçalo began to suffer from insomnia and nightmares. But he was an exemplary Secretary of State.

JOSÉ SOARES, who had served Padre Vieira as secretary and faithful companion for more than thirty years, died at the ripe old age of seventy-four. Fifteen days before his death, according to Andreoni, Padre Soares saw Antonio Vieira in a vision "with his eyes raised to heaven and inviting him to join him", a vision which "brought him immense joy". Several days later he took to his bed. "In the middle of a conversation he suddenly asked that a bell should be rung, as was the custom, announcing that the end was near. No sooner had the prayers for the dying been said, than he passed away, leaving everyone present envious of his edifying death."

JOÃO DE ARAUJO GOIS, as usual, set out from home each morning at nine o'clock. At five minutes past nine he passed in front of the church, signed himself, and kissed the Cross of the Holy Order of Christ he wore around his neck. At fifteen minutes past nine he walked into the Tribunal to begin the day's work.

One April morning in 1683, anyone hoping to check his watch as the magistrate appeared would have been taken by surprise. For the first time in the twenty-one years he had worked in the Court of Appeals, the son of the clerk of the Misericórdia Alms-house did not leave the house. Instead, a buxom female slave came dashing out to blurt out the news: Gois was dead.

He, too, had succumbed to the plague which had overtaken the city. The deadly epidemic spread throughout Bahia, decimating the population, as it did in India, Thessaly, Macedonia and the

Mediterranean where it had penetrated Southern France, parts of England, Germany and Poland.

In the colony, there were endless outbreaks of smallpox, measles, syphilis, endemic goitre, infections and diseases, fevers and dysentery. The Jesuits, assuming the role of native quacks and black witch-doctors, used medicine as a powerful instrument for conversion. After some practice, the Jesuits became skilled at amputating limbs and sucking out the poison when labourers were bitten by snakes. But their methods were arbitrary. In a number of colonial towns there were no pharmacies apart from those provided by the Jesuits who became the healers of souls and bodies, although their notion of medicine was primitive, and they kept neither notes nor records.

Alongside the Jesuits, the Jews and Jewish converts to Christianity who had migrated from Europe, some of them qualified, also practised medicine. But the handful of fully trained doctors in the colony were mainly civil servants employed by the Crown, the Council and the military. The barber-surgeons, physicians, or licensed practitioners were only allowed to carry out surgery. However, because of the shortage of professional doctors, apprentices, herbalists, anatomists, faith-healers, witch-doctors and quacks prescribed medicines without supervision.

Delegates and commissioners responsible to the chief surgeon appointed by the Crown rarely made any attempt to enforce the rules. They supervised medical practices and sanitary conditions in the most superficial manner. Nurses had little or no experience, medicines were scarce, there were no proper hospitals, and few surgical instruments. Given this dismal state of affairs, the plague spread like wildfire in Bahia.

There began a reign of terror. Haunted by the fear of death, by the sorrow of losing their loved ones, the city's inhabitants started to avoid each other. Confused, disorientated and close to madness, they were afraid even to remain indoors.

The streets were deserted. Devout Theatines went from door to door trying to persuade people to confess their sins and do penance. Families died en route as they tried to flee the city. News arrived of the entire population of nearby towns being completely wiped out.

Ships avoided mooring in the harbour where only a few vessels remained, abandoned by crews who had been stricken or killed by plague. Activity in the city came to a standstill, the hoist no longer lifted or lowered cargo. The taverns put up their shutters, the brothels closed down.

People lined up outside the shops hoping in vain to buy supplies; there was no salt, flour, oil, dried cod, wine or cloth. People ate what they could grow despite the questionable hygiene and nutritional value. There were no stockings, hats, sacking, armaments, smelted copper, equipment needed for the sugar-mills, druggets, serge, brocade, thread, paper. Prices soared and a black market began to operate.

In the cemeteries, slaves were ordered to dig large pits and the clergy often buried as many as six corpses in the same grave, after mumbling a few short prayers. The infirmaries and convents were overcrowded with the sick and dying. Within three months, most of Bahia's inhabitants were dead and buried.

The Archbishop João da Madre de Deus and Judge Palma also succumbed to the plague.

Antonio de Souza de Menezes, the twenty-fifth Governor and Supreme Military Commander of Brazil, never relinquished his hatred for Padre Vieira. He lived the rest of his days tormented by resentment and remorse for the sin he had committed during his years of confinement on the Estate of Olivais. Padre Vieira was the only man who knew of his treachery, but he revealed nothing. The Jesuit had learned of the Governor's guilty secret in Lisbon when Braço de Prata, who by then had been nominated Governor of Campo Maior, had come to ask him to plead on behalf of a sailor arrested for murdering a woman of the nobility.

Captain-General Teles was granted a royal pardon through the Governor João de Lencastre. He discovered, some years after his brother's assassination, that the discord between the Menezes and Ravascos had arisen over a noble lady glimpsed in the shadows of a shuttered window, or through the curtains of a palanquin. Rumour has it that the lady in question was probably Dona Bernardina Ravasco.

ANTONIO DE BRITO was summoned before the Court by order of the King. He was ordered to clear his name and publicly refute the accusation that he had been involved in the criminal attack on the Captain-General. De Brito carried with him a letter of recommendation written by Padre Vieira and addressed to Dom Marchão Temudo. In his letter, Vieira tried to justify De Brito's actions in the name of honour and self-defence. Vieira wrote: "Kill, and be assured of the King's goodwill!" for he truly believed that that most prudent monarch would prefer to retain men of valour rather than lose them.

Antonio de Brito was sentenced to exile until 1692 when he was pardoned by Dom Pedro II through the intervention of Pope Innocent XII who wished to gratify the Grand Duke of Tuscany, the brother of Cardinal d'Este.

The RABBI SAMUEL DA FONSECA left for Amsterdam almost immediately after Braço de Prata's dismissal. He married Judith, the young, good-hearted daughter of a rabbi. She died soon afterwards.

He became a member of the Rabbinical College and occupied this post until his death in 1698. His fortune had been converted into books. He sold all his possessions, keeping nothing except the printing press, and published an illuminated edition of the Sefer Torah. He devoted his last years to reading and printing books, thereby fulfilling a lifelong ambition. He was buried in Amsterdam.

Councillor LUIZ BONICHO, after escaping on the flagship bound for Portugal, arrived safely in Lisbon.

Once the wound from where his hand had been cut off had healed, he sought out the same silversmith in Oporto who had made the artificial arm for Antonio de Souza. Unable to afford an artificial hand made of silver, he had to settle for an ordinary iron hook. He begged the authorities and the King to remove Braço de Prata from power.

Having lost everything when he fled Brazil, and reduced to poverty, he joined the crew of the ship taking the young Viceroy, the Count of Vila Verde, to India. They set sail from the Tagus in March 1692. Between sickness and storms, the voyage was disastrous. A forced landing on the disease-ridden island of Mozambique wiped out so many passengers and members of the crew that when the flagship, *The Immaculate Conception*, finally reached Goa, there were only eighty-four survivors out of the original five hundred and eighty. Bonicho had suffered scurvy and fever and it took him months to recover.

Left behind in Goa, he travelled on to the Persian Gulf where he joined the crew of a pirate ship at Bandar Kung. He took part in a number of assaults on Portuguese, Spanish and English ships. Seriously wounded by gunfire, he lost a leg.

Disabled but wealthy, he returned to Portugal in December 1698 aboard the São Pedro and from there headed for the delights of Paris, and no more was heard of him. Some say he moved from one chateau to another, surrounded by handsome youths and every luxury money could buy. Others claim he retired to a monastery where he took holy orders and repented his sins.

ANICA DE MELO was allowed to reopen her brothel and kept open house there for some years. Though married, Gregório de Matos was a frequent visitor.

When the poet was exiled, Anica went to Angola in the hope of finding him again. But her ship capsized near the African coast during an assault by Dutch pirates. She drowned not so very far from where Gregório was living. He never learnt of her death.

MARIA BERCO, who had returned to Bahia after the departure of Braço de Prata, waited in vain for Gregório de Matos to reappear. Now a rich woman, she constantly received proposals of marriage notwithstanding her disfigurement, but she turned all of them down. It deeply distressed her to hear of the poet's marriage to the widow Maria de Povos and to know that he had a son.

She departed for Lisbon on the flagship taking Antonio Luiz da Câmara Coutinho back to Europe once his term of office had ended.

In Portugal, Maria made the mistake of telling neighbours, who were jealous of her wealth, that Jews in Brazil were decent people. They denounced her to the Inquisition. In December 1697 a warrant was issued for her arrest on the grounds that she was suspected of practising Judaism and had uttered words "offensive to Christian ears". During the trial she continued to insist that there was much goodness among Jews. Intimidated by threats of torture, she broke down and begged for mercy and promised to recant. But she was careful not to mention Samuel da Fonseca, who had helped to secure her freedom and offered her sanctuary on his plantation.

The Tribunal, which had declared her a heretic and apostate, passed sentence in October 1699. Maria was to be excommunicated and her property sequestrated by the Fiscal Authorities and the Crown Council with some minor concessions. She agreed to obey the Court's ruling that she be reconciled with the Church and publicly renounce her heresies. She was to be sent to prison and wear penitential robes for the rest of her life; exiled on the Island of São Tomé for two years, she was forbidden to return to Portugal. Her excommunication was to remain *absoluta in forma ecclesiae*.

She died on the island of São Tomé, penniless and disfigured, stricken by the same fever which had killed Gregório de Matos. Maria never forgot the poet, and in her final moments she remembered a line from one of his poems: *"I've sung my verses and all is ended."*

The young AFRICAN SLAVE who had helped the assassins by detaining the Captain-General's litter at the crucial hour was never found. Some alleged he was Moçorongo, who served Tomás Pinto Brandão.

On one occasion, Gregório de Matos claimed that the youth had been one of several rebellious blacks who, after drawing swords on a party of judges some years later, were arrested, put on the rack, and quartered for their crime.

BAHIA prospered and changed. But it would always be a place for pleasure and sin, and continue to delight all those who belong there or come to visit, whether they be humans, angels or demons. And Bahia would forever be known as the city where Gregório de Matos, the Mouth of Hell, once lived.